The Prison Compendium

I0533932

Edited by
Jennifer Word

EMP PUBLISHING

The Prison Compendium

CONTENTS

Editor's Note

EMP Publishing has this nifty little horror quarterly, *Creepy Campfire Quarterly* (the CCQ). When submissions are open for that monster, we get over one hundred stories each month. That's a lot of reading for me and my small associate editing staff to slog through. Every so often, buried in the slush pile amongst the expected tropes and horror staples of monsters (vampires, werewolves, zombies, and even Bigfoot), as well as serial killers and typical psychos, not to mention ghosts and other dark supernatural and paranormal themed tales, we'd get something dramatic, disturbing, and utterly moving... set in prison. Of course, those stories simply didn't fit with what the CCQ was accepting, but I found myself keeping them on the sidelines, not quite ready to send out that rejection notice for a story that wasn't right for our horror quarterly, but was still *good*, and effective storytelling, containing all the desired qualities for acceptance and publication.

In short, amongst the monsters and ghoulies, creepies and crawlies, I noticed a random theme appearing in the slush pile, more so than any other recurring motif, yet often not traditional 'horror', per se (you'd probably be surprised just how *many* subs to the CCQ are *not* horror in any fashion). There are other recurring topics that span multiple genres that creep (no pun intended) into the CCQ slush pile, to be heaped in with the spooky and creepy horror stories that the CCQ regularly receives. Enough dark speculative, dramatic, and literary pieces abound (to name just a few genres) for example, to spawn the idea of having one whole issue of the CCQ (releasing on January 28, 2017) be specifically Science Fiction/Horror themed (and even that has some fantasy/steampunk genre stories in it). Still, again, enough stories (aside from prison-themed) have come in to inspire yet another, whole new anthology with a specific theme (you all really should see this crazy slush pile that comes into the CCQ – Jen laughs until she cries) to be announced next year, with the open call beginning in the Fall of 2017. To give you a hint, that anthology theme (expected to be a tome not unlike *The Prison Compendium*, of well over 100,000 words) will be titled: *Dystopedia*.

But I digress. I kept saving all the prison themed stories. I couldn't justify rejecting them. The writing was strong, the stories emotional and effective, the pacing great, the stories coming in were *good*. No, scratch that, many of the stories coming in were *exceptional*. And I never realized how many ways a story revolving around the idea of 'prison' could be told. Mixed in with these exceptional and deeply emotional "Shawshank" style epics, there were also the funny and light, or otherwise basic tales, perhaps nothing to shout about, but still competent beyond a lot of the horror stories that were predictable and sub-par. Even the silly prison stories were well-crafted to a degree that astounded me.

I happened to be visiting with a 'relative' one weekend for a 'holiday' not long after I noticed the prison theme rebounding in the slush pile. I mentioned a few of the stories to this person in passing, which finally got them 'talking' a bit, albeit, still in a very limited capacity, sharing some of their own stories. I cannot repeat those, specifically. I must be cryptic here, because this person works as a prison guard. I remember when they first got the job, over six years ago, how shocked I was to hear their initial stories, about how they can't use their real name in the prison, not even with the fellow guards, in case a co-worker accidentally refers to them as such. Even their closest work colleagues don't know their real name, and the guards are not allowed to 'hang out' or be friends outside of work, to reduce commiseration issues and other conflicts of interest.

Prison guards lead very guarded lives, all around, and to varying degrees, depending on whether they work in a low or maximum security prison, or Death Row; or whether they are an outright prison guard, or a correctional officer (CO) in a county jail. Depending on the job (just as varied as the story genres in this book), the level of security for CO's and guards across the country also varies. Not all guards are as 'guarded' as others, they don't *all* share the same rules of conduct and work policies, but none of them are as open as typical civilian jobs, because all guards, no matter *where* they serve, are *not* working a civilian job, but a post that requires some level of vigilant secrecy for their own protection, as well as their family, friends, or other loved ones.

In fact, my family member only tells very close family what they do. Friends who are not as close to this person, or more casual acquaintances are told this person has a different, more inconspicuous job. This person can't post on social media, at least not in any way that might allow an inmate to locate them online and figure out who they are. I asked this family member, "Why?", and they explained to me how their entire family (that could include me) would be in danger if they were known or revealed to prison inmates. Again, I asked, "Why? And how?", to which they explained that inmates still have friends on the outside, who are sometimes ordered to pay visits to family members and even friends of the guards, should their true identities be discovered, and suddenly, that guard is compromised and becomes the blackmailed bitch of that inmate, to keep their family on the outside safe from 'retribution'. Yes, even guards can become somebody's 'bitch' in prison, if they aren't careful. And I mean, *very* careful.

I was utterly shocked to learn how far my family member had to go to try and keep their true name, even their hometown from being known or ever found out. After all, inmates have access to the Internet... and the ones that don't, their friends on the outside do. And inmates *listen*. Guards must be on their toes. They cannot talk or interact with the inmates they watch over about anything personal. The tiniest tidbit could be a hint or clue to help track them down online and find their family or ascertain their real identity. No social media, not under their real names, or at the very least, with fake towns that they don't live in. No posting pics of family, especially their own kids, and never themselves or their face. These are some of the lighter rules for *minimum* security level prison guards.

This family member is not even allowed to drink while off-shift, because they can get called in for an emergency at any hour of the day or night, so must remain sober always. And the stories this person would tell me about their experiences with the inmates were equally as interesting and mysterious. Stories about other inmates' stories. I began to realize that this, combined with the stories I'd been sidelining from the CCQ slush pile were more than just a theme for an issue of *Creepy Campfire Quarterly*, but an untapped and unexplored *world* of stories, that walk the line along nearly every genre that exists in literature, from speculative to horror, dramatic and literary, to science fiction, fantasy, and erotica, and anything else in between. You can spin a prison tale in any genre that exists if you've got the imagination to try, and suddenly, *The Prison Compendium* was born. In one afternoon, the entire anthology, idea, and theme simply came alive.

I immediately had a cover designed, and within less than two weeks, the open call was launched. It lasted less than six months (I'd originally slated it to run well over a year), but that proved too much time. I had enough amazing stories to fill the entire collection in less than half a year, and then had to cut authors short, and send out rejections to more great stories. So, perhaps if this Compendium entertains people and word of mouth creates some decent sales (a publisher can only hope), we'll be able to launch the open call for *The Prison Compendium Volume II*. But let's just see how this one goes, shall we?

There is also an Indiegogo Generosity fundraiser attached to this project, called 'Books for Prisoners', inspired by many stories I've also come across or heard from various sources about how important books and reading are as entertainment to prisoners who, in some cases, might otherwise lose their minds from utter boredom. In many cases, the shared sentiment is that books, more than anything else, are what make prison even remotely bearable to inmates, to pass the time or otherwise mentally escape confinement, if only inside the creative worlds and imaginations of the authors spinning these tales.

I had one person point out that if prisoners read stories to escape, why would they want to read stories about prison? I said, "Good point," and then recalled receiving a report about a prisoner who'd been seen in their cell reading a book that *I* had written and published... and the prisoner was utterly engrossed in the book, and *smiling*. Well, that book is all about people who are incarcerated, and although the theme is science fiction, it's still mainly about people locked way, in a form of prison, who've lost their freedom. I realized it doesn't matter if the stories are about prisoners and being locked away... the prisoners reading these stories can find entertainment and escape so long as they're not reading their *own* story.

After all, as I've already stated, there are a myriad of ways and genres to spin a prison-themed tale, and most of these will not be what you might assume in your mind when you begin reading. There should be plenty of entertainment and escape in these tales for prisoners to enjoy, as well as the general reading public. Many of these stories might surprise you, or otherwise not be what you're expecting, but they all share the theme, in some form or other, of prison or similar forms of incarceration (some take place in mental hospitals), the loss of freedom, and everything to do with and around that idea. Some of these stories tell the tale leading up to prison, or how the person ended up there. A lot of the stories take place and tell what happens inside the prison. Most are from the point of view of the arrested, sentenced, and imprisoned inmates, but a scant few are from the guards (or in one case, an executioner's) experience. Still, other stories take place and tell the tale of what happens to prisoners *after* they get *out*; and some of these stories involve prisoners that aren't even human, and don't reside in prisons on Earth...

Prison is a monster of a theme, without even needing to go near or limit the idea to the horror genre. To be certain, there are a few classic horror stories in here... involving prison, but not nearly as many as some of you might be expecting. So, returning to the Generosity fundraiser, we've managed to fundraise $215 as of publication date, to purchase and send books to various prison book donation programs that deliver books to prisons all over the country. In the back of this book, you'll find a page with information and the link to the Indiegogo Generosity fundraiser, should you enjoy the Compendium enough that you decide you'd like to help us get more copies into the hands of prisoners and into prison libraries across the United States.

While I can't say for certain that this Volume is one hundred percent unique or groundbreaking, I do feel confident that it is one-of-a-kind in the level of variation in the stories and genres. There may, in fact, be other fiction anthology collections out there already that are prison themed, I really can't say. But then again, for all I know… maybe there aren't.

This is for all the writers with such varied and creative imaginations, as well as all the prisoners out there who need a good story to help them escape their barred cells for only a few minutes each night, or to make them more bearable, if even just a small bit. And lastly, this is for readers who simply enjoy a good story, and like reading tales centered around and exploring a specific theme, who find the topic of 'prison' to be of interest.

However, what I discovered, and what you are now about to, as well, is that prison is *anything but* a specific theme; it's an entire *world, realm, and reality all its own*, and this Volume only just begins scratching the surface.

So, welcome, and enjoy the ride (or read, as it is), and let's all escape into the imaginations of these creative and talented writers for a bit, and live inside these tales. Some of these stories might haunt you, move you, horrify you, make you cry, feel sad, shocked, disgusted, or perhaps even make you laugh. Guaranteed, a few of these will stick with every one of you long after turning the page and closing the book. Which *specific* stories will touch or grab each individual reader, I can't say. That's all yours.

'Time's a-wastin', as the saying goes. Without further ado:

Get to it, everyone. Let's go to prison. Welcome to the Yard.

Jennifer Word – Senior Editor
EMP Publishing
Atchison, Kansas
December 8, 2016

A Farewell to Apotheosis

Gregory L. Norris

I.

Ares spooned an extra portion of food onto Seth's tray.

"Manna again?" the Egyptian complained, oblivious to the gesture.

"Get used to it," Ares said.

Seth sighed through his nostrils, a pathetic reenactment of desert winds from eras long ended, and moved down the chow line.

"Take over for me, would you?" Ares asked.

Hermes nodded, accepting the big slop spoon. Another Egyptian shuffled closer—Osiris. Soon, the Yucatan prisoners would enter the line. They didn't miss much. Time was short.

Ares grabbed a tray, dumped two bread rolls on it, and skirted around the last of the Norse. He headed toward the farthest table in the cafeteria where, for days—or it could have been centuries, given the state of time beneath the prison's roof—Horus had sat alone for his meals. The Egyptian was there again, separate from the huddle made by the rest of his brethren. Either the Egyptians had made him a pariah, or Horus had chosen his recent solitary status. The reason didn't matter for Ares' needs.

"You still hungry?" he asked.

Horus, presently in the process of bending and unbending a spoon with his thoughts, glanced up. A flicker of fear worked through Ares' insides, an emotion he hadn't suffered for unknown years. Not since his sentence had been handed down and he began serving hard time in the big house. Horus, like the rest of the Egyptians, had been imprisoned longer than the Greeks, the Norse, and the rest of the general population. Thus, it was clear by the glow in his eyes that the other prisoner had gone quite mad.

"Unless you're on a hunger strike..."

Ares set down the tray and its meager though symbolic offering. Horus eye-balled the two bread rolls and nodded. Ares took that as enough of an invitation to sit and did so across from the Egyptian. The two prisoners faced off.

"You're likely wondering why I'm here," Ares said, his voice barely above a whisper. The Aztec, Incan, and Mayan Alliance were keen trackers when it came to reading lips, but the Warden's hacks were all-ears.

"You're here for the same crime as the rest of us: blasphemy."

"I meant now, here, sitting with you when I should be back there with the rest of the Greeks serving this consecrated slop. I need your help."

Horus smiled, a disquieting expression that showed golden teeth, gaps, and rotting black nubs alike. "Did I hear you correctly? *My* help, Greek?"

A foul breath washed over Ares. He resisted the urge to turn away and saw that Horus still had the spoon in his hand. While spoons could be filed sharp, the cheap plastic ware was more likely to snap than pierce flesh, even after the prisoners had been transformed into the Warden's image, another of the punishments carried out after the sentencing process.

"We need to put aside sectarian prejudices, at least for now, and help one another."

"And how can you help me? Or the rest of the Egyptians?"

Ares tipped a glance, corner of the eye. The nearest hack stood at the head of the table three rows over, arms folded, a dour smirk on his lips as he studied Atlas, Cronos, and Oceanus, the last of the Titans, through a look of contempt.

"We all still have powers," Ares said. "Nothing like we used to, but if we pooled them together we might have enough to—"

"To what?" Horus demanded.

Ares saw the fire in the Egyptian's gaze had intensified. The madness no longer seemed there.

"To escape."

II.

The exercise yard brooded under a sky filled with storm clouds—an ominous sign that the Warden was still in one of His Old Testament moods. He'd made it particularly clear that he didn't appreciate prisoners who'd compared themselves to the sun. The last time Ares had seen radiant light in a blue sky eluded his memory.

Hands tucked into the pockets of his hoodie, the hood concealing his face, Ares tromped away from the rest of the Greeks and skirted the inside of the fence. Beyond, rose the walls of the Female Penitentiary Unit, white against the day's moody gray palette. Ares searched their exercise yard for

Hera, Pallas Athena, Artemis, or any of the Nine Muses. The women imprisoned behind the towering fences that he could see, sported blonde hair, braided, or pinned up—likely Frigg, Eir, or Frigg's handmaid, Fulla. He risked another glance and thought he recognized Isis standing off in one corner, alone.

Focus, his inner voice urged.

Behind Ares, Hermes ran laps in the Greek's section of the exercise yard and Apollo lifted weights. Ahead, the Norse were engaged in similar distractions from the reality of everyday prison life. Heimdallr and Thor tossed a medicine ball back and forth. Loki twirled slowly in place—*the first of the Norse to crack*, thought Ares. All the Norse prisoners stopped what they were doing, even the mad trickster, and turned to face him as he approached.

"Please, resume," Ares said lightly.

Thor folded his arms over his bare, glistening chest. "If I had my hammer, I would resume pummeling you hard enough that your shrieks would carry as far away as Olympus."

"Olympus has fallen. So, too, Valhalla, or do I need to remind you?" Ares said. He dug in his soles. "I've come to offer an olive branch."

Thor studied him. The Norse prisoner tipped his head. The rest of his kind carried on. Loki resumed spinning.

"What do you want?"

"Your ear, for a start," said Ares. "And then your help."

III.

They met in the laundry room, two representatives from the three factions of newly allied prisoner clans. Water cascaded, in attempt to remove the endless supply of dirty socks, underwear, and uniforms of their sweaty funk. A dozen dryers fed by stratus clouds dried the linens, endowing everything with a clothesline-fresh smell. Two hacks armed with stun sticks watched over the facility.

"This plan," asked Thor. "What makes you think it will work?"

"I don't think it will work," said Ares. "But I hope it will."

"You *hope*?" Horus growled.

"Don't you get it," Ares said, while pre-treating a handful of sour-smelling socks, "we're already dead. *Dust*. When was the last time any of you had a visitor? A millennium? Because they've stopped coming. Those worshippers no longer exist. Look around you."

Ares slopped the socks into a basket.

"Look for the ones who are no longer here, gone to ashes. And think— because before long, all those empty cells are gonna be full up with new prisoners once the Warden gets around to resuming His blasphemy trials. Fresh meat from the Hare Krishnas and the Falun Gong and the Scientologists. Do you really want to be here during the next gen-pop explosion?"

The speech worked. All the emotion ironed off Thor's face, save for shame. Even Horus the Insane looked humbled by the Greek's words.

"So yes, *hope*," Ares continued. "As much as we've left to spare."

"What about the Yucatan Alliance?" Thor asked. "Should we bring them in, double our numbers?"

"Do you really want to risk the chance of Tezcatlipoca stopping to offer up a blood sacrifice to himself right as we're running through the main gate?"

Thor said, "I see your point."

A voice sounded behind them, powerful, as though trumpeted. "Break up your little huddle," the hack said. "You know the rules!"

The air crackled with electricity, precursor to the thunderbolt readying to fly at them if they didn't disband. Ares turned to see the guard, dressed in his uniform scapular vestments, holding the stun baton in a threatening stance. He nodded and moved along, as did Apollo. Horus and Ra continued toward the dryers. Heimdallr started to obey the hack's order, but Thor stood where he was, the bravery back on his face.

"I said *go*," the hack trumpeted.

"You don't have the right to order me around," Thor said. "Do you know who I am? I am—"

The hack drove the point of the stun baton into Thor's chest. Furious lightning bolts dropped the Norse prisoner to his knees. Two more hacks hastened through the laundry facilities, alerted by the discharge of ozone and cosmic weapon's fire.

"Take him to solitary," the first hack bellowed.

The two newest arrivals extended their wings and carried Thor away.

IV.

Loki met him in the supply closet.

"We don't have much time before Horus's spell wears off and the ruse is exposed," Ares said.

The Norse trickster seized hold of Ares' arm, showing a level of strength more appropriate for Thor. "He's down there, in Helheim, as you planned."

"Helheim, Hades, Hell—solitary confinement, you mean," said Ares.

"The Underworld has many names and layers. Too many. Why did you send him there?"

Ares straightened. "The Warden's day of rest approaches, when we make our move. Aren't you curious about the others?"

Loki exhaled through his mouth. "You mean my father, Odin?"

Ares nodded. "If he's still down there…"

Loki swung, catching the nearest mop handle with the back of his hand and shattering it in two. Lightning-quick, the sharp edge of the small spear was flush against Ares' throat.

"Confess, Greek," the Norse prisoner said. "All along, this was really about *your* father, Zeus!"

Ares swallowed, aware that his mouth had dried up to desert. "Yes, but before you run me through, understand my intention. We knew that our fathers—Zeus, Odin, Geb—and their fathers before them went into solitary, at the very start. If they're still down there, and if we could free them, add their power to what we've got, through our combined numbers—"

The splintered edge of the spear pressed forward another fraction of an inch before it backed away from Ares' flesh.

"I know how deeply the art of deception runs among you Greeks," the Norse prisoner said. "As you must surely know how my people value the truth."

"An ironic statement, coming from the mouth of one who resembles Loki."

"Attempt to deceive me again and I will run this blade through your throat without hesitation."

Loki trembled. His entire visage rippled out of clarity and, for a second, it was Thor who stood holding the impalement. Shanked, his lifeless corpse left in the supply closet? Ares considered the merit of such an outcome. Other Greeks had evaporated before him, their bodies giving up the ghost in an unspectacular puff of dust.

First, he had to at least try to free his father and regain his freedom.

V.

Ares moseyed down the corridor, aware of the mucus-green industrial paint on the walls, the odors of sweat and flesh, and the absence of all comfort. His mind wandered back to the olive groves, the acanthus leaves, the days of life's blessings as savored through wine, daydreaming, and carnal pleasures.

The trumpeting of loud voices from the hacks shocked him out of his reverie of simpler, happier days. Ares fast-marched into the Greek cellblock, ascended the stairs to the upper level, and lined up in front of the pod he shared with Hermes.

"All right, let's do this quickly and without incident. Roll call," the head hack barked. "Dionysus…Hephaestus…Poseidon…"

Ares imagined similar routines being carried out in the Egyptian and Norse cellblocks. The Warden liked an organized prison, no detail overlooked.

"Okay," the hack said, after all Greek inmates had been accounted for. "Lights out."

Everything went dark.

VI.

The biggest question raised—by Horus—had been where to go.

"Even if we make it out of this dungeon, the Warden will hunt us down. He won't rest, not even on the seventh day."

"He's got more to worry about without focusing on a bunch of escapees from extinct religions," Apollo had offered. "But first, we must free the women. We owe it to them."

Ares' brother had invoked Hera's name and, again, he mourned for his mother and sisters.

"Too risky," said Ra. "My old charts noted a singularity far past Triangulum 2-2-9. What they now refer to as a 'wormhole' through space."

"Where does it lead?" This, from Heimdallr.

Ra had shrugged. "Somewhere *other* is all I know."

Sleep eluded Ares. The mattress felt unusually unpleasant on that night, and he kept pondering the Norse trickster's ability to pass himself off as Thor. Beyond the prison's walls, in that other life before incarceration, Loki had been believed capable of moving entire stars out of alignment, as well as possessing the ability to shift genders from male to female. Even after being stripped most of his powers, maintaining Thor's façade shouldn't have been too great a stretch.

Masquerading as one of the hacks to escape solitary confinement was another thing entirely.

At some untimed point in the night, hours, or centuries after lights out, a shadow of movement teased the corner of Ares' slitted eye.

"Wake, Greek," a familiar voice whispered.

Ares sat up, slipped out of bed, and hurried to the cell door, where Thor stood, flanked by other escaped Norse prisoners. Hope flared. The plan had worked!

"Soon, the escaped Egyptians will cause a distraction, and we'll be on our way!"

The cell door's lock turned. The bars slid open.

"Come, Hermes," Ares said. "Run fleet of foot and free our brothers!"

Hermes had unlocked seven more of the Greek cellblock's cage doors before the lights switched on, alarm klaxons shrieked, and all hell broke loose.

VII.

Greeks spilled out of pods, joining the Norse prisoners. Hacks lay stunned and bloodied, their wings torn from backs, their feathers ripped out in great handfuls and gathered as gruesome, practical prizes.

"For travel to the wormhole," said Thor.

The Norse leader handed Ares two feathers. Ares nodded, all the thanks he could offer. Then, the Greek turned toward the real Loki, easily identifiable in the stark white glare by the madness in his gaze.

"Did you learn the truth regarding the fate of our fathers?" Ares pressed.

"Only dust," said Loki.

Thor clamped a hand around the meat of Ares' upper arm. "Forget them now—time is at a premium!"

Ares glanced at the Norse prisoner's hand. The audacity that he should touch one of the sons of Zeus in such a familiar manner! That crime should have earned Thor the separation of his head from his shoulders. But Zeus was gone, per reports brought back from solitary confinement in Hades. The urge to return to his cell tempted. Yes, return to imprisonment, curl up, and disintegrate. What was the point of rioting further and escaping to whatever reality awaited on the other side of the Triangulum singularity?

If Zeus was truly dead, there was his answer. To carry on in their father's name.

Thor pulled him out of his uncommitted state. "Hurry, Greeks!"

Ares nodded. "For the honor of Zeus—forward!"

He tucked the bloody feathers in the elastic waistband of his prison uniform bottoms and charged toward the opened security checkpoint. A dozen other barriers awaited between the Greek cellblock and the prison's main gates, but he figured Horus, the surly magician, had carried out that part of the plan to perfection.

VIII.

Fires raged through the Prison of Dead Religions from overturned mattresses, toilet paper set ablaze, and the pious books in the prison library. Some hacks had barricaded themselves in safe rooms while others hastily donned riot gear and readied to march behind ballistic intruder shields.

Greeks and Norse prisoners converged on the front gate, where they joined the Egyptians.

"We are freed!" exclaimed Apollo.

Osiris and Hermes rolled aside the disc of carved rock. Glorious sunlight spilled through the gap, the first rays Ares had seen in... *centuries*?

The prisoners hastened through that final barrier to freedom and into the marble courtyard beyond. Ares withdrew the pair of feathers ripped from the wings of the hacks and aimed them aloft.

"None of us stops until we're beyond the wormhole, my brethren. I'll see you on the other side!"

And then he was flying up, up, higher, and higher, toward the sun. Emotion tickled the inside of his stomach. In the lightness that followed, he dared dream thoughts of lust, drink, and indulgence. A smile tested the corners of Ares' lips. Perhaps, the universe beyond Triangulum's wormhole would offer a return to the old ways of the world, a new Olympus. This, he prayed.

Sunlight rained down from the sky, too radiant to behold directly, even through the eyes of a Greek.

"*Blasphemy*," a mighty voice bellowed.

It was all around him, thunderous. Ares' ascent slowed. He gazed into the light. It wasn't the sun.

"The Warden," Ares said.

IX.

"Who instigated this escape?"

The words echoed in his thoughts and rang in the absolute darkness of Ares' cell in solitary confinement deep beneath the prison.

"Who was the ringleader?"

He figured it was Loki who gave him up, or Horus. None of the Greeks would have rolled over one of their own, and Thor wasn't the type to squeal. Not that it mattered.

The cell was cold, dark, and absent of all hope. Or so Ares thought until, untold days or centuries into his confinement, he heard an old man's voice speak through a chink in the volcanic rock wall.

"Son, can you hear me?"

Ares pressed his cheek against the icy stone. "Father, is that you?"

Ares waited for Zeus to answer. Eternity dragged onward.

Swing a Sparrow on a String
Ken Goldman

Angela opened her eyes to a new day, not knowing if it were morning. There were no windows in her room, and it could have been the middle of the afternoon, or even midnight. She heard no sounds except her own breathing, and when she awoke, she inhaled and exhaled heavily, as if she'd just completed a marathon race instead of having slept for hours. Perhaps she'd slept for days. She stopped wondering about time, months ago. Now, she simply slept if she was able, then stayed awake as long as necessary.

She knew she'd have to eat, they would soon come with food, and if she felt stronger, she might spit it back at them as she had when they first brought her here. But she'd swallowed that rage a long time ago. Now, Angela ate whatever morsels they gave her, and recently, she'd begun restraining herself from thanking them. She feared the day might come when she would feel grateful that they allowed her to live, when she might find herself smiling at them, as if she understood and accepted the perfect correctness of her captivity.

She looked at herself in the small, cracked mirror above the sink. Although her hair was stringy and unwashed, she remembered how golden it had once shimmered in the sun. Her face was still quite pretty, and once, she heard one guard tell another that he had never seen eyes quite that blue. The other whispered what a pity it was.

If only she had a piece of paper, a pen, even a crayon. Maybe this time she would show them that she could create something useful and lasting that mattered to them, something that, in turn, would make *her* matter. When Angela first arrived, they had eagerly granted the request of the eighteen-year-old girl, and waited to see what gifts her imagination might offer them.

She succeeded only in producing a few formless scrawls that they said were not art, and some rhyme-less gibberish that they told her wasn't poetry. They took away the paper, the pens, and the paint brushes.

Not long ago, the tall blond guard who wore the keys around his neck, asked her if she might like to sing. Any tune would do, he told her.

"Please, oh please, let me try!" Angela begged.

15

The next day, he brought her a small cassette recorder with a blank tape. "Perhaps we'll find the songbird in you where we were unable to find the artist. Sing, and we promise to listen," he assured her.

For days, Angela sang alone in her room, remembering what her mother had sung to her many years ago. *"Hush little baby, don't say a word. Mama's gonna buy you a mocking bird..."*

A week later, she handed the cassette to the man with the keys and simply said, "Please..." He stuffed the tape into his pocket and left without a word.

The next day, the guard sat alongside her bed and informed her that he and the others had decided she was no songbird. For a moment, his words sounded like an apology. She knew she would never see the tall guard again.

The wasted papers that Angela filled with nonsense, and the inarticulate squawks she tried to pass off as music, had convinced them that further efforts on their part would be foolish. From that day forward, the guards, who silently delivered her food, seemed unwilling to even look at her.

Angela heard the key slip into the lock on the other side of the heavy door. She no longer pretended to be asleep when they came, because they didn't care whether she was sleeping or awake. One of them always waited outside as the other entered. She heard the heavy jingle of keys and looked up; they were around the guard's neck.

"You," she said, but the word was only a statement of fact, not sparked with the warmth that accompanies the recognition of a familiar face. Once uttered, the word sounded idiotic.

"Yes," he answered, closing the door behind him. He didn't look at her as he set the tray of food on the stand alongside her bed. She expected no further conversation, and when he spoke again, his words startled her.

"They told me to say the other guard had caught the flu." He pulled up the small wooden chair and sat, although the seat was too small and he seemed not to know whether to fold his legs. "There is no flu. They wanted us to talk."

His statement was ludicrous. She hadn't conversed with him in months, and those few talks she remembered were pitifully brief and one-sided.

"I don't understand," she said, as she selected a small bread crust on her tray. She had learned to keep her responses short, for the guards tired of her quickly.

"I'd like to know about God," he said, as if this were meant as an answer. "Tell me how you feel about God. Tell me about your religion, your beliefs."

"I have no belief in God. I have no religion. Don't you have some sort of records about that?" She felt immediately sorry she'd asked, but the guard ignored the question anyway. He fidgeted in the small chair.

"You're an atheist, then? Or an agnostic? You have opinions regarding God's existence, or the lack of it?" He sounded almost hopeful.

"I'm apathetic…an apathist. I don't much think about it," she answered, as she nibbled at the crust. She picked up a slab of egg yolk with her left hand, ignoring the silverware, leaned her head back, and dropped the yolk into her mouth.

Her response oddly pleased him, although, he did not smile. "An apathist? That was a joke you just said. Admittedly, not a very good one, but it *was* a joke. Then, you have a sense of humor. Tell me another joke."

Angela looked hard at the man, uncertain how earnest her guard's question was. "A joke? You mean like, why did the chicken cross the road?" The absurdity of her question seemed to increase the guard's excitement.

"Yes! Yes! Tell me, why did the chicken cross the road?" There was anticipation in his voice as if he sincerely were interested in the chicken's intentions, and when he leaned toward Angela for her response, his face revealed the hint of a smile.

"Perhaps the chicken was an apathist," she said.

The guard's smile disappeared quickly, as if erased. "That isn't funny. I'm sorry, but that isn't funny at all." His tone became flat, expressionless. He sounded like a man keeping score. No points for humor. Sorry. Next category.

"Can we talk politics?" he asked.

"No."

"Sociology? Science? History? Law? Philosophy?" His questions had become a formality, a checklist to be completed, filed, and forgotten.

"No... No... No... No..." Although Angela couldn't remember ever having a discussion this long during her stay here, she wanted this conversation to end. "Perhaps I could tell you why the philosopher crossed the road? No, I guess you're right. That wasn't very funny either. I suppose you'll be leaving now?"

Her question anticipated his next words. The tall guard rose from the chair with difficulty, trying to maintain his dignity when he could not get up with his first attempt.

"I have one more question for you, Angela," he said.

He had never called her by her name before, and his doing so struck her as odd. He walked to the foot of her bed and turned. "Do you know why you're here?" He asked without malice or emotion, with only the desire to know her answer, as he had wanted to know about songbirds and chickens.

"I'm here because you see me as a useless bird." Having said the words, she knew they had always been on her tongue, waiting to be spoken.

"I beg your pardon?"

"You know: the sparrow who can no longer fly becomes useless to the other sparrows, a burden to them. I've broken my wing, isn't that right? And the flock has no further need of me."

"I'm impressed," the guard answered. "That's quite an inventive analogy from one who knows so little of creativity."

He sat on the edge of the bed and moved close to Angela, as if to reveal a secret. Instead, he reached under the blanket and grabbed hold of her right hand, yanking it out from where she'd kept it hidden. He held her arm straight up, and the pain caused her to wince. "But this isn't exactly a broken wing, is it, Angela? It's a wilted arm, a useless limb. It's not pleasant to look at, it serves no function, and it belongs to you. It *is* you."

The words came in furious bursts now, like machine-gun pellets, and he shook her withered limb as he spoke. "You see yourself as a wounded sparrow, do you? What happens if we take that sparrow and tie her leg to a string, and swing her around in circles, in a desperate attempt to make her fly? She struggles against hope to use her useless wings, and meanwhile, we swing her around and around and around, wasting our energy, our time. And in the end, when we stop swinging, she comes crashing down to earth, anyway. Our time has been wasted, and her hopes, destroyed. What is the point? Why even bother?" He let go of her arm, allowing it to drop.

For a moment, Angela stared at the shrunken arm, as if it were a foreign thing that did not belong in the bed with her. She spoke without removing her eyes from it.

"A sparrow who can no longer fly, can still sing. And if she can't sing, she can still feel, she can still—"

"Love?" the guard interrupted. "That's exactly right, Angela! We asked this sparrow to sing, and she couldn't! Then we realized she may still be capable of love... but the feeling could only result in frustration for her. Because the real question is not, 'can she feel love?' but rather, 'is she capable of *being* loved?' Do the words she writes encourage love? Does her beauty or intellect, in any way, inspire it? It's unlikely that anyone would even try to love her because of that hideous limb. Not that all physical impediments are repulsive. Perhaps, if she were only blind..."

"Stop... Please, stop." Angela pleaded. Her brief taste of defiance had made her want to gag.

"You want to cover your ears, don't you? You want to block out the words, make me go away. Maybe you would even like to strike me," he continued. "But you can't do it, can you? That limb just lies there, like a dead weight. Do you see my point?"

"I have my other arm..."

"Whose only function is to hide its companion. No, Angela, I'm sorry, but the time has come for us to stop swinging the sparrow's string."

His anger slowly dissolved, and he fell silent for a moment. He attempted to hold her wilted hand in his, but she pulled it away. Instead, he took her other hand.

"But first, I have something I want to show you, something you need to see." He placed her fingers on his left leg, below the knee. "Rub your hand along my leg, Angela. Does the calf feel peculiar to you? Congenital defect, they call it, like they call yours. The leg is gone, at least, from the knee down. Amazing, what they can do with prosthetics, today.

"But, you see, I have my particular talents. I happen to be quite good at drawing people out, at enabling them to find a way to compensate for their physical shortcomings. And I can be quite decisive when called upon to make decisions that others would find distasteful. No one ever asked me to sing, or to fly. But, when they came for me, I simply told them what I could do."

Angela struggled to pull her hand free, as her anger rose inside her like hot bile. "But you also decide who is to be exterminated! You decide who the state no longer regards as useful! What gives you the right—?"

"*This* gives me the right!" he shouted, his breath hot on her face, as he tapped her hand on the hard wood of his prosthetic leg. "This has forced me to find my usefulness to others, just as your pathetic limb has forced you to admit that you have none. And I have no intention of relinquishing my usefulness by allowing you to continue your hollow existence. I refuse not to matter!"

The guard's renewed anger embarrassed him; he turned away from Angela. He ran his fingers through his blond hair, an attempt to collect himself, and when he again looked down at his leg, he noticed that Angela's hand grasped it. She knew he was unaware of her touch until he looked. When his eyes locked with hers, her mouth curled into a bitter smile.

"I *feel* this," she said, as she ran the tiny hand of the wilted arm along his wooden leg. "I feel this with both of my hands, even the one you call useless. Tell me what you feel when I touch you. Does this prosthetic device extend all the way to your heart?" Angela tapped on the artificial limb, as if she were expecting a reflexive kick.

"A curious question," he answered. "You might have made a fine idealist, if you believed in God."

She moved close to his face and whispered, "To get to the other side. That *is* why a chicken would cross the road, isn't it?"

He paused for a moment, looking at her. "Such blue eyes," he said. "Such exquisitely beautiful, blue eyes." He called for the guards to take her, and within moments, three entered the room and another two waited by the doorway.

She presented no struggle, and went quietly with them. She wondered, as they walked, if one of them would take her hand.

Mastress of Light and Dark

Catherine A. MacKenzie

(Mastress - female of Master)

I pretended I was a terrible housekeeper. Only then could I forget I was incarcerated in a Mexican prison.

The tiny window, filmed with years of grime, yet see-through in places, was like looking through a greyed veil that had been stored in an attic for a century. The round, thick metal bars on the inside of the glass were spaced far enough apart that they didn't obstruct my view, not once I stuck my nose between them. I could pretend when I didn't notice those black vertical barriers.

Looking out that lacy window wasn't a sight to behold—nothing but a stone wall covered with dried vines and a dirt floor between me and the wall. I was unable to see the sky. The view wasn't worth the effort of moving the sole chair and climbing atop it, but I had nothing else to do. Though moving the chair equated to exercise, hopping onto the seat was a chore. At sixty-seven, my knees weren't as pliable as they once were.

But I had to see something other than four concrete walls, one marred with the steel door that shut me off from the world. If it weren't for that door, which clanged against me three times a day, I could be home, surrounded by pictures of my family, seated in a comfortable chair with a book on my lap and a glass of wine in my hand. Or even in bed, comforted by the down bedspread, my head resting on feather pillows. In that cell, I had one pillow, flat and stubborn as slate, and one sleazy sheet to warm me.

The naked light bulb above me, which I could turn on or off by unscrewing it from the socket, illuminated cockroaches scurrying across the dirt floor. (Unscrewing the bulb was a discovery I made after the first night when I realized lights weren't magically adjusted via a main switch as seen in television prisons.) In one corner, a pile of dirt grew while my eyes, entranced by the busy ants, remained glued to it. What the ants did, I didn't know, but they hustled as if chores had to be completed before dark. And the dark was in *my* hands. For when I sickened of staring at them — what else was there to do? — that's when I unscrewed the bulb. Then I

21

shivered with trepidation, my heart pounding into my head while I waited for a guard to jangle keys into the lock and rush in with a bayonet or some such weapon. But that never happened.

I became mastress of the light and dark.

The ants were there the next morning. Whether they woke when the bulb shone and began working as if they had never ceased or whether they laboured through the night remains a mystery. I wasn't privy, nor did I want to be, to the ants' world.

I knew night fell because of my watch. Due to my slim wrists, the stretchy bracelet sat midway between my wrist and elbow, hidden behind my long-sleeved shirt. The officials missed it. I'm not sure how I would've survived without my watch, but although I constantly looked at it, I could've estimated the hours by the regular timing of the meals passed through the door.

Sleep never came the first night before I discovered I could control the light. Boldness came the second night, when I unscrewed the bulb and slept off and on. I wasn't sure I'd make it to the third night. I became weaker, due to lack of sleep and sustenance. Despite having lived in Mexico for almost five years, I didn't particularly care for Mexican food. Beans make me fart and poop, and tomatoes are acidic. Tortillas add pounds.

Tortillas—always tortillas—and a conglomerate of mashed eggs, peppers, and onions constituted breakfast. Lunchtime brought a bowl of refried beans, two hunks of bread, and tortillas. A stringy piece of paper-thin, tasteless meat (which I prayed was beef), slices of dried-up tomato, a scoop of refried beans, a pile of rice, a spoon of hot salsa, and several tortillas made up dinner. No coffee, just grimy tin cups of water, and only three a day, one with each meal. If they'd given me a bottle of wine—even a cheap, sweet house variety—I'd have been a tad happier.

Dirt filtered in through cracks in the window. With every gust of wind, more dust collected on the six-inch-wide ledge. I'd run a finger through the layers, forming my initials or my first name, as if to leave my imprint, lest I be forgotten. Often, teeny insects crept through the crumbling grout to reside on the ledge. One puff and I'd make them disappear.

Light bulbs shone constantly in the alley, mimicking twenty-four hours of daylight. Incessant light filtered through the dull window, but faintly, like the glow from a lone star attempting to comfort me. And it did soothe me for, other than cockroaches, ants, and an occasional fly or unknown critter, there was nothing else.

***

22

"I can't see what's behind me, Neela," I said.

"Let me get out and see." Neela, my best friend and confidant, said.

A stone wall loomed at my left, a parked car on my right. A building and more parked cars were behind me. I didn't want to hit anything. I tried to be extra careful.

I backed up slowly, angling my head to see my friend. The May Mexico heat rushed in the windows. Neela was silent. I figured that was a good thing. I backed up a bit more.

"Neela, all okay?"

"Yes, back up, to your left. Lots of room."

I still couldn't see her.

I backed up a little. Gave the car more gas. Braked. Pushed the gas again.

A bump. The tires rolled over a hump. Just a rise in the uneven Mexican road.

A scream.

"Neela?" I whispered.

Until I alighted from the car, I hadn't realized I had run over her. A woman—not Neela—still screamed.

***

They say your life flashes before you in slow motion when you take your last breath—your entire life floating by like a colourful parade: flaunting, haunting, daunting, with clowns sporting their garish grins—but it also parades before you when you have nothing to do but stare at achromatic walls. You wonder at your inadequacies, your failures—never your triumphs—moments that draw out your hidden tears. That's the way it was with me. My tears streamed. Not so much for me but for those I missed, and years that flew by before I had a chance to stop and ponder them. And my regrets.

Neela.

I tried to push away unhappy thoughts, swat at them like insignificant flies, but they remained a stain upon the colourless walls, there to torment me as if I wasn't tormented enough; holographs of my life, photographs I wished I could shred or burn, videos of incidents I'd sooner forget. All imaginary, of course, but as real as the fingernails I chewed to the quick until blood flowed that I lapped up like red wine.

My guards were three beefy men. I wasn't frail when they first locked me up, when those metal circles clasped around my wrists. I was theirs then; frailty came later. It crept up silently, aged me, made me wonder who I was. What kind of woman kills her best friend? Voices taunted me.

Murderer, they chanted. *Murderer! You killed my mother. You killed my grandmother. You killed my wife, my sister.* Neela was all those people. And I snuffed her out as one would extinguish a candle. Decimated the flame that provided light. And love. And life.

I hadn't meant to do any of it. It was an accident. An accident!

But I was still a murderer. I killed someone. No matter how I looked at it, I eradicated a life. Someone's last breath was taken because of me. Because I hadn't seen her. I looked in the rear-view mirror. Even in the side mirror. I've never been involved in an accident previously except when a stranger barging through a red light rammed into my car and nearly killed *me*. My neck had hit the steering wheel. "A quarter of an inch farther down and you would have died," the doctor said. I was in my twenties then, when I was going to live forever, as young people assume. I could have died. Instantly. But I didn't.

But Neela did.

I could've become an alcoholic—had wine been provided in the prison. The bugs were getting to me, mocking me, grinning. I knew they were. *Stop! Stop!* But they persisted. Ants continued to work for their useless pay, carting leaves on their backs like motorized boats with their sails unfurled. Flies buzzed around my face. Cockroaches zipped across the floor, like miniature horses clumping down cobblestoned streets. *Clomp! Clomp!*

I let the insects take over, the insaneness that rang around my ears. They came at me, charging like soldiers readying for battle, careening down the mountainside. I was the villain, the enemy in the walker who waited patiently as if I had nothing else to do and nowhere to go. (Which I hadn't.) I existed solely to take the brunt of whatever those creatures threw at me. I was a murderer. A killer.

I didn't want to rot in jail. I wanted to go home. I was sorry for my friend—still am. More than sorry. I've cried and cried for her, but it was an accident. An accident I'll remember for the rest of my life, and not a day will pass I won't relive the scene. It'll be the first thought on my mind when I wake and the last sight I'll see before I fall asleep, but in that horrid Mexican cell I fought for *me*. My life took precedence then. More grief for Neela would come later, when I was safe at home. When I didn't have to worry about me.

The fourth day, the steel door groaned, stealing me from my thoughts. I jumped from the bed. Could it be—my freedom? It was in between meals. What else could it be?

No, they were going to drag me away, stand me over an open pit, loop a rope around my neck. Or prop me against a stone wall, pull a burlap bag over my head. But not quickly enough before I glimpsed the nameless, leering faces and the aiming rifles. Gone! Dead! *Terminado!*

A noose or a bullet. It didn't matter. Death was the same.

A guard, one I didn't remember seeing previously, entered the cell. He spoke Spanish and motioned me out. Two other guards framed the door. Despite my years in Mexico, I didn't know much more than the perfunctory words *gracias* and *nada* and *Buenos Dias*. Even if I had, the heavyset, bronzed man's words were spewed too fast for a Canadian to understand. Daylight hovered ahead. I yearned to race down the drab hall before he realized his mistake, shackled me, and tossed me back into that four-by-six enclosure with insects invading my space (or perhaps I invaded theirs).

I felt the sweltering sun, visualized the waving palm trees and vibrant coloured flowers scrambling over stone walls. I tasted the dirt skimming over the cobblestones, inhaled the balmy air and fragrant flower scents. I heard street dogs, choruses of birds, chickens' chatter, clicking of *cicadas*. The rushing vehicles blasted their tunes and talk, jovial and awkward. I pictured everything as I never had previously. Yet, the sights and smells and sounds were far in the distance.

They spoke their gibberish: those dark men in their well-pressed, clean but menacing uniforms, the guns at their side. So young, they barely looked as old as my grandsons, surely not as bright as my kin. If they made a mistake with my release, perhaps they wouldn't realize it until it was too late, not until after I'd climbed that stone wall dotted with pinks and purples and yellows.

***

The taxi dropped me off at my rental in Ajijic, about forty kilometres from the tiny, obscure village Neela and I had visited. Yet, ironically, the village hadn't been too small to be without a jail. I was thankful the Mexican authorities had returned my purse with my money intact. I had signed numerous papers before they freed me, none of which I could read, all of which I signed in a haphazard manner. Perhaps later I could claim insanity if I had signed something I shouldn't have, though non-knowledge of the Spanish language wouldn't count as a defense. I had proclaimed my innocence every time those nameless, squat men opened the cell door. Obviously, they didn't understand me, but someone must have been on my side. After the statement I had given at my arrest, no one paid any further attention to me, save for my three meals a day. That must have been law—*each prisoner must be fed three times a day*. I wasn't even allowed the requisite phone call. Wasn't that against the law?

***

After a drink to calm my nerves, I telephoned Pam. She and I, along with Neela, had been best buddies. Pam hadn't been feeling well the day Neela and I had taken off on our day trip. Perhaps Pam was the culprit. Four eyes are better than two; circumstances could have been different. But I harboured no ill will against her.

But why hadn't she come to visit me? Why hadn't anyone come to my aid?

"You okay?" she asked. "Where were you? What happened?"

What happened? "I was in jail. In Hell."

Pam didn't seem to have a clue. Where in the heck had she thought I'd been? Hadn't anyone missed me? Hadn't anyone cared?

"What!?"

"It was pure Hell," I repeated. "I never thought I'd be free. I'm not even sure why I am now."

"I'm so sorry. I had no idea."

Really?

"You okay?" she asked again.

"Yeah, I think so. I'm just glad to be home." I considered Mexico, my adopted country, home.

Silence.

"You there?" I asked. Mexican phone lines weren't the most reliable.

"Yes, still here."

"Did I miss the funeral?"

Silence.

Then, "It's tomorrow."

"Tomorrow? We should go together," I said.

Silence.

"Grace, I don't know how to tell you this. The family. They're here. They're pretty upset. They said they want nothing to do with you. That you aren't welcome."

My stomach lurched. I almost threw up. "I don't understand... it was an accident."

"I know. But that's what they said. Neela's daughter and son. Both here. From Atlanta. Met them yesterday when I went to Neela's home."

"Oh." *You went to Neela's home?*

"Pretty mad. They... feel you killed her."

"Yeah, I did, I guess. But it was an accident. You know that."

"Yes, I do," Pam said. "It's a private service. A cremation. Then they're taking her back to the States. It's not a big deal, really."

***

We had connected several years ago, the three of us, who had come to Mexico for a more relaxed lifestyle and temperate climate. Neela had arrived first. I followed a couple of years later, with my husband, Arnold. Pam, who had been divorced for seven years, arrived after Arnold and I. Neela's husband had died four years before my arrival, yet she had stayed. So had I, after Arnold's death, despite the chagrin of my two children. I hadn't wanted to go back to Canada's cold winters. Ajijic's warm weather enticed me to stay. Even the draw of my grandchildren, young adults by that time, couldn't pull me back. I had made my home in Ajijic. Thankfully, Arnold and I had never bought a house, merely rented long-term, which gave me the flexibility after his death to stay or leave.

If only Neela and I hadn't driven to that village, somewhere north of Guadalajara—a name I couldn't even pronounce—to check out a pottery exhibition. I hadn't wanted to go. "Too far, Neela. I'm not comfortable driving in places I'm not familiar with," I had said. I owned a car; Neela hadn't. If only I hadn't gotten stuck in that alley, penned in between the wall and the other car. If only I had stuck to my instincts. If only I hadn't wavered. If only...

If only... Too many ifs.

***

"Gracie, I'm sorry." Pam sounded contrite. But was she? I felt abandoned, much as I had felt for several months after Arnold passed on. Alone.

"I don't understand," I said. "It was an *accident*. Don't you believe me?"

"Of course, I do. Don't be foolish."

I heard tears behind Pam's words. Mine were coming.

*But it **was** an accident. I didn't **mean** to...*

"It's okay," I said. "I understand. I just wanted to pay my sympathies."

"I know you do." Pam hesitated. "Let's get together for lunch on Thursday."

"Yes, sure." I hung up, but I knew I wouldn't go for lunch or anywhere else in Mexico except to the airport. I wanted to go home, to my children

27

and their children—my grandchildren, perhaps whom I had neglected for too long. Mexico, despite being my home for the past several years, would be my home no longer. I was glad I had listened to my son and had Arnold's ashes spread in Calgary. If I hadn't, I feared I'd be stuck in Mexico forever. I couldn't have gone and left Arnold behind.

I stared out the bedroom patio. Magenta petals of *bougainvillea* splashed across the stone wall, the thorny vines creeping upward, higher, and higher, as if racing from me, running away, just as I wanted to. The three-tiered fountain, cascading its usual soothing tune, wasn't working its magic. The water spilling from the smallest top bowl, down to the middle, and then into the bottom, largest bowl, sloshed like buckets of tears.

I had always wanted a fountain.

***

I picked up the phone. Carol answered on the third ring. "Mom, how are you?"

"Fine," I said.

"What's wrong?" Perceptive Carol always knew.

"Mom?" she said when I didn't reply. "You there?"

"Yes, sweetie, I'm here."

"You okay?"

My tears flowed, matching the bubbling fountain in the yard. My insides felt as if they would gurgle up through my esophagus and spew to the floor. "I just got out of jail," I blurted. I hadn't meant to tell her, yet I had to continue. I had to tell someone who loved me, and always would, no matter what travesties I might have committed. "I... killed someone. A friend."

"Mom! What?" she gasped. "Mom, what happened?"

"It was an accident. I didn't mean to." I brushed at my tears. I heard Carol in the background. Another gasp. *Her* tears. "Oh, Carol, I don't know what to do." I paused and took a deep breath. "I'm coming home. For good. Pick me up at the airport?"

"Mom, of course. I don't know what to say. You sure you're okay? When's your flight?"

"I'll book it tonight. Send you an email."

"Yes, good. Mom, sure you're okay?"

"Fine." I wiped my cheeks, which sported more, and more tears. A steady stream of them, like the fountain. "I gotta run. I'll see you later with my flight info."

***

I pulled myself together. My rent was paid until the following month. I'd leave some cash for the utilities. My deposit of a month's rent would be lost. I'd be breaking my lease, but that was okay; I wouldn't be sued. Who could sue from Mexico? No one had my current address—the address I'd assume when I returned home to Alberta.

I possessed nothing in Mexico. My pension, which I accessed at ATMs, was deposited into my Canadian bank account. I owned a few knick-knacks, items Arnold and I had purchased when we first made our home in Mexico. Some I would take with me. I could handle two suitcases, even more if I wanted to pay extra to the airline. I could take what I wanted.

I sat at the desk and jostled the mouse. My computer came alive—a wondrous blue and white. I searched for the earliest flight. I'd be in the air before Neela's service even began.

In the Jailhouse

Bruce Harris

♩♪♫♬

Name's Bugsy. What am I in for? It's none of your business, but I'll tell you this: if not for me, the music scene would look a lot different.

My friends called me Bugs, if you can call them friends. Take Shifty Henry, for example. He always called me Bugs. Bear with me. All of this will make sense shortly, I promise.

Shifty Henry fancied himself a ♪ musician ♪. That might be the case, I never heard him play. The man served 5-10 for aggravated assault, ironic, because he was nothing more than a thief. Petty stuff. You know the type, a lowly pickpocket. He loved Times Square at New Year's Eve, not to mention the throngs at the Kentucky Derby and crowded subway cars. He was on overload in those arenas, the son-of-a-gun. But, the coppers never could catch him red-handed. That's how he earned the name Shifty.

So, several years ago, an alcoholic public defender struck a deal with a couple of crooked cops, and believe me, there ain't no shortage of them around, and this disheveled mouthpiece provoked Shifty Henry and finally got under his skin enough times so that Henry lost it and slugged the lousy lawyer in the jaw. Next thing you know, Henry was serving 5-10. I got to admit he'd been mostly behaved all right for all of them years behind bars. His fingers got sticky every now and again, but he was pretty much the model inmate.

Henry was only a couple of months away from having served his sentence and set free. But, the fool wanted to bust out! Can you believe it? Fact is, that isn't so unusual. The guy served so many years of his term, and then as he got closer to his release date, he wanted to break out. Social psychologists have a name for it, but I don't remember what it is. Something like approach-avoidance maybe? Hey, I've had a lot of time to study in lockup so I took advantage of the prison library. I'm no dummy. Sorry. Let's get back to Shifty Henry and his fool escape plan.

♩♪♫♬

The music blared. Abe, Joe, Raymond, and Izzy were on fire. Abe was at the drums...boom...bang. Ray-Ray's bass was low and fierce, while

30

Izzy was anything but; He was ♫♫ *one* ♫♫ with the piano. Joe handled the guitar like a pro. Funny names for these four faux celebrities who comprised the entire rhythm section, it's no wonder they took so fondly to the Purple Gang tag.

There was nothin' funny about them, however. Rough group they were, but they said they was always good to their mother. That night, they felt the music and the event. Ever wonder how they got their collective moniker? Simple. The brothers, yup, they was all siblings; recklessly decided to rob yet another bank. I mean, they weren't satisfied with the booty they collected from the first four robberies. No, they had to do another job. This group ain't the brightest chandelier in the dance hall. Well, the good folk at the Central National Bank of Detroit were a step ahead. They had planted purple dye in the moneybags, and when Abe, Joe, Raymond, and Izzy opened the stolen bags – poof! Dye flowed everywhere. The four of them looked like the dark iridescent shade of rotten meat. They were easy pickins, and the law had a good laugh, but the Purple Gang sure knew how to play.

Speaking of play, that young'un with the pimply face from Illinois – I never did find out his name – but it could have been Buddy Rich, Jr., this guy was *that* good. You'll have to take my word for it.

♪ Crash…boom…bang ♪! He was all over them drums.

Like I was sayin', that's when Shifty Henry turned and asked me if I wanted to make a break with him! Can you imagine? He said it was the perfect time since everyone was absorbed with the Purple Gang's music and no one was lookin' at us. The guy was only a couple of *months* from freedom!

♩♪♫♫

Music wailed. Everyone danced. Had I gone along with Shifty Henry, music history would have changed. I hate to think of it. Thank goodness *one* of us was thinking clearly at the time.

I should point out Shifty Henry wasn't the only one who played a pivotal role. There were others. For instance, Spider Murphy. Guy stood over six feet, six inches tall, yet he was as scared of spiders – all kinds – as any schoolgirl. But the Spider knew his sax. Word had it that he trained under the personal tutelage of The Bird, Charlie Parker. That's some heavy stuff right there.

Spider Murphy worked long and hard to perfect his skills. I swear he was just as good as Coltrane himself, but that joyride he took in a stolen jet-black convertible Cadillac cost him several productive years of makin' a legit living. Shame, really. But, Murphy had nothing on Little Joe.

Poor guy stood barely a few inches over five feet. That's a hell of a way to go through life. The slide trombone was his thing. I suppose it still is. It was as if he was born with one in his mouth. Little Joe made it look easy. Wailing, he was, when Shifty Henry asked me about breaking out of the joint. It was a hair-brained scheme then, and it's the same the more I think about it now. It wasn't as if it had been carefully planned or anything. It was spur-of-the moment stuff and made no sense to me.

I looked at him. "And how do you propose we do that, Henry?"

He glanced around, all jumpy. "Whadd'ya mean? We just make a break for it. It'll be easy. Keep it simple. Everyone, even the warden, is focused on this stupid music. They'll never see us leave. Look it. Everyone's jigglin' and shakin' and rockin'.'"

Just then, the two lovebirds, numbers Forty-Seven and Three, walked over to Henry and me. The two held hands.

Forty-Seven said to Shifty Henry, "We've been watching you, and we'd like to know if you'd like to have lunch with us tomorrow in the mess hall? The two of us think we'd make a nice threesome."

With that, the two let out little girl-like laughter. Number Three was an old queen. Rumors had it that he dated original inmates Numbers One and Two, not to mention Four through Seven!

Henry's jaw dropped. I raised an eyebrow.

"No one's looking? What do you say now?" I asked Shifty. "Those two," I pointed toward Forty-Seven and Three, "watched your every move. What makes you think the guards aren't as well?"

He balled his fist and started toward Forty-Seven. I quickly intervened. "Whoa. Stop!"

Then, to Shifty, "Just ignore his comment. He didn't mean anything by it."

I turned toward the lovers. "Did you?"

Both Forty-Seven and Three recoiled back a few steps. Neither spoke a word. Both shook their heads before they retreated and disappeared behind a huge block of stone where Sad Sack sat. The poor devil looked more morose than normal. Who could blame him?

From what I'd been told, Sad Sack had been a successful business owner of a dry cleaner store. He was married with a couple of nice kids, lived the American dream in a suburban house with attached garage, white picket fence, the whole nine. Only problem was, Sad Sack was caught in the sack with a prostitute down in the seedy side of town. The papers *loved* it. The entire ordeal turned a productive member of society into a reclusive and depressed convict. Neither the warden nor the prison psychologist, a quack if there ever was one, could raise Sad Sack's spirits.

I watched as the warden approached Sad Sack, but I couldn't hear what he said over the raucous music. Whatever it was, it elicited an uncharacteristic reply from Sad Sack.

"Why don't you go screw yourself with a wooden chair instead, Warden?" screamed the depressed one.

Don't get me wrong. I had nothing against a plan to bust out of the county jail. Hell, it was nothing like the prisons I'd seen in movies. The place reeked. It was damp and cold. Time had its own way of functioning in there. Days dragged. Nights were longer. The food stunk. The other incarcerated societal losers complained to everyone and anyone who'd listen. If I've heard it once, I've heard it a million times: "I was framed. I'm innocent. I had a crummy lawyer. It was nothing but bad luck. The deck was stacked against me," etc., etc.

*Sure, **that's** why you're in prison.* I just wanted to slap everyone and tell them to their collective ugly faces the reality – they had been caught. They were lousy criminals. They needed to man up and do the time.

♩ ♪ ♫ ♬

Forgive my rant. I promised all this would make sense. I also said that, had I gone along with Shifty Henry's plan to bust out of the joint, history – or more specifically – *popular culture*, would have been impacted. I'm as good as my word.

You see, when Shifty said no one was looking and that was our chance to split, if I had said, "Good idea, let's go," then the world would've been robbed of the warden's party in the county jail where the prison band wailed.

I answered Shifty Henry's question about breaking out by looking him in the eyes. I told him straight to his slimy mug that I wanted to hang around a while and rock with the others. His shoulders slumped, but I knew I'd done the right thing.

'Cause, you see, thanks to *yours truly*: Bugsy; everybody – and I mean *everybody* – from the inmates, to the warden, to the guards in the whole cellblock, continued dancing to the *Jailhouse Rock* and **Elvis** had himself another number one hit in 1957.

~ ♩ ♪ ♫ ♬ ~

The Will to Lose

Laird Long

Lenny tugged the safety goggles off his bullet-shaped head and tossed them down onto the work bench. He mopped his receding forehead with a sawdust-heavy cloth and sighed. It was as hot as a summer holiday in Hades in the tiny workshop, but Lenny didn't care. He was content. He had only six weeks left to his release. He could do six weeks with one, four-fingered hand, handcuffed behind his pimply back. And he already had a job lined up on the outside – working in a woodshop.

The bandsaws, the planers, and the sanders hummed loudly and busily, and Lenny hummed a workman-like tune right along with them. He and the five other cons in the program were making playground equipment for a nursery school someplace where they were loose about safety standards. Lenny could picture the little tot's happy faces, lit up with excitement and sugar-filled treats, when they first glimpsed their new—

Choski jabbed two stiffened fingers into Lenny's short ribs. Lenny jumped three feet in surprise and pain. "Get 'er movin', Connors! We got another order to fill tomorrow!"

"Yes, sir, Mr. Choski," Lenny responded, rubbing his side.

"And put on them goggles, dammit! You know the rules!" Choski pointed a tobacco-stained digit at the five safety rules painted in big red letters right in front of Lenny's work bench.

"Yes, sir, Mr. Choski," Lenny reiterated.

Choski was a fat, sunburnt, cuspidor of a man, with a leathery neck and a red crewcut. He moved his chunky head constantly, in a pecking motion. That, and his chicken-like views on courage, had earned him the obvious nickname: Red Rooster. Or Cockhead, as some of the ruder inmates put it. But Lenny knew that Mr. Choski meant well. After all, he was obviously concerned about Lenny's health, since he was always pointing out various safety infractions and shortcomings of—

Choski slammed his extendible graphite baton across the back of Lenny's legs. "No injured cons on my watch, Connors! Too damn much paperwork!"

As Choski solemnly picked his nose, Lenny fumbled his goggles back on and resumed cutting the four by four. He looked up and smiled at

34

Choski. "No need to fret over me, Mr. Choski," he said. Mr. Choski shouldn't be called a rooster, he thought, he was more like a mother hen, always—

The bent saw blade jumped out of its groove in the wood and bit into Lenny's left pinky finger. Blood gushed from the wound, and half a finger swan-dived into the wood chips on the concrete floor.

A nurse with a face like a dollop of over-cooked mashed potatoes patched Lenny up. As Choski sweated and cursed over a mound of paperwork, Lenny started humming again. Only six more weeks.

***

"You tellin' me I gotta go to some damn vocational school?"

Lenny smiled, and shrugged his bony shoulders in a conciliatory manner, like he imagined Sigmund Freud or Dr. Seuss would. "Malcolm, I'm not *tellin'* you anything. I'm merely suggesting that when you get out of here, in five to twenty years, you're going to need some sort of trade or—"

"Hold that thought, cracker." Malcolm held up his hand. A guard was approaching them from across the yard.

Lenny nodded patiently. He had made it his burden, his personal cross to bear, to try and help his fellow prisoners; advise and counsel them – especially the hard-time losers like Malcolm. If he could help a con with his rehabilitation, then—

Malcolm stabbed the guard in the gut with a sharpened screwdriver. The guard screamed, fell to the grass, and rolled over. A gun jumped into his hand and began barking orders. A bullet tore off Lenny's left earlobe.

The yard was bedlam. Prisoners ran in circles, yelling and gesturing, and shots rained down like Hell's hailstones from the guard towers. Lenny took off after Malcolm. He was the one who had leant Malcolm the screwdriver – to fix his bed. They scaled the chain-link fence, jumped over the razor wire, raced through the prison cornfield, and hit freedom head-on.

That night, after the wounded and the slain had been tucked away in the prison infirmary, Choski slowly and painfully wrote out his own, sweat-stained version of the day's events. His view of the riot had been partially obscured by the closet he had locked himself in, but then, he didn't carry a union card for nothing. He ran a furry comb through his red hair and cackled. Lenny Connors, escaped and at large. The imbecile only had six weeks left to serve. Choski popped a sunflower seed into his mouth and clucked his disapproval.

***

Malcolm shoved Lenny through the front door. A shotgun blast rattled the dilapidated farmhouse and painted the wall with a coat of lead. Lenny sprawled onto the dirty floor. The homeowner squeezed the trigger again but nothing happened. Jammed. Malcolm charged, and he and the farmer wrestled over the gun.

As Lenny got to all fours, a woman burst through the swinging door of the kitchen and charged at him with a cast-iron skillet. It clanged off the side of his thick head and stretched him out flat. Through blurry eyes and bloody teardrops, he saw Malcolm win the struggle for the gun and line the woman and the man up against the living room wall. Then he went bye-bye.

"Welcome to the world of the livin', boy!"

Lenny had to stare at Malcolm's hard, shiny face for a long time, before recent events came into focus. Lenny was spread out on a sofa. The man and the woman were sitting at the dining room table, while Malcolm occupied an easy chair, the shotgun nestled across his lap.

"What happened, Malcolm?"

Malcolm grunted with laughter. "Your fool head cracked like an eggshell when Miss John Deere here whomped you with a fryin' pan, is what happened."

Lenny heard the Deere woman giggle. She was obviously the farmer's daughter. She was about half his age, and there was a definite family resemblance that—

"Hush, wife," the farmer said.

"Take it easy, old man," Malcolm warned, raising the shotgun like an erection. "If that pretty little lady wants to open up her sweet mouth with laughter, that's okay by me." Malcolm nodded at the woman. The woman winked back.

"I just wonder what else that mouth can hold," Malcolm pondered.

The farmer got halfway out of his rickety chair before the pointed shotgun set him back down. Lenny rubbed the fresh lump on his head and stared at the two strangers. The farmer was thin, with a tired, worried expression and nervous hands. He had his work cut out for him – seeding in the fields and in the home. The woman had a fleshy face that was as subtle as a glory hole, enormous breasts, and an inner-tube gut to keep the breasts from doing serious damage to her knees.

"What are we going to do, Malcolm?" Lenny asked.

Malcolm licked his thick lips with his tongue and glanced at the woman. "We is goin' to chill, brother. Enjoy some country livin' for a spell."

After dinner, the woman cleared the dishes from the table. Malcolm shoved the farmer into a closet, and then he and Lenny pushed the sofa across the door, barricading the farmer in. Malcolm handed Lenny the shotgun. "Keep an eye on that cornpone cracker, Lenny. I'll be in the kitchen if you need me."

Lenny sat down and watched the closet door. He thought it was nice of Malcolm to help the farmer's wife with the dishes, even though the food had been lousy and—

The woman screamed. Lenny jumped up and kicked the kitchen door open. He watched, bewildered, as it came back and hit him in the face. He nudged it open with the shotgun. Malcolm had the woman up on the counter. His pants were down around his ankles.

"Get away from her, Malcolm!" The shotgun jumped around in Lenny's shaky hands, impatient to spout off. "There's no call for raping that poor girl." He looked at the woman. "I apologize, ma'am, for—"

Malcolm had turned around. Lenny stared at his hardened penis. It was as small as a twelve-year-old midget's. Lenny grinned. Malcolm couldn't do much damage with that thing.

"Put that shotgun down and get over here, stupid!"

That was the woman yelling at Lenny. He looked at her, stunned. Her heavy-duty tube top was pushed up around the rolls of her neck, and her tree-trunk legs were spread wide. Her huge breasts quivered with every bad breath. Lenny became so mesmerized by the woman's spread that he didn't notice what Malcolm was doing until it was too late. Malcolm snatched the shotgun away. He turned to the woman.

"Baby, this guy's got a yardstick! Short on brains but long on—"

"Well then, bring him on over," the woman interrupted. "I'll see if he measures up."

Malcolm shoved Lenny between the woman's marbled thighs. "Just what is going on, Malcolm?" he asked, confused.

Malcolm answered with his hands. He pulled Lenny's pants down and began fondling him. "You gonna be our human sex toy," he whispered into Lenny's ear.

The woman guffawed obscenely. She climbed down off the counter with a grunt and hunkered down on her haunches in front of Lenny. "Come to Mama," she said greedily. She was hungry.

***

Lenny gingerly sat down on the edge of the hotel bed. He was still sore. Malcolm and the farm woman were noisily scarfing down fried chicken at the little table they had set up in front of the tiny TV set. They were watching Saturday morning cartoons in their underwear.

"You didn't kill that poor old farmer, did you, Malcolm?"

Malcolm swiveled his greasy face around to look at Lenny. "'Course not, fool! I didn't have nothin' against that old coot."

Malcolm and the woman looked at each other and grinned. He licked some chicken skin off her face and she licked back.

Lenny lay back on the lumpy bed, relieved. Maybe he could get used to this, he thought. Being on the run wasn't so bad, as long as—

The door crashed open and cops boiled into the room. Malcolm let out a whoop, shoved the woman at the cops, and opened up with the shotgun. The woman squealed with anger and pain as bullets tore open her front and buckshot peeled away her back. A cop's face disappeared with a splash, and then Malcolm was doing a jig up against the wall. He pitched forward, his head smashing through the TV screen. Parts of his body showed daylight. Smoke, flame, thunder, blood, and chicken parts filled the room. Lenny rolled off the bed and onto the floor, stiff as a board.

***

He gazed blankly around the familiar yard. Most of the despair-ridden faces, he recognized – and would for a long time – two hundred years had been added to Lenny's original sentence. The sky was grey and low, constipated with snow and ready to dump. The air was cold, the wind biting. *Well, at least I'm back in the shops program*, Lenny thought. 'Idle hands are the devil's workshop', he was told his mother used to say, before she had died giving birth to her only son. *Maybe I'll join group therapy this time, help some of the other fellows—*

"Hey, Lenny the loser! Good to see you back, man!"

Lenny looked up, *way* up. "Oh, hi Razor. How's it going?"

"Lousy, man." Razor turned his huge body slightly, dipped, and then threw a hook-uppercut at Lenny's benevolent face. Lenny's teeth rattled around in his mouth as his head whipsawed back-and-forth from the force of the blow. "I was 'sposed to go with Malcolm, before you screwed up the break-out!"

Lenny sat down on the frozen ground with a dizzying thud. Stars flashed in front of his eyes and birds fluttered around his head.

"Your ass is mine! For all time!"

Lenny watched Razor walk away, the ground shaking with each step. He looked up at the dead sky. His head slowly cleared. *Maybe, just maybe*, he thought, *I can get Razor to control his anger, channel it into something constructive, like—*

The Will to Lose

Bird crap slapped Lenny full in the face. A relieved pigeon flew over the prison fence and away.

Parole Violator

Laird Long

Don Bradford checked his watch — 12:35. Ervin Rudd still hadn't appeared at the dented, red metal door of the Boulevard Hotel.

"Wake up, sleeping beauty," Bradford muttered to himself, sitting in his car by the curb.

A bum stumbling by on the sidewalk glanced at him. It was a hot day, and Bradford had all the windows open. He stared back at the bum, and the guy shuffled on down the cracked sidewalk with a broken-toothed grin and a wave of his dirty hand — just as Rudd pushed through the door of the hotel across the street and walked out onto the sun-blasted sidewalk.

Bradford didn't have to look at the picture cut-out of the newspaper he'd been given. He easily recognized Rudd's long, lean, wolfish face, the shaggy black hair and slouched shoulders. The man's height and weight matched up with the rest of his physical description. Completing the positive ID was the paleness of Rudd's complexion – not a hint of tan, despite the summer sunshine. A jailbird, fresh out of the pen.

Rudd squinted and put a skeletal hand up to his bony brow. He glanced briefly at Bradford's car, but it didn't mean anything to the ex-con. He'd served half of a ten-year sentence for killing a man, was out on statuary parole. His obligation to society was now merely to report in with his parole agent on a regular basis, and appear to stay clean.

Rudd scrubbed a finger under his nose and hunched his shoulders, then loped on down the sidewalk. Bradford keyed his car to life and rolled after the man.

There were all kinds of amusements for a guy just out of the joint, on Front Street. Bars, massage parlours, booze cans, crack houses, shooting galleries, pool halls, gambling dens, prostitutes on patrol almost every hour of the day and night. Rudd obviously had a thirst on, from too many years swilling cell-made shine, because he cut across Broad Street and shoved through the door of the Occidental Beverage Room on the corner.

Bradford cruised on down Front, found a parking spot and pulled in. He turned off the car's engine, then checked the gun tucked away in his jacket pocket. He got out of the car and crossed Front, pushed into the bar.

It was cool and beery inside. Bradford let his eyes adjust to the gloom, walking slowly into the big room. There were dark, round tables, and red, padded chairs laid out on the floor, a stripper stage thrusting out into the middle from the far wall. There were only ten or so men, scattered around the room, nursing beers and watching the Asian exotic dancer grind out her moves up on the stage. Rudd was sitting at a table by himself, alongside the platform, a pitcher of beer and a glass in front of him.

"Wanna try the buffet?"

Bradford turned his head and glanced at the fat man in the food-stained white shirt, standing behind a buffet set-up against the near wall. Piles of chicken wings and a couple of logs of meatloaf shone greasily under the heat lamps.

Bradford shook his head, said, "Gimme a beer." Then he sat down at a table far from the stage.

He sipped his watery beer and watched his quarry, looking for an opening. But there were just too few witnesses, the place too dark, for Bradford to make his move. So, he waited patiently. Until, just after one-thirty, Rudd finally unfolded his lanky form and got to his feet, stretched like a contented animal.

Bradford hadn't moved from his seat the entire time. Now, he jumped up just as Rudd arose, was out the door of the bar before Rudd had even turned to look in his direction. Bradford jogged across Front Street, back to his car, the bright sun blinding and dizzying him, for a moment.

Rudd slipped out of the bar and proceeded on down the sidewalk, heading north. He covered two blocks, then stopped at the Aragon Pool Hall between Smith and Rutland on Front. He looked around, nervous, like all newly sprung cons, then jerked the battered aluminium door of the joint open and slipped inside.

Bradford stopped at a red light, then pulled into a parking spot just beyond the intersection. The day had gotten even hotter, and he was sweating under his jacket. But his hard face was impassive, his strong jaw set, his blue eyes cold. He'd been on many such shadow and surveillance missions when he'd been a cop, and he knew that if he just played it cool, he'd come upon the perfect opportunity to nail Ervin Rudd. It was just a matter of patience, steely nerves, and grim determination — then swift and violent action when the opening presented itself.

Bradford exited his vehicle and crossed Front Street, pulled open the aluminium door and entered the Aragon Pool Hall.

Rudd was bent over a green, felt-covered table at the back of the smoky-smelling room, shooting a stick at a white ball, lit up by the bank of lights hanging over the pool table. He was playing against another man, a short, round guy, with a shiny moonface. The man was jabbering away, as Rudd slammed a red ball into a corner pocket.

There were two pairs of men at two of the other tables, a threesome at another. There were ten pool tables in all, a few scattered card tables and chairs in front of the snack bar next to the door. The men playing snooker and billiards were heavy-set and bearded, dressed in dusty blue jeans and black leather vests. Biker types.

Bradford didn't like this set-up, either, as he surveyed it. It was the kind of place where all sorts of things happened that went unreported, were covered up; and these were the types of men who kept their mouths shut, especially around cops.

"Want a table?"

Bradford glanced at the dark-skinned dwarf perched up on the stool behind the snack counter. "No, thanks. Just sight-seeing." He turned and left the building, crossed the street back to his car and settled in for another wait.

Rudd re-emerged just after four. He stood on the sidewalk and straightened out a crumpled ball of bills, then glanced sharply around and shoved the money into his jeans. He was on the move again, loping down Front Street, still headed north.

Bradford pulled out of his parking spot and slowly followed, like a shark cruising a swimmer. He shifted over into the boulevard lane. The sun beat down on the car. It was an oven inside. But Bradford was undeterred, a man on a mission.

Rudd turned left onto Graham Avenue, just before Front plunged into an underpass and popped up again into a low income residential district on the other side. Bradford sat out the light in the left-hand turn lane, watching Rudd snake through a group of exiting customers and into the Shanghai Express restaurant.

Bradford turned onto Graham. He had to drive two blocks down the street before he could find a spot to park. City Hall was close by, and things got busy this time of the day. He jumped out of his car and jogged back up Graham, pulled open the two sets of glass doors and went into the restaurant, anxious not to lose Rudd, now that he'd put in all this hot trail time.

He needn't have worried. This time, the set-up was perfect.

A grim smile creased Bradford's pressed lips. He wiped sweat off his broad forehead with a swipe of his big hand.

"Just one, sir?"

"Just one," Bradford replied to the gaunt Chinese guy manning the service lectern. "I'll find a table myself."

The restaurant was half-full, some sort of office function taking place in the middle of the long room, a series of tables pushed together sideways. There were pairs and groups of other patrons, mostly seniors and civil servants, off early. The dinner buffet opened at four.

Bradford adjusted his jacket, checked the gun in his pocket. These were good, clean, honest citizens who would make credible witnesses and wouldn't hesitate to call the police, pitch in themselves in an emergency. And the room was well-lit. Rudd was sitting at a two-chair table against the far wall, a pair of plates loaded with Chinese cuisine in front of him, wolfing the food down.

Bradford weaved his way through the cheaply-decorated room, past tables of happily chattering customers. Until he came to the table next to Rudd's, against the wall. He yanked out a chair, slamming the back of it into the back of Rudd's chair.

The man jumped, choked on an eggroll. He twisted his head around and glared up at Bradford. "Hey, what the fuck!?" he angrily spluttered batter and bean sprouts.

Bradford grinned, humped his chair back a bit. Then he took a step even closer to Rudd and looked over the man's bony shoulder. His heavy, booted right foot landed on Rudd's light canvas sneaker.

"That looks pretty good," Bradford said, leaning over Rudd and looking down at the man's plates of food, pressing his boot hard into Rudd's foot, putting almost all of his weight into it.

Rudd's wolf-face burned red, his knuckles flared white, gripping his knife and fork. "What the fuck you doin'!?" he rasped in a strangled voice; his eyes popped and a purple vein leaped to beating life on his bony forehead.

"I just said: that looks pretty good," Bradford repeated, continued grinding his boot into Rudd's sneaker, piling on the pressure.

He knew Rudd had a hair-trigger temper. That's why he'd killed Mike Tomko, when the little man hadn't handed over his wallet quick enough for Rudd's liking. It was those so-called 'anger management issues', and the fact that Rudd had pistol-whipped Tomko with his .38, instead of shooting the man, that had allowed Rudd to plea-bargain a second-degree murder rap down to manslaughter; get away with only a ten-year sentence, reduced down to half under statutory release provisions.

"Get your fuckin' foot off!" he snarled at Bradford, trying in vain to pull his injured foot away from Bradford's crushing boot.

The hair-trigger temper hadn't gone anywhere, despite the 'rehabilitation' programs.

Bradford slowly lifted his foot up, still grinning. Rudd jerked his leg away, his right hand rising with the knife. No one else in the restaurant had noticed the incident, Bradford's bulky body screening the scene.

"Just saying," Bradford said pleasantly to Rudd. Then he turned his back on the man and walked over to the line at the buffet, picked a plate up off the stack.

He glanced briefly back at Rudd. The man was watching him, his eyes narrowed and his face frozen in hate. The table was set, Bradford figured. All he needed to do now was serve up the main course — Cold revenge.

He walked back to his table, balancing a food-laden plate in one hand and a hot cup of tea in the other. Rudd's wolf-eyes watched him every step of the way, the man twisted around in his chair. When Bradford was within three paces, his foot accidentally-on-purpose caught on the carpet. He tripped, stumbled forward, his cup and plate thrusting precariously up into the air.

Rudd's eyes went wide and his mouth dropped open. He threw up his arms, protecting himself from what looked like certain catastrophe, as Bradford lunged at him unbalanced.

But the big man easily jumped to a stop, steadied himself, two feet away from where Rudd sat startled and staring. Bradford smoothly brought his cup and plate back down to chest level. Then, looking Rudd square in the eye, he leaned over and spat into Rudd's half-eaten plate of food.

Rudd gaped, stunned. Bradford grinned.

The ex-con exploded, pushed past the point of containment for a man of limited self-control. He leapt up from his chair with a roar and slammed his fists into Bradford's broad chest.

"Hey, what are you doing!?" Bradford innocently yelled out, tossing the cup and plate back over his head and staggering backwards with more than a hint of theatrics. Crockery shattered in a violent blast of noise, food and drink splattered everywhere. A family of three at a nearby table took the brunt of the sharding china and drenching liquid and eats. While Bradford's big body banged into another table where a couple of women had been pleasantly dining, sending the table rocking and clattering, setting the women to screaming.

Rudd charged at Bradford. Bradford set his feet and grabbed onto Rudd's shoulders, as Rudd pounded away at his chest and stomach. Shrieks and shouts filled the electrified air, as the men grappled, one obviously beating at the other, all eyes focused on the pair.

Bradford wrestled Rudd back closer to the wall, using his superior strength and training. Rudd pummelled Bradford's ribs, his mouth and nose foaming.

When they were back alongside Rudd's table again, Bradford pulled his right hand off Rudd's left shoulder and shot a short, vicious jab into Rudd's stomach. The man blew food and saliva, jerking over. Bradford quickly slammed his fist up into Rudd's jaw, knocking the man back against the table, dazed. It all happened so fast.

"Call the police! He's got a gun!" Bradford yelled over his shoulder at the crowd, sitting Rudd down in his chair. He covertly dove his hand into his jacket pocket and came out with the cold .38, dumped it into Rudd's lap.

Then he jumped back, pulling the semi-conscious man forward so that the gun clattered onto the floor, as Rudd's body sprawled out like he had slipped. The gun was the same make and model that Rudd had used in the pistol-whipping murder of Mike Tomko.

In the ensuing pandemonium, heroic citizens sprang forward and kicked the gun away from Rudd, jumped on top of the stunned man and pinned him to the floor en masse, as others frantically punched 9-1-1 on their cellphones. Meanwhile, Bradford quietly slipped away from the yelling and gesticulating crowd and right out of the restaurant.

Back in his car parked on Graham Avenue, Bradford used his own cell phone. "It's been all arranged, Mrs. Tomko," he said, hearing the sirens already wailing down Front Street. "He'll be arrested for causing a disturbance, busted for possessing a stolen weapon; his parole violated and the scumbag sent back to prison to serve out his full term."

"Thank God!" Mrs. Tomko exhaled. "*Thank you!*"

Bradford heard her swallow, hard. "It just wasn't fair... that he killed my husband and got away with such a light sentence. That he got out early on parole. I... I had to—"

"I know, Mrs. Tomko. Don't worry, it's done." Bradford paused, letting the woman catch her breath. "You can mail the remaining $2,500 to the post office box number I gave you."

"Yes, yes, of course! I... it just wasn't—"

"I agree, Mrs. Tomko," Bradford cut her off, watching the flashing blue and red lights in his rearview mirror, as police cars skidded up to the curb and the crowd in front of the Shanghai Express. "Sometimes justice has to be... forced."

He tossed the cell phone onto the seat and keyed his car to life, pulling away, a grim smile on his hard face.

It's a Kinda Magic

Jeremy Mays

"Do you believe in magic?"

You might expect to hear those words on a children's playground. At a franchise family amusement park. Hell, even in the hands of a cheap prostitute. But never, *ever*, did I expect to hear those words being uttered from a 6'7, three-hundred-pound man...

In prison.

"What the hell are you talking about, Juice?"

"Magic. You know, that Abracadabra shit. Presto, chango." Juice was using the elaborate pantomime of a stage magician.

"I don't know," I replied, still looking for my toothpaste. The CO had dropped off our toiletry supplies that evening, while I had been in the infirmary getting my nightly sleep meds. When I returned, Juice had already accepted my supplies and put them away for me. I still hadn't been able to find them.

"My Ma always believed. I remember goin' to the fairgrounds and watchin' the cheesy magician there. One even came to our school. Picked people's cards outta the deck and even made some things fly," Juice sounded like he was in a faraway place. "Watched that guy a time or two on the television. You know, the one that made the Statue of Liberty disappear? You know that one?"

I shook my head, "Yeah, David something or other. Dammit, Juice. Where in the hell did you put my...," I turned and saw the big man on the bottom bunk. He had his head in his hands and his shoulders were heaving up and down. I set my toothbrush on the edge of the metallic sink and sat down next to him.

"Your Ma sick again, isn't she?"

Juice looked up. Tears streamed down his dark face. "They thought the cancer was gone. She went back to the doctor just a few days ago. Found it again. My sister says there ain't much they can do for her now."

I put my arm around him. "When's the last time you got to talk to her? Seen her?"

"She's been too sick to come for visitation. I talked to her last week, but I ain't got no more time on my card. I would ask my sister to see if she would put some more money on the books for my phone card, but I know things are rough for her, too, right now."

"I have time on my card. I could slip you the number. Help ya memorize it."

Juice smiled. "Thanks, man, but I don't want you gettin' caught and lose your privilege."

"Who do I have to call? My ex-wife? Her new flavor of the month? Might as well let someone use it." It was the cold, hard truth. Once I had been incarcerated for the armed robbery, everyone who I thought mattered in my life had disappeared on me. The life of a convict could be lonely.

"I just wish I could get out and see her. Would make a world of difference, ya know?"

"Have you tried talking to the warden? Ask her about a possible visit due to the circumstances?"

"Yeah. Since Mississippi is a few states away, she would have to get special permission and such. Could take months, even if they allow it. My Ma don't have that much time." He handed me a small, leather, spiral-bound book. "So, you think this is all bullshit, then?" I could tell he'd had enough talking about his mother and was ready to change the subject.

I looked at the cover and read the title out loud, "1,001 Magical Ways to Amaze Your Friends. Where did you get this?"

"Got it from Spence. He found it while working detail over on G Block."

G Block was the area of the prison where inmates who suffered from mental disorders were housed. Most of the time, those housed there didn't last too long. They either hurt themselves or others. When this happened, they were either carted off to another facility, or off under a sheet. Either case, their personal belongings became free stake.

I began flipping through the pages. Each one was numbered and had a title centered at the top in bold, capital letters. "The Vanishing Coin. The Disappearing Knot. Number Magic. Most of these are sleight of hand type things. Simple street illusions." I handed the book back to Juice. "You thinkin' about taking it up or something?"

Juice put the book in the waist of his pants. "Gotta do something to get my mind off things. Besides, there are some pretty cool tricks towards the back. Whoever had it before me kept some pretty wicked notes."

"Unless it has a trick on how to make disappearing toothpaste reappear, I'm not really interested." I got back up to continue my search.

"It's under your pillow, Bry. Why didn't you just ask?"

I reached for the plastic cup that sat on the side of the sink and turned to give it a toss at Juice's head. But when I turned around, he had already rolled over and faced the wall, the magic book out in his hands, thumbing through it. I set the cup down and retrieved my toothpaste.

Poor bastard, I thought.

The next afternoon, while playing ball in the yard with some other inmates, I noticed Juice had quite a crowd gathered around him, including two COs. I subbed myself out and went to get a closer look. Usually, a crowd of that nature in the pen was a sign of bad news. But as I got closer, I actually heard laughter. There, in the center of the stairs, sat Juice, towering over the other inmates around him. In his hands, he held a deck of cards.

"Ok. Now I want you to think of your card and *only* your card, Sir," Juice was talking to one of the COs, standing at the bottom of the stairs.

"Okay, Juice. I got it. What is it?"

Juice put the deck up to his forehead and closed his eyes. He squinted as if concentrating very hard, mumbled some sort of gibberish I couldn't make out, then opened his eyes. "Is it the nine of Diamonds?"

The CO shook his head. "Nope."

"Nine of Spades?"

Again, the CO shook his head.

"Are you sure?" Juice began thumbing through the cards. The inmates that had surrounded Juice, began to disperse, laughing and heckling him as they departed. I moved to one of the open seats next to my cellmate.

"Looks like you need a little more practice, Juicy Boy," the CO said, as he started to turn away.

"Hey, James! What the hell is that?" It was the other CO. He was pointing at the back of CO James's hat. CO James stopped and pulled his hat off. A single card fell to the rocky ground. Those of us seated around that area leaned forward.

"Well, I'll be damned. It's my fucking card!" He turned to look at Juice. "How in the hell did my card get there?"

Juice just smiled and shrugged his shoulders. "Magic?"

Juice handed the deck of cards back to CO James, who left, shaking his head. The inmates that had remained throughout the trick patted Juice on the back as if he had just pulled out the winning shot at a high school championship basketball game.

"That was pretty impressive!" I said. "From your book?"

Juice patted his waist. "You betcha! I have a few more I've been working on."

A tone sounded throughout the yard, signaling the end of recreational time. "I guess it'll have to wait until later," I said, standing up. "I gotta work the chow line."

"Chow line?"

"Some disagreement during prep. Someone got ahold of a bag of Jolly Ranchers, melted them down, and made a gigantic shank out of them. Guy pissed off the wrong person and got it right through the neck. I turned to walk away and then stopped. "How's your Ma?"

"Gonna call her in a bit. They have a phone set up in her room. Thanks again for the number."

"No problem. We'll talk later," I turned to follow the herd into the barred doorway. I took a quick glance over my shoulder; Juice was buried back into his magic book again.

Dinner detail actually went pretty smooth that night. I watched the line for Juice. About fifteen minutes into dinner, he came through the line. Those with him were pestering the man with questions and requests about magic and tricks. Juice was one giant smile. As he passed by, he gave me a quick and courteous nod and then took a place at a table in the corner. Numerous inmates followed, eager to see Menard Correctional Facility's newest standout.

As I filled tray after tray, I couldn't help but sneak a glance or two Juice's way. Just as in the yard, a small crowd had begun to gather. I could hear things like, "How the hell did ya do that?" and "Make that salt shaker float again, Juice!" The COs started to get a bit nervous, due to all the inmates gathered in such a small location. The crowd was broken up before I could personally walk over and enjoy the show.

Once I had my detail cleaned up, I made my stop at the infirmary for my sleep medication and then headed straight to my cell. I was surprised to see Juice already there, sitting on the top bunk, legs dangling over the side. I could tell right away, something just wasn't right.

"Juice?" The big man didn't move. "Juice?"

He looked up. His eyes were wide and filled with confused emotion. "Ma ain't gonna make it through the night, Bry."

I moved forward. "Ah, pal. I'm sorry."

He slid down onto the concrete floor. "I called. Talked to my sister first. She said things were really bad. The doctor wasn't expecting her to make it through the night." He rubbed his nose onto his dark, hairy arm. "Then Ma got on. She… She *begged* for me to come see her. To hug her. To hold her hand."

That was all he could handle and the big man collapsed into my arms.

Prison ain't like they show in the movies. A great many of the people behind bars are good at heart; people that have made mistakes or been in the wrong place at the wrong time. Yet, no one wants to hear that aspect of the pen. They only want to hear about the violence and the hatred; of the evil that can reside behind bars. They could care less about the emotional scarring, the goodness that can exist in a desolate place such as this. They could care less about someone like Juice.

"I gotta get outta here. I gotta get to my Ma."

I pulled Juice from my shoulder. "Ain't gonna happen, pal. I know you want that more than anything right now, but it's not possible. First thing tomorrow morning, you and I will go see Warden Snow. We'll tell her what's going on. Find out what we can do to get ya over to see your mom."

"There's not enough time," Juice said. I knew that he was right.

The door to our cell slid shut and the lights dimmed. It was "Lights Out". Juice walked over to the bunk area and crawled onto the bottom bed.

"What gives? You get top bunk."

"Not tonight, Bry. The top bunk is yours."

I could feel my sleep meds already starting to kick in. I was in no shape to argue. I shimmied my way up to the top cot and lay my head down. I hadn't even pulled the covers all the way up when I started to drift. The last sounds I remembered were Juice mumbling something incoherent and the sound of pages being flipped in his damn magic book.

***

"Phelps!"

I tried to open my eyes, but I couldn't. I was warm. I was at peace. I was free.

"Damnit, Phelps! Get your ass up!"

I opened my eyes. Standing eye level to my bunk, was CO Crane, and he wasn't alone. Five other correctional officers were with him. None of them looked pleased.

"Yes, sir?" I said, sitting up.

"Where the hell is Rodotz?"

"Huh?" I still wasn't fully awake yet.

"Juice. Where the hell is he?"

I rolled over the side of the bunk pointing, "He slept on the bottom…"

The bunk was empty.

"He did what?"

I looked again. The bed was empty.

"Damnit, Phelps. Where the hell is Jason Rodotz?"

I climbed down from my bunk. "I don't know, sir. He was here last night."

CO Crane pulled the radio from his belt. "Warden, Inmate Rodotz is NOT in his cell. I repeat, NOT in his cell." Crane looked over to me. "If I find out you know something about this, I will see to it you never get your ass outta here. Got that! Close cell 213."

I watched as all of them left and went in separate directions. The cell block was alive with all sorts of chirping and murmurings as an alarm was sounded. I turned away from the bars of my door and went back to my bunk.

"What the hell?"

When I sat down, I bumped something in the middle of the covers. I pulled the sheet back; it was Juice's magic book. I picked it up and rubbed my hand over the worn, leather cover. I noticed one of the pages was dog-eared. I put my index finger in its location and flipped the book open.

"The Disappearing Man."

I began laughing hysterically as I read the title of the magic trick. I closed the book slowly and walked back over to my cell door. I watched the frenzied chaos around me as they searched frantically for a man I knew they would never find.

"Do I believe in magic?" I asked out loud. "Hell yeah, I do."

I flipped the book back open, and began reading…

Solitary Man

Adrian Ludens

"Hello Tyler, it's Dad. I'm sorry your mother isn't with me. Seeing you in here like this is awful hard on her. You know how she got last time. Most mothers, you expect them to break down sometimes. Crying and carrying on some. But screaming out blasphemies against God until she foamed at the mouth? I didn't know she had it in her.

"I thought it'd be best to leave her at home. You understand. Besides, it'll give me a chance to visit with you about my work. You've exhibited an interest before but I always kept what goes on in prison to myself. I never took the time to tell you about my job and now I wish I had. I can't help but think it's too late, but it's worth a try. Maybe something I tell you today will get through to you somehow.

"I'll tell you about the prisoners on death row another time. Ditto for the yard fights and some of the contraband we've found smuggled in. Believe me, I have a lot of stories I could tell. But tonight I want to tell you about the block. A few of the guys call it 'the cooler' and the official term for an area that I'm in charge of is 'solitary confinement'. It's a special form of imprisonment where the prisoner is denied contact with any of the other prisoners and doesn't get any visitation. Most prisons do allow for minimal contact with staff; guards conduct room searches and somebody cleans every once in a while. But I run a tighter operation. The only contact the prisoners in the block have is with me. And I can be tightlipped when I want to be.

"The prisoner holding the record for longest stay in the block under my watch is this guy who beheaded a Catholic priest in the late 1970's. He never gives me any trouble – he's a model prisoner, believe it or not – but any time we ever tried to move him back into the general population, guys would try to kill him. Usually the Irish Catholics, but the Hispanics can be overzealous about religion, too. So this guy stays in the kind of protective custody that only the block can supply.

"There are other prisoners confined to the block; crazy bastards who relish the chance to inflict suffering, loose cannons with faulty wiring. But they're not the ones I want to tell you about either. I keep dancing around the subject and I don't know why.

"I want to tell you about one prisoner in particular. I need to get it off my chest. Part of it is your old man wanting to clear his conscience. But part of it is me needing to understand just what the hell is going on.

"This prisoner, he's quite famous. He's a writer. Specializes in horror and mystery. He's cracked the bestseller list several times. Let me whisper his name...

"Maybe you recognize him, maybe you don't. I guess I have to admit I don't know if you're much of a reader or not. But this author – he's always shunned the spotlight. He refuses interviews and he's never done a single book signing. Hell, his publisher doesn't even print his photo on the dust jackets because they don't have one.

"But he's got a cult following like you wouldn't believe. Awards, accolades, respectable sales... he still gets it all. You know why? Because nobody knows he's in prison! His fans think he's a recluse, like that guy who wrote 'Catcher in the Rye'. Only a handful of people – his agent, his editor at the publisher, the previous warden there and me – we're the only people who know that one of America's most popular horror and mystery authors got himself incarcerated with no hope of parole. Think on that for a bit.

"None of his fans know it, but this guy was convicted of premeditated first degree murder ten years ago. He was sentenced to life without parole but no one ever knew. Know why? Because money talks. His publisher spent a fortune keeping the whole thing a secret. I'm not saying the system is corrupt; if it was, he would have walked away a free man. I'm saying sometimes certain exceptions are made.

"You know what he told me when he first arrived? Said he just needed to know that what he wrote was realistic. Can you imagine? Said he did it 'for love of the craft'. Not the craft of murder, but writing. Told me now that he'd experienced it for himself, he could write for the rest of his life and never worry about the quality of his output. I just shook my head and told him he'd never get to write again.

"Man was I ever wrong.

"His editor at the publisher made a deal with the old warden. It was all under the table and the powers-that-be were incredibly guarded when it came to who knew what. The public was – and still is – hungry for new books by this guy, and I have a key part in making it happen. My cut over the last ten years has paid your college tuition – if you ever go.

"I know by now you must be wondering what it is that I do for this author, exactly. My only duty is to smuggle in paper each day and pens whenever he needs them.

"A lot of the guards are on the take, either turning a blind eye to certain situations or bringing in contraband on their own to make some extra cash. I never got involved with any of that. But this was, and still is, a whole different set of circumstances. One day, this guy in a suit buys me coffee. Turns out he's the author's agent. He flew all the way here just to visit me personally. He laid it all out that day; I get a package once a month: a ream of paper, a few pens, and stamped, pre-addressed manila envelopes.

"Whenever the prisoner completes a new story or a chapter in his latest novel, I slip it into one of the envelopes and drop it in the mail. His latest book got him a Stoker nomination. I read the first draft before anyone, including his agent and his editor.

"Not that I'm gloating. I'm taking a serious risk doing what I'm doing. It's gotten more dangerous now that there are fewer of us who know about the arrangement. The warden the publisher made the deal with passed away last winter and the new warden's not in the loop. I'm the only guy they need on the inside when you think about it. I'm the only person he has any contact with in the block. The author's agent knows but the original editor died a few years ago and as far as his new editor and the staff at the publisher knows, the author's just a recluse. So, I'm mostly responsible for keeping this guy's work on the best seller lists.

"It feels good to tell you all of this. There are worse things I could do, don't get me wrong. But to finally confide in someone, well, it feels good, like I said. I guess I'm a little selfish in telling you, but part of me thought you might be interested in my famous-but-secret prisoner.

"I also thought you might relate to him. I mean, he's in there, locked up in solitary confinement. We don't ever directly communicate. He is truly alone. Like you, son. Locked away someplace where it seems no one can reach you.

"That you even survived the accident is nothing short of a miracle. It's not too often a motorcycle rider survives a collision with an eighteen-wheeler. The doctors say you might wake up tomorrow – or not at all. So, I wanted to tell you the story about the man cut off from everyone and yet he still manages to thrill his readers with his words all these years later. That's an amazing accomplishment. If you can hear me, Tyler, I hope it helps you cope, even if it's just a little. If you can hear me, know that your mother and I – and a lot of other folks out here – hope you can find your way. We hope to be hearing from you again real soon.

"Speaking of your mother, I'll bet she's got supper on the table and is wondering where I am and what's keeping me, but I wanted to stop by after work to talk for a spell. One more thing, Tyler; this is the part that has your old man completely confounded.

"This famous author; he's been in the block under my care for ten years now. But I haven't actually entered his cell in quite some time. I don't even look in there anymore. I'm too afraid. Every day, I bring him his meals and his smuggled paper on a flat tray that I slide through this narrow horizontal slot in his cell door. And every day, like clockwork, I'm there to get the pages and the meal tray when the prisoner pushes them back out.

"The pages are always full, front and back, with handwritten lines every time. But for the past four and a half years, the food trays are returned untouched."

A Rose is a Rose?

Larry Lefkowitz

Jeffrey Rose had committed a white collar crime. A business transaction, or manipulation, which was in a gray area under the stock market law but to which a judge applied the black letter of the law. Unfortunately for Rose, his little transaction had caused considerable monetary loss to an influential politician – and so, Rose found himself not in a white collar prison for economic offenders, but in a blue collar prison where the only 'neckties' were worn by guys at necktie parties who had come afoul of a prison clique. Worse, he found himself in the cell of the formidable clique that ruled the prison, again, thanks to his political benefactor.

If you happen to be a white collar prisoner in a blue collar prison where your bedfellows have violent criminal records only approached by their recidivist records, the gap between you and your fellow cellmates is markedly apparent.

And so, Rose's first days among them were not particularly pleasant. He was, in short, the low man on a roughly chiseled totem pole. In a society where sobriquets flourish like subpoenas, they called him, mockingly, 'The Cincinnati Kid', because, first, he hailed from Cincinnati and, secondly, like the hero of the eponymous movie, Rose had been a gambler, his cellmates rightly considering playing the stock market as gambling. In addition, he was "the newest kid on the block." To wit, their butt. Until one morning when the cell and prison leader, Perini, whom his cellmates called 'Lifer' Perini in deference to his sentence, cocked his head at him. "Hey, Rose, you aren't by any chance, a relative of *The* Rose?"

"*The* Rose?" he paused. "Are you speaking horticulturally? It is unlikely that genetic engineering—"

"*Pete* Rose."

Rose hesitated. For the first time since he was "inside," not every face was hostile. They were curious, suspicious, but overt hostility had left them... but, for how long? Jeffrey Rose was an honest guy if we discount the questionable transaction that had brought him there, yet absolute honesty in that place, in those conditions, was hard to maintain. And so, he dissembled: "A Rose is a Rose is a Rose."

'Twenty Years' Dalton said, "You telling us something?"

Perini squinted at him. "He even *looks* a bit like Pete. A kind of professor-like Rose, if you'll excuse the comparison."

Rose. Our Rose, the faded prison Rose, saw their faces soften. Still, years of honesty (save for his one lapse) made it difficult for him to claim consanguinity with their Rose. "A Rose by any other name..." he dissembled once more.

"What's that?" Perini's softened face took on its regular, gun-metal mien.

"...would be unthinkable."

"So, you *are* Pete's relative?"

Four scowls scrutinized him.

Who can fault him for wishing to come up smelling like a rose?

Our Rose nodded.

The change was instantaneous. Four grins met his hitherto avoiding countenance. 'Fifteen years' Colson went so far as to pat him affectionately, if heavy-handedly, on the back. Small wonder he felt like the death row recipient of an eleventh hour reprieve.

"Sure, he even stands a bit like the way Pete stands in the batter's box," opined Perini. "After he's brushed back by the pitcher," he added with the guffaw that, over the years, he'd honed to reflect his perverse sense of humor.

"Have you ridden in the red chariot?" asked 'Baker's Dozen' Baker, reverently.

Fortunately, our Rose was a baseball buff. He knew that Pete Rose was the owner of a red sports car that could park in any non-parking zone in Cincinnati and be as un-ticketed as if the Police Chief's car itself had been parked there.

"Once or twice," he lied. Lying is a minor infraction in the hierarchy of crimes, yet, like any misdeed, it is one that becomes easier to commit with practice.

Awe, reverence, even a kind of soured love shown on the faces of our convicts. Perini could only bang his ham-fist against the bars in appreciation. Almost immediately, other prisoners in the cell block began beating on their bars. Because Perini was the leader, they thought he was beginning a riot. He quelled it with a vociferous, "Knock it off! It's not the food. Pete Rose's cousin lives in *our* cell."

There ensued a total silence, broken only by the far away clank of a cell door being slammed in the slammer as a new prisoner was locked in, or an old one, locked out. Silence was as usual in that bailiwick as that following a strikeout by their idol in his.

From then on, Jeffrey Rose had a prison-wide moniker: 'Pete Rose's cousin.'

Even the guards whispered to each other in almost saintly tones when 'Pete Rose's cousin' entered the dining hall.

Meanwhile, 'Pete Rose's cousin' had risen about as high as one can within the prison pecking order for one who lacks the credentials of a capital crime-committer. For the first time, he felt the truth of the adage that, 'it pays to have friends in low places.'

We have already pointed out that our Rose was a baseball buff. And, like a good one, he was full of statistics. What the legendary Abbadabba Berman had been to horse racing odds, our Rose was to baseball facts. He began throwing them around with the regularity of a pitching machine. If there had been doubting Tom's, Luigi's, or what-name-you's, as to the convergence of Pete's and our Rose's bloodlines, they faded whenever our Rose threw out a statistic about his cousin. Sometimes it was in the form of a poser to his cellmates to whom he supplied the answer when they could not come up with one. More often, as a statement, since our Rose thought making his new 'buddies' look bad could be costly. Such nuggets as, "Pete Rose was named the National League's Rookie of the Year in 1963."; "Pete Rose broke the club record for most hits in a single season previously set at 219 by Cy Seymour in 1905."; "Pete Rose set the major league record for career hits with 4,256." (To which, Dalton responded, "Gee that's even more 'hits' than you made in your career, Perini.")

These statistics, more than those of any probation report, helped bolster our Rose's blood-kinship claim in the eyes of his fellow prisoners. But, what removed any lingering doubts, was Jeffrey Rose's desire to go beyond the statistics to sum up the essence of his Rose's — their Rose's — greatness. Imbued by his stock-selling technique, he launched into a ringing oration: "Peter Edward Rose's value to his team goes beyond his ability at the plate. He is the team's spark plug, the type of player who runs into outfield walls to catch a fly ball, slides into a base headfirst, and runs full-tilt to first base when he draws a walk. A guy who can jar a lazy teammate with a few caustic words or push a less talented one to the limits of his ability with some judicious praise. It is not for nothing that Rose is known around the National League as *'Charlie hustle.'*"

As one, his convict audience leapt to their feet and applauded vigorously. "Better than any gangland funeral eulogy I ever heard," was Perini's ultimate accolade.

Perhaps because our Rose had gilded the rose just as he had over-gilded his stock transactions into manipulations, fate decided that events were going too smoothly for Jeffrey Rose. Even prisons are not immune from the proverbial fly in the ointment, with the proviso that the fly is likely to be particularly obtrusive in a place where ointments are frowned upon, at least as hand creams – there, however, being a limited demand for them in oiling locks and door hinges conducive to silent escape attempts.

In the case of our hero, the fly in the ointment took the form of another inhabitant of the prison, one Mat Benson, who really *was* a relative of Pete Rose, if a distant one. Naturally, he was suspicious of our Rose's genealogy when it reached him, and he was jealous of the achieved status of one whom he considered a likely pretender.

Benson resolved to investigate the matter, but was somewhat handicapped in this resolve, due to the fact that he sat on death row. He repeated to whomever he could find to listen to him – and there weren't many given his present surroundings – that *he* was a relative of Pete Rose. Nobody believed him. "He's just trying to cash in while he still has his chips," they said. And his surname was not Rose. "His only connection with Pete is that he murdered somebody like Pete murders the ball" made the rounds of the prison social network.

The only one who did not scoff at Benson's claim was our Rose. Not without feelings of guilt (since hitherto, he had been against capital punishment) he now began watching the calendar marking time to Benson's final paying of his debt to society. This, in the devout hope that Benson would 'go' before the truth of our Rose's non-kinship to Rose willed out. If Benson didn't 'go', our Rose could '*go*' and his 'going' at the hands of Perini and his friends would be more than metaphoric.

While Pete Rose's distant cousin waited impatiently to see if the governor would act before the executioner did, his professed closer cousin waited expectantly for an early release, even though it was unusual to receive a parole on the first round. Before Benson could be executed or saved, Jeffrey Rose was paroled, which rendered Benson's fate academic to him.

Rumor had it that the unheard of first-round parole resulted when somebody whispered to the Parole Board that our Rose was related to Pete Rose. But the story that kinship to Rose tipped the balance, may be only an urban legend. What is known, is that a crime reporter who had apparently heard the rumor as well, approached Pete himself on the question of his family connection to Jeffrey Rose. "Never heard of him," he spat out.

Whether this response reached the prison and 'Lifer' Perini, 'Twenty Years' Dalton, 'Fifteen Years' Colson and 'Baker's dozen' Baker is unknown. Our Rose prudently did not wait to find out, emulating 'Charlie hustle', himself.

Soon after, reports began circulating that he'd been variously spotted in Mexico, Tahiti, and Israel. We thought Cuba or Japan more likely because, in these countries, there dwelt rabid baseball fans, and our Rose would feel more at home; a surmise substantiated when rumors surfaced that an American baseball fan had gotten a cushy job in the front office of a Havana baseball team. Seems our Rose parlayed his claim, that Rose meant 'red' in German or Yiddish, into proving that he was spiritually – if not physically – related to Che Guevara. And yet, knowing our Rose, and mindful of his 'success' in prison, we suspect that he probably hinted as well that he was related to Pete Rose; a fact that would stand him well with a veteran baseball fan like Fidel Castro.

It is even said that a new Cuban cigar recently appeared bearing the label 'El Rosa' in tribute to Rose – but whether it honors our Rose or their Rose – is not yet clear.

Second Chance

Tom Larsen

The week before the break, he got Lucille to white-out the names and dates on her birth certificate. Told her to make a copy and type in a new name, any name, as long as it was easy to remember. She picked 'Buck Clayton', and that's who he became. One might think having the same name as a famous jazzman would get him some attention in life, but they'd be mistaken. Only twice did someone make the connection, and one of them had the wrong horn. Such was jazz fame.

Lucille left the birth certificate in the glove compartment, along with a hundred dollars, a change of clothes, and a short note.

Dear Buck,
Lotsa luck.

He still carried the note in his wallet, though he hadn't seen Lucille in thirty years.

He'd just turned twenty-four when he walked away. Half a mile through scrub pines to the local MacDonald's and a brown VW with the keys inside. Lucille was as good as her word. He changed clothes in the parking lot, ordered a Big Mac with fries, and drove off to his new life in his own goddamn car.

In Denver, he hooked up with a girl in a bar. Didn't remember her name, but never forgot the way she moaned when he took her from behind. Had her knock on the door a few minutes after he'd gone in to see the notary, and while the man was distracted, he slipped the seal from the desk. Spent a month in Reno, waiting for the driver's license, then, on to California for the Jerry Brown years.

Got the checks, got the food stamps, and at the end of six months, enrolled in nursing school for the standard six bits. Didn't use, didn't steal, and steered clear of the low life.

Every move he made, he thought of Dexter. Breaking out was the easy part, Dex would say. It was staying out that most couldn't manage. Buck chose nursing for the ratio of women to men. In a year's time, he was managing nicely.

***

He met a girl named Peyton in a health food store, and within the year, made her Peyton Clayton. Funny thing, all those nurses, and he married a lawyer. They bought a house in a small town on the Carquinez Straits, across the street from a massive weeping willow. The man who owned the tree said he stuck a branch in the ground on his wedding day. Three grown girls and a grandson later, that old tree was a hundred feet high. The man's name was Jack Walters.

On the day Buck's son was born, he stuck three of Jack's branches in his front yard. It'd been over a year since he'd seen his son, but he could see those willows a mile away.

They were regulars at Juanita's saloon, where they would sit on the back porch and watch the tankers slip past. Buck kept a bucket of flat stones out by the railroad tracks, and would skip them over the water and off the hulls; a distant bonk followed by curses from the crew. After his punch-out with a biker from Hayward, Juanita named a drink after him. The Bloody Buck – a Bloody Mary double with Old Bay and clam juice, served in a mason jar with a single, spicy string bean. The Bloody Buck was an instant sensation, and over the years, it made her a bundle. Buck declined the brass barstool and commemorative plaque, but as long as Juanita owned the place, the Claytons drank for free. Saturday nights, they'd close the bar and join her across the street for an absinthe or two. Just the thing for the walk home. Buck's hand in Peyton's back pocket. Main Street in the moonlight and not a car in sight.

Peyton quit the downtown firm and opened a practice at a nearby community center. It meant living on less, but the hours were better and she was home for their son. Her work involved her in local issues, and their house became a gathering place for artists and activists. Jake was a California kid. Buck watched him grow and marveled at how easy it was for him; parents who loved him, money coming in, every day as perfect as the day before. He worried that Jake wouldn't be ready for the harder knocks. He was a good kid, and smart as a whip, but he didn't know what his old man knew.

Buck worked the ETC unit at Martinez General. It was an easy job with good benefits, but the days were long and he missed being home. He helped a neighbor put an addition on his house, to see how it was done, then put one on his own, just to see if he could do it. He learned enough in the process to sidelight as a home inspector. Loved crawling around in people's houses and giving it to them straight. Bought a truck and some overalls and when the developers came, Buck was sitting pretty.

***

In the years Jake was away at school, their little town was "discovered". First, the gays; then gourmets; then, the tourists. On weekends, the restaurants and galleries were packed, and the line of cars stretched a mile out of town. Like all the locals, they bitched about it, but in the smug way of insiders. There were attempts to mobilize, but they bogged down in meetings or ran out of steam. Hard to get worked up when business was booming and houses were worth five times what they'd paid for it.

Buck ran a clean business. Not a bribe or kickback in a dozen years. Paid his taxes to the nickel, and gave a man his money's worth. He didn't think about Lynnewood, except for Dexter. Kept his old life buried under layers of new.

Still, there were moments. Once, Peyton asked him to attend a conference with her in Atlanta, but he wriggled out of it at the last minute. He read about a fugitive from New York who was captured in a Sausalito bar after 28 years, and it gnawed at him for months. He'd done a good job of covering his tracks, but he worried about the chance encounter. As he passed into middle age, he took comfort in knowing that his old friends wouldn't recognize him. With his white hair and prosperous paunch, he looked more Rotarian than robber, and he welcomed each change like a man growing younger.

***

He knew nothing of his mother and sisters back in Georgia. Couldn't say if they were alive or dead. It pained him to think he would never see them, but that was the price and he was willing to pay it.

The hardest thing was keeping it all from Peyton. When they'd met, he'd told her he was from South Carolina, but his family moved around a lot. Different towns and schools to explain away friends. Along the line, his folks had died, and he'd come out there. A simple story, and easy to dodge around, if a bit too sketchy to pass for a past. For a while, he tried fabricating recollections or altering events, but he saw the trouble that would come of it, and kept the story straight. The few times Peyton had pressed him; he'd steered her questions into a fight.

He always thought he would tell her someday, but time went by and he never did.

***

Jake graduated Stanford at the top of his class. For most of a year, he tripped around Europe, then took his Masters at the Sorbonne. Of all the things that had happened to Buck, this was the one nobody could touch; his son the scholar, man of the world. Few in his family ever made it through high school, and most had never left the state. Jake could speak three languages and quote Voltaire. Buck's mother had it wrong all along. It was ignorance, not misfortune, that ran in the blood. Jake was living proof. A person might beat the world or be beaten by it, but they couldn't be stupid if they didn't know how. When he'd walked away from Lynnewood, Buck walked away from a world of trouble, and now, that world had ceased to exist.

On their twentieth anniversary, Buck took Peyton to Paris to visit Jake. They booked a top-floor apartment on Isle St. Louis, with the terrace view alone, worth the price. The strange course of his life never seemed so dear as it did looking out on the city lights.

Every day was a gift, he knew, and he'd done his best with the cards that were dealt him. It wasn't getting caught that scared him. It was where he would be, had he served his time: If he'd done a single thing differently or made one wrong move. His one life had been a good one, and he had Dexter to thank for that.

***

"I'm gonna save you, little dick. I'm gonna teach you how to use the only two things you got." He does the preacher routine, pacing and waving his hands. "I'm gonna show you how to live a life."

"These two things you say I got... What are they?"

Dexter turns on those headlight eyes. "You got a brain. I know you got a brain, 'cause you knew what my origami was. Ain't no stupid people know 'bout origami."

"What's the other?"

"Your sorry, white ass. Wouldn't waste my time on no brother," Dexter drops into a crouch. "Too many times, a brain does a nigger no good."

"What do you know about living a life, anyway?"

"When I came here, I didn't know shit, but time is time. You can put it to use."

"In here? Not exactly role model city, homes."

"Save it, little dick. You ain't black and you ain't bad. It's why I picked you."

"What do you know about my dick?"

"It's white, ain't it?"

"You got the wrong guy, Dexter."

64

"You're not listening to me. I'm gonna make you the right guy. I'm gonna teach you everything you got to know, and then I'm gonna set you free."

"Why?"

Dexter sits with his arms around his knees, staring down between his legs.

"Let's just say, it's research."

"I think I'll pass, Dexter."

Again, the headlights, high beams this time.

"Ain't no pass, boy. You're the one."

***

That first night in Paris, they met Jake for drinks at an outdoor bistro. The kid was a marvel. Chatting with the waiter, flirting with barmaids, speaking of things they knew nothing about. After two days of sightseeing, Buck was happy just to watch him work. It was what he'd been waiting for. A chance to revel in it. That his sorry line could have made this leap was inconceivable. And yet, there he was. The blood of his blood.

"So, I had to fly to Philadelphia to see the Soutine," Jake was saying. "This Doctor Barnes had more artistic vision than all the curators of Europe."

"And more than a little luck, sounds to me."

"Not luck, dad. He was absolutely passionate and his taste was clairvoyant. Monet, Picasso, Cézanne. Do you know there are more Cézanne's in Philadelphia than there are in Paris?"

Buck did not. What he knew about art could fit on a postcard, but he never tired of listening to Jake.

"It makes me nervous to think of you flying all over the place," Peyton eyed him over the rim of her sunglasses.

"It's not so bad, mom. The customs people are very accommodating."

"So, did you see it? The Soutine?" Buck steered him back to the subject.

"Yes, and it was the strangest thing. Barnes stressed that the paintings should be accessible so there are no barriers. I was standing as close to it as I am to you," Jake faded slightly at the thought. "…Too close to process the effect, the depth of field, the distortion of light."

To live a life, Buck thought to himself.

"Soutine's style is very distinctive. Almost as if he used a trowel instead of a brush. The surface of his painting is like a relief map, sharp ridges and depressions, as much textural as visual. It was all I could do not to…"

"Touch it?" Peyton filled in the blank.

"Worse. I wanted to pick off a piece of it. It would be easy enough. Just take my fingernail and… snap!"

"But, you didn't."

"It was the fear of getting caught that restrained me. I would be disgraced, so I didn't dare. But, I wanted to."

"But, why?"

"It's difficult to explain, mom. These paintings are creations. You take the basic elements – canvas, paint – put them in the hands of a genius, and he brings them to life. It's a physical transformation. A product of the artist's hand. But without the elements, there is no painting. He must work with them, touch them, breathe them in. It is the accumulation of paint that we see, after all. Stroke upon stroke, directly applied. A series of movements combining one element with the other. It is the intimacy of man and material. The painting, as striking as it may be, is merely the result."

"Like French cooking," Buck grinned like an idiot.

"Exactly. You can taste the food and you can see the painting but you are not part of the creation. Only the artist and the elements have a role. And since the artist is dead…"

Peyton looked to Buck. "You have only the elements."

"Exactement, mom. Right there for the taking. A tiny paint chip. Who would miss it?"

Buck would bet he had it on him.

***

They were back from Paris for less than a month when Buck suffered his first dizzy spell. He was leading a young couple through their basement when his vision began to blur. To the couple's astonishment, he walked face-first into a support beam, nearly knocking himself unconscious. The second time, he was having a beer in Juanita's and had to grab hold of the bar to keep from collapsing. At first, he wrote it off to age, but a black-out at the wheel argued against it.

Got the CAT scan, got the MRI and prayed to God he would be all right. A few days later, they called him in and he saw in their faces it wasn't good. They'd found a tumor in the brain stem. Small but inoperable. Four to six months was the best they could do. Buck just sat there, crunching the numbers. Multiplied four times thirty, then six times thirty, then rewound the calendar to get an idea. The PA system crackled in the hallway, and laughing voices passed the door. Sixteen weeks to the end of the story. After nearly three decades, his luck had run out.

Second Chance

***

"A smart man don't do no crime. At least crime you got to pay for. Only way to pay is with your life. One day at a time. A smart man knows how much you got to rob and steal to make a living. Ain't never been worth the effort. The more you steal, the more they catch you."

Dexter rolls his collar up against the wind. From the top of the bleachers, they can see across the clearing to the edge of the swamp. Premium seats, off limits to lightweights, but he's there with Dexter, so everything's cool.

"Tell me, Dex. If I'm so smart, how come I'm in here?"

He just shakes his head. "Never said you was smart, little dick. I said you got a brain. Look at Leon, down there," they watch the big man cross the yard. "Old Leon robbed more banks than Jesse James, but the last time they caught him, he was sleeping in a car. A smart man don't sleep in no damn car."

"Old Leon's dumb as a stump."

"Check it out," Dexter stares out over the wall. "If you was to find yourself alone by those trees, with nothing but the clothes on your back, what would you do?"

"Run like hell and boost the first car I saw."

"Just what Leon did. Big Daddy had him hog-tied in the hole before the sun came up." Dexter yanks a knit cap from his pocket and pulls it down over his head.

"How did he do it? Get out, I mean."

"Prison's like a living thing. Runs on habit, mostly. Sooner or later, someone gets careless. A smart man is always ready." Dexter gives a wave to the watchtower. The guard leans out and flips him the finger.

"They're gonna be watching you now, boy," Dexter chuckles. "I was you, I'd watch my step."

"You say you know a way out of here. How come you don't go, yourself?"

"Another three years and I'm free and clear. No way I'm gonna fuck that up."

"What about me, Dexter? I'm up for parole at the end of the year."

Dexter laughs out loud at this one.

"That boy that died, how old was he?"

"I had nothing to do with that."

"Seventeen? Eighteen? They'll have the whole damn family down here tearing their hair out. You ain't goin' no place, son."

He doesn't say anything. Keeps watching those trees, seeing himself out there.

***

Buck told no one about the tumor. He kept it secret to spare Peyton and postpone the burden of sympathy, and because saying the words would make it so. He'd seen how friends reacted to a death sentence. The deference, the strained exchanges, the not-so-gradual phasing out. He'd been guilty of it himself. When Jack Walters' liver shut down, he hardly saw him towards the end. To keep his secret, Buck went for treatment at a Richmond clinic, and filled his prescriptions at the hospital pharmacy. He could feel the days slipping by but he did his best to act like himself. Once word got out, there'd be no taking it back.

Just before Thanksgiving, Jake called to say he was getting married. The girl's name was Genevieve, and the wedding was scheduled for the last Saturday in June. Peyton booked a flight the very next day, round-trip for two, with a weekend in London. She'd spent a year in England when she was in college and couldn't wait to show Buck around.

"Oh, I wish it was already June," she would grumble.

"It'll be here before you know it," he tried to sound cheerful. Depending on the doctor, he'd be gone a week to two months by then.

By Christmas, he'd dropped twenty pounds and the dizzy spells were taking a toll. He cut back on his workload but doctored his schedule so Peyton wouldn't notice. Used the time to put his affairs in order and made arrangement to sell the business. When Peyton voiced concern over his weight loss, he told her he was getting in shape. Even joined a gym to back it up. Then came the migraines. Once or twice a week, in the beginning, but increasing in frequency and duration as the weeks passed. Pain so fierce, he lay in bed weeping. Peyton beside him, out like a light.

He told her on a Sunday morning. She was in bed, stroking the cat, watching the sun inch up the window. A thin coat of ice melted in the time it took him. Not looking at her. Speaking in a level voice. Gave it to her straight, then rocked her in his arms as she fell to pieces.

***

"California? I don't even know how to get to California!"

"That's the point, little. They'll be turning over every rock in your skunky old town while you're three times zones away, laying on the beach."

"I don't know anybody out there."

"Point number two…"

"But… why California?"

"Highest per capita income. You go where the money is. It's the de facto state where they got no niggers and they pride themselves on their tolerance," Dexter's "pride" is a mile wide.

"So, I go three freakin' time zones, so folks will be nice to me?"

"There you go."

"The real reason, Dexter. I can go to Memphis for that."

"You ain't ready for the real reason. But I got time, so I'll tell you anyway. Three thousand wetbacks a week. This is a state that's not big on documentation. Get you some I.D. and you're a citizen. Think about it, man. No sheet, no priors."

He thinks about it.

"Number two, hippies and homos bookin' in by the boatload. These are folks with a program and soon they'll be running things. Which brings me to three. Political climate. Don't look at me like that, cracker. You got things to consider."

"Political climate? What the fuck?"

"Consider this. They got more liberal guilt in the Bay Area than they know what to do with. They're just dying to help," Dexter gives him a grin. "Throw yourself on their mercy, son."

"Sounds like I'm back in the courtroom."

"You ever hear of a one-time loser? Which brings us to number…"

"Four."

"Four. No death penalty in California. They catch you out there and you best kill somebody, cause Mr. Big Daddy will be waiting for your ass."

"You don't seem to think much of my chances."

"Without me, you got no chance. Do what I say and you walk away. Not just from Lynnewood, from all of it. The robbing and fixing, the whole sorry mess."

"I just want out. I don't need to be born ag—"

Dexter has him pinned to the wall before he can finish. Those headlight eyes fused to his own. His words coming in a low, even tone.

"I told you, it's been decided. You bail on me and I set the dogs loose. You got that? Fuck up and there's no safe place for you. That's a promise, little dick."

He nods furiously and Dex lets him go. This isn't even about him. He could feel it in the force of Dexter's grip. Not fury, but restraint. The man could snap his head off in a heartbeat.

"You meet me here every day. You hear what I tell you, and you take it to heart."

"It's Big Daddy, ain't it."

"Six breaks in sixteen years, all but one of 'em, back in a week. All of them dead within the year. The man takes it personally."

"And the one?"

"Dogs got him at the edge of those trees."

"Killed him?"

"Not before tearing him limb from limb. Daddy left him out there for two days."

"Ugh..."

Dexter gives him a couple of light slaps.

"Remember what I said about watching your step. They see us together and they're bound to start thinking. Can't be helped, y'understand?"

***

The inmate has no right to privacy. They take his name and give him a number and if you know the number you can always find him. If you don't know, you can call and ask for it. Doesn't matter who you are. A vengeful victim, a long lost relative, a lawyer looking to make a deal. The inmates' whereabouts are a matter of record.

Buck landed in Tampa on the first day of spring training. The first pennant race that would finish without him. He rented a car and a cheap hotel room and passed the night in a morphine haze. In the morning, he showered and shaved, put on clean clothes, and studied himself in the bathroom mirror. The face of a stranger stared back. Not just older, but worn out, lined with worry. Skin the color of damp concrete. He'd stopped all treatments weeks ago, out of vanity and despair. He was thinner, but far from emaciated. The tumor would kill him before he wasted away.

On the drive to Lynnewood, he thought about Peyton. Tried to imagine how she'd feel when she learned the truth. Would she judge him by their years together, or would the depth of his deception prove overwhelming? Either way seemed likely. His life with her was already fading, as if distance was a measure of time. Or was it the proximity of his old life working a change. The loss of one adding to the other. Peyton's love was the thing he could count on. How much did she count on him being Buck?

He tried putting himself in her place but it was like trying to see through a prison wall. Couldn't be done, no matter how he went about it. Whatever he'd done would be irrevocable. For Peyton, for Jake, and for all things Clayton. A borrowed name with a life of its own. A hooker's gift to a junkie thief.

His visit was scheduled for 10:00 a.m. He bought a road map at a convenience store, and traced his route with a magic marker. Strange to spend two years in a place and not know how to get there. He'd told them he was an insurance investigator tracking a stolen painting. The name Dexter Gannon had surfaced in an interview. He'd worked out the story in great detail, even had business cards and a letter of reference with a notarized seal. It was a good story, but hardly necessary. In the end, they didn't give a damn. The inmate, Gannon, was still in confinement, and "Big Daddy" Mercer still ran the show.

***

At half past nine, he pulled off in a cutout overlooking the complex. There were new buildings and ill-fitting additions, but the main structure, the towers and the distant swamp were as they had been. He watched a group of prisoners killing time in the yard. Fifty or so, clumped in groups of five and ten. A basketball game was going, despite the heat. He saw a single figure, high in the bleachers, but too far away to make out. Dexter would be close to seventy, and Buck wondered if he'd been there the whole time. If so, it was easy to figure why.

The prisoners glared as he drove through the gate. A cage now contained the laundry exhaust fan housing, and the tin shed where Dexter stashed the bolt cutter had been removed. He parked the car in the space marked for visitors and signed his name to the entry log. His voice was even, his hands steady. A dying man with nothing to fear.

They led Dexter in through an unmarked door. His hair was speckled in white and he'd grown a moustache, but he still looked solid, still had the swagger. He took his seat and stared hard at Buck, then leaned forward and picked up the phone.

"What do you want?"

Buck gave a glance to the guards but they paid him no mind.

"Can they hear what I'm saying?"

Dexter said nothing.

"It's me. Little dick."

His face barely registered the news, and for a second, Buck wondered if he'd somehow forgotten. But then, a frown turned the corners of his mouth, and he looked away, as if embarrassed.

"I'll be damned," he said softly, then shook his head, and said it again.

"What do you think, man?"

Dexter just kept shaking his head. "I think you better get the fuck outta here, before I do something illegal."

"How you been?"

Dexter leaned in and turned on the high beams. "I'm not playin' with you, boy. One word to those bulls over there, and you're back on the inside, lookin' out."

71

"That's the whole point."

"I guess I was wrong about the brain."

"You saved my life, Dexter. Now, it's my turn."

"I'm done here," he moved to hang up.

"Wait," a quick check of the guards. "It's over for me, okay?"

"Say what you mean, boy. I'm a busy man."

"Cancer. It's terminal," Buck gave him a shrug. "No possibility of parole."

The high beams flickered, then died. Dexter looked instantly ten years older.

"I'm sorry to hear that."

"Don't be. I lived a life. That's what it was all about, right?"

The old con settled back in his chair, ran a hand over his face. "Part of it."

"Now, we take care of the other part."

"The other part took care of itself."

"Big Daddy took it hard?"

"Still takin' it hard. Got so worked up, he had himself a stroke. Must be fifteen years ago, now. Been walkin' with a cane ever since. Like I told you, with him it's personal."

Buck smiled until Dexter smiled back.

"Let's finish him off, Dex."

"You don't know what you're saying."

"You have a lawyer, right?"

"On a thirty-year retainer?"

"Okay, we get you one. You go to Big Daddy with a deal. An even-up swap. You go home, he gets a dead man. What could be sweeter?"

Dexter laughed.

"Hey, Dex, what do you have to lose?"

"Look around you, little. This is my home. They say I've been institutionalized. You know what that means?"

"Fuck what they say. I'm getting you out."

"I been out. First time, for three months, back in '74. The last time was two years back. I didn't last a week."

"Big Daddy?"

"Shiiiit. He didn't have nothin' to do with it. Comes a point where you can't make it outside."

"That's bullshit, and you know it."

"Tell me something, little. You have kids?"

"A boy. Get this, he lives in Paris."

Dexter's eyes glazed over, and for a moment, Buck thought maybe he'd killed him.

"Got me two little girls." His voice came from a distance. "'Course, I suspect they ain't so little, anymore. It happened during my three-month vacation. Twins, little! Ain't that a bitch?"

"You see them?"

"Never laid eyes on 'em."

"This will be your chance."

"I wouldn't do that to 'em. Whatever life they got, they don't need me in it."

"So, you're just gonna lay up here and die."

"In time. First, I gotta out-live the man."

"You can't be serious," Buck felt a pounding above the cords of his neck, spreading almost to his ears. He had to end this quickly, if he hoped to make the motel.

"Listen, Dexter, promise me you'll think about it."

"Nothing to think about. Too late to assimilate. That's what the old timers say. Out there, you see all the million ways you fucked up. The world just rubs your face in it," Dexter looked away. "If it makes you feel any better, there ain't a day goes by, I don't think of you, little. Hell, I knew you could be dead or doin' time, but there was always the chance you made it. Sometimes, it was the only thing that kept me going."

Buck held on to the edge of the table as the first wave of nausea passed.

"Easy, son."

"Yeah, listen. Can I call you?"

"Go on home. Leave an old nigger alone."

Dexter smiled until Buck smiled back.

"You lived a life, didn't you, little?"

"That I did, Dexter."

"I'll see you soon. You'll tell me all about it."

"I believe I will."

***

He takes the injection, then counts the seconds. In the moment between agony and oblivion, he dreams he is on a train looking out on a full moon. A private compartment like the one they took to Canada years ago. The trees across the Straits shining silver; light reflected in a jagged line across the water. He hears music playing in the next compartment. The end of a tenor solo he knows by heart. Giving way to a trumpet's trill, high and sweet, sliding to a whisper, famous jazzman playing the blues.

They pass the water tower, the lumberyard and the soft light from Juanita's back porch. He sees Peyton waiting for him at the wrought iron table, searching the windows, straining for a look at her boy, Buck. The trumpet falls silent. He doesn't move, just lets the sight of her fill him up.

Prisoner Reincarnated

Calvin Demmer

Joey Sullivan, standing in the center of his jail cell, looked towards the bars that he'd gotten to know well. He could have named the bars had he wanted, and the thought did cross his mind once, but more important thoughts replaced such trivial matters. Soon, however, the nameless bars would be gone, but they would not be replaced with the illusion of freedom that the early morning light alluded to. No, the next time Joey got to step outside his cell, he would be on his way to meet his maker.

He'd lost track of all the appeals and had long since ceased caring about being on death row. In fact, he'd grown to like the idea of an early exit from this realm. He had not been spiritual before prison, but in the small, colorless room, he'd found hope.

Turning to face his bed, he inhaled the stale air that hung around the room like an invisible noose. The bed, neatly made, hurt his back, but he didn't complain. Sometimes, the ache let him know he hadn't passed on, and was not merely living out some eternal dream.

Joey got to his knees, and reached beneath his mattress for a book he kept. Why he kept it hidden underneath the mattress, he was not sure, he'd been allowed to keep the book for good behavior years ago; some of the guards even helped him fill its pages.

He figured old habits die hard.

He ran his wrinkled hand over the plain notebook's cover. Inside lay the hope that he'd found.

There were always old books to read in prison, and one, a story about a man who became reincarnated as an animal of his choice, resonated with Joey. There was one animal, in particular, he had always loved, and the thought of coming back as one of them, with a clean slate, saw electricity bounce around within. It was not hard to believe in something extraordinary when he had nothing but time on his hands, and he became convinced he would become reincarnated after death.

He turned the page.

A tear ran down his dusty cheek, as he paused on the first page. He inhaled deep, and continued flipping through the book. Every page had a different species of bird, most of them in-flight. The colors lit up the world around him.

He felt his aging hands shake.

The images calmed, but the idea of coming back as a bird, free to roam blue skies overhead, was overpowering.

Joey shut the book.

Soon, he told himself.

He hid his book, climbed onto his bed, and turned to face the wall. As his eyelids grew heavy, he couldn't help but think back to how he'd ended up in jail.

***

Joey, seated in a white lawn chair, looked over his back yard. He'd done it; he'd finally created the perfect utopia for all the birds that visited. From bird baths to feeders, even little wooden houses he'd built in the trees, for some to nest. He sighed, as he allowed the view to soothe. Slowly, he began counting, and when he had reached in excess of forty birds, he stopped. Content, he put his hands behind his head and stretched out his legs.

Out of the corner of his eye, he spotted a light blue bird flying overhead. Joey didn't recognize the species—a rarity for him. He got up to try and get a better view. He wondered which tree in his yard the bird would select to perch on; he considered rushing in, to fetch his camera, but canceled the thought when the bird didn't start to fly lower.

Scratching his head, he watched the unknown bird head straight over the high, white wooden fence protecting his back yard, and head straight for his neighbor's house. An icy current rippled over his chest, as he thought of the neighbor's cat, but he relaxed when he realized the feline was too fat and slow to have any chance at catching a bird.

Still, he was curious about what drew the bird to his neighbor's house, as all the others had clearly chosen the paradise that he'd created for them.

He made his way to the fence. There were no gaps to look through, something he'd made sure of, so as to protect against stray animals, particularly the fat cat next door. He did the next best thing, and stood on his tip-toes to peer over the fence.

The bird wandered over the lawn, near a bush of wilting roses. The scene raised Joey's nerves again, as it resembled a battlefield. There were all sorts of toys and other rubbish torn up over the back yard. Clearly, the cat was not as lazy as he'd thought. Of the feline, there was no sign, however, and Joey felt some tension release.

He watched as the unknown bird pecked at something on the ground.

If it's food he wants, I have an endless supply, he thought, holding his right hand up, as if the bird could see and understand the gesture.

He got no response, and tried making "cheep-cheep" sounds, in the hopes of getting the bird's attention, but this was also to no avail. He tried a few other calls he'd heard, but nothing had any effect. Frustrated, he shook his head, and frowned at the bird, as he continued watching.

A rustling sound came from a bush nearby. Joey crooked his neck, as he tried to see what was making the noise.

More birds? he thought. *No, that's too loud.*

Whatever it was, it didn't present itself, it stayed hidden. The bird started moving again, and Joey cursed when he saw it was headed straight for the bush. He figured it was as curious about the sound as he was.

But you have more to lose, little guy, he thought, and clapped his hands.

"Shoo-shoo," he said, after clapping didn't work.

Still, the bird did not respond. A dark shadow fell over it. The neighbor's cat had been waiting behind the bush. Joey felt his adrenaline pump as he watched the cat's claws come down. The bird, realizing its situation, spread its wings, and attempted to make an escape.

"Holy shit," he said, as he banged on the fence. He knew it would not budge, as he had made it strong to keep others out.

He looked back at the bird. It hadn't managed to escape. The scene was gruesome, as feathers and blood lay around the cat. He turned on a dime, rushed through his home, and headed straight for his neighbor's.

The elderly couple answered, but he didn't have time for them. He ignored their protests, pushing his way past, and then ignored their shouts and threats as he made his way into their back yard.

It was too late. The unknown blue bird lay torn to pieces in the center of the yard, and the cat was nowhere to be seen. Joey felt a sharp pain in his heart.

He turned back to the house. The elderly couple stood on the back porch staring at him. They were no longer moaning, the old man now seemed to be sporting a grin.

"Your cat," he said. "It killed a bird."

The old man took a step forward. "And? It does that all the time, keeps all the troublemakers out of my yard. I'll be sure to give him a treat later."

"But..."

The old man chuckled, but then stopped abruptly, as the wrinkles in his tanned, aged face, hardened. "Now, get out of my yard, you nut, before I call the cops," he said, shaking his head. "You come and disturb us, over a stupid bird. Why, the missus and I were just about to have a nap."

Joey felt all his senses leave his body; a peculiar numbness took over. At first, he thought he might pass out, but he didn't. Instead, he felt his neck turn, as his eyes looked over the back yard.

A few feet from him, a spade rested.

***

The sound of approaching footsteps awoke Joey.

He knew his time had come and did not fight the guards, as he was led to another small, cold room. He saw the stretcher, which would be his final place alive as a man, but he didn't flinch. He believed now, more than ever, and he focused his thoughts. He pictured all the different birds he'd seen; he imagined the wide-open sky that would be his world to roam. The fear of death dissipated, and was replaced by excitement.

***

Strapped down, he saw the poison enter his veins: death by lethal injection. The world around him shuddered. The light became hazy, and slowly, like a loved one that had to leave, it retreated. Soon, he'd know the answer to the afterlife question. The darkness didn't show the same care as the light had; it spread quickly across his vision, like a thousand spiders crawling up the walls.

Black became his world.

***

Joey opened his eyes.

Light danced before his view, sharp, bright, and it took him a moment to adjust, as his view was blurry. He felt different, lighter, and his backache was gone. He looked down, and slowly, the blur around him began to clear. He saw talons perched onto some type of branch. Warmth flooded his core, as he looked at the rest of his body. Colors exploded all around him. He sensed it, then felt and *knew* it.

Joey was a bird.

His dream had come true. Gone, were the trappings of man, and the weight of past deeds on his conscience. He stretched out his colorful wings, the feeling, natural. He had no doubt he already knew how to fly.

He left the perch, eager to soar into the heavens above.

A loud bang ringed within his head, as he crashed against an obstacle. Joey dropped down, seeing some strange, black and gray floor, rushing towards him.

He hit the ground, and tried to find equilibrium. A high-pitched voice echoed around him. He remembered the sound; it was that of a human child, a girl.

"Grandpa, grandpa, come quick," the girl said, giggling. "The silly bird flew right into the bars of the cage."

Just a Spoonful of Horror

Gary Ives

Of the boys at the Malloy Farm, Mickey Markham was by far the prettiest with blond hair, fair skin, full lips, blue eyes, and long eyelashes like a girl's. Let me say that, here—pretty counts. This, he traded on among other boys but especially with the warden and screws. He could smooth talk candy bars and cigarettes out of the screws without, according to him, having to drop his pants. It was just on his looks and a certain charm. Work lists for the cotton field or mucking out the stalls or the tannery never saw Markham's name.

This charm got him a soft permanent job in the kitchen, but everyone knew he was a sweet little pet to at least three fairy screws. His only duties were to help with clean up and to keep the napkin holders and salt shakers filled. Just the salt shakers, as pepper was not allowed at Malloy farm. I think we – all of us – hated him for the ease that his face and frame allowed; a primitive jealousy, I suppose, but I loathed Mickey Markham not just because he seemed to lead a charmed existence — but because he was evil.

Late one night during my first week at Malloy, he and two other thugs had forced upon me a most unpleasant situation for which I had no defense. Since that time – I, as the smarter boys here – carried a shiv. Me, I kept my distance from Mickey, as well as from his companion, Jeremy Toomey, Malloy's 250 lb. yard shark. Toomey, mentally challenged, was serving his term for having killed his father and two brothers with a kitchen cleaver. It was ironic that his work station was as dishwasher in the scullery. My work stations were divided between mornings in the turnip fields and afternoons on the garbage truck making pickup rounds, which seldom placed me in contact with either Markham or Toomey.

Some may think the lot of us at the Malloy Farm are evil individuals. After all, weren't we *all* convicted youthful felons; condemned and sentenced by courts of law to the state's hundred-year old reform school? But even here, among us bad boys, evil – *true* evil – is never prevalent. Wickedness is here, to be sure, and vile things occur, but such things happen on the outside, too. Most are here due to stupid choices often made under the influence of peer pressure, poverty, ignorance, and often drugs. Even here, the good outnumber the bad and the ugly. Certainly, the truly villainous are present, but in reality, these are few.

If Mickey Markham had any kind of pathos at all it was surely an inversion of true empathy. He enjoyed witnessing suffering. He had been sent up for having blinded his little sister by dowsing her with gasoline and setting her aflame. At Malloy, he exhibited no shame, rather, he sometimes boasted of this travesty, and often threatened some boy with the same. Frequently, he set two boys against each other just to revel at the fistfight and then the screw's subsequent punishments. He was clever at manipulating weaker boys for sex or their commissary credits.

A double row of fencing and razor wire separated Malloy from the state's adult men's correctional farm where prisoners raised hogs and cattle for the penal system. Markham often lingered at the fence, which afforded a clear view of the slaughter house. He joked that the squeals of the hogs gave him a hard-on. Such was the stuff of Mickey Markham.

Work in the turnip fields was the pits. We planted, we hoed, we thinned, we cultivated, we harvested. Mornings were always wet, and working without gloves, the rough wooden hoe handles blistered the hands. Once the sun burned off the dew, we baked on that miserable red clay like burned biscuits. The afternoon garbage run was almost a relief. True, the truck stank to high heaven, but moving most of the time passed a breeze across my face. And the real perk was the plunder, like magazines, sometimes articles of clothing, and scraps of metal good for trade on the shiv market. Our last stop was the kitchen. What wasn't eaten or carried home by the screws got tossed into a special bin for delivery to the hog farm next door. However, many times there were cookies or portions of cake easily salvaged. So, duty wise, the turnip fields sucked but the garbage truck rocked.

**

One screw, Mr. Paxton, was onto Young Master Markham and unfazed by the boy's charm. Paxton let no opportunity pass to upbraid or embarrass him.

"Markham, I saw you jump line, you scrub, don't deny it, so back to the dorm with you, dearie. You know the rules, pretty boy; no supper for line jumpers!"

Indeed, he kept a steady eye on our young Prince Mickey. While Markham disdained all the screws, he had a particular hatred for Mr. Paxton.

Mr. Paxton kept a cat, for which he set out food behind the mess hall. When this cat delivered a litter, Mr. Paxton took care to see that their little, orange crate home was warm with a cast-off blanket. One afternoon, Markham, smarting from a recent rebuke, summoned three of his toadies.

81

"Watch this," he commanded.

With a mess hall table spoon, he deftly thumped each of the tiny, five-day old kittens' heads, cruelly ending their brief lives, with one of his infamous chuckles.

"Betcha never seen that before, ha, ha, ha."

A place like Malloy will not hold secrets, and soon enough, one of our rats cuddled up to Mr. Paxton's ear with an account of the poor kittens' killings. That evening, the boys reckoned that the rat had put the finger on that dumbass, Jeremy Toomey, as that evening, Mr. Paxton was on duty and had called Toomey into the office for nearly an hour. He didn't leave the office until after lights out.

Later, about midnight, the dorm filled with screams. There was a scuffle in the dark. When the lights came on, gore covered Markham's face, and on the floor by his bed lay, like crushed grapes, his two gouged-out eyes, beside a bloody spoon. Markham lay screaming with his crimson-soaked hands pressed against his eye sockets, his yells choked by blood. Soon enough, the night screws had an ambulance at the dorm, and blind Mickey Markham was trundled off. The screws put each of us at attention at the foot of our bunks.

Mr. Swann, a particularly stupid and very fat screw, walked up and down the aisle smacking his nightstick into his palm.

"Any of you little punks move one inch, you gonna git you a kiss from Missus Hickory here. They's gonna be an investigation – a police investigation. Highway Patrol is on the way, you goddam smartasses. So is the Sheriff. Ever who did this horrible nasty thing to poor Markham is gonna wish he wasn't never born. Anyone ready to speak up? Huh?"

Of course, no one said a thing. Eyes drifted all over the room but the obvious focus was on Jeremy Toomey, who stood in his underwear before his bunk, his fat pig face impassive.

Detectives arrived and conferred with the screws. Jeremy Toomey was called out for interrogation in the duty office, and the rest of us were allowed to go back to bed. Before lights out, two uniformed cops tossed Jeremy's bed and locker, filling a giant black garbage bag. However, once the lights were out and the night screw left to eavesdrop at the duty office, there was a buzz of speculation. In the dorm, boys needed no light to navigate. There was a nightly traffic in drugs and sex which one learned to take for granted. We boys easily sussed out what had happened.

Hadn't Mr. Paxton called him in that afternoon and confronted Jeremy Toomey with having killed his kittens? Of course, Toomey denied this, but Mr. Paxton was insistent, claiming an eye witness. Although stupid, Toomey figured it out, with a few clues accidentally dropped by Mr.

Paxton, that the eye witness was none other than Mickey Markham, peaching on him for killing the kittens. Toomey's knowledge that Markham had killed the kittens, and was now fingering him, got him enraged. He told Mr. Paxton that Markham was the lying-sack-of-shit eye witness.

"Well, Toomey, that's the way it stands. Markham says you're the one killed the kittens. It'll be up to the warden who to believe, you or Markham."

It wasn't that difficult for us to figure the whole thing out.

***

I'd come by the spoon a week ago in the kitchen's garbage. The ripped size 38 pants had been in the trash picked up from the guard's locker room. The clever part was wearing the fat man's pants while I gouged out that bastard's eyes, then running the bloody pants with Mickey's blood and tossing them under Jeremy's bunk in the dark during the confusion.

I wouldn't call Malloy Farm a nice place, but it's more pleasant nowadays than it was just a week ago.

Seven Conversations in Locked Rooms

Alex Shvartsman

The lawyer looked at his watch for what must've been the hundredth time.

"It's a good thing that they're taking this long. Means the jury is seriously considering our argument, at least. A quick verdict would've likely been bad news."

Lewis couldn't tell if Malcolm meant it. Was he merely trying to offer a glimmer of hope or, perhaps, just calming his own nerves? He watched his lawyer pace back and forth in the small holding room.

"I want you to promise me something, Malcolm," Lewis said, after several more agonizing minutes of waiting.

"What's that?" The lawyer quit pacing and turned to his client.

"Claire's been telling me how there's all sorts of hoopla about my case. Talking heads discussing it on the news programs and all that. You and I are practically celebrities right now, fifteen minutes of fame sort of thing. That about right?"

"Well, yes. There's quite a bit of media attention. The ethical and philosophical implications of this case are rather important."

"Yeah, whatever. My point is, whether I win or lose, you're gonna win. You'll be the famous lawyer everyone saw on TV, and with that comes the big bucks."

The attorney made no comment, waiting for Lewis to continue.

"So, I figure, you owe me. Whichever way this goes, I want you to promise that you'll keep tabs on Claire and the girls. Help them out if they get into any sort of trouble."

The lawyer made all kinds of fancy sounding assurances. It was easy to make promises, Lewis thought, to a man who probably wouldn't even remember asking if they lost this final appeal.

Guards unlocked the door. "It's time," one of them said. They escorted Lewis back into the courtroom.

***

"Thank you for agreeing to this interview."

Talking to the lady Lewis used to watch on TV was a bit surreal. She looked older in person, sitting right across the table from him, with cameramen and guards positioned a few steps behind.

"No problem. It's not like I have much else to do with my time."

He agreed to the interview because the network offered to pay twenty large for the exclusive. The money would help Claire catch up on her bills, and there would still be some left over for Linda's and Betty's college funds. But he wasn't supposed to mention getting paid during the interview.

"Time is something you have in abundance," the journalist said. "The judge sentenced you to fifteen years in prison after it was ruled that you had a right to decline medical treatment. That's an awfully long time to spend behind bars. Do you now regret opting out of the memory modification?"

"If you're asking whether I'm happy to rot in here for the next fifteen years, then no, of course I'm not. But it's loads better than a lobotomy. What you call *memory modification* is really mind murder."

"You equate treatment with murder," she said, "but your own actions resulted in a real, physical murder, to which you pleaded guilty. What do you say to those who might feel that your attitude toward treatment only makes it a more fitting punishment?"

"I didn't mean to kill that guy. It was a stupid bar fight gone wrong, and I'm sorry it happened. I take full responsibility, but erasing who I am won't bring him back. It would be a deliberate act, an eye for an eye punishment as final as a lethal injection."

"There's overwhelming scientific evidence that selective memory removal is a safe and effective way to treat sociopathic behavior," countered the reporter. "It has been proven very efficient in people who've committed violent crimes with almost no incidents of recidivism. Don't you want to be cured?"

"I ain't sick," said Lewis. "I am guilty of a crime, and I'm being punished for that now. I'd rather spend time in jail than have my personality wiped by one of those Memory Eater abominations. I read up on the 'cured' people you're talking about. Shrinks went in and deleted whatever memories they say shaped the patient's personality and predisposed him to violence."

Lewis became animated as he spoke, causing the guards to tense.

"Whatever the research you quote says, it's not an exact science. There are side effects. People whose minds are messed with like that, they come out different. Their tastes, desires and temperaments are not what they used to be."

"Why is that such a bad thing?"

Lewis leaned in, his voice overcome with emotion.

"Because no one knows *exactly* what kind of changes the memory wipe will cause. Because there's a chance I wouldn't love my wife, or my kids, anymore. I'm not willing to risk that for anything."

***

"Where's your mother?"

Linda looked down at the floor, avoiding eye contact. "She's working tonight. She's been putting in overtime hours now that I'm old enough to take care of Betty."

Lewis frowned. Claire used to come by every week, like clockwork, during the visitation hour. Sometimes she brought the girls, sometimes not. After a couple of years, she began to miss a few weeks here and there. Nowadays, he was lucky to see her once every two months. This was the first time Linda came to visit him on her own.

"I'm glad to see you, Kiddo," he said. "But fourteen-year-old girls shouldn't come to a place like this by themselves. It's not like Claire to send you over unattended. Does she even know that you're here?"

Linda looked down at the floor again.

***

Malcolm dropped a thick stack of paperwork on the table.

"Divorce papers," he said.

"The guy she's with now—what's he like?"

"I don't really know. I ran the background check like you asked, and he's clean. Other than that…" Malcolm shrugged.

"I don't blame her," said Lewis. "Seven years is a very long time." He leafed through the pages filled with tiny print. "I still want you to keep your promise and look out for her and the girls. *Especially* the girls, with a stranger in the house."

Lewis picked up the pen and began to sign.

***

Malcolm walked into the room and shook his head.

"Goddamn it!" Lewis punched the table. "They wouldn't grant me furlough for Linda's wedding, and I get that, but for this… How could they say no?"

"They're holding a grudge," said the lawyer. "Do you know how much money it's costing the city to keep you incarcerated? Not to mention, the others who chose prison sentences over the Memory Eater, citing *your* case as precedence? They're being petty."

"Did you find out how it happened?"

"Betty overdosed at a sorority party. The cops are still looking into it, interviewing her roommates and such. It looks as though she might've been using for some time. The other girls were too scared to call for an ambulance and by the time somebody did, it was already too late. I'm so sorry, Lewis."

"They say fathers should never live long enough to bury their children. But not being able to attend your own daughter's funeral has got to be even worse. If only I was there for her, things might've turned out differently."

Malcolm put his hand on Lewis's shoulder.

"Don't beat yourself up," he said. "This kind of tragedy can happen to good people, families, whether both parents are there or not.

Lewis's eyes were moist as he stared past Malcolm at the bare, gray walls.

***

"I came to say goodbye."

Linda was a young woman now, twenty-two years of age and carrying herself with an easy assurance and optimism of youth.

"Peter and I have been accepted into the Prometheus program," she went on to say. "We're a young, healthy and educated couple, just the sort of people they're looking for to establish the Mars colony."

The speech sounded rehearsed, practiced in front of a mirror. His Linda was like that – even as a kid she always had to work up the courage to deliver bad news.

"It's a one-way trip, Dad," she said slowly, as though he didn't understand the implications, the finality of her decision. "We won't be coming back."

Lewis managed to hold himself together long enough to wish her luck and say proper goodbyes. There was plenty of time to cry after she left.

On the day the colony ship landed safely on Mars, he told the guards that he wanted to see his lawyer.

***

"My name is Malcolm," said the stranger. "I'm your attorney."

"Thank God," said Lewis. "Finally, someone who can fill me in on what's happening. These people, they won't tell me anything!"

"That was one of the conditions of your deal," said Malcolm. "You asked to undergo a Memory Eater procedure in lieu of serving out the remainder of your sentence. You also asked that certain painful memories be edited out. As per the negotiated terms, you'll be given a new name and allowed to reintegrate into society with relative anonymity. As far as everyone else knows, you're still incarcerated."

"A new life sounds better than prison," said Lewis. "I don't even get how an old me could stand being cooped up in here for years. I wonder, though, if there are any friends or relatives, or maybe a girlfriend that I should contact? Any people who might be worried about me?"

"Afraid not," said Malcolm. "You're all alone."

Smaller

James A. Miller

After her third attempt at the eggs, Jen placed the fork to the side of the plate. Their last breakfast was going to be a nice one. No talking about it. But the conversation had grown trivial and quiet. She couldn't stand it anymore.

"They're still going to put you in, even after what happened to the rest?" They had both seen it on the news. The first guy came out naked and trembling after a month. The next time they tried, the guy came out white as a ghost, laughing like a maniac. He never spoke, just kept laughing. The cameras cut away when they went to sedate him. There was no more news on him after that. Andrew was the third guy – the third time was the worst. Once he was out, he took off running. He just ran and ran and no one caught him. He didn't even stop when he had to go to the bathroom. He just kept running, urine and feces all over his inmate uniform – running like he was being chased – right up until he ran in front of that truck.

***

In their last few moments together, it didn't help for either of them to be thinking like this.

"Well, that was before," Rudy said. "It's different now. Now, they make it so you can't see back around. It helps to keep you from going – well… you know."

"It just seems so… untested. What if something else goes wrong? I just don't know how they can make you go in there."

"We're past all this. It wasn't much of a choice, Jen. I've been a bad boy, so they say I can't play with the other kids for a while."

"But a *year*?"

Rudy tilted his head to the side and tightened his lips in resolve. There was no chance of early parole, no matter how well he behaved.

"The attorney said that they want to set an example. We should plan on a year. I couldn't have done it the other way. I can't do thirty years. Thirty years would be the end of us."

She bit her bottom lip, tears welling up in her eyes. After a few moments of silence, she flashed to anger.

89

"It's wrong on so many levels."

Jen sank back in the chair. Rudy didn't need to say anything. He knew she what she meant; the sentence *was* severe. There had been political pressure to make sure of it. He could only guess at the amount of money and promises made behind the scenes. Covert workings set in action to create precedents and change public image. Their little family becoming a small – but pivotal – cog in the whole ugly machine.

***

They had talked about the consequences before going ahead with the plan. In the end, they had both decided that getting their daughter the help she needed was worth the risk of stretching the truth on a few insurance documents, and paying off a few people to look the other way.

Even after the surgery and how they only expected a year more for Sara, given the same choice, Rudy would do it again. For a chance to save their child – no matter how small the odds – he would do it again in a heartbeat. Jen would, too.

It was the *guilt* that was harder on her. The guilt came with the deal. If they played ball, only one of them would have to do the time. He would go in and she would stay out. That was the deal.

***

After they decided who, there had been one last choice. Do the thirty years straight-up, or do a severely reduced sentence in the WRAP as the fourth guinea pig. It was a slippery kind of decision that Rudy circled around for days. There were discussions with engineers where they swore they had solved all of the problems; how this time they were one hundred percent certain.

And then there were the talks with Jen, carefully walking through the options, outlining the pros and cons and wrestling with confusing uncertainty of parole and good behavior, and whether it was better to be in with criminals or all alone – until they got to the point of flipping a coin. But before the coin had stopped bouncing, Jen slapped her hand down on it, pulled it back and into her pocket, concealing the outcome. The decision, she said, was ultimately up to him. In the end, he finally made it alone; deciding the promise of extra years with his family was worth the risk of whatever he would face inside.

***

Before he had been sentenced, rumors of the WRAP had given it an almost mythical quality. Inmates who had no reason to know anything about it knew and could recount horrifying tales of its very nature. Back when he was being held for trial, his nervous, chain-smoking cell-mate, Alan – a man who was continuously fascinated by Rudy's options – had his own self-derived and erroneous understanding of the way the WRAP functioned. And he couldn't help but to give Rudy his two cents on it.

"I heard it's like livin' inside a microwave. It cooks your brain until you lose it. That's what they are really doin' – gettin' inside your head. Seein' what you're thinkin' – takin' out all the info they need and feedin' you the messages. I think you're a li'l bit crazy for goin' in. Thirty is a lot, but it ain't all of you – you still get some time at the end."

* * *

After being presented with his choice of sentencing, and before the talks with the Engineers, Rudy took the opportunity to research the WRAP and found that it had actually come about when a Quantum Physicist and his Mechanical Engineer brother took on the question of how to build the perfect prison. Their answer: build a cell that had no doors at all.

And not only did the WRAP have no doors, it had no windows or visible entrance or exit of any kind. The space inside the cell was finite, but with no discernible beginning or end. It was similar to the concept that some hold of the universe – in that there is no limit to its expanse – yet, finite in the way it curves back onto itself. The WRAP was its own little universe, but on a much smaller scale.

* * *

*The door buzzed and two guards came in, ready to return him to the holding cell. On his way out, Rudy turned back to watch Jen leave. He had wanted that last image of her shuffling around, getting her purse and coat, unaware that he was watching her, but this time, Jen was sitting there watching **him** as he left. His last image of Jen was of her face, sunken in deep sadness.*

* * *

He had no idea how long ago that image of Jen had been. It felt like forever. It was possible it never happened that way, or maybe it never happened at all. His mind may have made it up. In here, there was nothing to fear but his own thoughts and where they could take him; nothing to fear but his own mind turning to devour itself, just like what had happened to inmates one through three.

Rudy looked out over the seemingly endless desert that tapered off into a fog in all directions. His world ended in whiteness after about a half-kilometer. Outside, in the real world, he knew he was actually standing inside a 1.5 meter cube. Part of the design requirements mandated that they be able to retrofit a standard prison cell. Eventually, all of the cells would be like this, as the expanse of virtual space inside of them supposedly made for a more humane prison environment.

Humane, that is, if inmates could keep from pulling out all of their body hair, or shitting themselves while running naked.

Time seemed to hold no meaning in this place. For some reason, there were no clocks, and day and night were controlled from a switch. He had tried to keep track of his sleep cycles, but left to his own devices, with no job or other reason to keep up a cadence, his pattern quickly muddled into multiphasic napping, making any count of sleep a timeless, and otherwise useless, metric.

***

This was the first time he had been able to see himself. That wasn't supposed to happen. They had told him the wrap-around view was the most likely reason for the insanity; people couldn't stand to see the back of themselves at all points of the compass, so they had created the fog to shield the images of oneself from view.

But his image was there. Ahead, in the distance of the fog, Rudy could make out a shadowy outline of himself. He waved his arms and watched as the image waved its arms in perfect synchronization. It was like he was looking into a distant, hazy mirror, only this one reflected his backside. He brushed it off as an interesting phenomenon. Maybe the Techs didn't have the fog set quite right.

The next day, Rudy again squinted at the figure of himself in the distance. He seemed closer. Thinking it might be a good idea to measure the cell, he drew a long line in the sand, put his heel to it, and started pacing. He had made 1,018 steps by the time he came back to his original line. He repeated this for seven days and by the end of the week, the number had declined to 789 steps.

By then, he didn't need a number to tell him the world around him was getting smaller. He could clearly see the backside of the guy ahead of him doing exactly what he was. And along with *that* guy, there were *three other* very clear instances at all points of the compass.

If this was what drove the other guys crazy then they were just wimps; yes, it was unnerving, seeing copies of himself, but it would take a lot more than that to shake Rudy off his rocker.

***

After two more days, he began reconsidering his stance on his own mental fortitude. His clothes had become too tight. He now stood naked in the sand, looking around at all the instances of himself. They were much, *much* closer now – only 180 paces or so, and there were *more* instances beyond the original. He could clearly see *three* new iterations. Since they weren't totally obscured by the first instance, he guessed that this meant the virtual space of his cell was slightly curved. He wasn't sure if this was knowledge that could help him, but he would have to do something soon. This balloon was losing air.

His sleeping quarters (which even at full size could barely be called a hut) had been getting smaller as well. Rudy had taken his bedding outside and now spent the next two nights sleeping on the sand with his miniature pillow and baby blanket.

He thought that somebody should be noticing this and call in tech support to stabilize and resize the field. Later, he realized that maybe they didn't know this was going on. Maybe this was what had been driving *all* of the others crazy. If that was the case, he just had to stay calm. They were only iterations of himself – no more, no less. He was the only person in there, and if there was one thing he knew: he could live with himself. A quick laugh escaped him.

***

After two more days, he was able to throw a pebble and hit himself in the back. He made a game of trying to throw the small projectile and then move out of the way. It was surreal to be able to throw something in front of him and then see it fly past from behind. He picked up a rounded piece of gravel and recognized the defining crack. It was a rock that he used to sit on. It came apart easily.

Three nights later, he was unable to lie down without bumping into himself.

The next morning, Rudy put his hands on the hips in front of him – his *own* hips – and made an infinitely long conga line. He kicked his leg out to the side, angling to miss the iterations of himself, and watched as every instance ahead and to each side did the same; a googolplex of legs, throwing sand as they kicked. He and his iterations then sang the few words he knew to *The locomotion*.

***

That night, he was unable to lie back down without completely laying on himself, so he chose to stand. The full reality of being crushed by his own body set in when he felt his breath on the back of his neck. It was then that Rudy started screaming. The infinite monotone chorus of deafening shrieks continued until his voice was raw and the sounds that came from him were no longer screams at all, but dry, raspy bleats.

Only when he stopped screaming did the answer come to him. It would be his greatest escape of all; the way out of this place.

The only way out was to go in.

***

Rudy closed his eyes, feeling a second set of eyelids infinitely closing against the back of his head, and thought back to the tire swing. His father was pushing him higher and higher.

He made the distant memory very real.

"No, Daddy, no." Rudy was laughing so hard, he could hardly breath.

"Did you say you wanted to go higher?"

"No, Daddy, no!"

But he was laughing too hard and the words barely came out at all. He was dizzy, weakly holding onto the rope. It was so difficult to breath, as though someone were sitting on his chest.

"It's okay, Rudy," he heard his father say.

Rudy couldn't respond. Tears of laughter streamed down his face.

"Let go, Rudy… let go."

So Rudy let go.

***

"He's coming out."

Rudy opened his eyes to see a doctor standing over him.

His senses slowly returned, like so many lights in a house being turned on one at a time; he first felt the sensors attached to his head, then the sting of the IV in his arm, and then the intrusiveness of the catheter and NG tubes. Rudy realized that he was laughing.

"Get ready, he's gonna be bat-shit crazy."

"EEG looks normal."

Pinpoints of blinding brilliance from a small flashlight hit both his eyes.

"Rudy, can you hear me?"

Rudy tried to speak, but his throat felt cold and dry. He nodded his head instead.

"He's okay."

Rudy turned his head as much as the equipment allowed. He was in a hospital bed. Medical people swarmed around him. There was a nurse standing ready with a needle.

"We won't need that," boomed a voice, and the needle went away. The man behind the voice appeared in front of Rudy. He had a gray mustache and beard, and was wearing a suit.

"I'm sure you have a lot of questions."

The man waited for the sensors and tubes to be removed, then pressed a button that inclined the bed. Rudy winced.

"I'm sure you're pretty sore," said the man in the suit. "I am Dr. Alan Reeves." Rudy attempted to shake the man's hand, but his arm felt like lead.

"Don't worry about it," said Dr. Reeves. "I don't want you to move too much, until we get some bone density information."

A tube went into Rudy's mouth and he felt the roughness of a hospital-grade paper towel under his chin. Cold water trickled in. He hadn't even realized how thirsty he was. When he tried to swallow, he choked and the tube was pulled away. Dr. Reeves seemed to disregard this clumsiness.

"Rudy, first off, you need to know that you've been lying in this bed much longer than you think."

Dr. Reeves held up a mirror. Rudy saw that time had carved deep lines into his face. His eyes were sunken and his cheeks, hollow. He realized that someone must have been assigned to shave his face, he had no beard. The mirror went away.

"The program was too young for us to know this when you went in, but it was discovered that pulling anyone out had become a death sentence. The initial inmates not only went insane, but died about a year after they were transferred out. It was quickly understood that if we kept an inmate unconscious, the problem failed to manifest. But this was only a temporary solution.

"The whole project came under fire when the issue was leaked to the public. The ultimate decision was fast-tracked through the Supreme Court. You were five days from being woken up. Your face became a rallying point for activists on both sides of the debate, but the courts ruled in favor of keeping the prisoners under and waiting for science to catch up. Only, your fifteen minutes of fame died out, and the funding for the technology died away with it. The science took a lot longer than we thought."

Dr. Reeves held up the mirror.

"Rudy, you have been unconscious for seventeen years."

Dr. Reeves looked at his clipboard.

"There is still much we don't understand about how you were able to survive. The others who had been in this long were unrecoverable."

Even in his weakened state, Rudy knew that "unrecoverable" was really a polite way of saying "dead."

"I do have some good news for you."

Dr. Reeves walked to the door, pushed it open with one hand, and waved a 'come in' motion to someone outside. Two familiar-looking women walked in. One of them held the hand of a third female – a bashful, curly-haired little girl. Rudy initially placed the two grown women as Jen and her mother, but knew that wasn't quite right. His mind corrected for time and he recognized who they were. It was Jen and *Sara*.

The bald, dying girl he remembered crying over was all grown up. She now had long, dark hair, and a daughter of her own. The curly-haired little girl – his granddaughter – no older than four or five, hid her face in Sara's leg.

Return to Death Row

Fredrick Obermeyer

Although Ray Vosendak wasn't the one strapped to the lethal injection table, an electric current of fear crept up his spine. He looked into the eyes of Matthew Dean Pratcher. The fear in them made him look like a scared kid, despite the beard and the jailhouse tats on his arms.

At that moment, Vosendak felt empathy for Pratcher, even though he knew that he shouldn't. Ten years earlier, Pratcher had killed the Nogalko family in their home. Two of them had been children. Nancy, four, and Samuel, eight. And for what? A lousy three hundred bucks. Yet, despite Vosendak's hate for the man, he felt bad for him.

Although Vosendak had led Pratcher down the last mile, he didn't relish his job in the least, nor did he believe in the death penalty. He believed that every man deserved a chance at redemption, no matter how lost they were. But the people of the state of Pennsylvania had felt differently.

And now, here they were.

"Do you have anything to say before we pass sentence?" Warden Al Kelmore said.

Vosendak held his breath and thought, *what would I say if I were in his position? 'I'm innocent?' 'Fuck all of you. Go to hell.' Or just piss myself?*

Pratcher looked at a loss for words. He turned to the looking glass and stared at his mentally-retarded older brother, Brian, as if looking for inspiration. But Brian was crying his eyes out. Pratcher looked back at the governor and the warden, his face haggard with fear.

"I hope that God will forgive me for my sins," Pratcher said.

The warden nodded and then gestured to the other men in the room. They walked over to the lethal injection machine. Vosendak glanced towards the red phone, thinking about all the cliché prison movies where the camera holds tight on that phone, waiting for the stay of execution to come in, the protagonist looking tense and sweaty. Sure, in reality, Pratcher looked tense and sweaty. But Vosendak knew there was no way he was getting that call. Still, he looked at the phone.

The call didn't come.

The men activated the machine and the first injection of Pentothal came down. Pratcher's eyes twitched a few times, then closed. In less than thirty seconds, he was out. Saline solution cleared the line.

Vosendak tensed as the second injection of Pavulon came down and paralyzed Pratcher's lungs and diaphragm.

Had his victims died this peacefully? Becky Nogalko hadn't. She had been shot twice in the back and left to die, bleeding all over the floor.

Vosendak's stomach tightened with nausea.

Fuck the bastard, he thought. *He should suffer more. Or should he?* If there was a Hell—and Vosendak felt certain there was—Pratcher would burn in it forever.

Saline solution cleared the line again, then the third injection came down and pumped the toxic agent, potassium chloride, into his bloodstream.

Brian wailed and some people led him out of the room.

Vosendak was ready to join him, but Warden Kelmore gave him a look that said 'don't you dare'. Frustrated, he swallowed hard and remained where he was. Watching a man die in reality was hard—even if he was a scumbag who went out more peacefully than his victims.

A few minutes after the last plunger descended, a doctor walked over, put a stethoscope to Pratcher's still chest and listened. He took it off and said, "He's gone."

Vosendak fled the room, stumbled into the nearest bathroom, and threw up in the toilet.

* * *

When Vosendak arrived at work the next morning, he found Warden Kelmore down in D block. His face was white, and he was trembling. For a moment, he thought Kelmore was having a heart attack. He'd expected the Warden to ream him for showing sympathy towards such a bastard, but instead he looked petrified.

He rushed over to the Warden's side and said, "Are you all right, Chief?"

"No, I'm not." Kelmore shook his head.

"Why? What's wrong?"

"See for yourself."

Vosendak sighed and walked down death row. He had been on a suicide in the block two years earlier, and it hadn't been pretty. Marty Elms had somehow managed to hang himself from his cell bars with his shoelaces, and he had pissed and shat all over the floor in his last death spasms. His face had looked purplish-black, his tongue stuck out like a grotesque sausage, and his eyes had bugged out of their sockets.

Shaking the thought from his mind, he hurried to the end of the block. When he arrived, he stopped and gasped.

Pratcher was sitting in his cell, looking nervously at him.

"No," Vosendak said, and shook his head.

It couldn't be. Pratcher was dead. He had seen him die, watched his chest stop rising and falling. This was even worse than Elms. At least Elms had stayed dead.

Kelmore came rushing down the hall.

"This is impossible," Vosendak said.

"Tell me something I don't know," Kelmore said.

"What happened?"

"Bridger came on shift this morning at seven, and he... well, he found Pratcher sitting here."

"How?" Vosendak searched for some rational explanation. Maybe they hadn't administered lethal drugs? Maybe they had buried a weighted coffin and put him back in his cell? But he had seen the chemicals get pumped in.

And why keep a bastard like Pratcher alive? Aside from Brian, nobody wanted him alive. How could this be possible? Was he even real? Was he a clone or a ghost? Was he still in bed, dreaming all of this?

"I don't know," Kelmore said.

"Are you guys still going to execute me today?" Pratcher said.

"What?" Vosendak turned to him. "What do you mean?"

"The Warden said you guys killed me, but I... I don't remember that."

"How couldn't you?" Vosendak gaped at Pratcher.

"Today's August fourteenth, right?"

"No, it's the fifteenth."

"But, that can't be. I... I was supposed to die today." Pratcher looked as hopelessly confused and uncertain as Vosendak felt. Was this true? Had Pratcher somehow been miraculously resurrected? No, there had to be a rational explanation for all this. There had to be!

Curious, he reached through the bars and grabbed Pratcher's arm.

"Hey, what are you doing—" Pratcher said.

It felt warm and real, as real as it had yesterday. But it couldn't be. It just couldn't! Was he a twin, maybe? No, that was absurd. Pratcher had no twins.

He let go of Pratcher's arm and stepped back. He didn't want to be here. His mind couldn't handle it.

Was Pratcher telling the truth or was he lying? Did he know the reason behind his resurrection or was he really confused?

Looking for some kind of reasonable answer, he turned back to Kelmore.

"What do we do about this?"

"I have no idea." Kelmore reached into his coat pocket, took out a bottle of Tums and swallowed two. "But we can't let anybody know about this. Too many know already." He put the bottle back in his pocket.

"What about him, though? We can't just leave him here."

"Don't you think I fucking know that? But what else am I supposed to do? If the press gets a whiff of this, we're going to be swamped with reporters. And how am I supposed to explain to the governor how a prisoner we killed is back in his cell? Christ, I can't handle this shit."

Kelmore had a point. If they learned that this man had come back, it would only be the biggest news story ever. And what could they say to the victims' family? 'Oops, sorry, you know that guy who killed your family? Well, we're sorry, but he managed to come back today.'

Vosendak's mind reeled at all the wonderful and terrible possibilities of seeing Pratcher back in the flesh. Did that mean there was a God? And if so, why resurrect this piece of shit? Why not Becky Nogalko and the other victims? How could one believe in the righteousness of God when he brought back criminals and not victims? If it was in fact divine. Or, what if it was aliens or magic or something beyond human comprehension? In fact, was it even really Pratcher in there or someone else? *Or **something else***, he thought, with a shudder.

Confused and frightened, he turned on Pratcher and said, "Are you really Matthew Dean Pratcher?"

"Of course I am. Who else would I be?"

He sounded genuine, but what could Vosendak believe?

"What's the last thing you remember?"

"I went to sleep last night after eating a bologna sandwich and reading that book about France. And then I woke up here, like I did for the past eight years."

Vosendak remembered the book. It was the day before he walked the last mile. "And you don't remember anything else?"

"I swear to God, I don't."

"Don't say that."

Pratcher looked terrified. He was shaking. "I swear to you, I thought that I was going to die today. I *know* it's the fourteenth. You've got to believe me. It's still me, and I don't have a fucking clue what's going on."

"All right, all right, just…" Vosendak raised his hands, not knowing what to think or believe, anymore. "Just… stay there and don't say anything."

Pratcher laughed bitterly and gestured to his cell. "Where else can I go?"

Vosendak turned away from the cell and ran down to the bathroom, feeling like he was going to throw up again. But as he ran, a thought came to him. They were going to bury Pratcher today.

The coffin in the morgue. Maybe…

He ran past the bathroom and headed down there.

***

When he arrived, he found Kelmore there with the other two guards.

The coffin was empty.

Trembling, he sighed and leaned against the cold, white-brick wall. Its chill seeped into his bones.

"So, either this guy's a zombie or Harry Houdini," Bridger said.

Kelmore was shaking. "This doesn't leave the room. Understand?"

"Right," Vosendak said, nodding.

The other men agreed.

"What do we do? There's two other guys on the block. If they find out—"

"Put them in the hole."

"But, they didn't do any—"

"If word gets out about this, we could have a riot on our hands," Kelmore said. "Or worse."

"Right." Bridger and the other guard left.

"What do we do, Chief?" Vosendak said. "We can't hide this thing forever. Maybe we should contact our superiors and the media—"

"Oh, yeah, and then they can accuse us of aiding and abetting the escape of a known felon."

"But, they saw him die."

"Think, Ray. What other rational explanation could they have? If we say that he keeps coming back like a ghost, then they'll either put us in jail or the funny farm."

Vosendak sighed and nodded.

Kelmore paced around the table. "We need… we need…" His voice trailed off and he glared at the harsh light above them, as if he were lost in thought. "We need some time to think. Plan. We have to do something. That's right. Something."

Vosendak wasn't sure about Kelmore. His voice sounded shaky and he stared at the ceiling, as if searching for divine inspiration.

"I don't know," Kelmore said, looking at him. "You a Catholic, Ray?"

"Lutheran."

"You believe in God?"

He laughed, bitterly. "After today, I'll believe in just about anything."

Kelmore shook his head. "I don't know what to do. Honestly, I don't."

"That makes two of us."

Kelmore walked over to the door. "Give me an hour or two. I'll... I'll think of something."

"All right, Chief."

Kelmore left.

When he was gone, Vosendak closed his eyes and pounded the back of his head against the brick wall three times.

***

Two hours later, Kelmore met with Vosendak in his office, and said, "We have to take Pratcher down to death row and kill him."

"Again?" He stared at his boss with disbelief.

"What else can we do?"

Good question. He scratched his head. "What about the governor and the state of Pennsylvania?"

"Well, according to the state of Pennsylvania, Pratcher is legally a dead man. So, we can do what we want. And this might be the only way to deal with the... uh... the situation."

He frowned and scratched his stubbly chin. "Suppose he comes back again? I don't think he'll be too happy if we keep killing him over and over again."

"If you have a better suggestion, I'm listening."

He didn't know what to say. What could one say in a situation like this?

"Let's just get this over with."

He nodded and said, "All right." Then he followed Kelmore out of his office.

***

They found Bridger and the other guard and explained the situation. Both men looked stunned, but they agreed to go along with the plan.

Together, the men headed back to Pratcher's cell. Vosendak's hands shook as he approached. Would Pratcher come along quietly, knowing what would happen? Kelmore went to the death chamber to set up the injector machine.

When he arrived at the cell, Pratcher was gripping the bars, looking like he wanted to tear them apart.

"Open it up," he instructed Bridger.

"What's happening?" Pratcher asked.

"You're coming with us. Put your hands out."

Pratcher took his hands off the bars and retreated to the back of the cell. "What? But why?"

"Come on, Pratcher. Don't make this hard on yourself." *Or us,* he wanted to add.

"You're going to kill me again, aren't you?"

"Are you going to come along?"

"No." Pratcher shook his head. "You already killed me once, and you can't do it again."

"You don't have a choice."

The door opened. Vosendak took out his handcuffs and nightstick. His hands felt slick with sweat as he held them.

"No, please don't, please!"

"Come on, Pratcher, be a man about it. You were yesterday."

He crept inside the cell, his heart racing. Pratcher backed against the wall, looking like he was going to attack.

"You can't do this to me again, man!" Pratcher said. "You already killed me!"

"Pratcher, calm down!"

He screamed and charged towards Vosendak and the open door. He was so surprised that he stood there for a second, unable to react. Pratcher slammed him against the bars. The blow knocked the nightstick out of his hands and it went clattering into the far corner of the cell.

Gasping, he tried to grab Pratcher, but he was already outside the cell. Bridger and the other guard caught him and struck him in the head and chest with their nightsticks. Pratcher cried out and dropped to the ground. Once he was down, Bridger cuffed him.

Pain screamed through his back where he had hit the cell bars. There'd probably be some nice bruises there later, but it didn't seem like anything was permanently damaged.

He groaned and straightened up.

"Thanks, guys," he said. "I didn't think he'd try—"

"Let's just get him down the row before he wakes up," Bridger said.

"Right."

Vosendak took Pratcher's legs, and the other men took his arms and chest. They carried him down to the end of death row.

***

Unlike the last time, this trip to death row was devoid of any pomp and circumstance. Vosendak helped the men strap Pratcher to the gurney and his stomach tightened as Kelmore plunged the IV into the convict's arm.

"Shouldn't we say something?"

"Like what?" Kelmore said.

"Don't bother coming back again," Bridger said.

Everybody laughed, but it was the titter of nervous men.

"All right, let's do it," Kelmore said.

They walked over to the injection machine and pumped the poison into his veins. Vosendak hardly noticed when Pratcher's chest stopped rising and falling.

When they finished, Kelmore said, "Take him down to the morgue and make sure he's cremated."

Vosendak frowned. "Shouldn't we keep an eye on the body and his cell for a while, in case he decides to come back again?"

"No. It's probably just..." Kelmore groaned. His eyes darted back and forth, as if searching for some rational explanation to the impossible. "All right, I'll watch the cell for the rest of the night. But we're all very tired, Ray, and we probably just imagined this." He pinched the bridge of his nose. "Just, uh, just get rid of him."

"But he didn't request to be cremated—"

Kelmore gave him an annoyed look.

"Right, I'll change the forms. Come on."

They carried Pratcher's body out of death row. Bridger got a cart from the prison laundry and brought it back. They dumped Pratcher's body into it and led it down to the mortuary.

Vosendak hoped that it would be the last time.

***

Somehow, though, it didn't surprise him when he heard Kelmore's voice on the phone the next day. Kelmore had watched the cell the whole night, but he hadn't seen anything until after three in the morning.

Getting sleepy, he checked his watch and went to get some coffee from the break room. It was 3:05. At 3:11, Kelmore returned to the block with his coffee.

Pratcher was back in his cell.

Instead of sounding fearful or angry, though, Kelmore sounded almost resigned to the fact that Pratcher had returned yet again.

"Did you tell him about the—"

"No, I didn't," Kelmore said. "Why bother?"

"Right."

"What are we going to do?"

"Beats me."

"I'll be right down."

He threw on some clothes and raced down to the prison. When he arrived, he saw Pratcher sitting in his cell, reading his book about the history of France. He retreated with the Warden to his office.

"What happened?"

"The same thing as yesterday," Kelmore said. "Only Bridger wasn't quite as afraid." He scratched his head. "He still thinks it's his execution day."

"Is it?"

"I don't know." Kelmore shrugged, looking more helpless than he had the previous day.

"Maybe we should just let him go."

"Are you fucking nuts? He's a convicted killer."

"And what are we supposed to do? Just keep killing him every day?"

"Maybe he deserves it."

"Are you so sure?"

"No, I'm not sure of anything, anymore. Especially after the past two days."

"Let me talk to him."

"What for?"

"I want to see what he has to say."

"Fine. Do it."

Vosendak sighed and returned to Pratcher's cell. When he arrived, Pratcher lowered his book and glanced at him nervously.

Gathering all his strength, he recited what happened. Funny enough, Pratcher seemed to take it well. Or about as well as anyone could take it.

"Maybe it's a sign," Pratcher said.

"Of what? You think you're God?"

"No." Pratcher looked around. "Listen, do you think you can keep a secret?"

"Depends on what it is."

"Swear to me."

Annoyed, he groaned, and said, "All right, I swear."

"I didn't kill the Nogalko family. In fact, I wasn't even there when it happened."

For a second, he thought that Pratcher was kidding. Yet, the look on his face was quite serious.

"If you didn't, then who did?"

"Brian."

He blinked and gripped the bars. "You mean to tell me that your brother killed the Nogalko family?"

"That's right. I took the fall for him."

"Bullshit." He pushed off the bars. "I read the case file. They found your shotgun and the spent shells at the murder scene, with your fingerprints on everything. And they also found your semen in Allison Nogalko's vagina."

"Brian called me on their phone after he did it. And he was in hysterics. I came over and told him I'd take care of it. So, I took the shotgun, fired a second round to finish Becky off and then I... I'm not proud of it, but I..."

"You raped Allison Nogalko after she was dead?" His stomach churned.

"Like I said, I'm not proud of it. But what else could I do? Brian is a retard. He never thinks his actions through. He just... he went in and robbed them, thinking they were still asleep. About the only smart thing he did do was wear gloves, and that was only because I told him to do it a million times."

"Why did he bring the shotgun?"

"Like I said, he isn't smart. He thought that if they tried anything, that he could scare them with it. Unfortunately, Ben Nogalko also had a gun. When Brian saw it, he panicked and started shooting." Pratcher sighed and shook his head. "When I got there, it was a fucking bloody mess. I had to take Brian to my car and clean him up, then go back in and make it look like I had been there. I figured since I had a criminal record with theft, ADW, and attempted murder, the police would believe I went too far."

"Wait a minute. If you were all by yourselves, why not just torch the place and disappear?"

"Two reasons. One was that Brian owned a distinct car, and I knew that some of the neighbors must have seen it coming down the road. He would be a prime suspect. And he's not too bright, so if he ran, he wouldn't think to get a new car. The police would have caught him eventually."

"What was the second reason?"

"I felt bad for the Nogalkos. I felt somebody had to take the blame, and I couldn't bear to see Brian go to jail." Pratcher groaned. "You know what they do to people like Brian in here. He wouldn't have lasted a week in this shithole. So I took the rap for him. And the police were only too happy to send me away forever."

He stumbled back against the wall, feeling like a sledgehammer had struck him in the stomach. Had Pratcher really been an innocent man covering for his brother? Or was it just another lie?

"Why should I believe you?"

"You don't have to," Pratcher said. "It's just the truth." He laughed bitterly and shook his head. "You know... I swore to myself that I'd take that secret to my grave."

"So, why tell me now?"

"Well, seeing as how I've been to the grave two times, already, I figured I'd more than kept my promise." Pratcher folded his arms. "But if you tell anybody, I'll deny it." His eyes narrowed. "Brian's never going to see the inside of a jail cell. Not while I can help it."

Vosendak ran a hand through his hair and sighed. Deep down, he wasn't sure what to believe. Was Pratcher telling the truth or just lying to him? The more he looked at the man, the less he could be sure. His eyes and general demeanor seemed sincere, but then again, he had seen criminals in the past who could lie with utter conviction.

"Even if this is true, what do you want me to do about it?"

"Let me go," Pratcher said.

"Fuck you! I'm not putting my career at risk, even if you are innocent."

Pratcher folded his arms. "Then expect to have me around for a very long time."

"Who the fuck do you think you are? A ghost or something?"

"I don't know what I am, anymore. All I know is that I didn't deserve to die."

"Neither did the Nogalkos. But they didn't come back."

Pratcher stood up. "Hey, I'm sorry about that! But I can't change what happened, and I can't tell you why I was brought back. Just let me out of here." Pratcher gripped the bars and squeezed them until his knuckles turned white.

Vosendak turned and walked off the row.

***

What if he was telling the truth? Vosendak thought. *What if Pratcher were innocent? But what if he was guilty? What is the right thing to do? Could he really be innocent of the crime? Or was it all an elaborate trick? What if they killed him and he came back again and again? What about the Nogalkos and their rights?*

His head hurt as all these thoughts spun around his mind. He briefly flirted with the idea of taking him out of prison. It would be difficult. However, it wasn't impossible. Cut all his hair off. Get him a spare guard's uniform. No, he couldn't. It wouldn't be right. Or would it? If he were innocent, it would be right.

That was a pretty big 'if', though.

For the next few minutes, he paced around the break room, weighing his options, considering everything. He thought about telling Kelmore, yet, he knew the warden would have no part of it. Maybe he should forget it.

No, he thought. *There must be some reason for him coming back. Maybe he is innocent. Maybe not. But he can't stay here forever.*

After some more soul searching, he decided — *fuck it*. He would help Pratcher escape.

***

The following night, Vosendak grabbed an extra guard uniform from his closet and smuggled it into the prison. He also took along a straight razor, scissors, and some shaving cream. He waited until the block was quiet, then he came in with his supplies in a brown paper bag. Pratcher was lying on his bunk, looking distraught as he stared at the ceiling.

"What do *you* want?"

"I'm helping you get out of here."

"Yeah, right."

"I'm serious. Here, take this." He looked around nervously, his blood thudding in his eardrums.

Pratcher shot up from his bunk and walked over to the bars. He looked stunned as Vosendak handed him the bag with the shaving cream, razor, scissors, and uniform.

"Shave your beard and hair off and put this on," he said. "And be quick about it."

"Right."

Pratcher carried the stuff over to the sink, wet his beard and hair and started cutting. As he worked, he said, "What made you change your mind?"

"Maybe God brought you back for a reason. I don't know. Just hurry up and get done."

When Pratcher finished, he looked bald as a cue ball. He put on the uniform and cap. It was tight on him, but not a bad fit, especially considering Pratcher was a few inches taller than him.

"Come on," Vosendak said. "Stay close to me, and do exactly what I say."

He felt a terrified thrill as he opened the gate. Pratcher stepped out and said, "Thank you, man."

"Thank me, later. Come on, this way."

He walked down to the end of the block and looked around. When it appeared clear, he led Pratcher down to the prison.

As they reached the entrance, he heard someone coming towards them.

"Quick, hide."

He shoved Pratcher into a closet and waited. Two guards passed by and nodded hello. Trying to act normal, he said, "Hi," then waited until they passed.

When they were gone, he led Pratcher out to the security gate. His heart hammered as they approached. If he screwed up, they would both be fucked. He took several deep breaths.

"Stay to my right and don't say a fucking word."

"Right."

He walked up to the bulletproof glass gate. Harry Lodormine was at the controls. He was engrossed in a Robert Parker novel. Usually, he had his snout buried in one detective book or another during the late shift.

"Harry, can you buzz me through?" he said. "I just need to go out to my car and get my other glasses."

"Yeah, sure thing, Ray." Harry buzzed them through while barely even looking at them.

For once, Ray thanked God that Harry was an intense bibliophile.

They walked through the security gate, onto the main yard. He hurried Pratcher to the front door and opened it for him. They stepped outside. Shaking, he peeked out and looked around. Nobody was there. It was a cold, windy night, and rain pelted them.

"All right, just go," he said. "Keep walking 'til you reach the woods. You can catch the bus to another town."

"Thank you." Pratcher held out his hand.

Ray didn't shake it.

"Goodbye, Vosendak."

Pratcher nodded, then hitched up his collar and walked into the rain, across the long parking lot, the wind howling.

Shaking with fear and uncertainty, Vosendak started back inside the prison. As he closed the door, he decided to say goodbye to Pratcher.

But when he looked back towards the parking lot, the man was gone.

Unlife Sentence

Eric J. Juneau

<u>Date: November 4th</u>

The guard gave me this notebook. Said it's so I don't go crazy. Then he gave me some cans of food and metal spoons and a can opener. "What the hell?" I asked him, "what's going on—I ain't supposed to have this stuff." He said, "It's just in case. I can't let you out. But it ain't humane to let a guy starve to death." Just in case what?

I might as well write something, seeing as I've got nothing else to do. My name's James Buck. I don't need to tell you my life story. I've told the lawyers and cops a dozen times, and it keeps getting better every time I tell it.

And if you watch the news, you know why I'm in jail. This time, I mean. I've been grabbing all my life, hold-ups and burglary, shit like that. This time it was a liquor store. But the owner was one of those neighborhood watch types—the ones who stow a shotgun under the counter.

I don't get people like that. That's a person who's willing to die just to save a few bucks. And the store's got to be insured anyway. Anyway, I got clipped pretty bad. They caught me sitting in a puddle of spilled milk and blood.

But get this—some news reporter found out I've been in and out of jail twenty times, and did an article on it. I think they're fudging that number. Some of those were juvy and holding cells. Different states, different names. That's why I slipped under the radar so long.

But the story split wide, so now I'm news bait. Guess there's some scandal about police budgets. Republicans are saying these slaps on the wrists are what's making me a repeat offender. Democrats are saying "no-no-no, jails are <u>too</u> tough. That's <u>why</u> he's the way he is." I tell you, I don't get politics. All I know is it's going to be one fucker of a trial.

The best part is, I ain't got no secret. Every time they cuff me, I play ball. I'm nice and polite, I say "yessir" and "nossir". As long as you don't tie up court, they can stack up all the evidence they want. Nothing can't be negotiated. Attorneys plead it down. Or it's a suspended sentence or community service, based on good behavior. At worst, I serve a tiny sentence and don't have to worry about rent for a month.

Maybe that's why the cops here don't like me—I'm a golden boy now. I'll get probation or something. Then I'll be living off my story, while those shitheads keep eating their corn at the county fair. Cops just want the power trip anyway.

This place isn't bad really. Taupe walls, got the old school iron bars on the cell, down in the basement. It's a good waiting jail. Waiting for trial, waiting for lawyers to call, waiting for paperwork. Guess that's why I'm writing in this, passing the time. Used to have a journal when I was a kid. Still don't know why I got it though.

Okay, here's what happened. The cop comes down. Real sad look on his face, like his mama died. All he does is check on me. I'm the only man in lockup right now, so not much to see. Then he goes back up.

He does this a few times past few days—each time he looks worse and worse. Then today he looks like shit on a stick. I even tell him so.

"Yeah," he says. "Long day." He looks like someone I knew after the INS deported his family—no home to go to.

Then he shoved a box of books and magazines into my cell.

"What's this for?" I asked.

"It's so you don't go crazy. I don't know how long you're going to be there for," he says.

"What? Is something going on with my trial?"

"Sort of. I think it's going to be postponed, at least."

I started sweating then. I've had friends who rotted in jail for years because of tie-ups and delays. And then got released without so much as an apology. "I want to talk to my lawyer."

"Sorry. Phones are down."

"Phones are down? What do you mean?"

"I mean phones are down." He turned back to the stairs.

"You can't deny me contact from my lawyer. That's illegal."

He sneered at me. "Shut up."

"What's going on? Why are the phones down?" I yelled back. But he was already gone.

Then he comes back. He's holding a box of canned food—peaches, Spam, that sort of thing—and he puts it right outside my cell. Plus some utensils and a can opener. I could pick up a can of corn and brain him with it, but he looks like he wouldn't even care.

"What's all this?"

"Just in case. So you don't starve," he says.

"Fuck you," I say. "You poison this shit?"

He didn't answer, he just went back up. I went through the books. Lot of car magazines from six years ago and yellow romance novels. And this notebook, with the pen inside. Now that I think about it, I'm not even sure if he knew it was there. I could pick the lock with the pen, but I won't get anywhere with the cops upstairs.

So now a few hours have passed and I'm wondering what the hell is going on. The only window is one of those frosted rectangle things up high. So all I can see is whether it's day or night.

***

Date: November 5th

Okay, now this got fucked up. I thought yesterday was bad, this is even better.

I'm writing this down so there's no one can convict me. Everything here's the God honest truth.

After I woke up, I heard the door open, and the cop came back down. If he looked like shit before, now he looked like shit on shit. His left shoulder's bandaged, his face is dirty, and he's limping.

"Jesus, what happened to you?" I asked.

Then—and this is the good part—he takes the ring of keys off his belt and drops them in the box of food. I swear to God.

"Here's the keys," he says.

"What?" I say. No way he's doing this, so I think I must have heard him wrong.

"The keys to your cell. I wouldn't use them if I were you."

Now I figure this is some kind of mind game. They're testing a psychology experiment on me. Or it's a practical joke. Either way, I'm not playing.

"Nice try," I said.

Then he got a call on his squawker. (I don't know how they understand anything on those things.) He said "yep" and hobbled up the stairs.

"Hey, what's going on?" I yell out, just before he reaches the door.

"I don't know if you're safer in there or what. And I really don't care. Do what you want."

"Safer from what?" But he was out the door.

So that's that. I haven't touched the keys yet. I bet they're trying to entice me to do something illegal because I'm going to get off easy. I'm not that dumb.

About time for bed, but the lights are still on. Sitting and trying to figure out what's going on.

***

Date: November 6th

No one came to give me breakfast or dinner. I was so hungry I opened a can of spaghetti. Even if it's a game, a man's gotta eat.

I'm damn well not going to use that key though. I know they're trying to trick me. There's probably some obscure law they're trying to get me with. I ain't biting.

***

Date: November 7th

I heard an explosion just now. I think something outside might be on fire. There's an orange glow out the window. Riots? Can't be because of me. I'm not <u>that</u> special.

I didn't see a single cop yesterday and I haven't seen one today. I'm still pretty sure this is an experiment. At least it better be. Or my lawyer's going to have a nice mistreatment defense.

***

114

Date: November 8th

No food. No cops. And now the power's out. What's going on?

***

Date: November 9th

Okay, after four days of not one person coming down, I finally decided to use the keys. This whole thing is giving me the creeps. And whatever was burning before is still there.

So this is just letting whoever gets this know. I'm taking the key, <u>which the cop gave me</u>, and I'm letting myself out, just to see what's going on.

You can't possibly arrest me on this. No one's been feeding me. No one's been here to let me make a phone call. I've been calling out for four days straight with no answer. That's got to be prisoner abuse.

Maybe there's a war going on. Maybe they all had heart attacks. Anyway, I'm just going to find out.

—

I'm back. So the key worked, and I let myself out of my cell. (I even yelled that I was coming out, not that it would have done any good.) And I went upstairs. <u>Holy shit.</u> Place was a mess. Looked like everyone left in a big damn hurry. Still coffee in the pot (cold as ice though).

I didn't touch anything, but I looked. No fingerprints, so no one could tell I'd been there. Books and papers and photos everywhere. Saw a lot of stuff about "Emergency State Protocol". Computers knocked over. Gun cabinet was left open, but nothing in there.

Oh, I touched one radio and one phone to see if it worked. The phone didn't. But the radio, almost all the stations were blaring the Emergency Broadcast Signal. The one that wasn't, some blowhard was yapping about the latest medical crisis. When isn't there a medical crisis in America? All I understood was that it wasn't airborne or in the water, whatever they were talking about.

Then I heard footsteps, so I booked it back down the stairs. Didn't want to be caught. Shut the door behind me. Locked my cell. Everything back to normal.

Except now whoever came is pounding at the door to the basement, like they don't know how to get in. I don't know who it is, they don't respond when I yell. Cops? Did they lose the key?

Over and over, it's pound, pound, pound. Not real hard, just slow and thumping. To be safe, I pulled all the food and shit in the box into my cell.

***

Date: November 10th

Well, I found out what's going on. I'm staring at it <u>right now.</u> And he's staring at me. He either figured out how to open the door, or it just gave.

The guy walked through, looking like you see in the movies—eyes all white, blood all over his shirt, purple-gray skin. He stumbled to the bars. Didn't even know he was reaching in, until I snapped to my senses and got out of the way. I was staring too hard, like at a car wreck. Almost grabbed me. But he can't get in, door's still locked.

<u>Zombies.</u> I swear to motherfucking God, there's a <u>fucking zombie</u> standing outside my cell right now. It's the walking

116

fucking undead right in front of me. I'm not sure if he's really a zombie, but he sure looks and acts like a zombie. I suppose he could be on drugs or something, but I doubt it.

I think he used to be a desk worker, before his jaw was torn off. Now it's hanging there like a dog's chew toy. I guess they lost the fight outside. Explains why no one came down. Too busy fighting zombies.

I don't know if he's following the same rules. Like if you get infected by getting bit or if it's like a disease. I feel fine so it's probably not in the air. Or maybe I'm one of those "special people" who's immune. Lucky me.

I don't know if he wants to eat my brains or my flesh or what. But I'm not going to find out. I'm staying right here on my side of the bars. I don't know what I'm going to do, but I've got some food and some time. Sooner or later, this idiot's got to realize there's no meal here.

***

Date: November 11th

I wish I knew what was going on out there. All I see is light during the day and dark at night. Last night I barely got to sleep with the groaning and moaning. I'm used to sleeping light—people always jumping your ass in prison. But at least the fudge-packers go to sleep once in a while.

This actually solves a lot of my problems, now that I think about it. If it's chaos out there, my trial's got to be postponed or something. Maybe even cancelled. There's no cops around to stop me. I could be king of this town. All I need is a few guns and lots of ammo. Can't be that many zombies around this hick town.

He smells awful. I think he's decomposing. Skin's all black and splitting, like a balloon's poking through. Maybe I can wait him out. How long does it take for a body to break down? Maybe his legs will collapse into mush. Then I can just jump over him.

Water went out, but I managed to break a pipe. Just a drip, but it works. Use a strip of clothing to filter it and collect it in an empty can.

I could dig my way out of here, but it's all concrete foundation wall. And all I have is my can opener and a fork.

Oh, fucking duh. I'm a fucking idiot.

***

Date: November 12th

This'll be the last you read about me. Took a while, but I made a shiv out of the fork. It's not much, but I can stab this fucker in the head. He's pressed right up against the bars. Gotta be careful he doesn't grab me though. And I gotta plunge hard. I tried to make it as sharp as possible. That's why it took so long.

Now I just want to say, this isn't murder. This guy's clearly dead—he hasn't slept in two days and his eyeball's about to fall out. Just want to make that clear to whoever finds this.

Next time you see me, I'll be ruling this town. Adios, fuckers.

***

Okay, I'm a fucking idiot. I admit that.

You can tell by the fact I'm still here that something went wrong. Everything started fine. I stabbed the asshole right in the brain. Blood spurted out like a fountain pen. Almost got in my mouth. I thought, _Jesus H. Christ, any closer and I would've become one of them._

But it worked. He spasmed a little, then fell down. I waited like fifteen minutes, made sure he wasn't getting up. Then walked out. Free and easy.

After that, I went foraging. Went across the street, picked up all the food I could carry. Only in this podunk, cousin-fucking town, you'd have the police station, grocery store, and gun shop right next to each other. Didn't see a soul, human or zombie. Packed everything useful I could find.

Best shit was already taken, but there was enough. Grabbed a huge bag of ammo and guns. I was fucking ready, man. I felt like king of the world. Took my shotty and blasted that fucking police station, broke the windows, the signs. Fuck those assholes for keeping me in the dark.

That was the big mistake. Zombies started crawling out from everywhere, behind buildings, out of windows. Must've heard the shots. Where the fuck were they before? It's like they were waiting for a signal.

I plugged a few of them, but I couldn't reload with two huge duffel bags on my arms. But I didn't want to drop them. I took too much time figuring out what to do. One of them grabbed my gun bag from behind. I panicked, dropped it. Shouldn't have done that. I should have kept that instead of the food bag, but I had half a second to think.

So I ran back into the station. It was the only place I could go, I was surrounded. Went back down to the cell, shut myself in.

Only three followed me so far. Fell down the stairs too, but they got up. They reach their hands in and scream, but that's it. I guess the others are too stupid to find a way in.

***

Date: November 14th

Four more zombies arrived. A biker. A guy in a college t-shirt. A guy in a construction helmet. A cop. We could have a Village People reunion if they'd bite an Indian and a cowboy.

Sometimes I have conversations with them. I say things like "What are you in for? Being a zombie? Yeah, that's a bad rap. The man's got it out for zombies. Don't worry, you'll get off." We play some fun games. I pull one guy's legs out from under him. Then all the guys shove him back, and I see how long it takes him to get back to the front. Right now, Anthrax has the record (he has an Anthrax t-shirt on), but Construction Man is catching up. Maybe if I get out of here, I can rope them and use them like cock fights. I could dangle some juicy brains overhead and watch them go at it.

Hey, it's not like they care. They're dead. And they'd eat me if I gave them the chance. Eventually these guys have got to get bored, or too rotten to stand. Then I can get out of here, free and easy. Or I'll get rescued, maybe. Someone's got to remember I'm down here. Except I wouldn't be surprised if they "conveniently" forgot. I'm not even worried about my trial anymore. I think that's long gone. They've got to be just looking for survivors at this point.

Date: November 15th

I didn't sleep at all last night. More zombies coming in. It's a big fucking party down here now. Starting to get crowded. I had just gotten used to the smell when they brought in some new funk. It smells like an asshole in a sewer in here. Can barely swallow my food sometimes.

Trying to make another shiv. No idea where my first one went. Maybe I can kill enough of them to clear the way. But there's probably more waiting for me upstairs. I can stay here for a while. I'll wait them out, then I can get back to ruling this town.

Why the fuck was I showing off like that? Why the fuck didn't I just shoot them all? Why'd I run back here?

***

Date: November 16th

More zombies keep coming in. This room's filled with them now—wall to wall. Some are just standing on the stairs, swaying back and forth, like they're waiting for their turn. I'm sick of looking at them all the time. They're so disgusting, all missing lips and ears. One has an arm hanging by just a stringy tendon. Lots of old ladies and fat people. I guess they got the worst of it—couldn't outrun them. And all they do is stare at me.

This fucking sucks. This fucking sucks so much. I hate writing in this thing, but I've got nothing else to do. I never know what to say. I've got nothing to say.

Date: November 16th or 17th

I'm not even sure what day it is anymore. I fell asleep during the day, woke up, and it was still day. So did I sleep through the night or what?

Finally got the shiv finished. Tested it on one of them and mission accomplished. He's laying in front of the bars, bleeding from his head like a stuck pig. Motherfucker.

Didn't take long before another one came to take his place. I can take them out one after the other. They'll just keep coming up, like lemmings. Got to be quick though. They can't get their heads through, but they can reach through the bars. One of them could grab me and bite.

All I got to do is kill the rest of them and I'll be free. Like I said before, adios, fuckers.

***

Date: November 17th or 18th

Okay, this isn't working. Everyone I kill, another one takes its place. They keep on coming. As soon as I take out a few, two or three more stumble down the stairs. It's like there's no end to them. And now there's a big pile of stinking corpses outside my door. Great fucking plan.

What the fuck am I supposed to do? Just sit here and die? I still got tons of food and water. But as soon as I use that key, they'll come flooding in here. I've been pissing and shitting in the corner, but I don't even smell it with the festering garbage stench already here.

Date: November 18th or 19th

I don't even care if someone comes to rescue me. Someone give me a shotgun so I can start blasting away heads.

I will never watch another zombie movie again as long as I live. I'll never do anything wrong again. Just someone get rid of these things.

***

Date: November the fuckteenth

I've looked back through my entries. I haven't seen another human for a week and a half at least. Do you need human contact to stay sane? Zombies don't count.

You think I should be used to staying in lockup. But I never did time with living corpses outside my door. They don't get bored. They don't stop coming. How the fuck am I supposed to deal with that?

No one's come to get me. They've forgotten or they've abandoned the town. Meaning they're probably going to nuke it at some point. Or they're leaving me down here to die.

It's some fucking cruel joke. I've got the world in my hand, right outside the door, and I can't get to it. What do you want me to say? I'm sorry? I apologize? Forget it. I'd sooner die here than bow down to you chumps. I'm getting out of here. Make no mistake.

***

Date: who the hell cares?

I stuck my hand out in front of one of them today. Just held it in front of him for the longest time. He gazed at me with his blank eyes. His jaw was filled with black teeth and drool. He reached out like he wanted to bring me in and tell me a secret. Kept clawing for me, like he didn't want a piece, he wanted the whole thing. They all did.

Is this punishment from God? Fate's doing the job the cops couldn't?

My skin is so itchy I can't stand it. Maybe staying in this cooped-up room is getting to me. But I'm not going to let a few zombies take me down.

***

Date: not with one of these fuckers.

My belly's full, but I'm so hungry. There's nothing but canned food. I'm dreaming of a rare steak, surrounded by gravy and potatoes. Raw and dripping. There's plenty of meat in these cans, but there's nothing like that fresh, just-killed-and-cooked taste.

Maybe I can eat myself. My friend told me about this book he read where a guy was on a desert island and he ended up eating his legs and arms to stay alive. Might take a while to saw through my limbs with just this shiv. Jesus Christ, look what I'm talking about.

I'll get out at some point. I know it. They'll leave or decompose or someone will come get me. I always get out. Prison ain't shit to me.

***

124

Date: the fucking apocalypse

How about this? I can either go out there and die, or stay here and die. I can decide to do something or decide not to do something. Either way I'm fucked. How about this? I decide <u>not</u> to decide. How does that fucking sound? Throw all the fucking zombies you want at me. I've got all the food and water I need. You think putting freedom six inches away is going to mess with me? I'm staying right here.

You think you put me in prison, but it's MY prison, mother fuckers.

***

Date: fuck everything

My stomach hurts so much.

They're always there. They won't stop. They won't ever stop. EVER.

This is my prison. MY prison.

A Ray of Hope

Paul Stansfield

When Ray saw his new cell mate, he was a little disappointed. The guy, Arnold, was about six feet tall. Dark brown hair and eyes. Neither fat nor skinny. Facial features all normal. No strange facial hair or devil tattoos. He was... average looking. The kind of guy you normally wouldn't look twice at.

But Ray certainly did, after all, he'd heard about Mr. Pitman, a.k.a. The Baby Killer. Was even given an audience with Warden Miller about him. It was only Ray's second meeting with Miller, and this time, the warden acted almost too nice. He spelled out a weird little tale. Told Ray that they were afraid that Arnold would be killed, given the prisoners' moral outrage against child murderers like Pitman. So they wanted to keep him separate from the others, in his own cell, own meal time, exercise, etc. But they were also afraid that Arnold would kill himself if left alone. Also, they'd heard Pitman might have killed others but hidden the bodies. Maybe someone could draw him out, listen up, be his friend, and learn some details. Let some grieving parents get "closure" (as the warden put it). Someone like... say, Ray. In return for rooming and being fairly isolated with this guy, Miller said, Ray's sentence could be significantly reduced. Like a whole year or so off the two years he had left.

It was a no-brainer: Ray agreed readily. The warden was ecstatic. Thanked him warmly, led him out of his office. Later, the other shoe dropped. A guard engaged him one-on-one, outside the cafeteria. He hinted strongly that everyone wanted Pitman dead, and that his assassin would get away with it. This was all couched in vague terms and clues. Stuff like, "Accidents do happen, and we certainly wouldn't blame an innocent witness."

Ray groaned inwardly at this; he was no assassin, but he knew he couldn't say anything, or complain. He couldn't prove anything. They all covered their asses well, used a chain of command to deflect responsibility. So he figured he'd wait it out, try to get some info, hope that was enough, and if not, absorb the threats and beatings and let them replace him with an actual button man.

Ray was a little confused about why they felt the need for this rather obvious ruse. Probably all the publicity surrounding Pitman, and the many previous "accidents" here. Miller doubtlessly wanted to hamper the efforts of later bleeding heart investigators. It was all such a stupid game that everyone played.

"So you're my protector," Arnold said. His voice, too, was normal.

"That what they told you, huh?" returned Ray. Pitman must see through the silly ruse.

"Yes. They're quite concerned about my safety." He smirked lightly. "Course, no offense, I've seen several guys bigger than you, and it seems we're going to be isolated from the others, anyway."

"Wow. This jail, doing something incompetent? That's a first." The whole point, of course. Using a gorilla or known killer would be too suspicious.

The smirk widened. "I'm sure," he paused. "Or am I?" Pitman gave Ray a challenging stare.

Great, thought Ray. *He knows the stupid scheme, or can guess it. The hell with it.*

He was already tired of this. He'd play Barbara Walters, later. He rolled over in his bunk, and after a while, fell asleep.

*** *

As it turned out, Ray didn't feel much like chatting with his roomie the next day, either. Or the next two. Their exchanges were few and brief, about practical matters: What the meals were like, library privileges, visitation, that sort of thing. Arnold apparently didn't want to speak much, either. However, by the fifth day, Ray was bored. He'd read all his magazines and it was hours before exercise. So, he asked if Arnold wanted to play Scrabble. He did. And luckily, knew how to play. Without further ado, they set up, tiles nestled in their brown paper bag, the abridged dictionary sitting on the floor beside them.

They played the first few turns in silence. Then Arnold put down 'B-A-R-G*' so it was on a triple word square. "That's barn," he said. Ray had explained that his set was missing a blank tile, so the extra 'G' with a star on it was that second blank. Ray counted silently and added the appropriate points to Arnold's total.

"Aren't you going to ask me about my crimes?" Arnold said, looking boldly at Ray.

He returned the gaze calmly. "Sure. I just figured there was no rush. You got the rest of your life." Arnold ignored the barb and kept staring. Ray shrugged. "Okay, tell me."

"First, I saved my little cousin's soul. Then I realized I'd be arrested, so I went to a hospital, put on a doctor's coat, knocked out a nurse, and saved ten more babies' souls. Then I was caught, tried, and sent here."

Ray groaned internally at this bare bones account. Clearly, this guy had a game, wanted Ray to ask questions. Something he didn't want to do, even though it was his job. Finally, he sighed and played the game.

"Isn't that a funny way of putting it, 'saved?' Didn't others call it murdering?" He put down 'lynx' and smiled. Thirty points with its bonuses.

"Not at all. I killed them, yes, but by doing that, I saved their souls. Ensured they're in Heaven instead of Hell." Again the expectant pause.

"What makes you say that?"

"Look at the world, Ray. It's a scumhole. People have gotten away from God. They're warring, killing, raping, stealing, destroying all that is good and precious. How many decent people do you know? Hardworking, loving people? Not many. Growing up and living in this world is no picnic. I just couldn't stand it anymore. I sat there, babysitting my seven-year-old cousin, little dear, all cute, all trusting. That's when I knew what I had to do. Knew I had to stop him from joining in with the horrible sinners. So I snapped his neck, real quick. Then, the innocent babies. After I baptized them, of course. Didn't want them going to Purgatory." He put down 'wagon' and wrote his score down.

"I'm no churchgoer, but doesn't the Bible say killing is bad?" He didn't want to hear more of this nonsense, but he figured he'd better.

"Certainly. And I'll be punished. Yet, the Lord works in mysterious ways. I'm doing a bad thing, but in another way, I'm doing the best thing. What's better than eternal salvation?"

"Isn't that God's decision to end life? Aren't you taking His job?"

"Yes, but I have the best of intentions. He had to see that. Besides, haven't you noticed, it is the good that die young. It's the bad people that live on and on. Don't you see? Life on earth is punishment! The truly blessed are those killed young."

"But you're denying them life. How do you know they wouldn't have lived a full life, done good things, gone to heaven on their own?" Ray placed 'ape' down and frowned at the meager point total.

"I don't, for sure. But look at the odds. The majority of people aren't worthy Christians. So, I saved those, and if I killed some who would have been saved anyway, so what? We're talking seventy, eighty years on this toilet. Know how long eternity is? It's no loss to them. But what a gain to those who would have been damned if they'd lived longer."

Ray was already tired of this conversation, sick of hearing this nut rationalize his behavior. He didn't respond, and didn't ask any more follow up questions, even though he knew Arnold badly wanted to continue the talk. They played the rest of the game in silence, Arnold winning 302-285.

***

Smack! The pink rubber ball caromed off the wall, bounced once, four feet from it, and ticked off Ray's fingers, onto the ground. "Damn!" he exclaimed. That was game. Arnold had won their best of five series, three to two. Ray bounced the ball moodily. The only equipment they were allowed. They only got an hour of exercise a day, separate from the others, out in the yard. They both got quite into their version of handball. Basically racquetball without racquet. And you caught the ball, didn't bat it. The points went quicker that way.

Arnold stood there, sweaty and flushed, glinting his slight, Mona Lisa smile. Ray was irritated by the way he didn't brag or get real emotional over a win, although he nonetheless was extremely competitive. It was more insulting, somehow.

Ray continued bouncing the ball. They only had about five-minutes left, not enough time for another game. "So," he finally said. "You gonna have Father Jenkins visit anymore?"

"No. We don't get along. At first I respected him, even though we clearly disagree on several important matters. Then he revealed himself as being a hypocrite, a tool of the warden." Arnold paused, then continued, having learned in his month with Ray that he wouldn't necessarily ask questions when desired. "He insinuated that suicide was okay for certain people." He looked straight at Ray, catching his eye. "Probably, he'd tell you that murder was okay in certain situations."

Ray shrugged. "Wouldn't surprise me."

"When are you going to get around to killing me? They must be upset with you."

Ray got annoyed, as he always did when this topic came up. "I've told you. I'm no killer. Let them be upset." He decided to return the favor, rile up Arnold. "I'm not like you."

The same, placid half-smile was Arnold's only response. Ray kept going. "By the way, I've been thinking, isn't your grand plan an excuse, at least partly? You saying you didn't like killing them, at all?"

Failure. "It's not an excuse, and I did enjoy it. I enjoy ensuring innocent souls go to heaven."

"I see. You're like Peter Pan, aren't you? Except your way of making sure kids don't grow up is more violent."

Success. Arnold's ordinary face clouded with ordinary-appearing anger. He was silent. Just then, the guard interrupted their conversation to bring them back to their cell. Arnold was sullen and quiet the rest of the night.

The next morning, Arnold went right back to what they were talking about on the court the day before, as if no time had passed. "What will they do to you if you don't kill me, do you think?"

"Don't know. Hopefully, nothing. More realistically, a beating maybe, some solitary as punishment. Worse case, delay my parole."

"So close to getting out. That'd be frustrating."

"Yeah, but I have no alternative." They were both silent for a minute or so. "If you know of their plans, why didn't you kill me before I killed you, back when you thought I might? What stopped you?"

"Christian decency. I kill you, I'm sending you to Hell, most likely. I don't kill adults, they're too sinful."

"What about a really good adult, then? Say like, Mother Theresa? Would she be worth killing, since she'd go to heaven?"

Arnold paused, considering. "Well... perhaps. Yeah, I guess so. Not that it matters. So few good adults..." he trailed off, and spent the rest of the day in a thoughtful pose, curled up on his bunk. Ray grinned. He really enjoyed playing with Arnold's head.

**

Ray sat moodily on the wet cement, watching Arnold run laps around the prison yard. It was raining steadily, too damn wet for 'handball.' Therefore, the alternative exercise for the psycho kid killer. Had to, "Keep the temple fit and healthy" as he said. The guards glanced down at Ray. They'd been quite ill-tempered lately. All of them thought that three months was more than enough time for an intentional murderous accident. He'd held them off by saying Arnold had mentioned other killings, but Ray had to go slow to stop suspicion. Ha, what a laugh. Like a retard wouldn't have figured out the scheme by now.

Back in their cell, Arnold asked if Ray wanted to play Scrabble or Hungry Hungry Hippos. Ray told him no, he wanted to write some letters. Arnold cheerfully replied, "okay" and then became unobtrusive, as he knew Ray appreciated. It was funny, Ray thought as he wrote, how nice Arnold had been of late. Chatty and engaging much of the time, having long talks with him, but shutting up deferentially when that was called for. Ray was starting to like the guy, despite himself. Still thought he was nuts and sick, but not a bad roomie. He found himself telling Arnold his life story, his inner thoughts, even, to which Arnold listened raptly. The night before he'd even gone back to sleep without comment after catching Ray jacking off on the can, (using the mayonnaise-filled sock Ray had found best approximated a vagina). Before, he'd launched into a sermon about why this was wrong.

He finished his letter. It felt good to write his girl. She was a real trooper, still supporting him through all the stress Ray had put her through. God, he missed her. Finished, he decided to get in a quick nap before dinner. Within minutes he was asleep.

***

Ray awoke with a start. Something was… he opened his eyes, and nearly yelled in shock and anger. Nearly, because his mouth was gagged. Some futile attempts told him his hands and feet were tied, too. Arnold was sitting astride Ray, his face inches away.

"Wanted you to be awake before I sent you to heaven, Ray. Thought I owed you an explanation, at least." He encircled Ray's throat with one hand and untied the gag with the other. "If you scream, I'll kill you right off. You can talk normal, if you want."

Ray did. "What are you talking about? I'm an adult, remember? Killing me is a bad thing, you said so yourself."

Arnold smiled broadly. "That's true. I did. But you've changed my mind. You were right. I have been negligent, only doing kids. Some adults are just as deserving. You, for example."

"That's not true! I'm a thief, remember? We're in a jail! I'm no innocent." He considered screaming for help, decided it was hopeless. Arnold would cut him off, and anyway, the guards gave them a lot of privacy, hoping for a murder of Arnold by Ray, of course.

"No, you're not innocent. You're a sinner, sure. You've done some sinful things. But I know you, Ray. Deep down, you're decent. You regret your mistakes, and I don't think you'll repeat your major ones again. You're like the good thief crucified next to Christ."

"But I'm not religious!"

"Not overtly, but I know you accept Christ. You follow His rules, His values. No, you're not perfect, but yes, you're good enough."

"That's not true! I don't accept God or Christ. I don't!" Ray's eyes bugged out in terror.

Arnold's voice continued, soft and soothing. "Now you're just trying to save your life. I know the truth. You'll be my twelfth. Twelve, like you're all my disciples, in a way." He cut off Ray's desperate yammering and his breath, with a long, firm squeeze. Waited. Looked at Ray's lifeless eyes and their glassy stare. Laughed.

131

And he'd thought his work was done. Maybe he'd get lucky again, and save yet another. Ray had helped to show him another road to follow.

The Life and Multiple Deaths of Virgil Eugene

Jennifer Word

The Robot *felt... wonderment.* He stared at the rainbow-haloed, luminescent bulbs above him. The colors made him *feel*; something he hadn't been able to do for quite some time. How long it had been, he couldn't be certain. He lay on the polythene-foam boxing mat, marinating in his own sweat and stink and frowned; something else he hadn't been able to do in eons.

In reality, his last facial expression depicting any type of emotion had come just ten months prior. It was the day he was brought into the Warden's office and told he would be part of a new 'experiment'. The Robot recalled that day as if he were reliving it in real time.

"You're going to be part of a cutting edge development in human mental conditioning," the Warden said.

Inmate number 186905, previously referred to as Virgil Eugene, frowned. He opened his mouth to protest, to inquire, to defend, but the door immediately opened and he was whisked away by five guards with batons. Fighting would be futile. Of course, had he fully realized what was about to happen to him – what was about to be done – he would have fought to no end: to the death.

His last memory as Virgil Eugene was of being laid on a table in a sterile white room, and a musky-smelling plastic mask was placed over his nose and mouth.

"Breathe deep, one-eight-six-nine-zero-five," the technician said in a lifeless tone.

Virgil Eugene breathed deeply. Then he closed his eyes – and died.

His next memory was hazy, as he now recalled it, lying on his back on the mat. He knew where he was, but it was like waking from a bad dream.

As his memories crashed back in on him, he merely converted from one nightmare to another.

"Do you know your name?"

Inmate number 186905 only stared at the man. Tabula Rasa; he was a blank mental slate. The man smiled. Inmate number 186905 — now bald and sporting an ugly-red, stitched incision laterally across his scalp — did not smile back. He wasn't programmed to.

"Do you know what has happened to you?"

Again, no response. The doctor nodded, looking pleased.

"Your brain has been altered; manipulated by a thin sheath of complex, spider-web thin wiring and something called a Motherboard, all outfitted with a transmitter: not unlike what you see in a standard RCA Victor. You're a prototype, number one-eight-six-nine-oh-five. Your brain is now being controlled by this device I hold in my hand."

The doctor revealed a gray box in his palm, with tiny buttons and a stick in the middle.

"Your limbic system has been 'rewired', so-to-speak. This system is part of a complex set of structures that lies on both sides of the thalamus and includes the hypothalamus, the hippocampus, and the amygdala. The hypothalamus is responsible for regulating your hunger, thirst, response to pain, levels of pleasure, sexual drive, your anger and aggression, and more. Your hippocampus is the area of your brain responsible for converting your experiences into memory. The amygdala, when stimulated electronically, further controls aggression. Tiny transponders in your brain are now in place, at receptor sites, to intercept the signals your brain receives. In this way, we can effectively cut off the sensory neurons that tell your mind you are feeling heat, cold, and even pain. Do you comprehend what I am telling you?"

The inmate only continued staring straight ahead. He had no thoughts of his own. He felt nothing.

"We've attempted this with prototypes; in machines. The problem is, it is simply far too complex to reconstruct a mechanical likeness of the human body. Robots, these are called. Or, in the event of full-bodied human likeness, the term 'android' has been applied. But my job was to take the actual human body, and simply convert the brain. Rather than build a whole robot, why not simply rebuild the human mind?"

The doctor had a mad gleam in his eyes.

"Of course, the experiments on human beings would be extensive and in most cases: deadly. There'd be an outcry, and who would volunteer for an

experimental procedure such as that? No one would. But no one cares about you, do they, one-eight-six-nine-oh-five? You're a hardened criminal. And criminals die in prison every day, don't they? Shanked by fellow inmates, or simply beaten to death in the yard. Or they hang themselves with their own bed sheets, and no one even knows."

The doctor stood. Inmate number 186905 did not follow him with his eyes.

"Many have died for me to reach this point in my research. You are the first to live. From this point forward, your name shall be 'The Robot'. It's what you are, after all. You will not feel hungry, tired, sad, or any other human emotion. You will not feel pain, or cold. You are under my control. The sections of your brain that control the production and excretion of adrenaline can also be manipulated, to temporarily increase your stamina and strength. Nod if you understand my words, Robot."

The Robot nodded. The doctor nodded back and smiled. The Robot did not smile in response.

"What you were before your conversion has been short-circuited. Your current mind has no access to previous events or memories from before today. You will not make new memories. Each day will be your first and only moment of existence."

But something had gone wrong.

For eight months, The Robot slept, ate, and worked. He made no new memories. Each day, he awoke anew and did what he was ordered to do. At first, he lifted heavy things, and his back did not ache. He built walls, structures, whole buildings. He hammered in the rain, worked in the snow, and never felt cold. He carried large boxes and handled inventory. He labored and did the work of ten men, and never became fatigued, nor did he once complain.

The Robot never spoke. He wasn't programmed to. He slept when told. He never defecated or urinated unless told to, at regular intervals. He was kept away from the other inmates, until one day, the doctor had an idea.

"I want to test control of your aggression and strength, Robot. You will box with another inmate. You will follow all the rules, but you will hit him until he goes down and does not get back up."

In the recreation room, The Robot was put into the ring with a fellow inmate. When the time came to fight, he felt a sudden surge of adrenaline-energy flood into his veins. The usual accompaniment of euphoria was absent. The Robot simply threw his punches at the other man. They hit with great force.

He was not perfect in his technique. He took many hits. His lip split open, his right eye swelled shut, and his nose was crushed. He bled profusely, but felt no pain. For every punch he took, he delivered a hit, until both men should have lain unconscious on the mat, equally destroyed, yet, The Robot stood in the end, over the unconscious body of the other fighter, feeling nothing.

His wounds were tended to and dressed. The Robot was treated, his body healed. Then he went back to working for the Warden and the doctor. They had begun a betting pool with all the correctional officers and guards on the floor of Cell B. The Robot could not be beat, and eventually, he was fighting several bouts a week, entertaining everyone, and the Warden and the doctor were making a nice supplemental income.

Ten months into The Robot's existence, he took a hit to the temple. Unbeknownst to the doctor, something shifted loose; some vital wiring, an intrinsic part of the webbing connecting his brain to the Motherboard. For the first time in the ring, The Robot went down – and stayed down – for he stared up at the lights in wonderment at their colors.

He lay in astonishment at the sudden return of his feelings. His body ached, his wounds stung madly. He frowned. Memories came crashing back of who he was; who he had been before he'd become The Robot. Every moment of his thirty-eight years upon the Earth flooded back into his awareness. Connections were made, between the past and the present, and The Robot suddenly comprehended what had happened to him.

The Robot became *Virgil Eugene* again. He was reborn, and he recalled his death, for that was what had happened to him. He had died. Losing himself in such a way, he was never so relieved to be who he was, as in that moment, despite his mistakes and even his crimes. For, he *knew* who he was. He knew that he was *alive*. He *felt*, and *thought*, and was *aware*. He began to cry. There was no control.

The doctor witnessed this. He grimaced.

"Damn."

A stretcher was brought. Guards in white coats and members of the medical staff carried inmate number 186905 off the mat. The broken man could do nothing but lay in shock, drained – traumatized by the reality of what he'd been made into, and what he'd been stripped of.

Every task, every long day of physical labor, spans of days without sleep, stretches without food, followed by surges of aggressive shock, in the ring, fighting; it all came back to Virgil with a shocking clarity.

It was all a blur that drained him of every ounce of energy his body was now manufacturing again on its own, without orders. His heart, his mind, his body cried out, and he screamed in a war cry.

"I am Virgil Eugene! I am Virgil Eugene! *I am!! **I am!!*** I am Virgil Eugene!"

He sobbed.

By the time he realized where he was and what they were about to do to him, yet again – it was too late. He fought feebly, but there were too many guards, too many medical staff members. Too much had happened to him, and there was nowhere for him to run. He could not get away. He'd already been stripped of his rights, for his crimes. He'd disappeared from the world. Already, he had ceased to exist.

They were about to murder him for the second time.

"Breathe deep, one-eight-six-nine-zero-five," the technician said in a lifeless tone.

With the mask covering his nose and mouth, his words were hazy, muffled, and lost.

"I am Virgil Eugene. I *am…*"

Virgil Eugene breathed deeply. Then he closed his eyes – and died – again.

His next awareness was in-the-moment. The Robot opened his eyes, saw the doctor, and sat up as he was ordered to. The doctor smiled.

"Do you know your name?"

The Robot only stared at the man.

"Do you know what has happened to you?"

Again, no response. The doctor nodded, looking pleased.

"Your circuits have been replaced. It's a miracle we were able to go back in and do the work without killing you. I suppose if I were a philosophical man, I'd surmise that you were *meant* for this experiment, Robot. Your new circuits are much more deeply implanted. I don't believe they'll come loose this time around. To be on the safe side, however, we'll avoid any traumas to the head for a bit, hmm?"

The Robot only continued staring straight ahead. Tabula Rasa; he had no thoughts of his own.

"We're going to move on from boxing, Robot," the doctor said. "Let's see how you do with assassination training."

The doctor smiled again. The Robot did not smile back. He did not know humor. He did not even know his God-given name, or that he'd been born twice and died as many times. He'd been stripped of that which made him a man: his identity, his personality — his soul.

In the end, The Robot felt nothing. He wasn't programmed to.

End a Days

Kristin Dearborn

He fingered the orange sleeves of his jumpsuit. Marlin Graves had suspected this day would come for quite some time. He lost his license in February. Tried to go straight after that. Tried to clean up his act.

But... sometimes he didn't make such good choices. He only drove from the bar to the house, and he wasn't speeding, he didn't hit anyone, didn't kill anyone, didn't even bang up his car. A taillight out. The officer had smiled at him when Marlin first rolled down the window, but the smile froze and fell off his face when he smelled the booze that wafted from the car.

And now, because three-strikes-and-you're-out, Marlin was here. Three months. Two days down. He had his cell mate, his jumpsuit, knew when to go to the mess hall, when the doors would unlock and he would have free time. He supposed it could be worse. It could always be worse.

Marlin's cell mate was a sixty-year-old black man, incarcerated for vehicular manslaughter. They'd joked a bit that they were two of the least dangerous guys in the jail, but often Ed liked to stare at the wall.

The first night, Marlin asked what he was doing.

"Prayin'," Ed said, irritated at being disturbed.

After that, Marlin kept quiet. He had a stack of books to work through. He never liked reading much, but found it a calming way to pass the time. There was no reason not to be Zen about his upcoming months. It wasn't as though he was leaving a job, or a wife, even a girlfriend or a cat. He had a cactus, but he didn't remember to water it very often, and suspected it would be fine until he got back. Marlin wasn't the type of guy who made much of a mark in the world.

"Storm's coming," Ed said, on the third night, his voice a deep baritone that would have been perfect for narrating nature documentaries.

"It's the season," Marlin said, unwilling to tear away from the latest Jason Bourne novel.

"No, man, storm's coming. Real bad one. Katrina-bad."

"Sure," Marlin said. Every year, a hurricane percolating off the coast was touted as 'Katrina-bad.' They never were.

"This one *real* bad. Talkin' 'bout end a days."

139

"I'd better read faster," Marlin said, and rolled over on his side, turning his back to Ed.

He heard about the storm the next day in the common area. The TV was turned to CNN, and amid the war in Afghanistan, the non-war in Iraq, and North Korea grandstanding about nukes, the commentators mused over a swirling mass off the Atlantic coast. It did look big, but out over warm water, they always did. Land and cool water always calmed them down. Here in Maryland, they would be fine. Some streams and creeks might swell up over their banks, but that was to be expected. Some wind, some rain, the power would go out, but nothing more.

So, what happened when the power went out in prison? What then? Did the doors pop open? Did people try and escape? Marlin pushed the thoughts from his mind.

***

The hurricane's name was Margaret, and it was indeed a doozy. A category four, it lashed and swirled over the mid-Atlantic. Meteorologists predicted it would head south to gain strength over the Caribbean, then head north up the Atlantic coast.

To Marlin, it sounded like any other late summer storm.

The day it made landfall in Florida—day five of incarceration—Marlin had other things on his mind besides a storm. Lunch sucked, and he managed to piss off a big, white trash, con-artist called Trunk. They were only in the jail, away from the real violent offenders, but some of these guys were bad motherfuckers, and Marlin didn't want to deal with them. Trunk was giving him shit, and Marlin couldn't take it anymore and made some wisecrack about the guy's mother. Not a good idea.

"You're dead, Graves," the con-artist said.

"Good to know, Tree," Marlin shot back before he knew what was coming out of his mouth.

***

The sixth day, Beth came to visit him. He told her not to a thousand times, but she wouldn't hear it. He didn't want her to see him like this, but when she arrived, he had to admit, it was good to see her face. They got to meet in a heavily supervised room with plastic furniture and a bunch of other guys. She brought him a Big Mac meal, said for some reason they hadn't let her bring in the Coke. He made a joke about cocaine, but it fell flat.

They sat in silence for a bit while she watched him eat.

"Thanks for coming," he said. They weren't the kind of friends where she would reach out and touch his hand.

"I told you I would. Once a week. Only eleven more visits. Though, I don't know about next week. The storm's supposed to be bad."

"Yeah?" The TV had been on the Learning Channel yesterday when Marlin was out in the common room. A very large, very gay con, who went by the name Horse was watching Trading Spaces reruns, and would not be moved. Horse was fabulous, but also lethal.

"Mmm, supposed to hit Sunday afternoon."

Marlin had to rack his brain to figure what day it was. Less than a week and he'd already lost track of everything except the number of days he'd been there.

"Two days," she said, seeing him struggle.

He managed a weak smile. "Thanks."

"I've got to stop at Home Depot on the way home, I want to board up the windows."

"You think it's gonna be that bad?"

"I'd rather be safe than sorry. I don't want anything to happen to the house. The kids are with me this weekend. I'm going to get them after I go to Home Depot."

"Ah." There wasn't much else to say.

"They keep asking about you."

Marlin wasn't upset about being there, but in the face of Beth's kids? That was when he felt like shit. He wasn't good enough for her. Wasn't good enough for anyone, really.

"Zack knows, but Amy doesn't." Zack was fourteen, Amy was nine.

The guard told them they had five minutes.

"Give them my best," he said. "Or whatever you feel like you should do."

"I will. Take care of yourself, Marlin. Hell, I may bring them here for the storm. You're going to be safer than anybody."

They had a quick, awkward hug—their relationship had never been a very touchy-feely one—and then she was gone. He could smell her on the orange coveralls and he cherished it.

"That your girlfriend?" asked a scrawny Hispanic named Parvey.

"No," Marlin said.

Parvey looked skeptical.

"Just a close friend."

Parvey still looked skeptical.

"We went to high school together. Just friends. Honest."

Parvey nodded, and wandered away. Marlin never wanted the taste of Big Mac or the smell of Beth's perfume to leave him, but knew both would, sooner rather than later. Ed was a nice enough guy, but he smelled vaguely of old man.

He wasn't in the cell when Marlin got back, probably at the infirmary getting his insulin shots. Marlin wanted to take a rest, but knew downtime was dangerous in his head. He found a poker game with four other guys and didn't win, but it was something to take his mind off everything.

After dinner, Warden MacLeod made his way to the front of the cafeteria, a big white man who'd been formidable once but had gone soft about the belly. He adjusted the brim of his hat and nestled his thumbs in his belt loops.

"Y'all know there's a storm headed our way." The crowd mumbled in agreement. They did all know. Although no one was heckling or cat-calling, Marlin wished MacLeod would get to the point. "I've made the decision that we're gonna wait it out here. We got food enough for a month, we're on high ground, we're in better shape than them that's outside. The guards and staff're gonna ride it out with you. Storm should hit later tonight. 'Bout eleven thirty." He scanned them, looking satisfied with himself. "Anyone got questions?"

There was a beat of silence. A black hand went up, tentative.

The warden pointed.

"Can I call my mother?" he asked, more articulate than the warden.

"She on yo' approved call list?"

"No, sir," the man said. "Could we maybe make an exception?"

"No 'ceptions. You men can make calls at the normal time only to them that's on your call lists. Any other questions?"

"We're gonna get fed, right?"

"What if the power goes out?"

"What if the AC goes?"

"What if the cable goes?"

No more useful information was distributed, and the warden sauntered off, looking pleased with himself.

Marlin made his way back to his cell, couldn't help overhearing two of the guards.

"I don't like it. I want to be home with my babies." LuAnne was a rat-faced bitch whose husband beat her. She liked to take it out on the prisoners.

"Jonas'll be home with them, won't he?" The other guard was Slim, a heavy guy in his forties who was actually a really nice man. One of the few who didn't feel the need to lord his position over the inmates.

LuAnne cast Slim a withering look, then turned her face on Marlin. "You got somewhere to be, Graves?"

Marlin tucked his chin down and made his way to the common area.

The agitation in the air was palpable. Marlin didn't like the energy one bit and headed back to his cell. Ed was out somewhere, probably in the common room. From down the hall, Marlin could still hear the shouting and stomping. They were going to get put on lockdown any minute.

Slim headed past, making a check. "You all right, Graves?" he asked.

"Sure. Little worried about my family." By family, he meant Beth and the kids. Beth rented a decent enough house on the outskirts of town. He didn't remember any streams or rivers nearby that could flood her out or give her trouble. She had a portable generator; she had water and food in the basement. She'd been around this block a few times, she wasn't stupid.

"Me, too," Slim said. "I sent my wife and daughters to her sister's place in Asheville."

"Not a bad move," Marlin said.

"They got there last night. Our house is going to be a total loss if this thing's as bad as they say. We're pretty close to the water."

"Sorry, man."

"It's insured, at least. We'll deal with it."

The yelling from the common room intensified and a siren blasted, lockdown indeed.

"Stay safe," Slim shot over his shoulder, before hurrying away towards the common room.

You, too, Marlin should have said, but it didn't come to him until Slim was too far away. He went back to his bunk and laced his fingers behind his head, staring up at the ceiling. Ed shuffled in and plopped down on his bed. The door slid shut with a resounding clang that Marlin would never get used to.

In their cells, the prisoners shouted and slammed things, beating themselves against the doors. Marlin stared at his novel, concentration impossible.

Then, around eleven, just like MacLeod had said, winds and rain buffeted the jail. The prisoners went quiet. The cells had small, thick windows, nearly impossible to see out. Ed and Marlin crowded next to each other, peering into the darkness, feeling the building shake in the wind. Ed's lips moved, in silent prayer, over and over. He put his hands against the concrete wall, fingers splayed. He had big hands.

Outside, Marlin could see tree branches jerking back and forth in the wind in front of an orange glowing street light. Then, the rain came and the night went black. There was nothing to do after a while but go to sleep, an uncomfortable doze from which he awoke often. In his dreams, there were things in the rain, in the wind and darkness, and Beth wasn't safe.

The power went out, and the cell doors all made a suspicious click a half-second before the emergency generators kicked on. For a second, the halls were dark and bathed in red light before the overhead fluorescents returned. Prisons were never truly dark, and Marlin relished the moment of dimness.

They stayed in lockdown, CO's patrolling the hallway, checking on them, blasting disruptive inmates with pepper spray. A skinny tax evader screamed about his lawyer too much and the CO's opened the door and sent LuAnne in with her baton. Not a sound came from the cell for the rest of the night.

As it always does, the rain stopped. Then, the wind stopped. The sun rose, like it did every morning. From Ed and Marlin's window, the view was of a parking lot. A tree had been uprooted in the night (*that's what that crash was*) and flattened a Corolla. Branches were down all over, but Marlin had seen worse storms.

With a scraping clang, breakfast was slid through a slot in the bars. "Come on," Marlin said. "It's over. Let us out."

"Fuck you," LuAnne spat. Dark circles sagged under her eyes. Her night was shittier than his, most likely. "Fucking Margrove Penitentiary is flooded. They're sending those shits over here to spend time with you. Get ready for a new roommate or two."

Then, she was gone.

"Whoa, whoa—" Marlin called after her. He hung on the bars, watching her go. Margrove? A ball of dread formed low in his stomach, churning and thrashing there. He stared down at his oatmeal, fried egg and toast. He'd better eat. It would take a while for things to get back to normal, if the boys from Margrove were joining them. Here he was with other drunk drivers, tax evaders, folks waiting to be sentenced. This was a jail. They didn't have to deal with murderers, rapists and the like. The food stuck in his throat, but he ate it anyway. He and Ed stacked their trays and slid them back out into the hall. Ed got his shot early; Slim flat out told him they didn't know when he'd get the next one.

The other inmates came at ten. There were twenty cells on the first floor, and each cell got one or two additional men. Why they couldn't group the jail boys together and the Margrove boys together, but separate, Marlin didn't know. Probably because they'd have to get too many prisoners out of their cells. This way, it was a simple matter of popping the door and depositing the new guys inside. Like animals at the zoo.

LuAnne appeared at their door, looking even more tired than before, with a Margrove guard and two mean-looking men. The door opened and the men shuffled inside, their ankles in chains. All the jumpsuits in the county were the same orange material, with the institution name stenciled on the back. LuAnne slammed the door shut, and the CO's unchained the men and moved on. Marlin wondered if this was a good move.

"Fucking hell out there." The smaller man's hair was in dire need of a new bleach job. "Water everywhere."

"It was a rainy summer," Ed said, sitting on his bunk, his long arms and legs drawn around him.

"Really hell. Like, really," the man reiterated.

"How'd you come?" Marlin asked.

"Crosstown expressway. Parts are underwater. They say it's gonna get worse before it gets better."

"Drove through standing water to get here," second guy said. "Felt the van start to move. Driver and guards were scared shitless."

There wasn't much to say after that. Though Marlin was curious, he didn't ask what they were in for. The second guy had tears tattooed down his cheeks, and the artwork on his neck gave the illusion you could see his jugular and tendons and muscles. It was a nice piece of work. But Marlin wasn't there to see about tattoos. When Slim walked by (he and LuAnne seemed to still be on duty) Marlin asked about making a phone call, noon was his time to call.

"Phones are down all over the city. Even if they were up, I can't let anyone out. You know that." Slim seemed exhausted, and Marlin felt bad for asking. Still… he wanted to know how Beth was. A few cells down, another prisoner started wailing about wanting to get out. That it was a death trap here.

Marlin heard the pop of the lock on the cell door, and heard muffled thuds. LuAnne having her way on him with the baton, most like. Then, he heard a girlish squeak from her—not the kind of sound he'd ever heard her make before. Sounds of a scuffle as the rest of the cell block went silent. Ripping fabric. She shouldn't have gone in there. Not when there were three or four men, some of them from Margrove.

A heartbeat later, Marlin forgot all about LuAnne, as a truck hit the side of the prison. No, not a truck. What was it? The whole building shuddered, kept shuddering, then again. And again. Earthquake?

Then, the sounds in the cell down the hall resumed. Someone was getting hit with the baton. Over and over. The two Margrove guys pressed against the door, peering out. Marlin wasn't going to get near that. He hoped it was the sound of LuAnne, reclaiming her baton. He listened for the sound of the cell door closing again… but it never came.

Ed stood at the small window.

"The dam," he said.

It didn't even compute.

"The dam," he said again, pointing. "Look."

He moved to the side to let Marlin see out. Brown water swirled through the parking lot. The Corolla and the tree that crushed it were both gone, carried away by the brackish, swirling tide. A truck drifted past, down at the bottom of a little hill, turning end over end.

More, different, panicked yelling started in the far end of the jail.

"Water!" "— fucking gonna drown!" "What the —" Loud cries of confusion and panic. The Margrove guys backed away from the door.

"Fucking hell," Tattoo said.

Blondie's breathing grew shallow and the color drained from his face.

Marlin looked down to see brown water swirling at their feet. Just enough to wet the floor. The lake was huge. As Blondie succumbed to a panic attack, Marlin tried to map the town in his mind. Where would the water go? What would happen when it met the swollen river? He thought about Beth's house and felt his own breathing quicken. She wasn't far from the lake. Her house would have (*been completely destroyed*) taken some damage. Where would she go? Where would the kids go?

"It's getting deeper!" keened Blondie.

"Shut the fuck up, you mother-raper," said Tattoo.

Marlin didn't want to know.

Outside their cell, a dark face appeared, sporting an orange jumpsuit. Marlin's stomach turned even harder. If he was out, then LuAnne… she was a bitch, sure, but didn't deserve… whatever they'd done to her. Where was Slim? Who else was on duty? No one. Only Slim and LuAnne, after two of the other guys left to check on their families. When Slim came back to the block, it was gonna be an ambush.

The con outside called in to Marlin's new cellmates "I'll get you out, bros. Don' you worry."

Having broken out of the cell, the inmates were essentially trapped on this cell block. They had to wait until Slim came in to make their move.

Or perhaps they could work sooner than that… the lights flickered and died, came back to life. The block went silent. Chatter, then yelling, banging, resumed, but stopped when the lights went dark a second time. The red emergency lights kicked on, and everyone was silent, letting their eyes get used to the dark.

Blondie was the first to break the quiet. "It's getting deeper!"

Marlin looked down off his bunk and saw water still swirled into the cell. How much water was in the lake? In the river? How much water did that dam regulate?

Would they drown in here?

He'd kill for a phone. Or a radio. Or anything. Any contact with outside.

"You know what that fucker said?" One of the Margrove guys said, his voice carrying above the din. "Said we're all criminals. We made our choice; we deserve to be locked up in this shit, no matter what happens. Deserve to die in here."

"I didn't do it," called someone else.

The voices, the shouting, the clanking of bars made a rhythm, a music. Marlin closed his eyes. He sat on his bunk, knees drawn to his chest. The Margrove guys huddled around the door, Ed clung to the window. There was nothing for Marlin but shutting his eyes.

***

He opened them when something wet touched his ass. He hadn't been in jail long, but he slept very light, and jerked up to his feet on the bunk. Disoriented and sweating, Marlin looked around.

His mattress was soaked. The Margrove men stood in knee-deep water.

Outside, the sun shone, and made one little bright spot in the room on Ed's bed. When the power quit, so did the AC. Marlin didn't like how pale Ed's face looked.

"You all right?"

"Son? None of us is all right. I wish you and I'd met in a different way."

"They'll come for us. They know we're here," Marlin said, not meaning it. Not really.

Ed smiled at him, revealing even, white teeth. "That wasn't no normal storm."

"Course it was," Marlin said.

"Shut up!" Blondie shrieked at him. "You just shut up!"

"This is the end a days," Ed said.

"Ed, they don't want to hear this." Marlin didn't like the look on Blondie's face. Too crazy. Too wild. Marlin scanned the room for potential weapons. He didn't see anything, but a man can use a pillow to kill with, if he's desperate enough. Or his fists. Not that Marlin would even know how to defend himself. Would die screaming, with less fight than LuAnne'd had. Marlin crouched on the balls of his feet on his sodden mattress.

Where was Slim? Probably, he'd seen that there were convicts out, and was staying someplace safe.

From outside the cell came rhythmic clanging, men trying to break free. All at once, the block went silent.

"Help!" someone screamed.

Marlin didn't like it… That moment of silence. "This man needs help!" someone cried, letting his voice go high with panic. "He's having a fucking heart attack!"

Don't, Slim, thought Marlin. *Don't fall for it.* He couldn't shout, though. They'd kill him. He could only silently hope Slim knew what was up, and wasn't going to come onto the block. The silence should be a dead giveaway. The anticipation hung palpable in the sweltering air. All these bodies, so close, and the rising water, made the jail stink like a shithouse. Marlin rubbed his palms together, slick with sweat. He was watching for Slim, but thinking of Beth. Hoping she was safe.

"He's having a goddamn heart attack!" the inmate called again, his voice cracking.

Marlin stole a glance at Ed. He watched the Margrove men.

The trance broke when something big (a tree, maybe a car) slammed into the building, shaking it to the foundation.

Inmates screamed and yelled, the slamming intensified.

Then… a clang. And cheering.

"Kick it up and off the track!" spread down the line like wildfire. The Margrove guys got on their backs in the rising water. Marlin watched it splash in their mouths and eyes… he'd be in it soon enough. With Christ knew what else. They kicked and kicked; their legs like pistons. Margrove gave the same shoes as the county jail, canvas sneakers with slight rubber soles. Marlin couldn't imagine how it hurt. Blondie gave a squealing cry every time he kicked, but Tattoo kept quiet. They kicked up at the cross piece, and examining the door from his bunk, Marlin could see how this would work.

Blondie gave a particularly stalwart kick, then started screaming, clutching his left foot. Four Margrove guys came to hover around their cell door. Marlin tried to make himself invisible. Ed had gone back to staring out the window.

"I broke my fucking foot!" It was impressive that Blondie could find the words to speak amid all his squealing. The guys outside looked in. Looked at Ed, who was paler than before, his dark skin gone ashen. He hadn't eaten since breakfast. A couple other guys needed meds, too. Someone knew, someone would come. But it wouldn't be safe for them.

Then, the guys in the hall turned their gaze on Marlin. "You."

Marlin wasn't a big guy. He was scrawny and not terribly tall, not terribly attractive. It made sense he was the guy who gradually developed a drinking problem without even noticing it, and it got so bad, he wound up in jail for a DUI. In that moment, he finally realized how pathetic he'd become, how amazing it was that Beth still talked to him or let him near her kids.

"You," the big guy in the hall, said again.

"Yeah?" Marlin said, voice cracking.

"Come help get this door open." He didn't bark the order. Just said it, like it was a normal, casual request. A "hey, hold this door for me because my hands are full" kind of thing.

"I'm, uh, not very good at… things," Marlin said, not moving from where he crouched.

"Get the fuck over here," the big guy said. "Stop being a pussy. Get us this door open."

Blondie draped himself over Marlin's soaked mattress. The water lapped at the upper edge now.

"Before the fucking water gets higher! Now, son-of-a-bitch!"

Marlin stood and looked to Ed. Ed stared out the window, ignoring what went on in front of him. Marlin stepped off the bed and into the water. It was warmer than he expected, and that repulsed him. A few degrees cooler than body temperature. It was brown and things floated in it. Leaves, twigs, a water beetle paddled past. He slogged over to the door, careful not to splash anybody.

The big guy's tone relaxed as Marlin stood before him. "I ain't gonna bite'cha. Lay back, and bothayous kick right here." He pointed at a cross brace on the door. "Should lift it up off its tracks."

The other Margrove guy dropped into the water. Marlin did the same, feeling his back get soaked, keeping his face up and out of the water.

"What's your name, brother?" the big guy asked.

He told them.

"I'm Davis, this is Afwon, and that," he pointed at Blondie, "piece of shit mother-raper is Keegan." Marlin smiled at them. He wondered if Keegan had raped his own mother, or someone else's. He didn't want to know. He wanted to be dry, and cool, and have something to drink. A tall glass of water. He could see it, condensation beading on the side. Could taste it.

"On three, all right?" Davis counted and they kicked. Counted and kicked, over and over, as the water grew higher around them and Marlin's feet began to ache and the water splashed in his mouth and eyes. One kick angled just right would do it, they were close, Marlin knew it. He began to feel invested in the project, even though the balls of his feet screamed. He hollered as he kicked, he *needed* the door to open. It shuddered on its frame, then crashed out into the hall. Without thinking, he found himself in Davis's arms, a celebratory embrace. He'd done it!

Then, Marlin looked around. About half of the doors were off, and guys were standing around in the hallway.

***

Time passed. The water rose, and with it, the stench of sewage and the temperature. Guys could sit on their bunks, still, but it meant they were more underwater than not. Most preferred to stand.

"End a days," Ed said, again. A handful of inmates, from the jail and Margrove, gathered around Ed and listened as he prayed. He spoke of the end times, and Noah, and how this cement building was no arc, they were all men with no hope of procreating to save the human race.

They're fine out there, Marlin told himself over and over. *We're the ones in trouble.*

And still, the water rose.

Ed stopped preaching about the time Marlin felt something thick and curious brush his leg underwater. He closed his eyes until it moved on. There was nowhere he could go, nothing he could do. Ed's eyes rolled back in his head and he slumped over, disappearing underneath the brackish water. Inmates dove in after him, and for a moment, three men were gone, the stinking, rippling water the only indication they'd ever been there. First, one came up, then, the next, hauling Ed. Sludge poured from his gaping mouth. It made Marlin's stomach turn. He remembered his breakfast of eggs and oatmeal, toast with butter and apple jelly. Tears came to his eyes. It had only been… a day? Two? How many times had the sun risen and set?

They let Ed go about ten minutes later. He was breathing, but they were shallow breaths, and his heartbeat was so slow. They said they couldn't keep holding him up. And he didn't float. Everyone moved out of the cell.

No one had the voice to cry out any more. The sobbing and the gentle rhythm of the rising water were the only sounds. Marlin's eyelids grew heavy. Sleep wasn't an option, the moment he dozed off, he'd fall into the water and wake up with a nasty lungful of… that.

***

"You alive in there?"

Marlin's eyes popped open. Who said that? Saliva pooled in his mouth. Must have been dreaming of food.

Struggling to remember where he was, Marlin nodded.

The water wasn't rising any more, it stopped at just about nipple height on his chest, and he stood at five foot eight. He wondered who was talking. He wondered if Beth had eaten her children.

He shook his head. Snap out of it. *No one is eating anyone.* Only... three days?

Water lapped at the concrete walls. Sounds and splashes echoed in the dark hallways.

End a days, Ed had said.

Maybe for the men in the jail. Outside, life still went on. But... he hadn't seen anyone out the window, not a soul since this all started. And it made sense, he guessed, why would anyone come up there to the prison?

Well, his mind argued. *It is high ground. Shit.* This was high ground? After Katrina, there'd been boats up and down the streets. Where were they, now? *Who wants to come to a filthy old jail anyway*, he asked himself? They hadn't been forgotten, just put aside. No one realized how bad things were in here. If they realized, someone would come. Where was Slim? The two other Margrove guards?

Honestly... where was anyone?

Marlin thought about what Ed said. If they were the only humans alive... even if they got out of this trap, that would be the end. A bunch of the shittiest guys in Maryland talking about what it was like before the floods, back when there were women and children and honest-to-goodness dry land.

A day passed. Two days? Or maybe an afternoon. Marlin was bone-tired.

Keegan died, and the whole cell block was a much quieter place without his howling and caterwauling. He'd shown them his foot, struggling to lift it up high out of the water. The sewage got in where he'd broke the skin kicking. It was twice the size of a normal foot, the skin stretched tight and shiny, bruised black and green and purple.

Another voice murmured assent.

Marlin waded to one of the windows in an open cell. Not all the doors had come off before the water got too high, and those men prowled like caged animals. He looked out at the parking lot. He couldn't tell if it was morning or afternoon. The shadows stretched long over the rippling water. Nothing moved but the undulations of the ugly brown liquid. Where were the birds? The animals? Anything. The windows were too thick to hear through, but Marlin imagined the world was silent, only the wind and the lapping of waves.

He dozed, leaning into the corner, forehead pressed into the green painted concrete. Green was supposed to be soothing. He heard the splashing near him, but didn't open his eyes. He didn't care who was near him.

"Well don' choo look good enough to eat."

Marlin opened his eyes. The man leered at him with several missing teeth. Trunk. Marlin hadn't seen him since all this began, had almost forgotten about him. His Caucasian skin looked almost like a black man's from all the river grime. The great racial equalizer. Marlin almost laughed.

Trunk held out a sharpened toothbrush, waggled it at him. His hand was shaking so bad, he almost dropped the thing. "Fuck you, pretty boy."

No way. Marlin was beginning to give up hope that he would make it out of there alive, that he would ever see Beth again, but it wasn't going to be at the hands of fucking Trunk. He slapped out at the man's hand. He'd forgotten how good it felt to move. The toothbrush dropped and floated in the brackish water. They both grabbed for it, but Marlin moved faster.

The man's jaw quivered as his easy target began fighting back. *Shouldn't have said anything*, Marlin admonished in his mind. *Shoulda just stabbed me while I was asleep and been done with it.*

Trunk reached for Marlin, swinging a paw at him, and Marlin countered with the toothbrush, opening the man's palm. It was nigh impossible for him to keep his wound out of the water. His hand would look like Keegan's foot soon enough.

So… it would be better to kill him, now. The idea of killing another human had never crossed Marlin's mind. Not even here, not even during the end a days.

Two figures appeared in the cell door, watching.

"We won't let him get away."

Marlin found himself nodding thanks to them. Sick camaraderie. These men would approve.

It wasn't hard. He lashed out once—and hit Trunk's other hand.

Where blood dripped onto the brown water, all Marlin could think of was a chocolate dessert with a raspberry swirl.

He lashed out again, and caught Trunk's stubbly cheek. More blood. Like ketchup. A French fry to dip in that would be divine. Marlin laughed. The men in the doorway laughed with him.

"—helped us get the door open. Quiet guy, little weird, but a good shit."

On this next slash, Marlin's sharpened toothbrush caught Trunk in the throat, opening up the artery there. Like a jackpot at the casino, blood poured and poured from his neck. He slumped in the water but Davis was there to catch him.

This. Trunk's corpse. This was Marlin's mark in the world. Finally, he was something.

"Good work," Davis said. He held out a hand, and Marlin handed over the bloody toothbrush. His knuckles ached from gripping it so hard, and the bristles had imprinted a funny pattern into his palm.

Davis let the body go; it slid under the water. Just a red swirl to show where Trunk had been, then, not even that. The cell block, for a moment, was quiet.

Marlin went back to his corner, and this time, everyone left him alone.

When he heard the metallic clanging of the door opening, he was too preoccupied with the cramps in his stomach. Maybe someone kicked another door down.

Yelling came from the cell block, and Marlin waded out to see what was what. Men in hazmat suits! They had flashlights and guns and they shot Davis when he charged with the toothbrush. So, there *were* people out there!

Maybe Beth was out there!

He wondered what she would say if she knew what he had done. Would she let him see her? Her kids? Would she let him into her nice, neat home, that always smelled like cinnamon and pie crust? It didn't matter, did it, Marlin realized, a sliver of hunger gleaming inside him. She was his. She'd always played coy. Never wanted to be his, always holding him at arm's length. But this time? She'd be his. He'd see to that. He'd find her.

A flashlight shone into his eyes, and he raised a hand to block it.

"Name?"

"Graves," he said, remembering his name. "Marlin Graves."

Steel handcuffs clasped his filthy wrists, and with the other men, he was led towards the door.

Misconceptions

Bryan Grafton

The father sat across the table from his son in the dull, gray-walled prison visiting room. The father was the visitor. The son was the inmate. The ritual of 'how ya doing' had been gotten out of the way and next, the father began the narration of all the news from home. As usual, the son asked about his aunts and uncles, his cousins, how they all were doing, was Uncle Jerry still going to buy a truck, was Aunt Susie just as feisty as ever, what's the news from the neighbors, their kids, etc. etc. The father responded to all the inquiries as politely and thoroughly as he could, the reports hardly differing much from last month's information. He did so every visit, but just like all the other times, his mind wandered aimlessly elsewhere as he answered.

His thoughts were elsewhere, but still thinking about his son, always worrying about him; thinking about where they – he and his wife, that was – had gone wrong in raising him. If they had only done *this* or *that*, then their boy would have turned the corner, gotten over the hump. He would have been all right, then. He would have been normal, wouldn't be what he was today: a felon locked away in a state penitentiary. Locked away for the safety of others, and ironically, also for his own.

***

Oh, they were so happy back when they'd first got him. Thankful that the unwed mother had agreed to put him up for adoption. So many unwed mothers kept their babies. They wore the child like a medal of honor, proudly bearing the title of 'single mom'. Others kept the child as if it were a puppy – a pet – a thing to be coddled and cuddled and played with. And others still, because it was the cool thing to do, all the kids were doing it. So happy that they had gotten him, but so soon, disappointed and sad.

***

The son looked at his father, and knew what he was thinking. Zooming in on the topic that always came up during these visits, he volunteered, "It's not your fault, Dad, that I'm here. *I'm* the one responsible, not *you*. I *always* screw up – remember? You *told* me I almost got kicked out of

154

preschool daycare because I couldn't follow the rules. I screwed up right from the start."

"Follow instructions. Stay on task. You're still having trouble with that, aren't you?" replied his father, knowing the answer. This was the first thing they taught at preschool and hammered home again in Kindergarten. His son couldn't even do that, never could. Something in his brain wouldn't let him. He was so oppositional. He did what he wanted, never thinking or caring about any consequences.

They sat there in silence. Like the bench and table bolted to the floor, they sat there, each bolted into the seats in their own way, neither knowing what to say next, the bare walls staring back at them, the silence speaking louder than words.

"I don't know why I couldn't behave in grade school. I tried."

"Well, your teachers didn't know why, either."

His first grade teacher had told his parents, "Give him an inch and he takes a mile." He never got along with kids in his class, always arguing with them, continuously verbally harassing. No fisticuffs, but he was so disruptive that he made things miserable for the other students and teachers alike. The principal had told his parents that whenever there was trouble, nine out of ten times, their son was at the center of it.

***

"Yes, that's why we ended up sending you to that private Church school," spoke up the father, repeating this for the umpteenth time, and for lack of knowing what to say next. The parents were lapsed Christians and would have sent him to any private school for the smaller classes and stricter discipline, and this one was conveniently located just down the road. They didn't care about the religious overtones, but thank God for those teachers. Their Christian benevolence enabled them to go out of their way in order to help and work with him. Without them, he would have never gotten through eighth grade. But the school folded the next year and it was back to public academia for high school, as there was no other such private school in the area. Ironically, they had bought their house in that school district just so their son could go there because of its excellent reputation.

***

"It's not your fault, Dad. You and Mom tried. I'm the one that never tried." He had repeated this like a broken record a hundred times. Nothing changed.

His father's mind continued to wander. It wasn't that their son was dumb. He tested out average, the high school guidance counselor had told them. But for some reason, when he got to high school, he just sat there. He never did his homework, or studied for a test. He never passed a course; never seemed to care. He did have an attitude, though. And for some reason – known only to him – he thought he had been promoted from freshman class to sophomore, even though he never passed a single course his first year. His parents could not fathom such convoluted thinking. His teachers had never seen anything like it before.

They asked the school officials if their son could be placed in special ed. "Oh no," they said, "because he tests out average."

What about alternative school, they then asked? "Oh no, he's not a violent discipline problem. He doesn't physically fight with other kids. Yes, he often gets detentions for minor infractions, but that does not merit him being sent to an alternative school."

In the end, there really was no place designed for one like him, and so, he fell through the cracks.

***

"Well, are you obeying the rules, here? You been in any trouble again, lately?"

"It's no big deal. I can handle it."

That's what the psychiatrist had said, he could handle it. They voluntarily committed their son for one week into a mental facility for juveniles after he got in some trouble threatening another kid. The other parents didn't press charges. Perhaps if they had, he would have been permanently placed in a juvenile facility, and maybe *that* would have helped him. Then again, maybe not.

Placing him under psychiatric care for one week was just one of many attempts they had made while trying to fathom the workings of their son's mind. He came away from it like a hardened criminal with a tough guy attitude; no big deal to him. The psychiatrist there said, "As for authority, he can take it or leave it, it's all the same to him. No right or wrong, and if there's consequences, he can deal with them."

That was the first time that he 'did time' in a sense. Now, once again, here in prison, he was the same. Nothing had changed. His brain was still stuck in its own place, as it always had been, the only difference was that, now, his body was physically an adult.

***

156

"You weren't mixing it up again, were you – bugging people? Getting in their face about something, were you?"

"I said that I can handle it, Dad."

"Uncle Jerry bought that big honking car that you told him about," said the father, hoping to change the subject.

"Tell him to save it for me when I get out. Tell him I'll customize it."

"When you get out, that car will be junk. It'll be worn out, rusted up. There'll be no point in sinking any money into it."

It will be worn out, just like you, thought the father, *and there's no point sinking any more money into you, either.*

His mind then jumped randomly again, now trying to recall the few pleasant times they'd had with their son. He had brought them so much joy at first, so much happiness and excitement, so much to look forward to. That all evaporated, however, as soon as he could talk and walk. He came up blank.

But, on the other hand, he had brought so much joy and happiness to his two grandmothers. The grandfathers had both died long before they got him, but whose two names, he nonetheless bore. Thank god neither lived to see how their namesake turned out.

For the one grandma, he was the only grandchild, and she doted on him to the extreme, and of course, he took advantage of it when he went to spend a month in the summer with her each year, in another state.

The father could never forget the incident concerning his son and soda pop with that grandmother. "My folks let me drink pop all the time," he told her. So she let him drink all the pop that he wanted, all day long. She was shocked when he and his wife later told her that they did not keep pop in the house. This was probably not the only fast one that he had pulled on this grandmother, but the parents didn't want to know what else he had told her, and therefore, didn't ask. Grandma would have been too embarrassed to admit to anything, anyway.

As to the other grandma, this boy, she knew, was to be her last grandchild, her other ones being teenagers and so, likewise, she also spoiled him.

When he was little, the time spent with the grandmothers was such a joy to the two of them, and such a relief to the parents, as they got a much needed break from the daily drama. He was always good for the grandmas. Thank God that they, too, would die before they saw how he turned out. They would have been beside themselves – hysterical, nervous wrecks – wringing their hands in continual turmoil and grief if they had seen how he turned out.

***

"He'll save it for me. I know he will, if I ask him. I'll buy it from him when I get out and get my job back," spoke up the son, zapping his father back to the present.

It was always cars with him. His son had been car crazy, cars, cars, cars. They thought that because of this, perhaps, once he entered high school, he would keep his grades up so he could take driver's Ed and get his license, buy a car – but no. He never tried at school. Instead of keeping up his grades and getting his license at sixteen, he just waited the two years until he was eighteen, studied the test booklet, took and passed on the first try. That was the second time that he did time, in a sense, waiting the two years to get his license.

***

"You don't have a license, remember? And the chances of you getting one again are slim to none."

Silence. His son looked up at the ceiling, avoiding eye contact with his father.

He had gotten his license and lost it within a year. Got traffic tickets. Blew them off. Never showed for court. Warrant issued for his arrest. Got picked up when he committed his next violation. Ordered to make monthly payments on his fines. Didn't do so. Got thirty days, did only half for good behavior. He was somewhat proud of himself for reducing his sentence from thirty to fifteen days. In a perverse way, this was an accomplishment, an achievement for him. He was good at negative achievements. In the meantime, his license was revoked, of course.

***

"I've completed the alcohol and drug program here. I'll get my license back."

No, thought his father. *You'll go right back to your old ways. You'll be older but not wiser. Live and don't learn, that's your motto.*

After the first DUI, he had warned his son to stop drinking and driving before he killed himself or someone else. But that was all to no avail.

"I won't drink anymore. I've learned my lesson."

But it wasn't drinking that had sent him to prison in the first place. It was theft. Stealing stuff, junk basically – but of enough value to make it a felony – out of a barn with a camera recording it all. He was between jobs then and this was easy money that he couldn't pass up.

Oh, he'd had jobs before; when they pulled him out of high school. They saw no sense in leaving him there four years, never passing anything, getting detentions, causing problems for the teachers, having them waste their time. He never would have graduated in four years. He had dug himself into a hole too deep to get out. It was better that he worked, they figured, then waste time in school, plus he actually liked to work. He didn't want to hang out all day and do nothing. He wasn't programmed that way, thank goodness. That was his one redeeming characteristic. So, an aunt got him a job washing dishes where she worked, and Uncle Jerry had him help out on the farm on weekends.

He was a good worker, everyone said. It was just that he couldn't get along with his fellow employees, and because of that, he eventually lost his jobs. Yet somehow, eventually, he always got another one.

***

"And I won't steal anymore, either." The conversation was going nowhere, like it always did.

He'd stolen before he was caught on camera and had sold those stolen items, his father had gathered, from prior conversations with his son. But since this was unbeknownst to the court – he had never been arrested – he got probation on the theft charge because he was a first-time offender. Got a chance to redeem himself. If he stayed out of trouble for a year, the felony would be dismissed. No conviction, his record would be clean. One more, last chance for him to be good, to his way of thinking in his childish mind.

But he blew that. His father knew he would. He couldn't control his drinking. Got drunk while on probation. This, his first DUI, plus charges of driving without a license, no insurance and speeding. The probation officer couldn't ignore all that. This was a blatant violation of his probation. So she sent him to a halfway house, where he went to his job during the day and was locked up nights and weekends.

One more last, *last* chance to behave. If he managed there, he could earn weekends away, provided he had a place and someone to go to that was approved by his probation officer. This, he could do, and did. Like always, if he wanted something, he could buckle down and do it. Even earned his GED as it was strongly suggested that he do so if he wanted out of the halfway house sooner. Never bothered to get it for his mom and dad, even though they constantly kept prodding him to do so.

Got out, but not for long. Got in an accident and a second DUI. His system genetically could not tolerate alcohol and he couldn't control himself. Probation revoked. Got new felony charges.

***

"Dad, I'll still be a young man when I get out. I won't be forty."

"Time's up," came the announcement over the P.A. system. "All visiting parties must leave now."

The father arose, walked over to his son, bent down and hugged his grown child sitting in his chair, tears in his eyes, wondering if this would be the last time he would do so. His wife had come each time, too, until she got sick and died last year. Their son was not allowed to attend her funeral.

His wife had been adopted, too; like mother, like son. Both he and his wife had thought this would be an advantage, raising an adopted child, but as their son self-destructed, they both realized it made no difference. Nothing they did – all the psychiatrists, school counselors, social workers, medications – made a difference. They debated whether nature or nurture ruled here and both parents came to the agonizing conclusion that nature had won.

Certain people were just born defective. They couldn't be fixed. Science wasn't advanced enough to let surgeons go into one's brain and tighten the loose screw or rewire the circuitry. Someday, it might get there, but it would be too late for their son.

***

"See you next month, Dad. I love ya, man."

"Love you too, Son."

Such misconceptions that they'd had about adoption. Their son had been doomed from the second he was conceived. That was the first misconception. The others soon followed.

The father reflected one last time. Twenty-five years for driving drunk and killing a fellow human being. He'd get out in half that time if he behaved himself, didn't run his mouth, obeyed the prison rules, but that wasn't likely. Even if he did behave, in a sense he'd never really get out, anyway. He'd never get out of his wheelchair and walk.

Impala

Timothy O'Leary

I was eleven years old when the man took us. It was my fault.

Mom made it clear we were to be home no later than five, even making us repeat "five o'clock" as if time were a foreign language. But at five-thirty, my little brother Dennis, and I, were in the arcade in the back of Sunset Bowling Alley, feet glued in place by Ms. Pac-Man's blue and yellow glow. Dennis whined every few minutes, anticipating Mom's fury, but there is no free will between little and big brothers. Finally, spurred by Ms. Pac-Man's gulping soundtrack and the violent applause of bowling balls cracking pins, I reached level twenty-eight, the highest score in the history of that particular game, and nodded as I entered my signature—GOD—into the name space in the top slot, then called it quits.

As we were leaving, I noticed the man, standing at the counter and handing in his bowling shoes. First it was the long, stringy hair and tattered army field jacket that grabbed my attention, the street uniform of the Vietnam vets that had been roaming around the last few years. When he turned, his face gaunt, eyes half-lidded, I envisioned Bruce Dern, the man who killed John Wayne in *The Cowboys*. I didn't notice him follow us out, so I didn't know it was him who grabbed us as we unlocked our Huffys from the light pole, his boney fingers digging into the napes of our necks and rushing us, like cattle through a chute, into that deep car trunk.

Dennis cried out, and the man slapped him hard on a fat, moist cheek, stunning us into submission.

"Shut the fuck up or I'll cut your goddamn head off," he said, in a low, serious voice. I wrapped my arm around my brother's face, urging him to be quiet as the lid slammed us into darkness. As the car moved onto the street, we bounced hard on spongy shocks, damp, rusty grit covering my cheek, air thick with oil and some other rotting smell. Sometimes I heard a muffled hum from the radio, Credence Clearwater Revival, the man singing along out-of-tune to *Fortunate Son*.

After maybe twenty minutes, we stopped, the brakes grating. I heard him get out of the car, a garage door rolling up, then rolling back down, after we'd moved in. When the trunk opened, bright light streamed in, the terror subsiding, momentarily. It was a garage like any other, a place where normal men like our dad stowed their stuff: a lawn mower in the corner, rakes and tools hanging neatly on pegs, a boxy freezer humming against the wall. But Dennis flew into a panic, springing out as if he might take flight; a bird locked for days in a room, suddenly freed. The man grabbed him, yelled, "Shut the fuck up, I warned you," and slammed him down outside of my sight line. I collapsed at the front of the car, covering my eyes when the man grabbed the short, square-headed shovel off the wall, swinging it as if he were about to bust-up stubborn dirt clods.

Impala. I concentrated on the chrome emblem on the car's grill, trying to block out the sheaving sound, metal into thick mud, and the more horrible silence when my brother stopped screaming. The man rushed to the front of the car and grabbed me by the hair, bloody shovel dangling in his left hand, and dragged me into the basement.

And that was the last time I was above ground for nine years.

***

Thirty-three hundred days. Eighty thousand hours. Five million minutes. I had plenty of time to do the math, to learn every inch of that twelve-by-twelve room. Fresh, hospital-green paint and gray linoleum, a new porcelain sink and toilet in the corner. I knew I wasn't the first. I crawled on the floor like a slug, forensically analyzing every inch of the walls, spent hours splayed on my back under the bed, pretending the crisscross of the box springs were clouds. I imagined my family in Pioneer Park, our parents laughing as Dennis and I struggled to get a kite airborne. And it was there I discovered the person imprisoned before me. He—was it a he?—I always assumed so, had notched two hundred and forty-one scratches, four vertical with the fifth a cross scratch, on the metal slats. *Did he escape?* I wondered. *Or was his time up?* I counted days in my head, until I could no longer keep track, panicking when I thought I might be close to that number.

Sometimes, the man brought me comic books, and I'd pretend they were letters from home; Archie and Jughead updating me on what was happening with the gang in Riverdale. After maybe a year, he started rolling in a black and white television for an hour or two every few days, just never at a time when I could see news or anything about the outside world. Reception was almost non-existent, but I'd twist and turn the rabbit ears to watch snowy episodes of Gilligan's Island, wishing I was trapped on an island, instead of here; swinging in a hammock and eating coconuts with the Skipper. Sometimes, the man would even watch with me. He'd hear me giggle, and slip in quietly to stand in the corner, a strange smile on his face, as if he were witnessing something magical. He might even have cookies or chocolates wrapped in a napkin, and he'd cautiously hand me one, gesturing toward his lips, as if I didn't know how to eat, then grin happily when I chewed and smiled at the sweetness.

After a while, I couldn't comprehend time, didn't know how old I was or how long I'd been locked away. At some point, the man gave me an electric razor and told me to shave every other day, though he wouldn't allow a mirror. My hands traced my face, the strange new sensation of whiskers, chubby cheeks now slim, trying to comprehend what I might look like.

I'd speak just to hear the changes in my voice as it grew deeper and foreign. Eventually, I forgot my parents and friends, my thoughts confined to Dennis and the one who'd made the notches. Praying I'd misunderstood what had transpired in the garage, I'd talk to my brother for hours, on the off-chance that he might be in the next room with his ear to the wall. With a lot of time to think, I thought a lot about time, and I often considered the importance of minutes. If only I'd followed my mother's instructions and left a few minutes earlier, we wouldn't be here. If it had taken me a few minutes longer to beat Ms. Pac-Man, the man wouldn't have seen us. Sometimes, I'd lie under the bed and carry-on long discussions with the one who came before me, the only one who could really understand it all.

One day, there was an explosion upstairs, rattling the foundation of the house, like a tank had brought down a wall, followed by angry shouting. My door burst apart at the frame, a helmeted man in black, with what looked like a cannon swinging from his arms, yelling at me to get on the ground. The room filled with other uniformed men, brandishing huge weapons. I couldn't comprehend what was happening and thought they might be aliens. Like *War of the Worlds*, perhaps the Earth had been overrun by creatures from another planet and the man and I were the last holdouts. Had he actually been trying to save me?

They whisked me from the basement, into a sinister-looking van, and for the next twenty-four hours, I rotated between hospitals and a police station. I soon understood the truth. I was now a twenty-year-old man that had spent almost half his life in a cellar, imagining he was friends with Veronica and Richie Rich, and communing with dead people.

My mother was gone. Some suspected suicide, Mom so grief-stricken that, late one night, six years earlier, she drove head-on into a telephone pole. My father had remarried, filled his house with new children, and after my initial homecoming, he didn't seem overly interested in seeing me; an unexpected, painful relic from a time he'd rather forget.

I was famous for a few weeks, even appeared on the cover of People Magazine, "The Boy in the Basement." But horrifying stories like mine have a short shelf life, and I was soon replaced in the public's imagination by a British movie star caught communing with a male prostitute, and a Nebraska woman that had given birth two dozen times.

Society loves blame, and officials that should have found me right after the abduction lost their jobs. Friends and classmates I barely remembered, now in college or otherwise living their lives, threw a party and paraded me around like a science exhibit.

Of course, there was counseling and concern, but I felt more like a specimen; doctors repeatedly urging me to confront the worst details. Those that made their livings documenting monstrous crimes, hovered around with the promise of fame and money, neither of which I craved. I had no desire to be the star of a freak show. I understood that everyone assumed a boy held in solitary confinement for half his life had to be insane, and people feared me, almost as much as they did the man. I'd been branded.

I suppose I could have gone back to school or learned some kind of trade, but mostly, I just wanted to keep moving. For a while, I tried to relate, to be human, but the world didn't seem any more real than those comic books, and I found myself drawn to ugly places that reminded me of the room. The counselors and psychologists expressed a grim understanding of my choices, my hollowness. I was defined by my diagnosis: post-traumatic stress and sociopathic tendencies brought on by years of captivity. And I suppose that at some point, even a compassionate society has to enforce its own rules and laws.

***

In Solvang, California, I was arrested for assault and armed robbery. My victim only spent one night in the hospital, but it cost me a year in prison. Next, they sent me to a halfway house and a job I refused to work, the hairnet and paper hat the last straw. I left for Texas, where they were less forgiving, after I shoved a beer bottle into a man's ear, landing me in an even smaller room for three years. Colorado: four years for drugs and a stolen Glock. In Idaho, I made a decent living robbing truck stops and convenience stores, racking up another half-decade in an institution surrounded by fir trees.

After that, I worked my way back home to Montana, even though there was nobody there I wanted to see. That's where I went big time: seventy-five to life for killing a bartender in Great Falls. Did I feel remorse for the man I murdered, the people I hurt? They were no more real to me than those blue and yellow circles I used to gobble-up with Ms. Pac-Man. I wasn't even sure I existed.

Impala

***

Montana only has one prison, Deer Lodge, a red-stoned fortress straight out of a medieval nightmare, built in 1871 as the territorial lock-up. You might've thought someone would do a little research, realize who I was, and decide it might not be a great idea to incarcerate me in the same joint as the man who kept me captive for all those years. Maybe they'd forgotten us. It had been over twenty years, and he was growing old, serving three consecutive life sentences, locked up in solitary when I arrived, so perhaps they thought it wouldn't be an issue. Might have even seen me as a solution, an easy way to trim the herd, assuming I would certainly kill him and save the taxpayers some money.

In my fifth year at Deer Lodge, they released him back into general population. I spotted him across the yard, head down, smoking cigarettes and shuffling back and forth on a six-foot stretch, near the wall. He seemed smaller than I remembered. He had to be pushing sixty, skinny and frail, thin-stretched skin the color of cigarette ash. I doubted he recognized me after twenty-five years.

I became the scientist and he my lab rat. He was always alone, eyes locked on his feet, only raising his gaze to keep from walking into a wall. I memorized his patterns, watched him retreat to the same safe space every day, carrying his tray to the back of the cafeteria to eat alone. I never saw him speak, an occasional head nod, the only acknowledgement of an outside world.

For a while, I imagined what I could do to him, the various ways I might end his life. Sometimes, the fantasy was brutal, dousing him in lighter fluid and sparking him up like a torch, or something slower; my knee, hard on his sternum, his eyes bulging in recognition as I slowly strangled him. Or a shiv pounded into his center as he watched the life leak out of him. But gradually, playing out every violent scenario, the urge to kill subsided, and I remained content just to watch, curious about what made him tick.

When I was in the basement, I'd spend my time anticipating his sound, my internal clock resetting to the man's rhythms; the weight of his steps foretelling how the visit might unfold. If he walked angrily, gait heavy and hard, sometimes cursing while he unlocked the door, I knew the day had gone bad and I would pay the price. I'd retreat to the corner, pushing in hard and covering my head, wondering if this might be the time he went too far. Other nights, he would sneak in lightly with a soft murmur, intent on using me to fill some other void, offering what he probably assumed was tenderness. Some nights, he could be almost childlike, a gentle big brother come to play.

***

One day, I heard from one of the cafeteria workers that he had stage-four lung cancer, a believable diagnosis, given the hollow coughs and thick phlegm he was always hacking up. His movements lapsed to half-speed; his complexion, the pale hue of the dying. I knew he would soon be moved to hospice and pumped full of morphine for his final days, a death that seemed unfairly peaceful for a felon of his accomplishments. So, I decided to sit down across from him in the cafeteria, as he took slow spoonfuls of soup.

He looked up without surprise, anticipating me. "Do you know who I am?" I asked. He nodded slowly, then stared down at his bowl and continued eating. Up close, his shoulders were narrow, a brittle, deflated version of the terrifying specter that shoved Dennis and I into that trunk. We sat in silence, the only sound, him slurping his soup. Finally, he put down the spoon and looked at me as if we were old friends.

"You and me boy, we just never really left that house, did we?"

And I realized he was right. In some crazy way, I would always be there, my head pushing into the car's grill, *Impala* burned into my brain; or lying under that bed, looking into the clouds of my imagination, wondering when I would hear him unlock the door.

Monroe and Warner

Morgen Knight

The subway wasn't as bad as it used to be, but it was still a shithole. Most of the graffiti had been cleaned off or painted over, and there weren't as many dried puddles of vomit near passed-out junkies. Those were positive steps. But the subway cars still smelled like a latrine, and small piles of trash accumulated in odd places, like some hoarder's stash. I guess an old whore can only be improved so much.

When I sat down, I didn't notice her. The car wasn't full, but there weren't large areas of open real estate, either. And by the door, beat down there, by that fat man and the snoring bag lady. I sat down and unfolded my *Conception Gazette* to the Op-Ed section. Kevin Lee had an editorial – thrashing Mayor Carburne – over the slash in arts funding. But all I really wanted was a beer. No, that was a lie. I was more professional than that. I wanted whiskey, and there was a half-bottle of Jameson waiting in my studio apartment.

Four stops away.

It was her book that I noticed first. *The Collected Works of Edgar Allan Poe*. It was in the bag on her lap. I read him my first year of college, which also proved to be my last. I was remembering a few stories, when the young woman looked at me. She had an oval face, simple and pretty. She hid much of it behind a fall of black hair so dark that it sheened blue in the nicotine-colored light. She was Hispanic, but she had eyes that were almost Oriental. Her long lashes were as dark as charcoal, curling gently away from the cinnamon of her irises. Her eyebrows were pencil thin, and two gold loops went through the slender end of her right one. The piercing on the side of her nostril had an emerald green stone. Her small mouth was shaded a heavy brown.

"What do you want, perv?"

She was very pretty, could be beautiful, but wanted to hide it. She had on a black skirt and shoes with metal studs on them. Her long-sleeved shirt was blood red with a black skull over her tiny chest, laughing. A rhinestone sparkled at the center of each eye socket, as if I stared Death in the eyes, I might glimpse the twinkle of his secrets. Her shirt was baggy, but I could see how thin she was. A waif, and I thought of those checked-out street kids you see huddled in dark doorways and beneath overpasses.

Her fingernails were done in black and chipping. She was a young woman, and not a day over seventeen. "Not a thing," I said. "I've read that book, a lifetime ago."

"Hooray and congrats," she said, dryly. She went to shove the book deeper into her bag. Lifting the mouth of the satchel up, I saw the overhead light glint off the nickel body of a .38 snub nose. She looked at me. She saw that I saw. What she didn't see, was how little I cared. The city was dangerous, and she wasn't a girl spending time at church choir practice. Instead, she panicked, grabbed the pistol and jammed it deep into my side. "Not a word," she said. It was a strange command, because I couldn't have uttered a sentence if I'd wanted to. I could feel the Reaper down the car, looking up from clipping his fingernails. She looked around, but nobody was paying attention to us.

"Why do people have to be so fucking nosy," she said. "I hope you weren't headed anywhere important. You're mine until this is done."

I was headed home. What was that? A pathetic, dirty apartment, below ground. I was going to sit in silence, drink, and watch a little TV. Maybe I'd masturbate in the shower while those tiny gnats watched from their perch along the channels of brownish grout. Until now, I'd never been eager to get there. It was ill-furnished and smelled (I suspected dead mice in the walls). I had cockroaches and only did the minimal housekeeping. I never had guests. The only thing I had to look forward to, was buying a drink for my 20s. I had to be a few drinks in before he showed up.

My 20s. Not a gray hair or an extra pound on him. He liked to smile and laugh. He didn't yet know about failure or regrets. He was still strong enough to take on the world alone and believed it would bow to him. Sure, he'd done some disgraceful things, but he couldn't see how they'd ever haunt him. How running away from everything hard didn't make life easy, but shallow. He was full of energy. He described dreams I could almost believe. If I kept drinking, my teens would show up, awkward and lost. Rarely, did I drink enough to invite my 30s. That man was bitter, pathetic, and angry. He hadn't learned to give up, yet, but he had no idea where forward was, much less, how to start it. He cried a lot.

But home felt good right then. Better than bleeding from a hole in my side on a dirty subway car aisle. And sometimes, if I played it right, my 20s allowed me to precisely remember what it was like to be him.

"What are you doing?" I managed to ask at the next stop. The doors opened and closed, people filed in and out, and I sat, taunted, like a man whose prison keys were just beyond his fingertips.

"What does it matter?"

"I have a gun in my side. It matters to me." I could hear my heart beating. It reminded me of Poe's story "The Tale-Tell Heart", that one noise driving a man mad. And then I thought of Poe, on a drinking spree, dying suspiciously on the empty streets of Baltimore on the way to his second wedding. I wondered if he felt the lonesomeness of his words, or the tension. And somehow, it seemed right, didn't it, that a man that wrote those things would die that way? And me, dying right there, would that be so extraordinary?

She leaned against me as if she were tired. Her head was on my shoulder, face turned upward, as if we might be lovers, her mouth close enough to my ear that when she spoke, I felt their hair-raising touch, ghost-like, as if words were the souls of ideas that died in the mind and sought freedom between lips, to forever roam the world. Her breath was warm. It made my spine tingle.

"Be cool. This is over in three stops. That's where I get off."

"Me, too," I said. "At Monroe and Warner. Whatever you're going to do, you don't have to."

Her laugh was bitter. "I do, if I ever want to sleep again."

"You don't want to hurt anybody. Trust me."

We came to stop number two. "Yes, I do. I want to kill him. I want to walk over to his kiosk, put this pistol in his face and blow his mind all over those magazines."

"How could you want to do that? You're so young."

"What the fuck do you know about me?" There was no emotion in her voice.

I closed my eyes. I knew that I should not interfere. Let this play out. What business of this was mine? When she looked at me, she saw a forty-six-year-old man with thinning hair streaked with gray. She saw a man that had fucked up most of his life, destroying what little he'd touched. Maybe she couldn't see all of my failures, maybe she couldn't see what a loser I was. Maybe all she saw was my gut and my weary face and the fact that I'd seen her gun. I hoped so, because I needed her to listen to me.

"Nothing," I said. "Maybe a bit of everything." I looked down at my knees. "You know how these stories end, right? If one of the transit cops don't shoot you, you'll die in prison."

She was quiet for a moment. The pressure of the pistol against my side lessened but did not vanish. I could hear the heavy bass of a man's iPod on the seats across from us.

"I don't have a choice."

My voice lowered. "If someone is making you do this, we can get you help." I pictured someone being held hostage or a debt held over her head. "Do you want to go to prison?"

She shook her head against me.

"And you don't want to be a murderer. Imagine what that means. I don't know if you believe in God. I'm not much of a believer, but that doesn't make killing right." I felt like I had a foothold, so I tried to advance as quickly as I could, grasping at any straw argument that came to mind.

"I've done some bad things in my life. Not like that, but bad enough. And believe me, it might not seem like it now, but this is something you'll have to live with. It won't be as easy in ten years, as it is now."

"So," she said, but she didn't sound sure.

"These are the actions that make the meaning of us," I said. I knew what I was talking about. My failures, my mistakes, my fondness for the easy road had all defined me. By the time I realized how much more I could have been, it was too late. Talent wasted, intellect unused. I'd always secretly believed that everything I wanted—fame, money, love—would find me. All I needed was to accept it. And I believed that all the way into my dull, lonely life.

"I've hurt people," I said. "I never killed anyone, but I've ruined lives in my selfishness." The gun moved from my side. She put her other hand over it, on her leg. "I could have been a father. I have a daughter about your age, somewhere. I ran off because a family sounded too hard to me. I've done that a lot... run. Now, I'm used up and alone."

She was quietly crying against me. "He killed my mother," she said. I was galvanized by the claim. And then, she detailed a story about a monstrous man. She told me about the beatings that she and her mother took, the verbal abuse. The mental games. How this man terrorized them, but they'd had no place else to go. His trailer was home, and home-life was hell. Her mother used to hide her in the closet to protect her, but those thin doors never stopped the sounds. Hearing something can be worse than seeing it. She told me about her own wounds, weeping into me. We made an awful sight. People's eyes lingered on us a moment. I could feel her tears wetting my collar. She trembled and it felt like mild seizures.

I reached across my body, holding her head against my shoulder. The man had destroyed her mother in every way. Then... he'd left. She'd been so mentally crushed that only pills had allowed her to function. And this girl had watched her mother wallow in the sediment of despair, until she come home one day and found her dead. She'd never known another family. It was state homes and foster care, afterwards. She was a bright girl, she said. All the tests said so. Smart and driven. But she could never sleep, hearing those sounds from the closet, seeing the vacancy in her mother's dead eyes, dried vomit on her chin and chest.

These memories were her own tell-tale heart, beating her into madness.

"You'll be okay. It's okay, it's okay," I whispered, holding this girl that I didn't know. But suddenly, I did know her, and I loved her, and I hated the world for all the wrong things it'd done. I was nobody's hero, but I knew that I could save this girl from this mistake. She *was* pretty *and* smart. She could be the contender I'd failed to be. My hand was over hers on the pistol.

"You have a chance. You've got so much life in front of you. This man already took so much. Please don't give him the rest." The train pulled from the third stop.

She pulled her hand back slowly, leaving the gun in mine. At first, I couldn't believe it. I slid it to my side and tucked it in my waistline. I knew exactly where I would throw it away.

"It can hurt so bad," she said.

"I know," I said. And I could see that no dark spirit had been cast out of her. When she sat up, she still had that haunted look. Her eyes were wet. A dark smudge of mascara ran down her face. She sniffled repeatedly, and tears marked her like melted wax. She would keep hearing those sounds and seeing that lifeless face, I knew. Beneath this dark, beat-up rind, was the tender fruit of possibility about to rot. I wanted to tell her all of the mistakes I'd made – I wanted to shield her from the wounds of regret – I wanted to explain why I sometimes sat on an empty park bench and wept uncontrollably in the middle of the day. I wanted to be something fundamental and everlasting, that could offer her a new perspective on life. I saw who I could be in her eyes, and I liked that man.

"I'm sorry," she said.

"You've got nothing to be sorry for."

"I just want to be free."

"You are, now," I said. "And you've got a good, long life ahead." The train was stopping.

"This is where I get off."

She cleaned up her face. I told her where I worked and how to get a hold of me. I told her, again, that she was free, now, but she didn't believe me. It was on her face when she looked at the open doors and the platform, beyond. Her lip quivered when she saw the man—older now—at the black kiosk near the restrooms. It was good that I had her gun. I saw the question of having it back, pass through her, before I stepped off. Glancing back, I saw her move towards a window, pushing herself against it, to memorize the man, as I walked away.

I had to see him. He looked about my age, but thinner. He had stringy hair that fell around his face, like he was in a grunge band. He had on a plain white button-up and jeans. When he looked at me, I saw the same things in his eyes that I witnessed in my own mirror every day. We both wore shame; we were sadness – we looked away when our dreams spoke – we saw youth and hope and potential, and cringed at our own wasted trails.

He nodded at me. He asked if I would like to see a magazine. I didn't know that he had been going to church for two years, or that he had a long-time girlfriend. I didn't know he gave blood twice a month or that he once pulled a man from a burning car. I learned that at trial, but what did it matter? I never believed him to be evil personified, but he was the object haunting a young woman. And what was I? I was merely a shell – alone – counting the days that crept silently by. My life had no value and this girl had a chance.

So, I pulled out her pistol and shot the man in the face. It was easy. All I had to do was think of the things she'd heard; imagine the dead face of her mother.

Poe wrote dark stories, but he also penned beautiful poetry. Sometimes people find light in unexpected darkness. The man's eyes widened, the bullet entered his brain, and all the horrors of that girl fell with him. I know it might sound oxymoronic, like one of those '60s protest signs I'd seen in movies: 'Killing for Peace is like Fucking for Chastity' or 'Equality Now: Kill the Rich!' But for me, it wasn't a slogan, or a lifestyle. It became a prayer, my catechism: 'I did a good bad thing'. And I could almost feel my 20s looking at me, trying to comprehend. I heard my 30s quiet down. But… something in my teens agreed.

And tomorrow?

Tomorrow would be visiting day. She came every week. She was in college, now, top of her class. Sometimes, she called me Pa, as she hugged me. And when she looked at me, I knew that I had changed her. I saved her life; and I had finally defined mine.

Brooms

Jon-Michael Kelley

"Tornados," Christian said.

"Recurring nightmares about tornados?" said the pretty lady psychiatrist, her eyes hinting no surprise as she scribbled something onto her yellow notepad.

"I wouldn't call them nightmares, really," Christian said, somewhat distantly. "I'm not frightened by them."

"What do you think they represent, these tornados?"

"Chaos, maybe. Loss of control." Christian nodded his head vaguely, staring faraway – way past the pretty psychiatrist; his eyes glazing placidly with something recalled just then. "Yeah, loss of control."

The psychiatrist obsessively pushed her round, wire frames back up the bridge of her nose, a long, feminine nail dully glinting valentine-red beneath the white fluorescent boxes that checkered the ceiling. Then, she silkily cleared her throat. "How long have you been having the tornado dreams?"

Christian slowly returned his gaze to those beautiful, intelligent green eyes. "I've been having them since I started seeing you."

There was a fleeting nuance of dread in those lovely green eyes; an evanescent twinkling of horror that Christian regarded with a mixture of exhilaration and guilt. He was excited to think that she knew what was lurking beneath his revelation, but also ashamed at having upset her.

The lady psychiatrist leaned back in her swivel chair, the corners of her eyes crinkling with veteran concern. "Let's talk more about this loss of control, Christian. To what were you referring? Something specific?"

Christian began fidgeting, pinching creases into his white hospital gown. "You know, the same old stuff. Girls, mostly." His eyes diverted embarrassingly to the floor. "Love."

"Well, that's perfectly natural, Christian. Love is a very complex emotion, especially for a young man approaching his seventeenth birthday," the psychiatrist said, then was suddenly afraid that she might have sounded condescending. She knew that Christian could never again pursue courtship with another woman; wouldn't be allowed. *Ever.*

There was only one thing more terrifying than the thought of Christian having developed a crush on her, and that was the thought of having made him angry, having insulted him. His intelligence quotient had been gauged at 140, but Christian was still an adolescent, susceptible to misinterpreting the good intentions of an adult, especially those coming from one of her stature. She had to monitor her every word and action while in session with Christian, and his powerful intellect made walking that fine line even more perilous.

And though he was treated with utmost respect (out of abject fear, no doubt) from the staff at the institute, he was still a prisoner.

But more than anything else, Christian was a guinea pig. In just two weeks, he was beginning to show signs of marked fatigue. Combined with the daily bombardment of sedatives and neurologic medications, he was usually torpid by mid-afternoon.

The apathetic expression on her patient's face went unchanged. She exhaled silently, feeling a little more at ease.

Three weeks ago, she'd been approached by a liaison with the United States Government, offering her a very challenging – and lucrative – job with the Manger Institute; a facility renowned for its dream research. Her job, it was explained, would be to work with a team of specialists involved in conducting extensive research on a teenage boy who had the extraordinary ability to manifest his emotions into tangible, living creatures. Her specific duties would be to counsel said patient, to look for and treat any pathogenesis or symptoms of schizophrenia, manic-depression, and the sort. She would also be involved in researching the patient's hypnogogic area of slumber; that ephemeral state just before the onset of true sleep.

More fine lines.

Evidence accumulated thus far, she was told, indicated this pre-sleep period might be the launching pad for the phenomenon.

She found the story a bit hard to swallow, but the paycheck and prestigious position persuaded her otherwise. She packed her bags and reserved first-class seating on the quickest airliner out.

Today, while in conference with the clinicians of the dream-lab, she had been briefed on Christian's nightly EEG patterns, which continued showing marked alpha wave activity just before, and during stage one sleep, and some peculiar delta wave activity while emerging from stage four sleep. REM, or rapid eye movement, they'd said, was suspiciously absent from the majority of normal dream-sleep, but present in pre-sleep states. They'd gone on to discuss periods of elevated blood pressure, pulse rate, and other physiological points of interest, but by that time, she had stopped listening. It was not her area of expertise.

The one thing that had evoked her interest, as well as her colleagues', was the fact that Christian was narcoleptic; uncontrollable sleep could accost him at any time. And hypnogogic hallucinations were common in narcolepsy. Although, it was still in debate whether the patient was eliciting this phenomenon from hallucinatory-sleep or from dream-sleep, it was unanimously agreed that Christian was a modern-day Frankenstein.

The governing staff of the institute had elected her as part of *The Team*, they said, because of her previous and most celebrated work with schizophrenia and neurological disorders. Thus far, she wasn't convinced that Christian was clinically schizophrenic, but his nocturnal passions had certainly displayed some pathologic behavior.

Up until now, all the victims had been girls on whom Christian had felt crushes, their deaths following some act of renunciation: spurned sexual advances, breaking off the relationship, showing interest in other boys, and so forth. But there was agreement among many at the institute that emotions other than puppy love could – and would, eventually – stimulate more murderous episodes. This was everyone's real concern.

So far, nothing had manifested itself in physical form in the laboratory setting, and no other bizarre murders had occurred since Christian's committal. This was to the delight of many.

And, she was certain, to the secret consternation of a few.

At the present, she was more compelled to help her patient learn to control and understand his feelings before they got the better of him. And, just as importantly, the better of someone else. This seemed to her the area in need of immediate attention, and one where her expertise lay.

"I have a feeling love is always going to be a problem," Christian said, a suggestion of disdain in his voice. "I mean, considering the trouble it's gotten me into so far." His eyes looked over into hers, where they sojourned unwavering.

Was it admiration she saw? *Infatuation*? Something centipede-like writhed up her spine.

She looked down and pretended to jot something onto her pad, not wanting to let Christian's eyes consider hers for too long.

She flipped to a clean sheet, her pen poised precariously between two, long and delicate fingers. "Have your parents visited you since the day of your admittance?" she asked, subtly changing the subject. She knew the answer.

"Naw," Christian smiled, a roadblock that was meant to stop the pain that was recklessly racing from his heart to his eyes. It worked, though feebly. "They just came the one time. They were... scared."

You'll never see them again, Christian. The government has seen to that.

"I'm very sorry, Christian," she said. "I can imagine how that must be hurting you."

Christian looked out the barred window adjacent to his chair. He stared past the high, encircling electrified fences and armed sentries, all there for his benefit; past the monolithic city architecture of concrete and glass that skirted the institution; past the vigorous traffic; past even the alluring day-dreams of him and the pretty psychiatrist – of how she finally falls in love with him, seduces him, *understands* him. Past everything corporeal, searching for the one cloud that would mercifully open its belly and give birth to a swirling, black funnel.

The available sky, however, was spitefully clear; a dusky blue, slowly fading to white, toward the horizon.

"Am I crazy only when I dream?" Christian said, still staring through the window, his eyes coveting the one thing he knew he could never again have: freedom. "Or am I just crazy, period?"

No, Christian, you're not crazy, she thought. *At least, according to the multitude of personality tests, electroencephalograms, magnetic resonance imagings, computerized coaxial tomographies, and a myriad of other mainstream and experimental examination results that, by the way, would be enough to list the Queen Mary to a very sloping starboard. You're a phenomenon, Christian. A curiosity that the doctors here would like to use to catapult their careers. And one the government would certainly like to keep around for its own, albeit clandestine, purposes. And a few have even suggested that you be killed. Oh, but that will never happen as long as the government continues to support your surreptitious stay at this institute. You're simply a very creative, extremely intelligent youth, who has the ability to manufacture assassins from an awkward, teenage subconscious. It's what every adolescent should be blessed with.*

She leaned into her desk. "There's no evidence suggesting anything so acute, Christian. Now, let's talk about the dreams, again. In our last session, you said..." — she busily flipped the pages backward, searching through her previous notes. "...that: 'I dreamed a lot about the praying mantis before Brenda died. When she was dead, the dreams stopped'."

"It's cunning, insidious," Christian said. "It knows the spider's vulnerable spot." He returned his gaze to the psychiatrist, pursing his eyes down into narrow slits. "Like lightning, it strikes."

"Interesting metaphor," she said, goose flesh blazing across her arms like a windswept grass fire.

"I thought that's the kind of cerebral bullshit you wanted to hear, what I think the mantis represents," Christian exclaimed, anger swirling up in his voice. "But that's exactly what it is – bullshit!" He caught his anger, controlled it. "You saw the autopsy results. They found enzymes and other proteins indigenous to insect saliva in the masticated flesh. *That's* what's important. Not what I *feel* the mantis – or any other fucking monster I've concocted – represents!"

The psychiatrist pensively scrawled more notes, painfully recalling that particular autopsy folder with its glossy, colored photographs of what was once Brenda Eckhart's head.

Her first three days at the institute were spent examining the mounds of data, which included police and autopsy reports, complete with black-and-white and colored photographs of all the victims, pre- and postmortem. Her skepticism of the whole affair had been quelled in those first three days.

It was day number three when she began feeling uneasy.

Day number five was her first session with Christian, and that was when she became *truly* frightened.

"And what was Brenda's vulnerable spot, Christian?"

"Her beautiful face," he answered without pause, summoning memories that preceded its desecration: warm smile; mahogany brown eyes, twinkling with life; long, smooth neck complemented by a perfect, angular jaw.

The psychiatrist, referring to her notes again, said, "And you believed you were in love with Brenda Eckhart, but she wasn't in love with you. In fact, she didn't want to have anything to do with you. And you resented her for that."

"Sure. But not enough to do *that* to her."

"So, you believe the mantis... *avenged* your feelings of rejection?"

"Of course!" Christian said, in a tone more infuriated than he intended. "That's exactly what it did! But I can't control my emotions when they have the ability to get up and walk out of my mind and hunt down anyone they desire!"

He took a deep breath, collected himself.

"I'm a victim of them, too, you know," he continued. "I just don't have the fortunate luck to be quickly killed by them. Mine is a painfully slow death."

The psychiatrist sucked on the tip of her pen, allowing a therapeutic pause.

Seconds pulsed from a long wall clock, swiftly building to a crescendo in Christian's ears: *tic-toc tic-toc tic…*

"A metronome on the mantel of sanity," he finally submitted, as if an actor in a Shakespearian play, "whose cadence hungrily embraces any period of utter silence, where it then taunts the vulnerable with its maddening, simplistic meter." His eyes followed an imaginary pendulum. "Tic-toc, tic-toc, tic-toc."

She regarded his performance cautiously, saying nothing. He often went on short, harmless tangents in the middle of session. She attributed them, however reluctantly, to his medicated state.

"Tell me about Deborah Bannon. She was the first, is that right?"

Christian looked down and answered to his white hospital slippers. "Yes."

"What did you dream before her death?"

"I started dreaming about the orphans after we broke up."

"The orphans?"

"I don't know what else to call them. They were really troll-like, ugly little creatures. For some reason, I just started calling them orphans. Funny, huh?"

She didn't respond.

"Villainous, distorted little men with hatchets..." Christian broke off, swallowing the memory down hard. He peered out the window again, his eyes clouding with distance.

"For how long did you dream of the trolls, Christian? These 'orphans'?"

He sighed, silently. "Until her body was found in the park. Or what was left of it."

"The dreams stopped after Deborah's death?"

Christian nodded groggily. "Just like all the others."

She was losing him again. She became fearful when he grew indolent like this; slothful from the medications. It was too similar, she guessed, to the furtive periods of sleep, when Christian was most vulnerable, most dangerous; too parallel with the frame of mind that accompanied such dazed periods, those just before drifting off, when consciousness was prostrate to the darker realms of the psyche.

When *she* was most vulnerable to *his* darker realms.

She knew all too well that to keep Christian celibate behind lock-and-key would only naturally promote more elaborate and consuming daydreams. *Night dreams.* And Christian was nothing short of Jack the Ripper when he was dreaming. There were five dead girls to vouch for that.

And why the governing faculty of the institute had chosen her, along with three other female staff, to shrink his head was becoming even more suspicious. She was a very attractive woman of thirty-one years, and was certainly not naïve enough to believe that a heterosexual, adolescent male patient would not include her, to some extent, in his sexual fantasies.

But to what *extent*? That was the nibbler.

God! She didn't want to get into Christian's mind – she wanted to get the hell *out* of it!

"You look tired, Christian. Would you like to cut the session short, today?"

Christian folded his hands in his lap, his eyes finally leaving the window. "Why? So I can go back to my nice, padded room? No, thanks." He glanced up at the wall clock. "There's not much time left, anyway. I'll stay."

"Very well," she said, trying not to let the slight tremor of fear in her voice reverberate to her eyes. She was being very careful not to let her anxiety show. *Animals can sense when you're frightened of them, can't they?* "Then let's continue with the orphan dreams. Did you start to suspect that something was wrong when you began having them? Did they upset you?"

"Just a pack of trolls stalking the shadows of my sleep," Christian said with a laugh, shrugging his shoulders. "I never once had the feeling they were after *me*. I knew they were looking for something else."

You mean some*one* else, she thought, icy fear sprinkling down her neck in pinpoint-sharp droplets. *God help me, if you are entertaining – or I'm nurturing – any thoughts about us.*

"Did any of the orphans ever talk to you?" she gently nudged. "Was there a leader?"

Christian rolled his eyes. "No."

"Care to offer any 'cerebral bullshit'?" she said lightheartedly; any attempt to quell her gnawing fear.

Christian smiled, embarrassed. "I guess not."

"What else have you dreamt, Christian, since the orphans?"

Christian's head lolled over, his eyes shut.

He was asleep.

For a moment, she could only stare and wonder. This was the first time Christian had suffered a narcoleptic episode in her presence. This was what everyone at the institute was praying to catch in the laboratory, where the sundry instruments could monitor the event.

What had they called it? *The launching pad?*

Should I wake him? Is he dreaming? **What** *is he dreaming? More orphans? More monstrous insects? Something for* **me**? *Dear God in Heaven, what if...*

"Christian?" she almost screamed. "Christian, wake up."

Nothing. Not a stirring.

She bounded from her chair, around her desk, knocking over file folders; billows of white rectangles cascading to the floor.

She grabbed the armrests of his chair. "Christian!"

Still, nothing.

Her brown hair fell in silky strands about her eyes as she shook the chair. "Christian! *Wake up!*"

Christian jolted awake, his eyes wide. He looked around the room, bewildered. "Did I..."

"Yes, yes. You fell asleep, Christian," she said, with a resounding sigh, feeling the adrenaline pool in her knees.

She returned to her desk, ignoring the carpet of felled papers. "Did you... dream?" Something inside her wormed adversely for asking, but she *had* to know.

His eyes looked away from hers. "No."

He's lying. Damn him if he isn't lying.

"You don't remember anything? A dream? Hallucinations…?"

"Dammit! Don't browbeat me! I'm sick of being treated like a criminal. You can't possibly imagine the guilt I feel, the helplessness. Everyone has spent so much time frantically monitoring my every waking and sleeping moment that they've overlooked the one thing that's most important: *Me!* —Well, this time *they've* created the monster. I refuse to take responsibility."

"What have *they* created, Christian? Please, tell me."

Christian leaned back into his chair, surrendering to its comfort. He ignored the question. "I've changed my mind about the tornados."

"Excuse me?"

"The tornados. I don't believe they represent chaos." He stared out the window one last time. "I'm beginning to think they symbolize brooms."

"Brooms?"

"Yeah. Maybe I have a subconscious desire to want everything in my life swept away."

"That's a... theory," she offered – dread, like ice-cold mercury – seeping into her veins.

Christian pressed a hand against the window's glass, his fingers curling inward, as if trying to grasp the receding reality of the world outside. "There's not just one or two, you know, but *thousands* of them – **millions**

– descending at the same time, from a black, hateful sky." His hand slid slowly down the glass, squeaking sorrowfully, proclaiming its emptiness. "Brooms, sweeping away the whole damned world."

"Did you dream them again? Just now, the tornados?"

"You're so scared, aren't you? So scared I've created another bogeyman. One that knows your name. But there's only one problem," he said, looking at her with sad, wondering eyes. "You've never *told* me your name. Why?"

"I... I suppose I was afraid to," she stammered, her chin beginning to quiver. "Giving someone your name is, is like…"

"An invitation? The first step in letting them in?"

She nodded; swallowed hard. "Yes."

"You believe I can't fall in love with you if you remain nameless to me?"

"Yes," she whispered. "Something like that."

Christian looked down at his gown and began pleating it again with trembling fingers. "It's too late. I'm already in love with you."

"I know," she said, tears burning in her eyes. "I know." She was no longer frightened for herself. Her fear reached beyond simply her – *much further now* – encompassing the entire world.

"Sandra Anne Connelly," she offered softly, avoiding his eyes.

Christian looked up, tears streaming down his cheeks. "I'm so sorry, Sandra."

***

Sandra's last memories, just before drifting off into a much-welcomed, pill-induced sleep, were of staring out her front living room window, just before nightfall. She remembered watching the storm clouds steadily build across the horizon, as far as the eye could see; how webbed lightning whisked dazzlingly across the storm's black belly; the distant gurgle of thunder. How the immature, lone juniper tree on her front lawn whipped back and forth like a convulsing child in the gales of the advancing tempest.

Remembered hearing the relentless sirens; like lost, wailing children.

All the poor, poor children.

Remembered thinking, lastly, that Christian must be dreaming.

Redemption

Lee Duffy

Steven Darlington accelerated his brand new, bright yellow Chevrolet Corvette to seventy-five. He could barely see the road. The car swerved from side-to-side on the dark, rural, two-lane highway, despite his best efforts to drive a straight line. The headlights reflected off the trees flashing past in a surreal black and green blur. He blasted through a stop sign that he never saw and continued north.

He had come to Mississippi to visit a friend from Harvard. His friend's party had been quaint, at best. The girls were mildly amusing, with their droll little southern-belle drawls. It all gave him the icky feeling that he had just starred in a comedy sketch about *Gone with the Wind*. The only redeeming quality of the gathering was that there was plenty of booze— and Steven had consumed his share.

And now, he couldn't get out of the Deep South fast enough. As far as he was concerned, the people here were all ignorant hicks who couldn't speak properly.

Steven wasn't entirely sure what happened next. He regained consciousness at some country hospital, beaten to a pulp. His pain was severe, but they wouldn't give him anything for it. The doctors and nurses treated him like some Yankee pariah. He was handcuffed to the bed, and a deputy sheriff sat just outside the open door, reading a newspaper.

Steven soon learned that he had run down a little girl who was crossing the road. It seemed the girl he'd killed was related to one of the deputy sheriffs on the scene—which soon swelled to a whole pack of deputy sheriffs—all of whom had proceeded to kick the living crap out of Steven Darlington.

He could only remember bits and pieces of what happened, but he did recall that before the pounding commenced, the deputies had dragged him out of the Corvette and pulled him along, stumbling, back to where the little girl's body was lying on the side of the road, all crumpled and bloody. For some bizarre reason, he remembered smelling chicken broth.

The beating, however, was really the least of Steven's problems. His blood alcohol level was 0.13, and the judge convicted him of involuntary manslaughter and sentenced him to seven years' hard labor at the county prison farm.

The Darlington family had tried everything to save Steven from southern justice. Their Ivy-League Boston lawyers employed every sly legal scheme they could imagine. One of Steven's lawyers even tried to bribe the judge in chambers. But it was all for naught.

That judge was a real Mississippi holy roller, and even the massive money and influence the Boston Darlington's could muster couldn't reach that far down into the bowels of the earth, and young Steven went to the farm.

At the prison farm, the guards didn't seem to watch him too closely. He was fairly free to wander around on work details here and there about the property. That was during the day, of course. At night, the inmates fought over Steven, until he finally worked up the courage to run.

He slipped off into the woods near the garbage dump where he'd tended to the reeking cans. He had heard the stories about escapees, but he ran anyway. He just couldn't take it any longer.

Damn if they weren't watching, though. He knew now that it was all true. He had heard rumors that you could escape, but they would hunt you down and bring you back in a burlap sack. It was said that no one ever came back alive—runaways all seemed to die resisting capture. Steven believed it, now. This would be the deputy sheriff's final revenge.

Steven was now on the run, but there was nowhere to run to. It was all woods and swamp. He didn't have a clue where he was. And the hounds that had been chasing him all morning had some kind of alien radar that could see through trees and steam and mud and leaves. Those acutely sensitive canine noses had been carefully bred for just one purpose—to track a man to his grave. And, of course, the dogs loved every minute of it. Steven had been running for hours, and the dogs had been hot on his trail the entire time. It seemed as though they were just toying with him.

Yeah, he thought, *those rednecks were waiting. I was so stupid. I did exactly what they wanted me to do—run. They just hung around, chewin' tobacco. Patient. Dogs ready. And when I ran, I know those rednecks just grinned, spit some tobacco juice, grabbed their shotguns and the dogs, and then started off into the woods after my sorry ass, just as happy as kids on Christmas morning. I'm the ultimate damn hunt, right boys?*

Steven Darlington inched himself shakily up a weed-filled incline. Thick mud gripped his still-submerged brogans, making loud, sucking noises, as he pulled his boots free from the swampy muck. He was drenched in rancid, brown swamp water and streaked from head to toe with sticky, green slime. His lungs seemed as if they might burst. He struggled in ragged gasps, to catch his elusive breath, while his heart palpitated violently in his chest.

The July heat beat down through the thick, southern forest, making Steven's misery even greater. Large beads of sweat dotted his handsome, angular face. Insects of a dozen varieties swarmed about his head and crawled over his sticky, sweaty skin—they buzzed, bit, scratched, stung, and swooped, 'til it nearly drove him crazy.

His once sandy-colored hair, was caked with mud and leaves from the forest floor, and every joint and muscle tormented him. But the physical discomfort was minor compared to the gut-wrenching fear that gripped his soul. He knew that he was about to die. He could feel death's hot, fetid breath pressing down against his sweaty neck. And it scared him, truly frightened him, for the first time in his royally pampered, young life.

This wretched southern swamp certainly was an unlikely place to find such a young man as this. The Boston Darlington's were wealthy socialites, more accustomed to jet setting about the world than being pursued through inhuman terrain by seasoned bloodhounds.

And because of his privileged roots, Steven Darlington had grown up a bit self-centered and cocky. Who wouldn't be self-indulgent after having grown up with a platinum spoon in their mouth, every whim catered to by family servants?

Boston, though, was a long way from this hellhole, and in a sudden surge of self-pity and utter despair, Steven Darlington realized just how very far from home he really was. He dropped his pounding head to the ground and sobbed.

I didn't mean to hit that damn girl, he thought, shaking his head from side-to-side. *Dammit to hell! Why was that stupid kid out walking on that unlit country highway, anyway? She didn't have any business out on such a somber road so late at night. Got what she deserved*, he thought, clenching his fists in anger. "It wasn't my fault!" he cried out.

Then, Steven cocked his head to one side and listened intently. For the first time all day, he couldn't hear the dogs. "Did they lose my trail?" he asked himself hopefully.

There was a merciful, exquisite moment of near silence. Then, that unmistakable, piercing, spine-chilling, whine-yelp of bloodhounds on the scent filled the heavy Mississippi air. A morbid chill shot up Steven's spine as he bolted over the small ridge just in front of him. He went crashing down the other side—briars, vines, and branches tearing and clawing at his already raw and ragged skin.

This is it, he thought. *They're louder. Only got a few minutes, now*, he mused, as he continued his blind dash forward. *Will they let the dogs have me? Or just shoot me?* he wondered fleetingly.

As he ran, Steven's thoughts were suddenly interrupted when he dashed over the edge of a steep bank and found himself falling. An instant later, he hit the dark, swirling water, hard, and for a long moment, he was sure he would never come back up. Finally, he surfaced, floundering in panic. Steven flailed at the water until he realized he would drown if he didn't calm down and get control of himself. The instinct for survival prevailed, and he managed to get his heavy limbs to tread the swift brown water.

The current in the Big Black River was fast, and the brown water was full of logs, limbs, and debris. Anxious moments later, Steven somehow found himself clinging to a log, his breathing somewhat restored, dully watching the trees drift swiftly by up on the muddy riverbanks, and still trying to figure out what had just happened.

I made it, he thought with wonder. *Even hounds can't track through water. Not even those damn rednecks can do that. Crap,* he thought, *I just might make it, after all. But they're clever,* he knew. *In their backwoods, redneck ways, they're clever. They'll pull back and try to get ahead of me. And they know this terrain.*

Then, a solution loomed, just overhead.

Steven clawed his way up the muddy riverbank until he reached the train trestle overhead. A freight train was passing by at a crawl. With extraordinary effort, he grabbed the doorframe of an open boxcar and pulled himself up onto the floor. He rolled farther inside, to conceal himself. Then, he lay there, flat on his back, soaking wet, gasping for air, until finally, exhausted, he fell fast asleep.

When Steven woke, it was dark. He could hear the engine's whistle reverberating through the still night air. The rhythmic, clickety-click of steel wheels on rails, vibrated beneath the car's rusty metal floor in an ever-slower cadence.

Steven pulled himself upright and peered out the open door of the rail car. The train was slowing. He had no idea what time it might be or where he was. A short distance away, he could see the lights of a town. The moon was high on the horizon, and it flooded the night with a shadowy, glaucous light.

Gotta get off this train, he thought. *Cops'll be checking it.*

The train seemed to be moving pretty slowly, so he sat in the doorway, eyes squinting, trying to pick an open, grassy spot to hop down. Then, sliding off the edge of the car, Steven dropped, seemingly forever. He hit hard, knocking the breath from his lungs. He tumbled down a rocky embankment—the train was moving faster than it had appeared in the dim light, and it was also a fifteen-foot drop down the steep, rugged slope below.

As the train rumbled past and disappeared into the night, Steven just lay there, gasping. Only a faint vibration lingered in the distance now, to mark its passage. Steven gritted his teeth in agony. He decided that it was ironic his quest for freedom should end here. He was sure he had broken something.

He lay there for a time, taking stock of his condition, testing his ability to move his limbs. Only youth and a bit of dumb luck had prevented Steven Darlington from breaking his neck. And miraculously, he hadn't broken anything else, either. He slowly gathered himself up and began making his way across the big open field before him, toward the lights in the distance. Moonlight laid a wax-yellow sheen across the slick, grassy pasture.

He soon arrived at the first house on the outskirts of town and helped himself to a towel and a set of clothes from the line. A few neighborhood dogs barked in the distance. None were in the immediate vicinity of this house, so he felt reasonably secure poking around in the backyard, stealing clothes.

Outfitted in jeans and a Mississippi State T-shirt, prison duds stashed in a drainpipe, Steven moved cautiously toward the town. He soon discovered a busy, all-night truck stop, situated on a state highway. He needed to make only one telephone call, he knew, and this gruesome nightmare would be over.

He bummed a quarter easily enough, and verifying that no one was watching, he settled into one of the truck stop's ancient, indoor phone booths, amazed that such things still existed. Secure behind the near-antique, folding wood and glass doors of the booth, he dropped his solitary coin into the slot and waited anxiously for the collect call to go through. Alexander Donaldson, of Donaldson, Donaldson, and Tate—the Darlington family's own private law firm—quickly accepted the charges and the operator dropped off the line.

"Steven? Is that really you?" he demanded incredulously. "Where are you? What the hell's happened? Are you all right?"

"Shut up, Alex," ordered Steven, through gritted teeth. "Yes, it's me. Just listen, for Christ's sake, will you?"

"Sure, sure," came the calmer reply.

"Listen," Steven said again, straining to control both his emotions and his fears, "I'm out. I ran off and got away."

"You what? Where are you?"

"I'm still in the state, I think, so they're probably all over the damn place, looking for me. I'm at a truck stop called Chuck's Place. A truck driver told me it's near a little town called Brook's Crossing."

"Okay, I got it, Brook's Crossing."

"Alex, get the Lear down here as fast as you can. Find out where the nearest airport is that it can land. Call a limo service somewhere and have them send a car for me here at the truck stop. When it shows up, I'll contact the driver. He can take me to the jet at whatever airport you can get into. I want to go straight to Europe, Alex. You understand?"

"Got it, kid. You can count on me. Your old man will be thrilled when he finds out we plucked you out of there. We'll have to make sure we don't implicate your family—but I'll handle that. This is great, kid," he stammered with childlike enthusiasm.

"Let's congratulate ourselves later, Alex. For now, just get cracking on the transportation."

"Sure, kid. Just sit tight. The cavalry's on the way."

Steven Darlington hung up the receiver and leaned his head back against the phone booth wall. He sighed a deep and satisfying breath of relief. *If I'm careful,* he thought, *I might actually pull this off. In a few hours, I'll be out of this god forsaken hellhole and have my clean, dry feet propped up in front of a hardwood fire in a high-mountain chalet in Switzerland. Some hot Swiss chick will be under my arm, and we'll be sipping Dom Perignon.* He closed his eyes, and with a slight smile on his smudged face, he pictured that enticing chalet scene.

***

On the other side of the county, Lester Pacheco's ringing telephone finally pierced his slumber. The heavy-set, slightly balding, fortyish-looking man, rolled over and groped for the handset.

"Yeah?" he asked sleepily.

"Lester, it's me, Wheeler."

"Yes, Mr. Wheeler," came the unenthusiastic reply.

"I've got a run for you."

Lester Pacheco forced his eyes to focus on the clock. It was 2 a.m. He had been asleep for thirty minutes. Running limos was only part-time work, and he had just gotten home from his regular job.

"Who wants a limo this time of night?" protested Pacheco.

"Somebody pretty important, I assume. There's a real hefty bonus in it for the company," he said, pausing. "And for you, too, of course," he hastened to add.

Lester Pacheco was exhausted. It had been a long and tiring day. He *did* need the extra cash, though, so he decided to gut it out and take the job.

"Okay, Mr. Wheeler, which car?"

"When you go by the garage, take the black Caddie. It's just been serviced."

"Okay, Mr. Wheeler, what's the location?"

"You've got a single party, male. Pick him up at Chuck's Place. You know, the truck stop on Highway 65 South?"

"Yes, sir, of course I know Chuck's Place."

Wheeler continued. "Take him to Raymond County Airport. There'll be a private plane coming in to pick him up in an hour or so. In the meantime, take good care of him."

"Right. I'm on my way."

"And Lester…"

"Yes, sir?"

"Treat this fellow like royalty, got it?"

"Yes, sir, that's the name of the game—limo service with a smile," he said hanging up the phone, though he was definitely not smiling.

Sixty-five minutes later, Lester Pacheco swung the big, black Cadillac limousine into the sprawling parking lot of Chuck's Place and pulled up to the curb in front of the main entrance.

Pacheco strode in and glanced around. If he ventured into the country store or restaurant, he would know just about all the regulars, plus all of the employees. But here in the lobby, he didn't recognize anyone—it was all out-of-state truckers, just passing through, heading someplace else.

He didn't have long to wait. A fair-haired but filthy-looking young man, quickly approached and made contact.

"What took you so long?" asked Steven Darlington testily.

"Sorry, sir. Got here quick as I could. Right this way." Pacheco opened the front door and ushered the young man through. He went quickly over to the limo and opened the rear door.

As Steven Darlington slid into the back seat of the limo, Pacheco pointed out the snack bar and the mini-frig. "Help yourself to drinks and snacks."

Pacheco climbed into the driver's seat and said over his shoulder, "I understand we're going to Raymond County Regional Airport, and we'll be met by your associates."

"How long?"

Starting the car, Pacheco said, "It's only about forty-five minutes from here." He eased the big limo out of the parking lot and onto the two-lane highway, headed east.

Lester Pacheco said, "I just need to call my boss and let him know that I picked you up. He'll inform your people that we're on the way."

"Fine," said Darlington, with a full mouth. He popped the top on a small bottle of champagne.

Pacheco picked up the car phone and pressed a button. He had a brief conversation and then hung up. "Okay, my boss will let your people know we're on the way."

"Great," came the reply. Steven took another bite of the Snickers he had found in the limo bar.

A short while later, Pacheco turned the limo onto a dark driveway leading into the regional airport. At this time of night, the building was deserted. A gate stood open, and Pacheco guided the limo through and out onto the airfield, past an old hangar bay. He brought the car to a halt about forty feet from a white Lear jet.

"Just hang tight here for a second, sir, and let me verify that they're ready for you."

Pacheco got out and walked away from the car, toward the dark hangar.

Looking over his shoulder, Steven Darlington muttered to himself, "Where's *he* going?"

And that's when all hell broke loose—both rear doors of the limo suddenly jerked open. State troopers in swat gear screamed at Steven from left and right.

Steven Darlington was so startled and jumped so hard, he smashed the Hostess Twinkie he was about to take a bite of into his face and nostrils. He tossed the bottle of champagne straight up into the ceiling; it bounced around for several seconds spraying champagne about the car.

One of the troopers reached in and grabbed him, roughly snatching him out onto the tarmac. As Steven went sprawling, face-first, spread-eagle, onto the hard concrete, he glimpsed even more lawmen, guns drawn, rushing into the gleaming white jet.

Deputy Sheriff Lester Pacheco, his badge now clipped to his pocket, and County Detective Josh Handler, strolled back over to the limo.

Pacheco had spent the previous sixteen hours pulling a double-shift in his patrol car, like every other cop in the state, searching hill and dale for Steven Darlington.

"Good plan, Lester," said Detective Handler. "We had everything set up by the time you called to tell us that you were on the way. This is good. We got the kid *and* the plane all wrapped up in a nice little bow. Just talked to the DA. The plane directly ties his family, and their law firm, to the kid's escape attempt. The DA is going to give it to the Feds. He thinks the Feds will be able to indict them *all* on federal charges of conspiracy to aid and abet an escaped felon across state lines—a felony charge."

"Glad to have this brat off the street," said Pacheco. "I was getting tired of looking for him."

"Yeah," replied Handler, "they'll probably send him up to super max, now, with the big boys, and additional time for the escape attempt. He'll have plenty of time to ponder the meaning of life."

The County Detective paused briefly.

"So," Handler continued, "how'd you know it was the kid, before you even picked him up?"

"Just a hunch. Who else would be sitting at a truck stop in the middle of the night, waiting for a limo and a private plane, but a rich brat on the run from the law? As soon as I laid eyes on him in the truck stop, I knew my hunch was right. I recognized him from his mug shot. Then, I called you, to confirm that I had him. My boss from the limo company is going to be mightily pissed he lost that big payday, but I guess he'll just have to get over that."

"Well, anyway, good work, Lester," said Handler, as he and Pacheco watched Steven Darlington and the Lear jet crew, wearing leg irons and handcuffs, being shuffled toward waiting patrol cars.

"Well," said Deputy Sheriff Lester Pacheco, "I can call my sister, now, and let her know that justice has been served."

"Your sister?"

"Yeah. I was on patrol that night, so I couldn't look after my sick wife, and that helpless, eleven-year-old little girl that punk ran down and killed, was bringing her some chicken soup from across the street. That little girl's name was Lillie. She was my niece."

The Joint

Randy D. Rubin

The King of Keys and Courtyard Jesters

So y'all must be the freshest fish to flop into this bowl
of felons, fools and fucktards -- freaks born without a soul.
You are now a part of the Mississippi Criminal Control
And Rehabilitational Facility Patrol.

We got our ways of doin' things, procedures tried and true
that ain't in no damn textbook them instructors made you chew.
The first rule is they's only us, just us. The chosen few
but if you ever buck me boy, you'll find they's only… you.

'Cause you ain't fit to hold my shit, just another blue shirt bump
that keeps the keys, says 'Sir' and 'please'. I say 'That High', you just
jump; we'll get along like Donkey Kong; you hearin' me there, Hump?
Don't come at me all amphibious or you'll draw back a bloody stump.

The second rule is watch your ass, mind your business and your back,
'cause "Crazy" runs up/down these halls with 'whoop-ass' in a pillow
sack, just waiting for some 'unawares' or signs of weakness to attack,
and beat you bloody, black-and-blue, then shuffle off, back to his rack.

We in a side show carnival, boy. This Circus of the Damned is streaked
with freaks and tattooed geeks, these cell blocks are slammed with sneaks
and tweekers, window peekers with their asses monogrammed.
It reeks of piss and log jam leaks and orifices crammed.

Follow close behind, Fishy, slam tight all them metal doors.
Our next stop's the Funhouse, where swishy boys and cell block whores all
meet to eat and grease some palms and palm some greasy meat. This
floor's for men workin' hard all week, then play hard, on all fours.

I'm a take y'all to the laundry house, the greenhouse and 'the hole',
and then we'll hit the mess hall and rustle up a big ol' bowl
of pinto beans with ham hock, and some cornbread or a butter roll,
with a glass of Sassy's sweet tea to sanctify my sorry soul.

Come on now, Fishy, hurry up. Ain't got all goddam day.
Slap leather to them horses, son, the wagon train heads this-a-way:
Laundryland, where 'The Chlorine Kid' and his sidekick 'Soapy' play.
They wash away the midnight sins of mad men led astray.

Now, out here is the greenhouse where our inmates grow the weed
for them terminally ill patients and other folks in dire need.
They also raise our vegetables; grow most ever'thing from seed,
and if you Fishies seen enough, I reckon we'll proceed.

I want to show you all that one place no con wants to be.
We call this four-by-four-by-eight, The Hole, as you'll soon see.
Offenders go in naked, an additional unpleasantry.
And three days bread and water... five days if they fucks with me.

And that's the grand tour, Fishies. It's time y'all swim upstream.
Remember what I learned ya, Guards, that we're all the same team.
These criminals are not y'alls' friends, no matter how they seem.
Congratulations, Fishies, y'all now livin' the dream.

Go bust some heads and toss some beds and make 'em toe the line.
Find contraband and reprimand 'em. Make a few eyes 'shine'.
You can whack 'em in the back, just don't crack that bony spine.
Play 'em hard, there, Prison Guard, and y'all will do just fine.

Your First Night Prison Lull-a-bye

Lock-a-bye, Big Guy. Por favor, don't you cry.
Poppi gonna sing you a prison lull-a-bye.
Now hush, mi amigo, don't shed a tear,
'cause that shit don't play out too well in here.

We got nada but time together to share,
so you just forget about your old life out there.
No more cocktail parties, no more 'Boys' Nights Out'.
You and I gonna party when they call, 'Lights Out!'

So, ése, stop crying, you whiny bitch whelp,
or Poppi will make you want to cry out for... 'help!'
You're the one, did the crime! You're the one who got caught, too!
You're the dumb Motha Fucka didn't do what they ought to, so...

The Joint

Lock-a-bye, Chica, locked up in here tight.
This being your first of a lifetime of night,
I'll give you this first night to cry crocodile tears,
but then you and Big Poppi are spending some years.

I'm your husband, your boyfriend, your dad and your brother,
your best friend, your auntie, your sister, your mother.
I'll be watching you shower, and smelling your shit,
Listen to you pissin', while we kissin', swappin' spit.

We both got thirty years to life; you might as well be mine.
I'm making you my prison wife. You better say, "That's fine."
Now get some sleep, mi corazón, as tomorrow comes so soon…
and when they call, "Lights Out!" tomorrow night's our honeymoon.

So lock-a-bye, baby, por favor, don't you cry.
Your Poppi is singing you this lull-a-bye.
Hush, mi esposa, don't shed a tear,
'cause Poppi don't play that sad bullshit in here!

Homicide Note in the Key of A Minor

Ay!
Asshole's dead.
Ask me how.
Aryan piece of shit.
"Another one bites the dust!"
Air-holed that tattooed, skin-headed,
Anti-semitic, swastika branded, sorry-assed Bitch
After the guards yelled, "Lights Out!"
And HIS lights went out.
All the kid's light.
A minor, huh.
Almost seventeen.
Aw…

'I' is for Infirmary… is for 'Eye'… is for…

I woke…
as someone softly spoke,

to find a million tiny fires
burning up my blackened soul.
My white hot pain keeps searing,
Crispy vision clearing,
Single eye is tearing…
(Eye before me except after see)
(from 'see' to shining white hot, foam-capped…)
I can't… see! THIS PAIN!
This icy, nice and spicy IV in my vein
that cools my battered, deep fried broccoli brain.
Drips vying for a spot to drop,
and chillin' with my homey, Amoxicillin, fights the illin',
spillin', fillin' me up with Fentanyl and
drops of salty Summer rain.
One single drip at a Tick-Tock time—
to ease this pounding pain,
an antibiotic, almost hypnotic, anti-psychotic nursery rhyme.
A solitary tear of sadness
from the nurse who fights this plague of cell block madness,
'ploinks' into the plastic pool,
as foamy, bloody, bubbly drool
escapes my swollen, stitched-up lips;
too weak to spit out bits
of some gritty shit,
like teeth chips.
Bummed by numbed, crushed finger tips
(All eight),
But wait…
Just one numb thumb.
The thugs too dumb
(to count all the way to ten!)
to stomp them all to glass shards. But then again…
And what about all those prison guards?
Those night shift ninjas, those saviors
of the dim lit night.
Those dimwit…
knights of 'I don't give a shit!'
Those keepers of the sacred keys.
Those 'sheople' shepherds of the sheepish pleas,
and sleepless people pleading, "please!"
Who beg for help on bended knees.

What about THOSE prison guards,
who whispered 'I' is for Infirmary…
'Eye' is for Infirmary!
My EYE… my scooped out, dangling
as I lay there gurgling, strangling,
struggling, they watched him smuggling
MY eye from MY socket;
scoop it out with some spoon HE pulled out of HIS pocket
and gulp it down,
and swallow it whole,
smiling and giggling crazily.
Now I can't see…
Now, no I can't. See?

Lock Down!

Lock Down! Lock Down!
Get yo' asses on the ground!
What up?
Shut up!
Put yo' mouth
facin' south,
and yo' narrow butt up!
Turn away from my voice!
No, you haven't got a choice.
Lace yo' fingers top yo' head.
Make the slightest move – yo' dead!
Lock Down! Lock Down!
Each and every cell block clown!
This ain't cool…
Who da fool?
Everybody out the pool!
Some half-crazy 'Fruit Loop'
tired of playin' in his own poop,
tried to fly our chicken coop,
here in Constantina Wire town,
'fore we shot and pulled him down.
Lock Down! Stay Down!
'til y'all hear the siren sound,
then get yo' asses up off my ground.

There it is. All clear!
Get yo' asses up out of here!
Hurry up!
Shut up!

WTF R U N 4?

A fortune cookie fortune
was tossed into my cell.
It hit me on my baby toe
from, hell... I couldn't tell.

I opened the piece of paper –
A folded origami shame,
then threw it on the cement floor
just wondering who to blame.

'Cause it read like someone's license plate.
This one line inquisition
both pissed me off and 'creeped' me out,
this phantom's brazen imposition.

"None your Goddam business!"
I yelled out 'cross the blocks.
"Don't bother me with stupid shit;
Go yank off in your spank-off socks!"

"Quit trying to be funny, Bitch.
I'll kill y'all in your sleep.
You'll hear giggling while you're gurgling,
I'll slice y'all open, wide and deep."

So don't be tossin' notes at me with
WTF R U N 4?
You ignorant, inbred dimwits
who think you know the 'score';

know I was once an English teacher,
some 'twenty-five to life' ago.
An "A" student, an accident,
a high school talent show.

Blame had to fall on someone, see,
they had to put a lid on rage.
A light bar broke its bindings
and killed that precious kid on stage.

So I was the Director,
and the adult that was shamed.
The School Board backed the Parents,
and I became the name they blamed.

They sued me and they screwed me,
and they 'had to let me go'.
They tried me and they fried me,
and I died inside, you know?

So leave my sorry ass alone.
I'm just wishing I was dead.
The last dumbass who asked me shit
was found with deep cuts in his head.

I'm not here, Bitch, to socialize
by written cell phone text.
Keep fuckin' with me, Asshole,
and I promise you'll be next.

Suicide Note #1 in the Key of B

Bars.
Bunk sheets,
braided and tied.
Barnum and Bailbond treats,
Big ticket items I tried
but could not find my receipts.
Blubbering with tears, I tie my feets.
Bending my head down I cried,
Because to everyone I lied.
Better tighten this noose.
Bug eyed blues…
Been real…
Bye!

Punch and Judy

There's this puppet show next cell to mine
that no one's ever seen,
'cept the puppeteer and puppet.
Punch and Judy's who I mean.

They share the cell beside me,
though "share's" a broken shiv.
Let's say it's really Punch's pad
where Judy's forced to somehow live.

Each night's a fresh performance
whenever Punch has nightly needs,
an hour or so past 'lights out',
the predator on his prey, feeds.

Punch's given name is Perry,
and Judy's name is really Jack,
but it got changed to Judy,
by Perry sometime two years back.

He swears to punch the teeth out
of any man who calls him Jack.
Just ask the five who challenged him—
All toothless from his last attack.

So Jack he was, now Judy is,
and will be from now on,
as well as Punch's mistress,
his punching bag and prison pawn.

My cell mate went to stop it once,
to hush the awful, anguished cries,
but for his vain, heroic stand,
Punch pounced and ate one of his eyes.

So Judy's left to screaming now,
through twisted, bloody pillow case,
and if his cries get too damn loud,
Punch lands a pounding to his face.

The whispering and whimpering
bring tears of rage to hardened men,

who lay there, fists clenched in the dark,
forced to listen to them once again

perform this show, this tragedy,
this cell block midnight passion-play,
this veritable travesty,
this kidney pounding butt-ballet.

He takes him and he shakes him;
makes him beg or say his name.
And finally he breaks him
down until he plays a bitch's game,

like, "Who's your daddy, Judy?"
"Don't you love the way that feels?"
"Let me hear you say you love me"
"Show me how a piggy squeals."

This asshole-taking asshole,
beating up a guy too weak to fight,
making us all hate him,
listening helpless almost every night

as Judy gets his ass tore up
and kidney punches take their toll,
while pieces of his mind peel off;
set sail with slivers of his soul.

But Perry doesn't give a fuck
from where his cell mate bleeds,
as long as there's a guy to suck
him off and fill his lusty needs.

"Who cares if Judy's pissing blood
and needs a new kidney?"
"Who gives a shit if he's got AIDS?"
"It damn sure didn't come from me!"

He yells out to his audience.
He screams it over and over each night.
He laughs a madman's cackle,
and we all know Punch's head ain't right.

We called the guards to save him

when he couldn't get up out of bed,
'cause Punch had punched him in the neck
so damned hard both his eyeballs bled.

They finally came and took Jack out.
That man was damn near dead.
They say he suffered broken bones
in twenty-two places on his head.

Punch wouldn't let them touch him.
He had to be sedated
with a tranquilizer pistol dart.
They shot him and they waited,

until at last, he hit the floor,
and then they brought a stretcher,
and a new guard radioed for the doc,
as another guard ran to fetch her.

Now Jack's in the infirmary
under a prison doctor's care.
The nurses claimed a miracle
or God's grace kept him breathing there.

The Warden sent Punch to the hole
for nigh on ninety-seven days,
to suffer for his madness
and repent for all his crazy ways.

Punch laughed, he cried, he 'tripped off line',
and hummed some dumbass whispered song
that only lonely psychos learn
when left alone for far too long.

Then halfway through them crazy days,
Jack paid his check but left no tip.
The waitresses and Maître D'
had teary eyes and quivering lip

when Jack whispered his final words
into a nurse's offered ears.
He closed his bruised and battered eyes
and said, "I'm out of tears."

The next day, Punch was visited
by our doctor and a nurse,
to perform a routine check-up
and ensure, "Punch wasn't getting worse."

His illnesses were diagnosed
(not documented, mind you).
The doctor had a 'Special Cure'
for Punch. "Nurse look behind you

and make sure no one disturbs us
while we do our tests and check
his pulse and O2 levels
with a syringe in his tattooed neck,

filled with sedative and air bubbles
to stop his evil beating heart."
"This should have been done years ago--
Punch executed from the start."

"So let's leave Perry sleeping,
to heal his wicked ways.
Do not disturb; no food or drink
for at least a couple days."

We'll call what he got, "Justice"
with payback as his costly cure.
If anyone deserves this fate,
it's Punch's sorry ass, I'm sure.

Cheap Chardonnay

I'm just a wino.
What the hell do I know?
It don't make a fiddler's fuck, end of the day.

I got twenty to life,
'cause I murdered my wife
on two lousy glasses of cheap Chardonnay.
Just two drinks too much and they put me away!

It was Holiday season.
I know, that's no reason,

but damn it, I don't drink that often, okay?

We had gone to these parties
at Mary's and Marty's,
but first there was Artie's Bar, there on the way.

We stopped for a few
(or like, three more than two),
but then looked at each other and swore, "We can't stay."

We finished the last one
and left some time past one,
or maybe one-thirty, I really can't say.

We were both doing fine
'til we purchased that wine—
Those two lousy bottles of cheap chardonnay.
That fermented grape juice that put me away.

So we drove and we drank,
and I've got God to thank
for not killing a soul 'fore that second soiree.

My old lady was sacked out,
and I must have blacked out,
'cause I can't recall that drunken melee'

that they all say I fought,
as I came in and caught
my drunk wife riding Marty and deep-throating Ray,
and holding a bottle of cheap chardonnay.

Mary got so upset and
kept cursing and threatened
us, "I'll kill you both if you don't go away!"

My wife climbed in the back seat
with no shoes on her feet
and then puked and passed out in my damned Chevrolet.
Barfed up cum, sour vomit, and that cheap chardonnay.

I slammed the door shut
on my fuckin' drunk slut
of a wife, and somehow, I can't say,

The Joint

I started the car,
but we didn't get too far,
before we drove off the bridge into the bay.

I jumped before impact,
but her neck and skull cracked
when she smacked the windshield and broke the ashtray.

The cops finally came,
and said I was to blame.
It took two teams of divers the entire day

to swim downstream and find her.
This constant reminder;
this inherent sadness I forever replay

is due to my drinking
and driving, I'm thinking,
that moribund vintage with dismal bouquet.
Those two deadly bottles of cheap Chardonnay.

Suicide Note in the Key of F (not so sharp, mostly flat)

Finally!
Fuck this.
Free at last.
Figured it all out.
First tie me a noose.
Fit said noose over my head.
Firmly tighten noose knot around my neck.
Fasten other end to top bars.
Feet tied together on chair.
Flip chair and dangle.
Falling forward... Floor!
Failed again.
Fool!

I Didn't Wake Up in a Killing Mood...

I didn't wake up in a killing mood
when I rolled myself out of the bed.

The demons slept peacefully most of the night,
and nobody ended up dead in my head.

I didn't wake up in a killing mood
when I shuffled to "Line Up!" at six.
Then somebody slipped some foul shit in my food,
that oozes most nights out their dicks.

I didn't wake up in a killing mood
when I went up to bus my own tray,
and a big burly bastard with bad attitude
decided to get in my way.

I didn't wake up in a killing mood,
but this huge tattooed dude said I owed him.
He slapped my tray away, which I felt was quite rude,
so I bit off his earlobe and showed him...

That I didn't wake up in a killing mood
when I walked in and sat down to eat.
It'd be best if they left me to my solitude,
and let me return to my seat.

I didn't wake up in a killing mood,
but the day's dealing 'aces and eights'
in a game of cards where this one-eyed Jack dude
beats four-of-a-kind and all 'straights'.

I didn't wake up in a killing mood
when I headed to work in the kitchen,
where they had this young new guy stripped totally nude,
and took turns raping his ass for snitchin'.

I didn't wake up in a killing mood,
but I swear to God, this guy in 'group',
they found his dead baby half-barbecued,
and his wife's head made into soup.

I didn't wake up in a killing mood
'til they made us go back to our cell,
and I could just feel myself coming unglued
when I couldn't locate that nasty-assed smell.

I didn't wake up in a killing mood,

The Joint

but then some asshole shit in my bunk.
It wasn't my cellmate; he isn't that crude,
and wouldn't put up with that funk.

I didn't wake up in a killing mood
as they herded us out to the yard,
where the 'Kings' can assemble each ethnic brood,
and flex muscles all sculpted and hard.

I didn't wake up in a killing mood
while I went out to bench press some weights.
It didn't take long 'fore the shit storm ensued
between two 'hulks' and two new inmates.

I didn't wake up in a killing mood
when they made us all lay in the dirt,
while they finally got all the fighters subdued
before anyone else could get seriously hurt.

I didn't wake up in a killing mood
'til this gay guy in group started sayin'
big words like, "verisimilitude"
with his HIV spittle a-sprayin'.

I didn't wake up in a killing mood
when I happened to find that damn shiv
someone obviously planted so I would get screwed
if they searched my cell... where I live.

I didn't wake up in a killing mood
when some prick wiped his ass on my towel
in the shower, when I was soaped up and shampooed
and I started to smell something foul.

I didn't wake up in a killing mood,
But, dear God, please give the strength,
and restore a small measure of man's faith renewed...
or a pipe about three feet in length!

I didn't wake up in a killing mood,
then I missed out on my evening meal,
because my 'mouthpiece' showed up and reviewed
my second conviction appeal.

205

I didn't wake up in a killing mood
when she told me there wasn't a chance
of overturning the ruling – "You'd
better get used to your dire circumstance."

I didn't wake up in a killing mood
when I found out they'd shredded my mail,
that told me my sister OD'd on Quaalude
the day after her release from jail.

I didn't wake up in a killing mood
when the warden said my 'Moms' was dead.
You see, these Fucks got no moral turpitude,
and the rest of these Schmucks are inbred.

I didn't wake up in a killing mood
after "Lock Down!" and "Lights Out!" are sounded,
when half of the fellas are forced to be lewd,
and the others are punched and ass-pounded.

I didn't doze off in a killing mood.
The demon dreams still held at bay
by a peaceful escape into quietude
until I wake up, homicidal, next day.

Suicide Note #2 in The Key of G Sharp

Go!
Get out!
God Damn him.
Give me that shiv;
Goin' to slit his neck.
Guy don't get to keep raping
girls and then hide in here forever,
giggling like some kind of lunatic.
Gurgling on his own juices.
Gravy oozing out his…
Gutted me good.
Giblets spillin'
Goo…

The Joker and Ol' One-Eyed Jack

Couple of old cards, these two;
wasting space inside these hallowed walls
and carved into the doors of shitter stalls
with the penis hieroglyphics, true,

but...

The Joker and Ol' One-Eyed Jack
been here a long, long time, Cuz,
and won't say zackly what they crime was
some forty-five years back

or

how they both ended up here
eleven presidents or so ago,
befo' yo' ugly mama was a thirty dolla' ho
and yo' daddy smoked a fatty and became a dumpster queer.

Hey!

Don't cut that look at me, Bitch.
I's only messin' wit yo' sorry ass.
Gon' pull out that piece of broken glass.
I'll cut you like I did that snitch.

Uh huh...

I was tryin' to tell the fellas 'bout
The Joker and Ol' One-Eyed Jack.
Some say they both attempted some damn terrorist attack.
Said The Joker took Jack's eye over somethin' he was jealous 'bout,

but then...

no one's really certain
'bout that A-rab and that one-eyed Jew
'cept if you fuck wit one you better plan to fuck wit two,
and you'll definitely leave there hurtin'

'cause...

207

they may be old but they don't play!
They'll leave you dying in yo' cell
or make it look like you just up and fell
wit that Israeli combat shit they learned way back in Moses' day,

like,

befo' the Pharaoh let his people go.
The Joker and Ol' One-Eyed Jack
been like brothers now since way, way back
when Moby Dick was just a minnow.

So...

The Joker and Ol' One-eyed Jack
ain't playin' wit full decks no mo'.
Time dealt them shitty hands fo' sho',
and now we leave them dinosaurs to just kick back

or

listen to The Joker tell his brand new daily joke
that's as old and tired as that ancient tella'
and Jack just grins at that crazy A-rab fella--
An unlikely pair of kings, those folk.

Straight...

But very much a touching tale of love.
The Joker passed away from a heart attack
and a stroke in the night took Ol' One-eyed Jack
back to The Joker and a better card game up above.

It's Showtime!

Ten more minutes until Showtime, folks.
(I have the best seat in the house – front row center.)
I asked for a drink. I got it. BAM!
Last night I ordered ribeye steak, baked potato, asparagus. BAM!
(You can't beat the service in this establishment.)
Holy-Moly! Would you look at the size of the audience for this –
it's standing room only back there!

The Joint

"Now I'm a Superstar!"
Whoa, show's about to start – places everyone!
They're about to dim the lights.
Leather straps… black hood…
(More cool water)
Metal cap fits good.
Gentlemen, dim the lights.
It's Showtime!

Responsibility

A. R. Shannon

Dating's a bitch when you're an executioner.

I usually end up telling my dates I'm a prison guard instead, but sometimes even that's problematic. A lot of men are used to the cheap premise of porn movies. They think there's some kind of hanky-panky going on, but it couldn't be further from the truth.

Hell, if they caught you making out at work, your ass'd be out on the street before you knew what hit you.

But I digress. Cheap porn aside, I flip the switch, pull the lever, or, in my specific case, push the button that starts the whole process.

They don't suffer, my clients. Not since the accident, anyway, unless their consciences hit them. We have a professional team, with an RN who places the catheter in their veins, and we make sure they're completely unconscious before the lethal dose goes in. If they have any pangs, then they're pangs of regret, not of pain.

Never any pain.

And you might think I'm mean and heartless, or I get off on death, but that's not true, either. I don't get off on doing it, any more than the trash man gets off on dumping the trash. It's just a job, and I treat it responsibly and professionally. And trust me, when the end comes for my clients, they usually have it a lot better than their victims ever did. So yeah, I'm interested in my job, but I don't get off on it.

What I do get off on is being spanked.

There are a thousand theories on why that is, but I don't know... I just like it. I can't explain why. Ever since I was a little girl, I fantasized about it. Maybe it's because I grew up without a father in my life. In fact, I'll bet it's because of that, because my fantasy spanker's always an older man dressed in a suit, or at least slacks and a button-down shirt and tie. He always takes me by the hand and leads me into his study or my bedroom and lectures me, and then he rolls up his sleeves and bends me over and blisters my ass. I pay a guy to do it now, but that's starting to lose its charm.

What I want is a spanker all my own; someone who'll be around to cuddle me after and take good care of me, someone who'll look after me.

In short, I want love. With spankings. And I want to be able to be honest about my career. A tall order, I know, but there it is.

* * *

I have a date on Friday with this handsome warden from the state prison in Visalia, a man who's already familiar with my work and who I won't have to lie to. I can't tell you what a relief that'll be. I sometimes think I sabotage my relationships so I won't have to live a lie. With Jerry – that's his name, Jerry Collins – I won't have that problem. He already knows what I do and we've worked together, so I know he even approves of and respects me.

When Friday comes, I wear a pink sundress – anything but black. I fix my hair and makeup so I look more my age, which is twenty-seven, and I wait nervously for my date. He's got a room nearby, since it's quite a drive from Visalia to where I live, and he's all set to spend the entire weekend here.

Suddenly, there's a knock at the door, and I know it's him. I ask him in while I finish getting ready.

The dress I'm wearing sashays when I walk and makes my ass look fantastic. If he's a spanko, like I hope he is, it'll make him zero in on my butt. However, he's one of those guys who are hard to read, so I really don't know if he likes to play. Kind of like me, he keeps to himself.

Oh, well. All I can do is hope.

It's been a long time since I went on a date, even longer since I've been spanked thoroughly, and I'm dying to be face-down over his knee, staring at the carpet. I hope he's not too soft on me. I hope he knows what he's doing.

"So. Thank you for coming all the way up here to see me," I tell him.

"No problem. You'd be surprised how few women want to date a prison warden."

"Not really."

"Oh, yeah," he laughs nervously. "You've got that whole zap thing going on."

"Don't be silly," I tell him. "We haven't zapped anyone in a long time. Not since Freddie Lasko burst into flames. Besides, we're the progressive state, remember?"

"What are you going to do if California abolishes the death penalty again?"

"Move to another state, I guess. Ready?"

"Yeah, sure. You'll have to direct me."

* * *

As we eat dinner and talk, I start liking him more and more. I know I'll ask him in after the date, but I still don't know if he's a spanko or not, and I feel shy about bringing it up. He's wearing a thick leather belt, but I try not to stare at it because I don't want him thinking I'm checking out his crotch.

What's a poor spanko to do?

"So, how about Nelson?" he asks, about a recent client of mine. "He was a tough one, wasn't he?"

"I hate when they put up a fight. I always feel like they should've thought of the consequences first."

"We used to be able to strap them if they got out of line."

"Times are changing."

"But I really miss the strappings."

As he says this, he looks directly at me, and I know it's an invitation to get the dialogue going, so I take it.

"Well, there are other outlets," I tell him.

"Yeah?"

"All you need to do is find yourself a lady who enjoys a little rough play."

"Maybe I already have," he says.

"Maybe."

"Let's finish up and get the hell out of here."

* * *

When we get back to my place, I'm unlocking the door and he's all over me, smelling my hair and caressing my ass.

"You have stockings on. The kind that use a garter belt."

"Yes, I do," I answer, finally getting the door unlocked and opening it. "Please, come in."

What man would turn down an offer like that? Certainly not him. He takes me in his arms and starts kissing me. He tastes of the Cabernet Sauvignon we had at dinner, and his breath is nice and warm. He's human, and I can feel his cock straining against his pants.

We flop down on the couch and start making out. He's a good kisser and he pays the proper amount of attention to my breasts, squeezing them and tweaking my nipples. He does that for a while, and then he moves in for the kill. He drops his hand and rubs me through my silk panties. I can't tell you how wild this drives me. I help him shrug off his sports jacket and loosen his tie, and then I start unbuttoning his shirt.

"Hold on," he says. "Take off your dress."

My dress just zips up the back, and I get up and let him unzip me. I shimmy out of it and lay it neatly aside, and I'm standing there in my bra and high heels, panties and stockings.

"Come here," he says, smoothing down his shirt. "Stand here."

He starts unbuttoning his cuffs, and I'm dying for him to roll up his sleeves as he watches me. With a stern look on his face, like he's read my mind, he does exactly that. My heart leaps with joy, and I crave the hard spanking I hope he'll give me. I need it. I need a good, hard spanking, and I need to be brought to tears. It's not easy to make me cry, since I'm not prone to tears and I can take a lot, but Jerry scoots back on the couch and pats his lap.

"Come on. Over you go."

I pause, because no matter how badly I want this, it's hard to put myself over any man's lap, so he leans forward and grabs my wrist, jerking me down until the momentum takes over. Once I'm down, he arranges me until I'm lying across his lap, all stretched out on the couch. He rubs my bottom, telling me how hard he's going to spank me and how sorry he'll make me.

"And when I'm done with that, I'm going to take you into that bedroom and fuck the shit out of you."

I picture him leading me by the hand to the bedroom, my sore, hot bottom throbbing. The image makes me squirm and he smacks my upper thigh.

"Be still," he commands.

I obey, and I know my pussy is slick and swollen. I want him to start, but he draws it out.

"First, I'm going to warm you up with my hand, and then you're getting the belt."

"Please," I say.

"No. You deserve this and you know it."

He tugs at my panties and makes me lift up so he can take them down, and I expect him to go about mid-thigh, but he pulls them all the way off. They get tangled in my heels for a moment, but he untangles them and hands them to me.

"You hold onto those," he tells me.

I feel marvelous lying there in my bra and garter belt, the garters framing my ass. Jerry reaches down and rubs my bare cunt, clicking his tongue to shame me.

"Look at this, you dirty, dirty girl."

I squirm again, trying for something to rub my clit up against, but he slaps my thigh again and threatens to skip the warm-up. I lay still, the suspense killing me, wondering how bad it'll hurt, wondering just how far I'll have to go to make myself cry.

"Have you got anything to say for yourself?" he asks me.

"No."

"No, what?"

"Sir."

"Then let's begin. First of all, let's address this arousal of yours. You're here for discipline, not for pleasure."

The first stinging slap hits my ass and I know right away he'll be a good spanker. He smacks my ass with crisp precision, making me gasp with pleasure. Before I know it, he's all over my butt, spanking it top, bottom, and sides.

Never before have I had the sides of my ass spanked, and the skin is tender there. I squirm and kick a little, and this time, he lets me.

"This is a long time coming," he tells me. "You've needed this for months."

"Yes, sir."

He stops, and I feel him working at his belt buckle, trying to get the belt loose. He does, and he loops it over, doubling it. I wait in heavy anticipation. The tension's thick, and so's the belt, and when he finally wields it, I let out a yelp. The belt catches me and wraps, and after about a dozen good licks like this, tears start to my eyes.

Something within me, some innate stubbornness, prevents me from crying, but I can sense he'll spank me to tears no matter how long it takes to break me down.

My ass is on fire, and I think about Freddie Lasko, poor bastard. I trembled there with my hand on the switch, but what could I do? The man's head was on fire, flames shooting three feet high. I'm an experienced executioner, and I've presided over a lot of them, but this time, even I had to turn away.

"Why are you being stubborn with me?" he asks.

"Because I feel bad about Lasko."

"You can't blame yourself for everything that happens to these men. They have to bear some of the responsibility, too."

I don't say anything else, so he goes back to spanking me. I kick and writhe to lessen the pain, but it's no good. In fact, it makes matters a good deal worse, since it makes him punish my thighs, too.

"Too hard," I tell him. "They haven't been warmed up."

"You want them warmed up?" he asks me. "Put your arms out in front of you and grab the arm of the couch. In fact, get up and bend over it instead."

I struggle up to do as I'm told, but I still have my panties in my hand.

"What do I do with these?" I ask, holding them out to show him.

"Put them in your mouth and bend over."

When I do, he comes up behind me and pushes my head down. I feel myself shudder as he reaches down and unhooks my stockings, and then removes my garter belt altogether. I feel naked without it, vulnerable. He gets right to work again, welting my ass and thighs. My butt's blazing, and I know I ought to just fake it and pretend to cry, but somehow I can't.

"You're a willful little brat, and you deserve every bit of this spanking. Spread your legs. I want to see everything. I want to see that cute little cunt clench up every time I lay one on you."

I've never felt so visible and open, so humble. The belt snaps against my flesh, wrapping itself around my thigh and coming very close to hitting me where it counts. The air whooshes between my spread legs, startling me, making me fear a lash to the cunt. I try to close my legs just a little, but he stops me.

"Keep them spread," he orders. "When I'm done with you, you won't sit for a month."

I think of Freddie Lasko again and wonder if he could've benefited by a few beatings like this. Then I think about myself and how hard I have to be in daily life, how chewed up and spit out I'm starting to feel, because legal or not, I'm little better than a murderer myself.

"Don't do that to yourself," he says, as if reading my mind. "You're a good, kind woman. It's your job that's ugly, not you. Right?"

"Yes, sir."

Not having to be made of stone feels good right now. I can be soft and ordinary, a dirty little slut bent over with her ass presented for punishment, panties shoved in her mouth and her stockings crumpled down around her ankles.

The thought makes me yearn for clothing.

I need something on me, but he reaches out and unhooks my bra, my last defense. It slides down my arms, but I want to grab it and put it back on.

I can't take the nudity.

He really knows how to work a sub over, old Jerry. He comes up alongside me and rubs my ass soothingly. With his other hand, he pinches my nipples. Being punished by Jerry is better than any trip to a BDSM club I've ever had.

He moves on from rubbing my ass to petting my pussy, which is shamefully wet. His finger makes a little squishy sound when it invades me, and he inserts a second. My hungry pussy swallows them up, and when he withdraws them, I feel bereft. Jerry stoops and picks up the belt again, and I ready myself for more.

All he does is run it up and down my legs.

The cool leather feels good as I lay there trembling. I'm wondering what's in store as he rubs the belt down over my cunt.

He can't be going to spank me there, too, can he?

"Can a belt give you an orgasm?" he asks. "Let's find out together."

I can't help but respond when he presses the cool leather up against my clit.

"That's right," he tells me. "Fuck my belt like a good girl."

I bite my lip and get started. The dampness in my pussy lubricates the belt as Jerry holds it up there tight. I hump away at it, thinking crazy thoughts in my head, that he'll think I'm a whore and never come back, that he'll spread bad rumors about me around the prison. These are things I'd normally care very much about, since I keep to myself, but I'm all stripped down and my legs are spread so I can ride this almost-total-stranger's belt, and that's all I care about right now.

"Responsibility," he says, grabbing a handful of hair and hauling me up to look at him. "You have to surrender all responsibility for what happened that day."

I nod, partly because I understand him and partly because that's all I can do with the panties still wadded up in my mouth. He drops my head back down and I concentrate.

"That's right," he tells me in a soft voice. "Fuck away all those bad memories."

I feel the tension mounting inside me, and I know I'm going to come soon. I also know I'll cry when I do, and suddenly, something twists inside me and snaps, like a rubber band that's been pulled too tight. I collapse onto the arm of the couch in tears, still fucking away at the belt until our goal is reached at last. Jerry tosses the belt down on the couch and comes to me, turning me towards him and guiding my head against his shoulder. It's a nice, warm shoulder, and I take advantage of it and cry for a while. He rocks me in his arms and pulls the panties out of my mouth so he can kiss me.

What he does then is, he slings an arm around my shoulders and leads me to the bedroom. It's just like I hoped it would be, and he lays me down gently on the bed. He sheds his own clothes and makes sweet love to me, just the way I always imagined.

And I know I'm safe.

And I know I'm cared for.

And I know I've finally found a new dom, or at least a way to get Killer Lasko – and all the others – off my mind.

Either/or's good enough for me, but both would be amazing.

Finding the Answer
Travis Richardson

Martha can't stand being here any longer. She's never liked being the center of attention, and this is too much. There's too much going on. Too much happiness. Too much joy. Her younger sister, Mary, Mary's husband, their children, their children's children. Perfect, idyllic bliss. She can't believe she has freakin' grandnieces. All of them pure and unscathed. They are all trying very hard, putting on brave smiles, though their nervous eyes reveal fear. She's seen that look plenty of times. Nice freakin' homecoming.

The silence is awkward as everybody stands in the shade of the barn, holding plastic cups of lemonade, waiting for the burgers to cook. Nobody's saying much. Definitely nothing of substance that means anything. Mostly, they're staring off at the cows in the pasture while stealing glances at the notorious legend, Auntie Martha. But it isn't the family's nervousness that motivates Martha to drop her cup and set off on a long walk to the Nathansons' farm.

No. It's a question that is burning inside her. Deeper than what could've been… What life might have been like if… Would she have a husband and children? A nice, cozy house? Acres of land?

"Martha," Mary says, running up to her. "Where you headin' to? The burgers are just about ready."

"I need to find out something."

"What's that?"

Martha bites her lip as she continues walking. She knows what she is looking for… sort of. But she can't express it. It's a question that's been burning acid inside her soul, yet to formalize it, to ask the question proper, she needs to be there. She has to go back to the place.

"Y'all carry on. I'll be back shortly."

"But…"

Martha shoots Mary a glare. She's not sure what it looks like, exactly. The expression is automatic. She's given it to hundreds over the years. It says, 'get the hell back or else.' Mary stops dead in her tracks, turning pale.

Although she feels bad and would like to apologize, Martha walks on. If she is going to continue in this world, she has to know. One footstep follows another as her canvas shoes peel off the sticky blacktop. She passes familiar pastures of her childhood, rows of okra, peas, and corn, with occasional cattle lounging under the shade of trees.

When she did this walk as a kid, it didn't seem like it took too much effort. Now, her joints, the arches of her feet, and pretty much everything else aches. To top it off, it looks like God has gotten into the mix. As if her physical suffering isn't enough, the vastness of the sky above, the infinite endless blue, is bearing down, trying to crush her into something puny and insignificant again.

Martha wipes sweat from her face. It would be easy to lie down in a ditch and curl up in a ball. Just curl up while the weeds grow up all around and let the elements do their damage. Anger surges through her body. She squints, looking up towards the white flaming ball of the sun.

"Sorry, Lord, I ain't gonna let you discourage me yet. I gotta go there and find the answer."

After five miles of trudging in the unrelenting Oklahoma heat, she stops at a rusted barbed wire fence with a 'NO TRESPASSING' sign. This is the place. There was a time when cattle and horses roamed under the pecan trees. Now, it looks like an ocean of weeds under the dying, webworm-infested trees. Holding up a taut, filthy wire with one hand and stomping on a lower one with her foot, she ducks through the little opening. Her knees pop, and her denim shirt snags on a sharp, rusted barb before she frees it.

Ain't as flexible as I used to be, she thinks. *Ain't a lot of the things I used to be.*

Pushing through the waist-high yellowing weeds now covering the old gravel road, grasshoppers spring upward to the sky and flap their noisy wings that only push them a few feet further. As Martha advances, it seems like the same hoppers keep jumping, caught in a cycle. She knows what it's like.

Finally, she comes upon the house in all its decaying glory. A dilapidated, two-story oracle that holds the answers. Except for a murder of crows cawing from the roof, it's long been abandoned. A smirk escapes Martha's lips.

"This is appropriate enough, Lord. Symbolism an' all that, with these harbingers of death."

Harbinger. Now there's a word she hasn't used in a long time. There was a time when she'd had a decent sized vocabulary. Winning the school spelling bee in front of teachers and family, she might've gone further if she hadn't frozen up with fright at the Greenbelt County Bee, with hundreds of strangers watching. Li'l ol' Martha Green.

A flood of nostalgia slams her. Hard.

She remembers folks talking about her decades ago. How could that sweet li'l girl have done such an awful thing?

What the hell did they know? Nobody knew what it was like to be Martha Green, the plump, awkward girl who wore long skirts and memorized Bible verses. Martha, the shy child who always obeyed her parents, who never swore, who never did anything wrong at any time, even when adults weren't around. Those idiots didn't know about her humiliation. What it was like to be teased by thin girls and ignored by boys, until Brandon…

***

Dreamy Brandon Nathanson was tall, strong, and popular. Every girl wanted him, but he'd chosen the shy nerd, Martha Green. He invited her to his home, this house, while his parents were on vacation. Within minutes of entering his bedroom, he savaged her virginity. Dressing afterwards, she flushed with excitement, tinged with guilt. She had marital relations with Brandon, doing everything he had asked without reservation. She had been his harlot for an hour. For Brandon, she would've walked a mile on her knees; she would've murdered her family for him. Her heart swelled.

Descending the stairs, Martha saw Brandon waiting for her. His muscular arms were crossed, and a sneer formed across his lips. She smiled at her lover. She saw their initials scrawled together on notebooks encircled with hearts. Saw their hands entwined as they strolled past Cindy Sinclair and Gwen Winslow in the hallways. She loathed those skinny bitches who taunted her and spewed hate.

"What the hell took you so long?"

She sauntered over to Brandon with arms open, wanting to hold him, needing to be held. A thought flashed through her mind, had they even kissed yet, or had they just skipped ahead to the sinful stuff?

He shoved her away.

"Get your hands off me, you filthy pig slut."

Martha felt like she had been punched in the gut. She could hardly breathe. He couldn't have said that. Not her Brandon. Maybe it was a joke.

"What are you waiting for? Get out of here, you disgusting fat slut."

Shocked, she couldn't move. Brandon grabbed her by the hair and dragged her out the back door. Shoving her outside, she fell, scraping her knees on the lacquered porch. Through her tear-streaked eyes, she saw him framed by the doorway.

"Don't you dare tell anybody what we did, or I'll kill you," he said.

Finding the Answer

Standing on the porch now, splintered and broken, Martha's eyes mist with tears. *Why did you have to be so cruel? Why, Brandon?* She understands now that he was probably using her to gain experience, but that bastard didn't have to be so cold-hearted to get her out of the house. Did he? She wipes away the tears and walks through the busted doorframe. She doesn't want to enter, but she must. She needs to see it all again if she's going to ask the question.

***

After Brandon booted Martha out of his house, she staggered five painful miles home with blood running down her knees. She cried all night in her room and missed school the following day. Her heart, which she had protected for years, was shattered and stomped into the ground. She desperately wanted to die. It was the only way she knew how to end the hurt. Opening her father's desk drawer, she pulled out his Colt semi-automatic. It was cold and heavy. So much heavier than she remembered when she had gone shooting with him. Turning the weapon towards her at a forty-five-degree angle, she stared into the dark hollow of the barrel, her thumb on the trigger. Taking a deep breath, she squeezed her eyes shut, but not the trigger. No. Absolutely not. She wouldn't do it. Martha Green would not kill herself.

She returned to Brandon's house the next day; the place where she'd become a woman and then died on the same day. She had a plan. She'd stick the Colt to Brandon's head and force him to apologize... and then have him touch her again.

Entering through the back door, she could tell he was home. His scent was strong. The house was dark and quiet. She crept upstairs to his room. Bullet chambered. Hammer cocked. Pushing open his bedroom door, Martha found Brandon, back turned, on the bed. But he was not alone. His hands cupped her tormentor's breasts.

"Oh. My. God. It's... her," Cindy Sinclair said in her snotty voice.

Brandon turned. The ugly sneer on his face was too much. She watched his lips part, hissing an *S*, about to form the word 'slut'. But Martha would not let him say it. *Bang-bang-bang!* She emptied the magazine into both of them.

***

Standing inside Brandon's room now, it is stripped bare. No bed, no posters of cars and bikini-clad women, not even the thick shag carpet. Only rotting fragments of the wall are left. Instead of bloodstains, green and black patches of mold are splattered throughout.

"This is the place where everything changed," she says, to nobody in particular. Four life-altering events happened in this house. First love, virgin sex, heartbreak, and murder. All in the span of twenty-four hours.

That was thirty years ago. The following years were full of bland food, crowded cells, icy showers, fistfights, improvised shivs – slicing and being sliced – and the inevitable, long stints in solitary confinement that followed. Life was hard in prison, so Martha had become harder. Nobody ever said a disparaging word about Martha and didn't regret it. Martha Green had become a force to be reckoned with. A woman that nobody forsook or used.

Descending down the rickety stairs and rushing outside, she takes a breath of air. Air that is free and unrestrained. Like she is today, right now at this moment. She turns.

It's time to ask the question that drove her here. Drove her from the welcome home party at her sister's house.

"Was it worth it?" she whispers. The time lost, the family she never had, the meek life she never lived.

The biggest crow of the murder caws, jerking its head up and down adamantly. A smile emerges, exposing Martha's gray teeth. She straightens her spine and eases her shoulders back.

"Yes, it was," she says to the observant crows. "It was *damn* worth it."

The Flea Jar

Layla Cummins

One of my earliest memories is of watching my mother pick fleas off the cat and hold their bodies underwater until they drowned. She'd sit on the sofa, or her bed—whichever was more comfortable—and scoop a cat up onto her lap. She'd scratch it behind the ears until it settled and then switch to long sweeping massages, probing its fur with her thin, skeletal fingers.

"I can feel them, you know," she'd say, smiling at me. "I'm a natural."

After the initial sweep, she would move in, focusing on a particular spot, green eyes darting like a vulture.

"The best places are on the neck and belly. The fleas feed at the neck, and the belly is dark and safe for them. But sometimes they will hide deep in the fur."

When I was younger and still learning, she'd show me all the tell-tale signs.

"Look, Carl, those little powdery black bits. Can you see? *Flea feces.* Do you know what feces is?" I shook my head. "It's shit, Carl," she said. "Flea shit. Dirt."

We'd spend whole afternoons sitting in our damp living room, me watching her at work. She'd trawl through fur and gasp when she saw a big, fat flea scurrying through the hairs. If the flea was quick, it would slip through her fingers and my mother would chase it, flipping the sleeping cat over when the flea vanished into a place she couldn't reach. Of course, even the most docile of cats didn't like this kind of treatment and they would try to scratch and bite her hands. If Mother lost a flea this way, she would explode.

"Come and help me find it!" she'd scream, and we'd spend hours trying to coax the cat out from some dark and dusty corner where it had tried to hide.

***

It must be Wednesday. Dr. Havilland has come to visit me again, like he always does. He sits on the same blue, hard plastic chair turned at a slight angle, wearing the same, fuzzy brown suit and matching tie. He

223

keeps a brass pocket watch close to his chest and sometimes pats it as if he's making sure it's still there. He is silent for a while, but then he speaks, always in the same low, steady voice.

"Carl, do you know where you are right now?"

I do, but I don't answer him. I've known since the beginning, when they wheeled me in, showed me to my room and introduced me to Nurse.

Dr. Havilland sighs and leans back on the chair. I hear this, but I don't see it. The straps across my wrists and head make it difficult.

***

Once a week, my mother would scour the local papers for unwanted kittens and bring home batches to experiment with. I was never allowed to go with her to these mysterious kitten farms.

"You'll get too attached, Carl. It's better that you stay here." She immediately weeded out the aggravators; kittens who were prone to scratching and biting.

"I've no time for difficult hosts," she'd say. "I want docile creatures. The kind that'll let you do anything to them."

White cats were preferred, as the dark brown, sometimes black fleas, stood out against the pale fur, although, every now and again, she'd choose a submissive black cat.

"The fur might be dark, which means a flea is harder to spot, but it's more of a challenge," she told me. Long haired cats provided a similar kind of joy: "The longer the fur the more difficult it is to pull them off. But there are always more specimens on a long-haired cat."

When she found the right kitten, she disposed of the others. "It's easier this way, Carl, I promise. I can't keep them all. Now, help me. Go and fill the bathtub."

The first time she drowned a batch, I was four. She kept a special, brown burlap sack rolled up in the cabinet behind the mirror and tied it tightly at the top with an old pair of flesh colored stockings. I cried for a week.

But then I got used to it. I think it helped that we never named any of them, even the ones we kept.

***

We went through a lot of cats. Never dogs. My mother was afraid of them.

"Big, dirty, stinking animals," she'd say, spitting out every word. "Filthy, angry, *wolves*."

I made the mistake of asking her for a dog, once. I'd seen a children's television show about a boy who owned a talking dog. A loyal, obedient companion who did exactly what you wanted, unlike the stupid cats that moved quietly around our house like living ornaments, all sinewy and thin because they only ate what they could hunt. I watched the talking dog and sat transfixed, excitement burning inside me until I couldn't hold myself back. I ran up our crooked staircase, two at a time. Breathless, I burst through my mother's bedroom door. She was lying naked on her bed, staring at the ceiling, breasts drooping lazily over either side of her chest.

"Mother! Can I have a dog, please? *Please*?"

She looked at me, suddenly savage. "What the hell do you think you're doing? Coming in here without asking."

I apologized. She patted the space next to her and I moved to sit beside her.

"Mother," I began, but she pressed a finger hard against my mouth. "No dogs, Carl, you know this. You know *why*."

Yes, I knew why. When Mother was younger and living in a small town, the next door's Rottweiler attacked her, tearing through flesh and muscle, down to the bone. The damage was irreparable, and the leg was amputated. The family who owned the Rottweiler insisted my mother had provoked it, that it was a good-natured and well-trained animal. My mother's parents were from an era where children were always wrong, so they believed their neighbors and punished my mother for telling lies. They made her limp to their front door and apologize.

"But I fixed it," she said, fingering the twisted, ugly scar below her knee bone. "I fixed it good. It was a dirty animal, filthy. So, I gave it a bath. A good, *long* bath."

***

"Are you comfortable, hon?" asks Nurse. I smile up at her, to show that I am. She smiles back. We're special friends, Nurse and I. She walks around me, fussing, checking the straps aren't too tight. Dr. Havilland sighs again and his pen rolls off his lap and onto the floor. I wonder if he's bored.

"I'm sorry about the restraints, but I'm sure you know why we have to keep you like this. Dr. Shaw is doing much better, now," he added. "His face is healing properly. Minimal scarring. I thought you'd like to know."

A glob of spit travels down the wrong pipe and I half-choke, half-cough, out loud, making Nurse jump in fright. She relaxes quickly, though, ever the professional, and double-checks my straps again.

"Carl," says Dr. Havilland. "I know it's difficult for you to talk to me, but communication is very important in a patient-doctor relationship. Perhaps we can work together and find a good way of talking to each other. What do you think?"

I say nothing and just smile at Nurse again, but she's too busy checking my stats on the clipboard to notice.

***

I never went to school. Mother taught me most of what I know, and for everything else, we had a television with good reception, and hundreds of books overflowing from the bookcases into tall, uneven stacks on the floor. A lot of them had been my father's before he died when I was a baby, and there they remained, gathering dust and droppings and bite marks from mice that lived and bred in the walls, their sole purpose in life to feed our many cats. We lived in the countryside far from any towns, and grew and harvested vegetables from the garden. People rarely visited us, although, once every year or two, a strange face would appear at the door, either lost or selling books that we did not need.

Mother handmade all our clothes, cutting up and recycling old things that I had grown out of. Everything in our house was tinted gray, as though our possessions had aged in sympathy with my mother. Our carpets, once the color of a strong red wine, had become mottled gray and threadbare in places where our feet rose and fell every day. She refused to change them.

"Carl, the carpets are where the fleas breed," she said. "We must keep them as they are. We must keep the fleas happy."

My skin was always covered in red welts. "Bites," said my mother, one day, after inspecting a small cluster of red itchy lumps on my groin. "The fleas like you, Carl," she smiled.

***

Whenever my mother caught a flea, she *harrumphed*. A victory sound.

"Get the jar, Carl."

She'd squeeze her fingers together so there was no chance of escape, and plunge them into the water and count. "One... two... three... four..." Then, she'd let go. I'd watch them drown, fascinated, their tiny legs kicking furiously. Some would die quickly; others would float on the surface and take hours, sometimes days to run out of energy and sink to the bottom.

"Mother," I gasped. "Look at that one!" A big, fat brown flea was twisting and turning under the water. It kicked feverishly, shuddered, then drifted slowly to the bottom of the jar. A thin crimson thread floated from a flea's rear like a tail. "What is that?" I asked.

"When living things die, Carl, sometimes they expel waste. What you're seeing is blood. That flea just ate."

***

We had a storage cupboard under the stairs. It was a tiny space, and you had to stoop to get in. It was lined with shelves that my father had built. Rickety and covered in holes from woodworm, they couldn't hold much. My mother lined up her flea jars on the shelves, hundreds of different shaped glass jars, some with lids, some without. Some were from old jam jars she'd collected over the years. But her favorite was an old bottle with two ring handles by the mouth, like the ones you use to make homemade beer or cider. It was filled up to the halfway point with water, and a school of dead flea corpses floated in the middle.

"You have to watch them carefully," she explained. "Sometimes, tougher fleas will try and crawl out of the jars. They crawl up the glass and if you're not careful, they'll escape, and then it will have all been for nothing."

"Why do the fleas stick together like that?" I asked her. She peered closely into the swarm. "I don't know, Carl," she said, finally. I remember feeling surprised, and more than a little disappointed.

***

We ate them, eventually, draining the bloated corpses of fleas using a sieve when the contents of the jars became more brown mass than clear liquid. My mother had a whole cookbook in her head. I watched her add dead fleas to sauces, or sprinkle them over soups, like a garnish. Sometimes, she'd dry them out in the sun, like I'd seen people on television do with shiny red tomatoes. When they were dry, she'd ground them into a dusty powder using a pestle and mortar.

"Gives it an extra kick!" she'd laugh, throwing a pinch of the brown crystals into a pan. We spread dead fleas on toasted bread, in salads with vegetables brought in from the garden, and we even tried liquefying the contents of one of her jars to make a smoothie, adding ice cubes because it was an unusually hot day.

"I don't like it," I said, screwing up my face.

"Oh? Don't you want to grow up big and strong?" asked my mother. She finished hers, sucking the last bits through a straw. "Here," she waved her free hand at me. "I'll finish yours."

***

"Carl, would you like a glass of milk?" asks Dr. Havilland. "I know it's your favorite." He leans forward, slightly, and pulls his chair closer. The sound of unprotected metal scraping against the polished concrete floor makes Nurse screw her face up in pain. I want to tell the good doctor to shut up, but the sound disappears as soon as it begins, so I say nothing. If I tilt my head slightly, I can see Dr. Havilland sitting with his right leg crossed over the top of the left. He pretends to study his notes. "Carl, the nurses say you don't eat any of the food they give you. Can you tell me why?" He sits back in his chair and uncrosses and re-crosses his legs, so now the left one is on top. "Do you not like the taste, is that it?"

He waits a moment, then glances at Nurse and gives her the slightest of nods. She disappears out into the corridor. I'm sad to see her go.

"Carl," says Dr. Havilland, softly. "Why don't you tell me what happened to your tongue?"

***

My mother was always handy with a knife. She'd carve vegetables from the garden into intricate patterns, like the way people do with pumpkins for Halloween. But she'd carve anything, my mother. She grew turnips and potatoes in the garden, peppers and fiery chillies in the greenhouse, where it was warmer. She'd work her magic, slicing out warped, misshapen faces in the skin, and we'd position them in the middle of the table, like centerpieces. My favorites were the peppers. Bright reds, greens, yellows. Shiny, waxy looking skin. My mother brought in three from the greenhouse and gutted them, flicking the tiny white seeds from her fingers. They smelled sweet and exotic and she smiled at me watching her.

"They look nice, don't they?' she said. "But remember, we mustn't eat them. They're poison, Carl, do you understand? Poison."

She stuck the knife into the peppers' flesh and twisted her wrists this way and that, thin red spines sliding down onto the table.

"We can light a candle and put it inside. Won't that look nice?"

The telephone rang, and she jumped as though she'd never heard it before. She put the knife down. "Wait here, Carl," she ordered.

The hem of her skirt disappeared around the kitchen door, and I was alone. I stood still, staring at her creation. The thin holes in the flesh, like paper cuts, the red off-cuts sprinkled like confetti. I touched one with my finger, expecting the poison to shoot up my arm, and for my brain to boil inside my head, but it didn't. I heard Mother someplace far away, speaking into the phone in her special telephone voice.

I took my hand away, and was surprised to see that the spindle I had touched was stuck to my finger.

I licked it.

"Why did you do that, Carl?"

Mother stood in the doorway, waiting for my answer. I spat the piece of pepper out, but it dribbled down onto my jumper, sticking to the fibers. Her face twisted and changed. Her fury, invisible to me, but no less real, pushed me back a step. Her fist clenched, and her knuckles popped and whitened. Then, she let out a sob; a fearful, choking cry. She rushed towards me and knelt down. Her eyes were bright blue and wet, and they bored into my skull.

"Carl," she moaned, "you must always listen to your mother, always, always, *always*." She gripped me tightly with one arm and groped blindly on the table with the other. She sobbed as she pushed me down onto the ground and held the knife against my cheek. It was wet from the juices of the pepper, and I saw there was a tiny, red speck of flesh still on it.

"I have to do this. It's poison, Carl. But I can still save you," she said, frantically. "Always listen to your mother."

Her green eyes were rabid. She forced her fingers between my lips and pulled out my tongue.

***

Nurse is standing over me, holding a cup of milk with a straw sticking out of the top. She guides the straw into my mouth and I suck up the liquid. Some dribbles out onto my chin, but Nurse is there to catch the mistake with a soft towel. She always manages to catch the drops. She's a natural. With her fingers so close, I see her nails, which she keeps trimmed and polish free, as per the hospital staff dress code. But I notice a tiny fleck of bright, post-box red in the corner of her thumb, just tucked under the skin. I wonder who she painted her nails for?

Such a vibrant color, red.

Dr. Havilland shifts in his seat again and checks his watch. It's almost over. He tries one last time.

"Tell me about your mother, Carl."

***

I was fourteen when she died.

I remember it well, because I was there with her, holding her head down under the water.

It was a beautiful and warm day, the kind where flowers bloom longer because they are so filled with joy. I spent most of my time outside then, with the cats. They showed me their secret hiding places, their little nooks and special ditches in the ground, where they liked to sharpen their claws and birth their young. Before, Mother stayed in bed for longer each day, then stopped getting out of it at all. She said she was tired all the time, weak. She cried a lot then, fearful of the death she suspected was waiting for her outside the door. She spoke very little, most days, and when she did peel apart her lips to croak out a word or two, it was always the same: "Feed me, Carl."

I carried up the flea jar and set it on the floor next to her bed. Her parched lips opened and closed like a fish at the sight of it. I poured out a small cup and helped her to sit up. I held the cup up to her mouth and she drank it in little doll-like sips. When she had finished, she pulled back her lips and grinned at me, a mother's smile, but all I saw were her brown, fetid gums, and dead fleas lodged between her teeth. She closed her eyes.

"Mother," I whispered, leaning in close. "It's time for your bath."

She nodded slowly, neck bones creaking.

I lifted her from the bed and her head rubbed against the pillow, strands of graying hair catching the fibers and pulling scraps of skin away from her skull. As I carried her into the bathroom, the cats stood silently, watching me and her, tails flicking from side-to-side. Steam from the bath had settled on the cracked mirror above the sink and heavy droplets trickled down in erratic little rivers.

I lowered her gently into the water. Her eyes fluttered a little, and her nightgown turned see-through. She raised an arm, as though in panic, but fatigue took her again, and she sank down to the porcelain bottom. She whispered something I could not hear. I placed my hand on her head and pushed her under.

***

The cats lined up against the hall followed me as I took Mother outside and lay her on a bed of wildflowers I had picked especially.

I sat there for a long time, sleeping outside and listening to the sounds of the forest. The cats avoided us at first, thinking it a trick. But they learned quickly. At first, it was a lick, a taste. Then, a desperate mother with many mouths to feed took the first bite.

And soon enough, my own mother was gone.

***

Dr. Havilland leaves me. I can tell he's not satisfied, but that's okay. He can always try again tomorrow. Nurse checks my straps one last time and wipes my forehead with a paper towel where fresh sweat threatens to slip quietly down onto my pillow. She smiles down at me and says goodnight. She walks away and turns out the lights, carefully closing the door behind her as she leaves. The moon shines through a gap in the curtains and creates a rectangle of light across my legs; a reverse shadow. At last, I am alone. This is my time. I smile to myself in the semi-darkness, and wait.

Then, he comes, padding along the bed. I've named him Oscar, although, I don't recall why. I just like the way it sounds in my head. Oscar. *Oscar.* I sit up in the bed and stretch my arms right out. It feels good to stretch. Oscar climbs onto my lap and I reach out to pet him. He rolls over, all thick orange fur and toothy smiles. He stretches out across my legs exposing a pink belly and almost immediately, a fat black flea runs across. Without even having to think, I trap it between my fingers. Oscar grins up at me. "Go ahead, Carl," he whispers, razor sharp teeth glinting in the moonlight. "Go right ahead."

Peeling back my fingertips, I see its tiny flea legs struggling. I quickly lick it up with my tongue before it can escape. It tastes like home.

Innocence USA

David Rachels

All the effort in the world isn't enough to get a man out of prison in this country. It takes a lot of luck, too. For three years, I had been doing what any good convicted killer does when he runs out of lawyers: reading law books, writing motions and briefs that I didn't understand, telling anyone who would listen about my innocence. I was driving my cellmate and everybody else crazy because nobody inside wants to hear about how innocent you are—watch how they roll their eyes!—but it was all I could talk about. I was possessed, obsessed with getting myself out of prison.

And then my luck happened. I got a letter from a woman named Melissa Tompkins who said she wanted to do a podcast about me. Now don't get me wrong, I *still* don't understand exactly what a podcast is, but Melissa's letter said, "I have serious reservations about your conviction," which pretty much meant she thought I was innocent, and that was good enough for me. I added her to my telephone list, and we talked on the phone for the first time four days after I got her letter.

The first thing Melissa wanted to talk about was Tonya Chilton and that was exactly what I wanted to hear. Tonya was the eyewitness who said she saw me and Naomi arguing in the parking lot the day Naomi disappeared. Tonya said she saw me make Naomi get into my car and then, supposedly, I drove away angry, burning rubber out of the parking lot.

It was all a lie. I have no idea why Tonya would want to do that to me—there were too many reasons, I guess, and I could never decide which one it was—but she did it to me. Even though her story changed from her first statement to her second statement to the grand jury to my trial, everyone believed her every time. She looked everybody straight in the eye, and she lied like she was a psychopath. I never had a chance. I had alibi witnesses—seven of them!—but my friends were all sketchy. Nobody was going to believe them, even if they were telling the truth.

"Tonya's testimony doesn't make any sense," Melissa said.

"Tell me about it," I said.

"Even if you set aside all the inconsistencies, there's no way she could have seen all the things she says she saw."

"Tell me about it," I repeated.

***

I talked to Melissa on the phone every week for the next six months. In the middle of the fourth month, the podcast started. I didn't get to hear it, but I got to read it, and Melissa found more problems with my case than I knew were there. The police department hadn't followed proper procedures with my first line-up. The expert testimony about my cell phone records was bogus. The coroner changed Naomi's time of death to fit with Tonya's testimony. Everything showed they were trying to frame me. Melissa said in one podcast, "The police, the coroner, the district attorney, none of them seemed even curious about the truth. They just wanted someone to put on Death Row."

Yes.

After the podcast, I got hundreds of letters from people who thought I was innocent, but what good was it doing me? In my situation, all the public opinion in the world was worthless. I was still a Death Row inmate doing his own incompetent legal work.

Then I got the letter that mattered. A lawyer from Innocence USA wanted to represent me *pro bono*, which means for free. The lawyer was named Jerry Fishbein, and I found out later that people call him Jugular Jerry because of how he goes for everybody's throat, which was appropriate, seeing how Naomi died.

Back when I'd run out of lawyers, I'd written a letter to Innocence USA, but they never wrote me back. I hadn't expected them to. In order for them to take your case, they have to think you're innocent *and* they have to think they have some way to get you out of prison or at least get you a new trial. So I was really excited to talk to Jerry Fishbein. He wouldn't be interested in me if he didn't think we had a chance. A *good* chance.

***

Lawyers aren't like podcasters, they have money, so Jerry came to see me in person. After we shook hands, he didn't mess around. I tried to make small talk and ask him about his trip, and he told me not to waste his time. He said, "I read a précis of *Railroaded*, and I want to get you out of here. Sign this." He put a piece of paper and a pen in front of me.

Now, I don't know what "précis" means, but *Railroaded* is the name of the podcast, and I wanted to get out of there, so I signed. The document didn't say much other than I would let Jerry be my lawyer. I slid the piece of paper back to him.

"So, what's your plan for getting me out?"

"DNA."

"What?"

"DNA. Deoxyribonucleic acid. It's—"

"I *know* what it is. I just don't know what it's got to do with my case."

DNA was never mentioned in *Railroaded*. There was no DNA evidence at my trial. DNA had nothing to do with how they convicted me. They convicted me because Tonya Chilton lied.

"When they did Naomi's autopsy, they recovered skins cells from under the fingernails of both hands. Those cells are from her killer. At the time of your trial, those cells weren't enough to test, but now they're plenty. I just have to pull a few legal strings, and then the lab does the rest. When the results come back, your release should be practically automatic."

I look a deep breath and let it out slow and loud. "How long till they do the testing?"

"Well," Jerry said, and he laughed a little bit, "technically, the court isn't *obligated* to order the testing, but with all the publicity in this case, I'm betting they will."

"You said you just had to pull some strings."

"In a manner of speaking. Given the substantial evidence of prosecutorial misconduct, they ought to grab at an easy chance to make things right, and they might even do it fast. I wouldn't be surprised if the testing is done in three or four months."

"Three or four *months*?"

"That's right! Not years—months! That's fast, my friend."

I knew he was right, of course, given how long I had already been dragging ass through the American Legal System. They say the wheels of justice turn slowly because justice takes time, which it does—it takes time from your life.

***

Back in my cell, Big Chuck asked me, "When are you getting out, man?"

He knew that I was meeting with a lawyer from Innocence USA, and he knew that Innocence USA only represents innocent people.

I didn't want to talk about it. "Don't jinx it, man."

"They got DNA?"

"You're jinxing it."

"Naw, man," Big Chuck said, "DNA don't jinx. DNA don't change its story. DNA don't get on the stand and *lie*. DNA is a direct line to the Promised Land."

"That's it," I said. "I'm jinxed."

Big Chuck robbed a convenience store when he was seventeen. He was high, and he shot the clerk in the face for no particular reason. She was a single, twenty-five-year-old mother of two who was working three minimum-wage jobs to feed her kids. They had witnesses, they had video, and the victim had parents who came to every parole hearing. Big Chuck was never getting out of prison.

"Come on, man," Big Chuck said, "let me live it with you. You getting free is as free as *I'm* ever gonna get."

"I've got a bad feeling about this," I said.

Big Chuck kept talking about it every day, and after a while I stopped telling him to shut up. For five months I listened to him jabber about how *we* were going to get free, until one day, a guard came to get me because my lawyer wanted to see me.

"This is it!" Big Chuck started shouting. "This is it!"

Only it wasn't. Not quite yet. Jerry had come to tell me that the court had granted my appeal, which meant they were going to test the DNA from underneath Naomi's fingernails, probably within ten days or so. So the *next* time Jerry came to see me would be it. I felt so nervous, I wanted to throw up.

I went back to my cell, told Big Chuck what was going on, and now he *really* wouldn't shut up. "Hell, yeah!" he kept shouting. "Promised Land, here we come!"

***

The testing took seventeen days. When the guard came to get me, Big Chuck was asleep. I was thankful for that. I shushed the guard, and I got away without Big Chuck waking up.

I'd been dreading this moment ever since Jerry said "DNA." God, was he going to be pissed.

"The DNA came back," he said.

"Oh," I said, ready for a smackdown, ready for Jerry to bawl me out for wasting the valuable time of Jerry Fishbein and Innocence USA.

Then he grinned big. "You're in the clear! You might be out of here by the end of the week!"

***

Actually, no. I'm out of here *today*. The *next* day. The state is saving face by getting me out of here as fast as they damn well can.

Now, a blur. Signing papers and more papers. Phone calls to tell my family the good news. A paper bag of clothes that used to be mine and that I don't remember and don't fit me anymore.

I tell them someone will be waiting for me, but no one will. I didn't ask any of my family to pick me up, and they didn't offer. I called them only because Jerry expected me to call people, and I didn't want to disappoint Jerry. So I called my brother and I called one of my cousins. They were polite, but they didn't care.

The gate closes behind me. I should feel thrilled, but mainly I just feel confused. All I want is for my head to clear so I can figure out what the hell has happened and what the hell I should do now.

***

I killed Naomi and I killed her good. I killed her like she *needed* to be killed. Tonya lied about what she saw. The coroner, the police, the prosecutors were all a bunch of dishonest fucks. But sometimes, *guilty* people get framed.

So I ask myself again: What the hell is going on?

I strung Jerry Fishbein along because what else was I going to do? I'm guilty as hell, and here comes this lawyer who says I'm innocent and he wants to represent me for free. I sign his paper, and then he mentions DNA. How could I send him away?

So what the hell happened?

I don't know much about DNA, but I know enough to know that somebody somewhere *fucked up*. But who fucked up and how?

They had two samples to compare: the cells from under Naomi's fingernails (supposedly) and the cells they swabbed from my mouth (supposedly).

So one of those supposedlys wasn't an actually. But which one? Does it really matter?

***

My mind clears, and I realize that it *does* matter. It matters a whole hell of a lot.

***

I look up and down the hot, dusty highway, and I think about which way to go. If they mixed up *my* DNA with somebody else's, then maybe I'm not *me* anymore. It might be that somebody else's DNA profile is now attached to my name. It might be that I can leave my DNA anywhere I please without it leading back to me.

Could it be?

I'm free, and I aim to find out.

Jeremy Knox

Jeffrey K. Blevins

I couldn't have known that it would be the reason for my apprehension when confined in an 8 x 12 room. I couldn't have known that it would become the reason for my unease when left alone inside this cell...

Westchester County Department of Corrections, situated three miles east of the Pocantico Hills, just five miles east of the historical village of Sleepy Hollow, New York – where the town's single footnote in the tomes of history was caused by a renegade, horse-riding demon known as the Headless Horseman, as the story goes. In those days, men carried flintlock pistols and the penalty for killing was simply that the losing combatant was dead. It isn't like today, where my life sentence serves as an everlasting reminder of early wrong-doings.

The weather is cold and the prisoners this facility cages are colder. We are a relatively small community, containing only the worst offenders – we are a motley crew of society's misfits, both criminally-educated and unwilling to be reformed. We are the violent, the murderers, the liars, the habitual thieves and some, though segregated, committed sexual atrocities that are unspeakable, and *still do*, but I'm not going down that road.

No, my unsociable accommodations wouldn't allow for that, even if I wanted it, which I don't.

Considered the highest threat level in this prison, and having attempted multiple escapes before, my skin-shivering sliver of real estate is located on the infamous D block's upper tier. Known by the officers as 'Never Row', meaning: we'll *never* go home. Its furnishings are basic for a man who will never see outside its walls: a transparent television set that's backing is made entirely of translucent plastic, so as not to hide contraband within its wirings; a shelf for my hobby equipment, of which is pitifully decorated; a few pictures of women from magazines that I'll never meet, and a couple of hand-carved soap sculptures I'll never show anybody.

My life is as this shelf; dull, pointless, and would look better if it were just cleared off. In fact, New York taxpayers would save a lot of time and wasted 'rehabilitation funds' if they were to just execute me. It would be drastically better than living in this ever-enclosing hole.

Naturally, my placement inside this particularly isolated cell is a consequence of my own slip-ups. What started me in general population, has overtime, transitioned me to maximum security seclusion. After several failed escape attempts, they put me in this lonely plot. In which I would probably rot away if it wasn't for Jeremy Knox.

Good ol' Jeremy Knox.

"Hey Jer," I call him by his shortened name, a more personalized version, "I'm back from the infirmary, just bronchitis, all it was. They didn't even know I was faking."

The old circuit-guided light fixture flickers above as he answers through the ventilation shaft.

"Did you get it?" His words echo through the vent that leads to an adjacent *separation* cell.

We call them 'cell' phones, which is entirely the play on words that it's meant to be – because we're separated from the 'honor' inmates, and our mail is thoroughly examined by the officers, our only form of direct communication is through these *cellphones.*

Jeremy is like myself, unfit to be around others.

I reach into the trouser line of my state issued jeans. The infirmary wing officer had been a new hire, an ideal candidate to overlook popular stash spots, especially when distracted by my complaints of the cell's cold temperature – most 'fish', as we call them, are worried about their performance evaluations, hypercritical about following procedures when regarding inmate rights; the last thing they want when fresh on the job is a human's rights violation.

I remove the razor-edged scalpel, careful not to slice my skin upon removal, "Yeah, Jer, I got it... the nurse was foolish enough to leave it unattended by her desk, just like you said she would."

Laughter pushes through the musty tube of the vent, clogged with years of mildewing debris. Odds are, it's never been cleaned. Because, in truth, they don't care about our quality of life here on D block's upper tier. Jer's doing a life stint for shooting some cop back in the nineties, has three beautiful little girls out there who will never see their dad. They never visit him during our miniscule allotment of visitation time, but he says, "It's too painful for them to make it here."

I understand, visitors stopped seeing me ten years ago, after my latest escape plan turned afoul and they stuck me inside this freezing tomb. My mother had recently passed but she was my final visitor. She said it was too chaotic trying to get cleared to see me since I was considered high-risk, and for good reason. I still have a brother out there somewhere and, if all goes as planned, I'll be reuniting with him next week. He just doesn't know it yet.

"Good, good," Jer states, mocking the guards for their flagrant lack of diligence, "We're going to need it because there's a series of service pulleys that need to be cut. I think they're the tethers for the laundry pulls. Regardless, they're in our way and we need that scalpel."

Good thing I acquired it – if it's going to help, I'm going to get it.

Jeremy's been formulating this escape route for fifteen years now. Naturally, his journey in this daring magic trick began earlier than mine. But, being the team that we've become over the years, he's coached me through all the initial stages; where to begin the excavation site and how to properly conceal its entrance. When the cell is subject to routine searches, a clever concealment is more important than the tunneling itself.

There's no point in digging if it's going to be discovered.

"So, when we crawl through tomorrow," I begin asking, "At what point are we going to require one another's assistance?"

"Roughly a hundred feet from the pulley obstructions. There's a loft that requires me to boost you up, then you'll reach down and help me scale it."

Jeremy's a good friend of mine and a gentleman – he understands that we're both seasoned criminals and offers me the certainty of being the first to go up; ensuring that he doesn't just use me and leave me stranded.

But he wouldn't do that. He's become my best friend, my *only* friend.

It seems easy enough, however. Under ordinary conditions, suspected crimes could be recorded on cellular devices, but these *cell* phones won't be recorded. Unless cockroaches and centipedes can tell tales, this is a one-way portal of communication between my cell and his. It won't be tapped.

The lights flicker, as they usually do when he speaks through the dusty vent-covered tube. It has something to do with the faulty wiring system, or so he claims. "All right, buddy, I'll be seeing you tomorrow to shake your hand – all these years," he laughs, "And we've never even properly met."

This is true, and I'm exceedingly excited to formally meet the mastermind of this masterplan... see, being in constant solitary confinement, the correctional staff aren't permitted to remove more than one inmate from their cell at a time. Normally, we could look through one another's splinter of a window on the outer door, but since our cells are aligned precisely in the middle, our pathways to the bottom floor are split: His to the right, mine to the left, with the steel stairs descending beneath our upper tier's walkway, making it impossible to create a line of contact.

Whether by coincidence or from our track records, we've been made to become the permanent fixtures in these two inconveniently placed cells... probably from track record.

"Good night, buddy," I state quietly, in the off chance I've misjudged the guard's proximity through the sound of footfalls. A man can develop supersonic hearing when stranded in a cage all day.

"Goodnight." The light above me flickers, and he presumably lays on his pathetically thin mattress, exactly as I do.

10:00 p.m. Lights out, sort of.

They dim to their relentless glimmer. In state penitentiaries, the nightly glow of lights never actually goes out. An elongated strip above illuminates each cell long into the hours of morning. They're never fully extinguished, like an ember that refuses to burn out.

How I long for the complete darkness of night, to sleep beneath its encompassing blanket of lightlessness, awaking refreshed with *real* sunlight as my morning gift. State requirements mandate that there always be twenty percent 'natural' lighting. But the hilarity of it is, the tiny rectangular window on the cell's steel door accounts for ten percent, and they've applied a thick film over the wall's even smaller window, making the other ten percent impossible to see through.

Too many days have been spent here on this anorexic mattress pondering what I'd do if I was physically capable of smashing through the glass peephole. It's honestly a blessing that I can't. The feel of icy air would be too excruciating – not because of its nippy bite, but because it would come from the other side of the prison's walls, where birds fly freely and people live of their own accord; no ten o'clock dimming of lights, but absolute darkness.

Yes, just a single night of utter darkness – sleeping through a lightless wonder.

Stale, poorly ventilated air breathes through the vent. It's too bad the quality of circulation isn't as great as my circulating thoughts. Tomorrow marks the beginning of my freedom, of my new life amongst the living – where I won't deteriorate with time and fade away in the remote recesses of this cell. Because unlike myself, these cemented walls, fortified with rebar, will be here long after this breakout... and as God is my witness, I will not meet my death here – but far away; vanished, disappeared like a magician through a theatrically placed trap door.

And my personal trap door remains undisturbed and undiscovered, beneath this chain-mounted bunk. Should my cell be "tossed", a circular portion of the cement cutout is covered with an ashy gunk that I've been collecting from underneath the stainless steel toilet bowl. Its color is almost identical to the cement flooring and has worked thus far. Its original architect – Jeremy. He explained how to do everything.

I thank the heavens that he needs my help, otherwise, he would've been gone long before my transfer here.

I gaze skyward at the vent, wondering what the man on the other side is thinking about; if he wonders about his three little girls, and if he longs for darkness instead of this drab grayish lighting. I'm completely lost in thought.

Then it starts…

As I stare distantly, the already cramped cell feels smaller; compressing like it's closing in on me. The dim lighting fogs over, as if its murkiness is actually growing dimmer. Gloomier.

The atmosphere is changing… taking on a bitter coldness, freezing more than normal.

Alarmed, I hear an improbable scratching near the vent. My eyes scan its thin, horizontal bars, and try to comprehend what's making the racket. "Nails," I say aloud, "It sounds like nails."

But that's impossible.

Fingernails couldn't drag themselves through a pipe that's no bigger in circumference than a 2-liter bottle of soda. This is, after all, not a scene from one of the many horror novels I've regrettably had the time to read. Yet, still, it scratches; scraping against the sides as if etching a trail.

Increasingly frightened, my eyes betray me. Suffering a futile attempt at ignoring the vent altogether, I instead focus on its grated faceplate more intently.

This is not a result of an overactive imagination. My years of confinement haven't led me to a lapse of sanity. This noise is *real*.

But what is it? Surely it has to be something.

Against all logic, elongated fingers, sharp and revolting, reach through the grated plate. Bloodied and darkened by decay, they wrap around each tiny steel bar, as if trying to escape from a prison *within* a prison. Nails, yellowed by rot, pull against the grate rather than push out. This is not a living hand, it's not even *human*… but then, what am I saying? That's not even possible!

Blinking avails me nothing… for every time I open my eyes, those fingers, with their dreadful nails, pull tighter around the vent's frame. As if it's trying to pull itself through.

I desperately rip out the stitching of my mattress's corner, slicing through my fingertip when retrieving the hidden scalpel. I fail to acknowledge that this half-inch blade wouldn't do much when face-to-face with whatever's trying to pull itself into my cell. Still, there's comfort in having some form of protection – like a child exploring the woods, armed with both a B.B. gun and the large ambition of taking down a predator should it surface.

Not much, but it's something.

Reasoning tells me to look away. It tries to convince me that the cinematic horror clichés are real – that by breaking visual contact, when my gaze returns, it'll be gone.

I can't. They're glued to the crusted fingernails of this demonic breach.

Now I can hear the crushing of bones and tearing of rotted flesh. Whatever's set on entering, is sacrificing its body to do so. Why?

Then, a loud tapping on my cell's steel door causes me to startle, slitting my abdomen with the scalpel. I've been taken by surprise and hysterically shuffle, trying to hide my illegal tool.

"Cell check!" the guard blares through with no regard to an inmate who might be sleeping, oblivious of the haunting that just took place.

Thankfully, he didn't care enough to peer through.

He moves on about his nightly patrol and the light's return to their normal, dim buzz. Nothing threatens to pry at the vent's grate. Part of me desperately wants to stand up against fear and call through the cell phone, asking Jeremy if he had seen the same set of sinister fingers. But I don't, I can't.

To think, me, a convicted killer and routine 'tough guy', falling victim to some form of illusion. Whether delusional or otherwise. Perhaps the surmounting stress involved with pre-escape planning has me on the brink of a mental breakdown. I've probably overworked my mind, constantly rehearsing the risky procedure. Breakouts are taxing on the nerves.

Yes, that's probably it... my brain has been so overworked that it needed to, pardon my pun, *vent*. It had to release itself from the bondage of labored thought, thereby fabricating this demonic deception as a bizarre form of distraction.

My heartbeat slowly returns, beating rhythmically at a slower pace. The gouge to my abdomen is minimal compared to the gaping wound in my pride.

I can't believe how absurd I've acted, nearly foiling my plot to escape by recklessly retrieving level 5 offense contraband – they would have me in a slightly smaller hole for months. And why; because my mind wanted to formulate an elaborate ghost story, a supernatural farce.

After intervals of glancing back towards the vent, I actually take comfort in laughing at my own foolishness. I feel like a child who convinces themselves that they see the eyes of a monster inside the closet. Our minds are powerful entities. They will synthesize manifestations if we think long and hard enough. They've built empires, and plunged into false realities. They can manipulate any situation, or manufacture stupidity.

My mind cradles on either side, obviously teetering from one end to the other.

What a silly notion – a ghastly demon squeezing through the vent. In retrospect, it sounds *ridiculous*.

Regardless, sleep does eventually find me and my mind rests without further disturbance. One fright for the night is all it needed to focus elsewhere. It was the jumpstart it needed to actually shut down. Quite the paradox, coffee of the mind, necessitating a restful crash.

The morning arrives in its usual fashion – the buzzing lights grow significantly brighter, the clinking sounds of unlocked cell ports signal that breakfast will be issued, the usual stuff – and notice, I use the word 'issue' breakfast instead of serve it; D block's food is scandalously foul, as are its inhabitants, both the criminally prosecuted and the employed staff. Ultimately, this is the disciplinary wing of the prison, where both the newbie guards and reprimanded officers are assigned. Some are under scrutiny for either depriving an inmate or requesting favors from them. Some remain employed despite internal investigations for using excessive force during routine inspections. Either way, this block is forgotten, as are the people within it.

Until today…

Our staunchly planned discharge from this stark reformatory is sure to create a rise in emotions. Reporters are going to have a field day. They'll want to know the intriguing details of how two homicidal 'maniacs' have escaped from a maximum security prison. Sure, my picture will be painted on society's television sets and newspapers will run countless articles, but I will somehow persist, despite freedom's fame.

These fools won't even know what's happening. They'll be the cajoled clowns of an otherwise elite prison system – how I'd love to see the look on Warden Monroe's face. See the angry gleam in his eye.

First, I must get out… then I can consider the conviviality of this master maneuver.

That requires me to speak with Jeremy.

Warily, I stand beneath the vent. I have exactly fifteen minutes before breakfast is issued. Usually, I spend this time watching people throw fish lines. It's always been amusing to watch men from across the way troll using improvised strings, sending notes and narcotics to other cells. Watching has always been my humorous morning ritual; one that even showed me that robbing a pill cart was entirely possible with a little well-placed aim, tacky adhesive, and ingenuity. But today, on this morning, I must summon the courage to call through and ensure the readiness of my associate.

Why am I delaying it?

"Quit being absurd," I whisper to myself, moving with the pace of what some call "The Bandage" technique, where it's less painful to just rip it off – only I choose the second option, peeling it off with gradual caution. As I near eye-level, standing atop my stainless steel sink (everything's stainless steel), I can't help but think that, if this were a stereotypical horror flick, a black cat would leap out and startle me half to death.

Yet, how is that any more irrational than seeing a set of demonic fingers?

Go, you fool, I tell myself in the silence of my mind, not wanting Jeremy to hear of my foolishness.

Finally, I inject myself with a dose of courage and pop up, seeing only the blackness of extensive tubing and cobwebs. Weirdly, I wonder if the spiders think of me as some gigantic monster staring in at them. Doubtful.

"Jer… Jer!" I call through with hushed eagerness. "You going to be ready?"

I wait… silence. Followed by more silence.

Either he's slept through the clunking sound of our opening meal ports or something's happened to him. And nobody could sleep through that.

"Jer!" I call through with an undercurrent of panic.

More silence…

What if something's happened? What if he isn't capable of departing? Or, what if that *thing* got to him?

In a frenzy, I place my ear against the grated plate as if by doing so I'll somehow have enhanced hearing; as if I'll hear his lifelessness in the adjacent cell.

It's worth a shot though – I press against it so hard that horizontal stripes will likely leave their imprints.

More ever-maddening silence…

I focus with every ounce of concentration. Then… "Buddy!"

Jer's voice reverberates in the channel of my ears. I leap back from the surprise.

Yes, cheesy horror movie cliché, transpired in real life, right before my ear. I would've actually felt better if it had been a cat.

After steadying my wavering composure, I return and make no mention of my actual nervousness. Instead, we discuss the operation in a coded text that only he and I have learned to comprehend – years of solitude will do that to people.

Just before my meal is issued through the port, I scramble to retrieve it. Because the guard on duty is Officer Blevins, pending investigation for multiple inmate mistreatments, he will simply drop the cardboard tray on the floor if a prisoner isn't there to catch it. Mine, he shoves through, hoping it will slip from my fingers.

I must've upset him in some form or fashion. As appropriately timed, my tray is pushed through with an exertion of force and he snarls, "Don't want trouble from you today, *prisoner*."

If my actions wouldn't affect the upcoming escape, I'd shove the tray right back and say, **"I'll be eating better by tonight, shove this tray where it belongs."**

"Thank you," I say instead, having never actually given him trouble. I'm confused by his ill-mannered attention.

"You're that guy who tried escaping a bunch of times, aren't you?" His questioning glare is irritating, but nevertheless, unprovoked. He's merely an angry human being.

"In my former days, in my former days," I say, while taking the tray to my chain-mounted bunk.

He leaves begrudgingly. I wonder if his day consists primarily of mundane tasks and the various contemplations of how to further torment inmates. Is that what they teach at the academy? In the end, it won't matter much longer.

The food, I empty onto the floor behind the toilet – I'm not interested in tasting its putridity today. With an institution-issued pen, I scribble, 'Take care boys, it's been a pleasure,' and leave it under my sheet where they are destined to discover it, too late of course.

It's a childish act, and an enjoyable one at that. I call through the vent, "Ready?"

"See you on…" he pauses, "… the other side."

"See you there, my friend."

No more time for conversation.

There's immediate work to be done. I have exactly fifteen minutes before officer Prick will be circling back around and I absolutely *must* be through the shaft before he returns. I'm thankful that Jeremy dug his own escape route long before I was able to start. He's been working on mine and I'm certain he's made it foolproof. Not only are we best friends – his departure also relies upon mine.

Now, the fun part…

Tightly squeezed under the bed, my headlong reach scrapes away the encircling gunk and removes the cement circle. I shimmy out and cover it beneath the sheet. It will be a stimulating farewell gift when accompanied by my note.

Because of a claustrophobic fear, I assume a pronated position atop my healing stomach. Then, I shimmy out, slithering into the hole with my boots leading the expedition.

So far, so good. I can feel the absence of cement from where I'm to be slurped into the escape route – just a little further.

Wiggling, I mutter, "C'mon, just a little further…" With a final glance before my torso is covered by the bunk, I look up toward the window.

To my untimely dismay, Officer Blevins scowls through, calling an alarm on his radio. The cell door is manually unlocked with a ridiculously oversized key, to match his paycheck, no doubt.

I feel Jeremy's grip around my legs, pulling me frantically, as if he can sense that we've been discovered. As his perspiring hands pull, clammy from nerves, they slip repeatedly. With each slip, so slips our chances of an exit.

Officer Blevins is quick to burst through, along with the trampling boots of nearing backups. He grabs me by the shoulders, tearing my prison-issued button down.

"Don't you think about it, you bastard!" he shouts, "I *knew* you were up to something!"

Jeremy's grip tightens, digging into my legs. His fingers shred through skin but I overlook the pain as he's only trying to rescue me.

Then, it dawns on me. *The scalpel! Oh yes, the blessed scalpel!*

I reach into my trouser line, pulling it free and swinging wildly at the officer. He plunges backwards defensively and unsheathes his baton. The moment I stop swinging, I know he'll beat me to a bloody pulp. Behind Blevins, more guards rush in.

Jeremy's fingers dig in so deep that I'm certain they've torn through my outer flesh and are reaching to the muscles beneath. With an explosive pull, the back of my head cracks against the bunk's metal ledge and my body is yanked midway into the tunnel, to just above my navel cavity, but I don't move any further. I am stuck.

Damn!

I must've underestimated the hole's circumference. Unless I'm stricken by a sudden and miraculous loss of weight, Jeremy's going to need to pull a *lot* harder, if that's even physically possible, and I'll literally be *squeezed* through the hole. Now I know how a cork feels when being jammed into a wine bottle.

"He's stuck! Get the son-of-a-bitch! He's stuck!" screams officer Prick, as the other guards react.

What they don't know is that I'm *not* stuck… Jeremy is right below me, daringly trying to pull me through.

Officer Blevins strikes my hand with the baton, shattering it in multiple places and sending the scalpel skidding along the floor and into the wall. If not for the barrier of my hand's flesh, bones would've gone with it.

All three grab at my shoulders, hair, and anywhere else they can sink their claws into. With Jeremy fighting below, I'm stuck in a brazen game of tug-of-war.

When all is said and done, free or imprisoned, I'm going to need reconstruction surgery on my abdomen from where it's literally being sawed in half – I took great joy in these last days comparing this escape to a magician during a magic show – only, I envisioned a vanishing act, not the sawed-in-half routine.

Large lacerations – maybe centimeters, or inches – *hell, maybe even to the bone*, saw around my stomach.

Strangely, I think only of Jeremy and that he makes his epic dash to freedom without my aid.

A final, earth-shattering stomp and pull, and I'm wrenched from beneath the bed, a baton whipping me across the skull.

6:15 a.m. Lights out… I got my request – complete darkness – when I slept. Be careful what you wish for, like they say.

Sometime later that week, I crawl through the weariness associated with awakening from a coma. First, the hazy outlines of figures standing above, then their distinct New York Correctional patches become visible, followed inevitably by the realism that I'm strapped to a hospital bed.

"It's about time you came to," says a voice that only confirms another dreadful nightmare come true, and the dashing of all my dreams of escape.

When my eyes focus, they clearly see Warden Monroe's face – needless to say, his countenance lacks any look of surprise… this is the second time my wishes have been bashed, along with my skull.

"Nearly got away this time," he laughs, acting as if my excruciating migraine is of absolutely no concern. "Yup, would've been extraordinary. A tale for the ages."

What a guy, capitalizing on my misfortune.

Still, I can think only about Jeremy's well-being during the beginning stages of the Warden's ranting. Surely, *he* got away. They must've been so distracted in *my* cell that he wisped away like smoke through a chimney, feeling the outside air caress his face, instead of a baton. My old dreams are quickly replaced by a new vision. My freedom is lived vicariously through Jeremy – a masterplan unfolded, with only its Master as the victor.

Minutes pass by when the Warden finally asks, "What was your plan? What were you thinking? Were you going to hide out down there and think we wouldn't know where to find you?"

This is the line of questioning I'd expect from a man whose about to call up a search party and wants to know where to start. I'm not falling for it.

I will tell him nothing... Jeremy is far too close of a friend for me to betray him. Despite the possible consequences, he sacrificed precious time in trying to save me.

Also, there's a code amongst the confined that speaking to an officer is unforgivable – then again, when you've been in solitary confinement as long as I have – who else am I going to talk to, now? Jeremy's gone, vanished, disappeared; finagled his way to the other side, a realm called 'freedom'.

"Well, looks like you aren't talking," the Warden says, superficially, stating only what's blatant. "You'll be here for a couple more days, and then we'll figure out what to do with you. Odds are, we're going to simply re-fortify your cell and send you back – call it a lingering reminder of your impudence... And I still don't know what was going through your mind. There was nowhere to go. You know, you should really count your blessings, you would've been killed trying to creep through those pipes."

As he stands up to exit, I can't help but ask. "What do you mean, Warden? There's a wall down there to climb over."

He stops, staring at me with a scrutinizing look, like he wonders if I'm still in a narcotic induced stupor. "Son, there isn't anything down there but a fifty-foot drop-off into a drainage dump."

What? Then how on earth did Jeremy escape? Why would he lie to me? Was it to keep me from discouragement?

"What do you mean, a drainage dump?"

He laughs with an odd, know-it-all tone. "Just a couple pipes at the bottom of a nasty fall. Last guy who tried it – almost *exactly* as you did – *died* down there. Couldn't have happened to a better fella, in my opinion. Convicted of kidnapping *three* girls; wouldn't tell us where they were. Probably dead, if you ask me. All he said was that if they tried to break out, they'd be cut to pieces by piano wires. *Sick puppy.*"

My body seizes with coldness – *three girls?*

I remember who had three girls. He said it would've caused them a lot of pain to come see him... Still not believing, I logically have to ask.

"Warden, who was this man?"

"Oh, he was a wicked human, if I ever saw one. Went by the name of Knox... Jeremy Knox."

I close my eyes, a wave of nausea washing over me. I'll be recovered enough in two days. I'll be returning to my re-fortified cell, the warden told me. In two days, I will return to that cell – with just myself, my thoughts – and the company of Jeremy Knox.

The Side Job

Joseph B. Cleary

Pain shot through Don's back as he picked up two cement blocks. A bead of sweat trickled down his cheek. He caught it with his tongue. The veins on his thin, muscular arms popped out. He wasn't used to working this hard but he didn't want to mess up another parole. He took two steps when he heard his boss, Mr. Hicot, yelling at him from his trailer's window. Don dropped the blocks and turned around. Hicot's scowl and finger pointing told him that the blocks had broken. *Fuck,* he thought. The jerk could call his parole officer. He strutted to the trailer.

"What's up, Boss," Don said. He started to run his hand through his wavy, sun-bleached hair when he realized it was matted from sweat.

"You broke the blocks."

"Only because..."

"Forget it. Come in here for a second. It's break time, anyway."

It wasn't break time, so Don asked if his parole officer had been there recently.

"Calm down, there's just some things I want to go over with you."

The trailer door was stuck, so Don had to force it open. He looked around. He wondered if the cot was used for anything other than taking naps. If it was, it was with women who didn't mind having sex in a room filled with dirty dishes and an overflowing garbage can that smelled like rotten eggs. He looked at Hicot, and knew the answer. His muscular arms and broad shoulders were canceled out by his receding hairline, weak chin, thick glasses, and beer belly. He looked like a ninety-pound weakling who had joined a fitness club.

"So, how do you like working for us?" Hicot asked, as he handed Don a can of diet Coke.

Don examined the can, and said, "Is this all you got?"

"So, everything's okay with you, here?" Hicot continued without missing a beat.

"Until I get the lead in a Broadway play, this'll have to do. Why, what's up?"

Hicot took off his glasses, cleaned them with his shirttail, and put them back on. "Yeah, there's a problem. You fucked up," he said.

"What, the blocks? Come on, I'm busting my ass out there."

Mr. Hicot flipped three photographs onto the desk. They slid across, and one fell into Don's lap. He picked them up. They were pictures of him giving an envelope to a well-dressed man. In two of them, the man, who had thick gray hair and was well built, was counting money.

"You had me followed? Man, what is this?"

"Do you know who that is?"

Don's stomach churned. He knew that he was in trouble, but he didn't know how. He sat back in his chair and examined a photo.

"Well, at least you got my good side, nice work."

"Keep it up, and I'll call your P.O. right now."

"What am I supposed to say? That's the guy you sent me to see last week. So what?"

"So, that's Iggy Dunes."

"I thought Iggy Dunes was dead."

"If you thought Iggy Dunes was dead, why are you giving him money?"

"Because you told me to," Don said, as he started to finger the knife scar on his neck.

"Don't even try that," Hicot said. "I'm a respectable businessman whose only fault is that he gives creeps like you a second chance."

Don sighed, shook his head, and said, "All right, what's going on, what do you want?"

"Nothing, you just have to do some work for me. Just a few side jobs. The type of thing you used to be involved with."

"Come on, I'm straightening out my life. I can't..."

"You're not doing shit, okay, so don't kid yourself. Why are you always doing that?"

"Doing what?"

"Playing with that scar on your neck. You worried it messes up your pretty-boy looks?"

Don put his hand down.

"I'll let you know when I need you, all right," Hicot said.

"Yeah, right, anything you say."

"Hey, come on, this is going to work out for both of us. You'll see."

On the way home, he didn't notice that the car in front of him had slowed down, until their bumpers were a yard apart. He slammed on his brakes and swerved to the side of the road. As the other car sped down the highway, he got out a cigarette and smoked it. Then, he started home again. He tried to concentrate on the road but it was futile. He could be sent back to jail for associating with a known felon like Dunes.

251

When he got home, he took some leftover Chinese food and a Coke out of the refrigerator. As he shut the door, he looked at his straight-A report card from the seventh grade that he had tacked on it. That was before his mother died and his father went from being a drunk to being a violent drunk. He had thought that when he went straight, things would go right for him, he even thought that his wife might come back. But it looked like what people said was true; you can't turn a pickle back into a cucumber.

The next day, Hicot called Don into his office. He gagged when he smelled bad fish. He almost vomited when he realized the odor came from Hicot's lunch.

"Okay, then, what I'm going to do is have you get these forms signed at this address," Hicot said, as he put some papers in an envelope, sealed it, and wrote a name and address on it. "Now, when you get there, I want you to check the place out. You see, we're professional. And don't worry about the woman, she's not too bright."

"Hmm, a finely tuned operation. How do I know you're not setting me up again?"

"You don't, but you don't have much choice in the matter, do you?"

"So, I do this, and then what?"

"Don't worry about the 'then what', just do the job. You know, that's why your life is so fucked up. You don't follow orders."

"Damn, that's good to know. I thought it was because I was a loser."

Don slammed the door as he left the office. He went to the construction site, and for once, he liked digging ditches. He dug the shovel in as far as it would go and grabbed as much dirt as he could. By the third shovelful, perspiration dripped down his forehead and into his eyes. It stung, but he liked it. He arms started to burn. His anger didn't dissipate, but it wasn't building up on him. He used to think that doing this for the rest of his life would be terrible; now, he would be glad if that was his fate.

The next morning, he went to the address Hicot had given him. It was a small brown house with white shutters. The lawn looked like it was two weeks past due being cut. A 1998 red Mustang convertible was in the driveway. It didn't seem like the type of place where a lot of money could be made.

Don stood on the porch and rang the doorbell. No one answered. He rang it again, waited, and then he rang it three more times. He took two steps down the stairs, and then he heard someone tapping on the window. Don turned and saw a forehead topped with blonde hair at the door's window.

The door opened and he smiled involuntarily. The woman was beautiful. He figured that she was about seven years younger than him, which would make her twenty-seven years old. She wore torn jean shorts and a pink t-shirt, and was smoking a cigarette. The only thing that took Don's attention away from her legs, was her face. It seemed to sparkle. Her cheekbones were so high, they looked like they could cut paper. No one would ever notice that she had small breasts.

"Can I help you?"

"Uh, yeah, are you Sherry Marx? Mr. Hicot sent me. I have some forms for you to sign."

"Oh, good. You know, I was just thinking about him. It just goes to show you; you can't judge a book by its cover. The man's a life saver."

"Uh, how's that?" He wanted to know what positive thing could be said about Hicot.

"Hey, fire and life insurance were the last thing on my mind, until he brought it up. Since my husband left, I sometimes just don't know what to do. What are you smiling at?"

He didn't want to say that he was glad she was single, so he said, "Uh, I thought Hicot was in construction."

"He is, but he introduced me to his associate, Mr. Sharpe. He does insurance."

"Oh, yeah, Sharpe."

Don had seen Sharpe around the office. He had slicked-back blond hair, crooked teeth, and a habit of wearing white suits.

"You know; I've got a pot of coffee on. Why don't you come in and have a cup and some cake, while I sign these papers? I'd hate for you to come all the way here and have to run back."

He had only driven a few miles, and didn't like coffee, but he said yes.

"You know; I'd read those papers pretty carefully if I were you. I mean, they are legal documents," Don said, as he walked into the house.

"I know, but I feel funny checking on those guys. They've been like saints to me."

The house was sparsely furnished with old furniture. The best thing he could say about it was that it was clean. On the coffee table there was a picture of her a few years younger, with a man. From the man's looks, Don figured the guy had to be amazed that he had a woman like Sherry.

He sunk into the couch. He watched Sherry's hips sway as she went to get the refreshments. When she turned around, Don expected her to say something seductive. Instead, she asked him what he wanted in his coffee.

He shifted in his chair as he waited for her. He thought about what he was going to say. This was rare, not because he was a great conversationalist, but because he usually didn't care what impression he made on people.

After a few minutes, she came back carrying a tray with chocolate cake and coffee on it. Her smile revealed a mouth full of perfect teeth. Her eyes seemed to smile as well.

Don sipped his coffee and took a small bite out of the cake. He asked Sherry if he could look at the forms. As he scanned a page, his hand started to shake. The house was insured for $750,000.00, about $600,000.00 more than it was worth, plus there was a $500,000.00 life insurance policy. Named as a beneficiary after Sherry, was a woman named Emma Barker. Don knew what stage two of the job was going to be.

He picked up his piece of cake, examined it, and then he put it back down. After a few more sips of coffee, he told Sherry that he had to leave. He put the forms in his back pocket and started toward the door.

"Uh, wait. I have to sign them before you can take them back," she said.

"Oh, yeah right. I thought you already did that," he said, as he handed her the forms. She scanned them, then signed, and gave them back.

"You know, you can tell something about a man by the people he employs, and you say a lot about Mr. Hicot. It was nice meeting you. Maybe you can come up with a reason for Mr. Hicot to send you back here."

"Yeah, that would be good," Don said. He thought about asking for her number, but he didn't want to complicate the situation. Instead, he asked her who Emma Barker was. Maybe if she thought about it, she would realize that something wasn't right. Hicot couldn't get mad at him if the woman suddenly became smart.

"Oh, that's my second cousin, or maybe she's my third. She was the one who told Mr. Hicot about my predicament. She works for him. I know it would never come to her getting anything, but I thought it would be nice to put her in it. Besides, the life insurance was part of the deal."

"I bet Hicot thought so, too."

"What?"

"Nothing."

When he got home, he threw the envelope on his kitchen table. Sherry had left her phone number on the back with a message to call her. There was a heart on it. If it was from anyone else, he would have thought it was corny, but she could have sung "The Good Ship Lollipop" and he would have thought it was appealing.

The next day, Don gave the forms to Mr. Hicot's secretary. He told her that he was going home sick. Mr. Hicot caught him in the parking lot.

"Where do you think you're going?"

"I'm..."

"Okay, now we go to phase two. You're going to torch the place."

"Oh, no, I don't do that type of work."

Mr. Hicot took out his cell phone and started to punch numbers into it. "That's it. I've got enough on you to send you back to the start of your sentence."

"Look, you've got to give me time. I've never done anything like this before. I need a plan. I can't just..."

"You want a plan? How about this; you light the place on fire in the middle of the night and then you get the fuck out of there. How's that for a plan?"

"What about the girl?"

"Don't worry about the girl, just do it."

On the way home, Don tried to think of a way out of doing the job, but he kept thinking about Sherry. That night, he called her. He still didn't want a relationship with her, but he didn't want her to think he was ignoring her. He was relieved that she wasn't home. He didn't leave a message, but he called back later.

"Don," Sherry said. "I didn't think you'd call."

"Why?"

"I don't know; I always think that. I guess I was afraid you'd think I was too bold."

"No, uh, I don't think any guy would have a problem with a girl like you giving him her number. To tell the truth, I thought about asking you for it."

"Then, why didn't you?"

"So," he ignored her question, "how are you doing? Everything okay?"

"You know, it's funny; I feel more secure since I got the insurance, and I didn't even know that I needed it."

"Well, you can't be too careful, nowadays."

Her high voice was as attractive as she was. He was about to ask her for a date when she had to answer her door. She came back on and said that her mother was there so she had to go. When he hung up, he was glad that he didn't ask her out. He would have felt like a bum going out with her knowing that she had been set up.

Don sat down at his kitchen table and drummed his fingers on it. There was no way he could do the job. He saw a picture of him and Iggy Dunes on the table, grabbed it, and tacked it to his dart board. As he hurled darts at Iggy Dunes' nose, it occurred to him that Dunes wouldn't like the picture, either. Even if he wasn't publicity shy, which he was, Dunes wasn't going to like Hicot keeping a picture of him receiving money. He was sure to do something about it.

The main problem was going to Dunes. He was known for having an irrational temper. At least, in his younger days, he was. In the past few years, no one heard much about him, other than an occasional mention of his activities. But since he didn't have the time to think of another plan, he was going to have to deal with Dunes.

Don put the picture in a folder and went to the building where he had given Dunes the money. It was in the industrial part of town. He rang a doorbell on the side of a warehouse. A fat man opened the door. He wore plaid shorts and a Hawaiian shirt.

"What do you want?"

"I was here the other day..."

"I know that, so, what do you want?"

"I want to see Mr. Dunes."

"Why, you have no business with him."

"It's about the other day."

"What about the other day?"

"That's why I want to see him."

The man's cell phone played the first notes of "Take Me Out to the Ball Game." He answered it, looked at Don, and said, "Okay." He put the phone away and told Don to follow him. He started to finger the scar on his neck, then he stopped. They went through a door in the warehouse and entered a living room.

Iggy Dunes was reclined on a leather couch, watching a Pat Benatar video with the sound off. His robe and pajamas looked like they were worth more than Don's entire wardrobe. When he saw the fat man and Don, he motioned for Don to sit down. The fat man stood behind his chair. Iggy Dunes sat up, leaned forward, put his hand on his knee, and looked Don in the eye.

"Now, what are you doing showing up at my door, demanding to see me? I don't know you."

"I thought..."

"No, you didn't. If you thought, you wouldn't be here."

"I thought you should see this."

Don took the picture out of the folder. The fat man snatched it from him and handed it to Dunes. Dunes looked at it and shook his head. He looked around the room, as if looking for someone else who thought the situation was crazy, and then he looked back at Don.

"Why would I be interested in a picture of me and a loser?"

"That's him," the fat man said.

"I know who it is," Iggy said, as he flicked the picture off Don's chest. "What I want to know is, what this idiot thought he could do with it."

"Uh, nothing. Look, I saw it on Hicot's desk and I knew it couldn't be good. And then I heard him mention something about you and the picture to that guy, I forget his name, he has slicked-back blond hair..."

"Sharpe?"

"Yeah, that's it. He looks like..."

"So, what's that got to do with you?"

"Because, I'm in the picture, too."

"So, what am I, some sort of an unsavory character you have to stay away from?"

"No, I'm saying that..."

"Then, you've got some sort of a problem with Hicot?"

Don knew that whatever Dune's relationship with Hicot was would dictate how the rest of the conversation, and possibly his life, went. He couldn't see a guy like Dunes thinking much of Hicot, even if they did business together. At least, he hoped that was the case.

"Well, I, uh, just don't think he's what you would call a stand-up guy."

Mr. Dunes took out a cigarette and lit it. He took a long drag, exhaled, and put the cigarette in the ashtray. He sat back, crossed his legs, and chuckled.

"No, he's not. In fact, he's a piece of shit. But it's lucky for me that he's a *dumb* piece of shit. Damn, I knew something like this was going to happen."

"So, it's a good thing that I brought the picture to you."

"For me it is, I don't know about you," Dunes said, as he glanced at the fat man.

"But, if I didn't..."

"Calm down, I'm just fucking with you. I just need to get something straight with you, and then, that's it. Now, you know you can't fuck with me. You know who I am."

"Of course, that's why I brought the picture to you."

"Hey, you know you might need a job, soon. You want to come work for me?"

"Uh, no. I mean, I think I'm going to get a job in a car wash or something like that, until I'm off parole. Keep things simple."

"Smart man, you can't fuck up in a car wash. Or maybe you can, I don't know. Look, just go back to work and mind your business, and things will work out for you."

Don lit a cigarette as soon as he got outside, and trotted to his car. His tires screeched as he pulled away from the building, so he slowed down.

***

Don never saw Sharpe or Hicot again. When Hicot's wife and Sharpe's boyfriend reported them missing, an investigation was launched. Once the cops looked into the company's business, they figured that the two of them had skipped out before they were caught. Since their bodies never turned up, they were both considered fugitives.

Don told his parole officer that he felt uncomfortable working for such a disreputable company. The P.O. shook his head as he gave him permission to work at a gas station.

Don liked pumping gas and then going home and doing nothing. He felt more free than he had in years.

PENALTY FOR MISUSE—$20
J. J. Steinfeld

He was on our side, Barzole the psychologist, used to say, and it was that damn expression that finally alienated me, made me want to put fear on his face. I was the only one to make Barzole look frightened – truly terrified. It was an achievement, believe me. Barzole had worked with some of the most hardened cons our God-fearing country had hidden away and he'd developed a fearless exterior that would be the envy of the toughest cop. Fearless or not, he was still effusive—this was a man who overflowed with ideas, and used the word *creative* with more emphasis and frequency than any word deserved.

Barzole would have been ecstatic that I am writing this piece for *Contemporary Prison Life*, a fancy journal he helped establish a decade ago, had I not, should I say, put the fear of God into the man. He would be shaking with approval, patting me on the back and saying, "Ah, flex your creative muscles... Creativity is the embrace of the gods... Don't abuse your creative gifts." He believed I was the most sensitive and creative inmate he had worked with in a dozen years of probing the criminal psyche. Problem was, Barzole didn't know what was in my heart, what made me tick and got me in the joint in the first place. He only knew the cold facts in my extremely thick file.

Barzole was always coming up with ways to retrieve and rehabilitate us cons—after all, *he was on our side*; the way he said that, you'd think he was our father or something, though he couldn't have been over forty. Creative Therapy was the foundation of his master plan to reshape the incarcerated. Through creativity, he wrote in an article for *Contemporary Prison Life*, he believed the hardest, toughest, most anti-social con could be transformed and rehabilitated. He used to apply his theories to us, then write about our therapy group in an article, except that it would be Prisoner A or Prisoner B or Prisoner C. I always seemed to be Prisoner E and was his favorite, the creative soul at battle with the criminal psyche. You'd think I was a maze-bedazzled rat he was doing meticulous experiments with.

The chain of events leading to Barzole's encounter with fear started harmlessly enough. After telling us it was his birthday— "But don't ask me my age, guys; one should never ask a practicing psychologist his age"— Barzole wrote on the chalkboard in our meeting room:

Describe the moment when you went down the criminal path. Write down your thoughts—those of you who can write—or tell your story from the heart. Be creative!

He read the instructions to us as he wrote, then read them twice more for good measure. From our heartfelt stories, Barzole was going to put together a play about our lives: *Doing Creative Time*. The bastard already had a title before we opened our hearts a crack.

Barzole had a theory—he didn't shit without a theory—that we were great actors who used our innate thespian talents in the wrong direction, that is, on the street instead of on the stage. He proclaimed in true Barzolean style, waving his large manicured hands, pacing around the room, tapping at the back of our stiff institutional chairs, that he was going to write *Doing Creative Time* and shape us into a reputable and dynamic theatre company. First, we would put on plays in the prison, learn about our acting craft, polish our natural talents, then, when we were all out of the joint, he would take us on the road, from St. John's to Vancouver Island. In the beginning, we all laughed at the idea, but his damn enthusiasm and persistence won us over; he had us believing we could actually be great actors. Us being the seven sweethearts in his Thursday afternoon therapy group. The prison groups he supervised were divided into specific categories based on either length of sentence or type of crime. Barzole was a stickler for categories and order. Despite his reputation as a prison reformer, he enjoyed telling us that prison was an orderly universe, more uniform than the world outside.

Barzole had literally built his career on crime. When he told us he eventually wanted to take us on tour—a bunch of ex-cons being nothing more than a traveling freak show—I began to question his motives: who did he really want to help: Barzole, or the cons? I'd have loved to have seen his curriculum vitae and how many of his listed accomplishments he had done at our expense. He was using us, like everyone else.

Barzole was encouraged that a few prison art shows he organized had done well and he was ready to expand his creative empire. Beneath that psychologist's skin was an impresario wanting to engulf the country with con talent: art, drama, prose, poetry – the works. He was going to merchandise us like Snoopy dolls. I have to admit, I wasn't aware of Barzole's deviousness right away. The air in the dungeons of Kingston isn't always conducive to clear thinking.

But I got to hand it to that slick dude, he thought my little story about when I realized I had criminal impulses and tendencies was brilliant. The other cons talked about ripping off stories or boys-will-be-boys vandalism on Saturday nights or kicking ass for the fun of it. But not me. I have, as dear Barzole was fond of saying, a literary bent. That profound assessment got me the nickname "Benty" in the joint. I wrote "PENALTY FOR MISUSE—$20" for the great Dr. Barzole, the least I could do since we both had attended the University of Toronto, except he finished with much distinction, and me... well, I'm sure the alumni and Board of Governors would rather forget me. My adroitness as a thief will never get me invited to reunions or asked to speak at commencements. I specialized in works of art, but I often stole simply for the sake of stealing, accepting my identity as a thief without question or apology. Yet, my criminality was developing long before I carried away my first Inuit carving.

In the large, gray room where we had our weekly meetings, a concrete room that could have doubled as an abattoir, I stood in front of my chair and read my little story to Barzole and my mates in captivity. It was just like being back at the good old U of T.

***

"'PENALTY FOR MISUSE—$20' by Prisoner/Recidivist 7367... I remember so clearly the sign, 'PENALTY FOR MISUSE—$20', that I would read morning after morning as I commuted by subway to classes. 'Post No Bills' and 'Keep Off the Grass' signs always gnawed at me and while I rarely violated their commandment in those obedient days, the desire to trample grass with tarantellas of rage stirred restlessly within me. I was fairly straight then, pursuing my education, living out the respectable fantasies of my parents and grandparents. But I was sick and tired of being obedient—I must have been a rebellious mutant at heart. I had fantasies about being a fugitive or revolutionary, even grew a Zapata moustache and Castro beard against my father's wishes.

"If I pulled the forbidden emergency handle, I used to speculate, I would be arrested, put in a dark cell on bread and water, subjected to a grueling and scandalous trial at which the enraged public would clamor for my privileged neck. Such outlandish speculating interested me a hell of a lot more than the economics courses I was taking. I'd had it with Kondratieff cycles, Keynesian gobbledygook, and the flushing of micro and macroeconomic toilets.

"The senseless, pestering urge to pull the handle—to forfeit the twenty dollars and embark irrevocably on a life of crime and degradation—would not relent. I wanted to see how the authorities would treat me, what my law-abiding, Queen's Counsel father would say and do, how a product of privilege and wealth like me would thrive in the sewers. That handle—and the unpredictable consequences it would trigger—was one of the mysteries of life that, if unraveled, could offer the sort of blinding insight only ascetic holy men and women or psychotics can get.

"*Besides*, I thought, with the logic of the trapped, *pulling that handle was the one way to keep out of law school, out of my father and grandfather's prestigious law firm.* Their dream of three generations of lawyers in one firm, I found obscene. That handle was important to me those dull mornings I rode to classes. In those scholastic days, busting my balls for A's and useless knowledge, I didn't believe I had the guts *not* to go to law school. The best law school in the country had a cell waiting for me, unless I could do some fancy footwork.

"The first time I became intrigued with the handle remains vivid in my memory. I moved to a seat near the alluring, summoning lever, the magnificent instrument of gray steel and even-grayer sin. Sure, I was overreacting, sinking my teeth into hyperbole, but I was a dreamer caught in the shell of one doomed to a life in the law; another link in an endless chain of legal minds bearing the same last name. Grandfather, once one of Canada's sharpest legal minds, was already talking about me siring a lawyer son, a 'Ripley's Believe It or Not' four generations under one plush roof. By the time I was at university, grandfather was allowed to deal with only the simplest divorce cases.

"In that subway car, an excited rhythm ruled my heart. I stared at the handle and read as if I were confronting the first sentence of Dostoevsky's *Crime and Punishment*: 'EMERGENCY—PULL TO STOP TRAIN'. The instructions—or perhaps divine orders—were clear, even an idiot without the benefit of higher education could follow them: *pull to stop train.* What would be the forbidden sensation? Would the passengers be tossed violently about? Would steel and bone meet in crashing and cracking symphony? Oh, how I longed for the twin joys of exploration and discovery. How I *needed* to bite from the fruit of the Tree of Knowledge. Try to understand, my life had been blueprinted for me, I was an Old Boy at birth. You had to see the opulence and anaesthetizing security I was embedded in. My one act of protest in those days was to take the subway to university and leave at home the Porsche my father had bought me when I was still at Upper Canada College. Maybe my mother accidentally looked at an accursed hunchback when she was pregnant with me; something sure as hell derailed me.

"With an assassin's ardor for his targets, I studied the others in the subway car—the regulars and the irregular riders—feeling I could influence each and every one of their lives with a single pull. One pull and the world would rumble, the earth would shake. 'PENALTY FOR MISUSE—$20'. What a paltry sum for such a grotesque tampering with the scheme of things. I imagined God sitting before billions of gray handles, pulling feverishly away.

"The passengers appeared as if they were protecting something valuable; locked within their flesh-armor, were treasures not for touch or sight. What a dedicated crew of automatons. I always imagined the worst about people in those days of confinement.

"'PENALTY FOR MISUSE—$20'. It wouldn't be misuse; on the contrary, it would be a noble deed. I had one, tiny gray handle and God had billions – was that fair? God didn't have to be a lawyer. His son merely had to die for the sins of humanity. I certainly smashed my head against outrageous images in those days, simply because I felt so absurdly trapped. But against the images in my mind was the reality of that gray handle. If I acted, the passengers would be expelled from their trances, forced to react, even if only with cries of surprise and inarticulate complaints.

"If I pulled the handle, maybe the deed would be recorded, spread near and far. How I longed to see my name in print, the encasing of rushing history, the halt of devastating time, the illusion of permanence: 'LAWYER'S SON—AND LAWYER'S GRANDSON—MISUSES EMERGENCY STOP... CANADIAN GOVERNMENT APPALLED...' And if some unsteady morning rider unfortunately should be maimed—or, perish the thoughts, killed in their rumbling steel coffin—then perhaps the evening news and the front page of the *Globe and Mail* would be mine. Only twenty dollars for disrupting the lives of ten commuters – twenty dollars to have immortality served up on a silver platter. What a bargain...

"An eleventh and twelfth blank face boarded the subway car, not suspecting the thoughts of the lurking coveter of the *verboten* handle. Maybe on New York subways people feared for their lives, but not in the tranquility that was Toronto in 1972, the best of all possible times. Twelve souls were now under my power, a new headline: 'TWELVE MEET THEIR GRISLY DOOM AS MANIAC, FORMER UNIVERSITY OF TORONTO ECONOMICS STUDENT PULLS THE HANDLE... PRIME MINISTER SENSES AN INSURRECTION AND IMPOSES THE WAR MEASURES ACT TO SAVE OUR SUBWAYS...' And still, more articles: 'Twenty-dollar fine protested as exorbitant; Famous defense counsel says ex-scholar victim of society; The glorious Canadian Dream gone amuck...'

"I stood, bringing my body closer to the handle. Just as I was about to defy the Establishment gods, a woman, squeezing a fat shopping bag and seeming one with her subway seat, looked asquint at me. Could she be a mind reader, blessed with extrasensory gifts? The evil eye swelled in her triangular and reproachful head. Would she attempt to stop me, to appropriate the glory that was *my* due? Would *she* be lauded in the newspapers, over the air waves?

"I lifted my miracle arm and reverently touched the gray handle with a lover's gentle touch. The woman squeezed her shopping bag tighter, a passionate, sexual squeeze. Some passengers got off, others got on; such is life – on-moving, never-ending – one long subway ride full of screeches and folly, signifying nothing. *Damn you, silent riders, I'll set your tongues flapping*, I thought.

"Suddenly mortified, paralyzed by my foolish thoughts of consequences, I lowered my miracle arm—the woman sighing the repeal of her curse—and gazed at the subway car's exit doors: 'DO NOT LEAN AGAINST DOORS'. I approached the solid, inviting doors, then leaned against them, waiting for my stop; ashamed of my Zapata moustache and Castro beard. I left the subway car, unscathed and temporarily denied access to the flowered halls of heroes. Odin would have to wait for my bonhomie. But I had glimpsed my salvation, my way out, and I promised myself that I would pull that damn handle before I really believed that Keynesian theories worked, before I got my degree from the U of T…"

***

Barzole applauded the reading of my story but the others didn't understand what the big deal was. My images and words threatened them. Curtis, a bungling, break-and-enter man, who had more tattoos than fingers, had read a story before me about the first time he sexually assaulted a woman, how he couldn't stop himself in the front seat of a '53 Chevy, claiming he loved the woman, offering the most salacious details. Then, like a cornered bully, he barked out at the group that he had never had a chance in the straight world. He capped his performance with a solemn confession that he screwed up everything he had ever tried to do. The man could do marvelous TV commercials for depravity and denial. The other cons thought Curtis was onto something good and let go with a spate of enthusiastic comments.

My story was more elusive to my fellow prisoners, but not to Dr. Barzole. *Irony, satire, crisp Swiftian and Shavian insights*: Barzole saw it all there in my humble tale. The touch of signing my story with Prisoner/Recidivist and my number, he found a deft stroke. He also saw the core of his play in my heartfelt outpouring.

Barzole put his arm around me as the other cons whistled pruriently and told me to rewrite my brilliant story because he was inviting some theatre people from Toronto to Kingston next week, and wanted me to be the featured reader. He then further embarrassed me in front of the cons by launching into a gushing paean to my creativity and sensitivity, reminding everyone that Oscar Wilde and O. Henry had also served time in the slammer.

The next Thursday, after the other stage-struck cons did their little histrionic numbers, I read my revised story with an abundance of feeling and foreboding mystery. Then, these theatre people from Toronto lectured to us about the "freeing" aspects of acting. One lopsided-faced dude had actually studied with Lee Strasberg in New York and pointed that out more times than I could count. They all agreed we had the makings of a first-rate play and an exciting theatre troupe.

"'Doing Creative Time' is going to free us all," Barzole exclaimed as loud as he could and began walking around our chairs. Getting higher and higher on his dream, our dear, effusive psychologist told each con how much he was on their side, how working together would produce vibrant and vital creative theatre. When he came near me, I grabbed the bastard and pulled a shiv out of the notebook from which I had read my story. I had the blade at his neck before any of the theatre types or my fellow prisoners could blink. I was on center stage, the way I liked it—*defying the script*. That's when I saw fear on Barzole's face for the first time.

I wasn't going to hurt Barzole—that would have been too easy—like punching an assistant professor when you hated the educational system or shooting a cop on the beat when you knew there wasn't a cat's-ass of justice in the world. I patiently massaged Barzole's jugular with my hand-crafted knife. One of the theatre types wanted to negotiate, and another told me to keep calm, violence never accomplished anything worthwhile, told me I was jeopardizing my theatrical career. The lopsided-faced dude who had studied with Strasberg didn't make a peep. The cons had all seen hostage takings before, but my little impromptu performance was relieving the monotony of their prison lives and they were thankful; *this* they understood in their guts.

"*Why?*" Barzole finally whispered. It was a beautiful word from such a damn, cocksure bastard. Again, "*Why? Why? Why?*" I waited a good, long dramatic time before I spoke, and then I let Barzole have it with all the conviction of a Stanislavsky graduate.

"Because I never pulled that goddamn subway-car handle when I had the chance," I told my fearful captive.

I allowed another minute to pass before speaking again, studying everyone in the large, gray room; the subway rumbling along as always.

"You didn't understand my story, did you, Dr. Barzole? You believed all that crap you learned at the U of T..."

I gave up my hostage after an hour, bored with the whole ordeal, and without so much as a nick to Barzole's smooth, theory-stuffed body. I got an extra eighteen months for that one-hour escapade; another eighteen months to write my stories, to find more gray handles to pull.

The True Vocation of
Sandy Brylirn

J. J. Steinfeld

My father, in his quest for respectability, named me: Alexander Sebastian Brylirn. By the time I was seven, I had changed my name to Sandy, and woe to anyone who persisted in calling me Alexander or Sebastian. The wobbly course of my life has been an effort to undo what my father has done or preordained for me. It seems that the one unbroken thread in my life, from the lavish surroundings of growing up in the Rosedale section of Toronto to my currently less-than-lavish quarters in Kingston, Ontario, as 1988 winds down, has been the battle against my father. Not that I'm objective, but I do think I've finally won. Now, I have stability and order and, most of all, work—on my own terms, not my father's.

I've spent most of the day working on a roll top desk in the carpentry shop. My instructor told me this morning that I could sell the piece for $800 to $900 on the open market, but the open market can go to hell, for all I care. I've become somewhat of a wizard with my hands after a lifetime of bungling and oafishness. I could be a fat-cat millionaire by now, honest, but the few bucks a day I earn is more than adequate. Money—or to be precise, wealth—was the core of my problem in the first place. I hated how my father measured his life: Possessions, assets, that horrendous museum dedicated to the glory of capitalism in our basement. But I never really settled on how to measure my own life except in terms of battling with my well-armored father.

I always wanted to work hard, to sweat, to get calluses like tiny medals of valor, but I couldn't sustain that physical kind of labor. I couldn't work for anyone very long, until I got the job working for Old Johnnie. The one job I found bearable led directly to this carpentry shop. Now, I find sense in my work, simply because it's the final defeat of my father.

So, how does the privileged son of a multi-millionaire find happiness working his butt off for next to nothing? Hating wealth made it easy. I can't remember exactly when I started despising my family's wealth, but now, at twenty-nine, as I think back on my life, I swear it was always part of me. Just like some fastidious people get all worked up over dirt in their immaculate houses, wealth disturbed me right into my guts. And the symbol of that wealth was the family business I was being groomed for from the earliest age—toy cash register, miniature transport truck pushed through plushily-carpeted rooms, games made of taking inventory and writing annual reports. Brylirn Foods Limited still creeps into my nightmares or prowls through an otherwise harmless daydream. The sound of a cash register – to this day – can make me shake like a scared kid.

After school and during summers, I was exposed to the workings and intricacies of Brylirn Foods Limited in preparation for the big day when I would oversee the family business. My first job was as a packing clerk, during which I took particular delight in placing eggs or fresh vegetables at the bottom of bags I stuffed. I can recall being especially thrilled when one of the gold-star—ten years or more at Brylirn Foods—cashiers called me the worst packer in Creation in front of a store full of customers and employees.

Whether instinctively or by plan, from my first day of work, I set the wheels in motion to ensure that I would not head the family business. I must have had some glorious Luddite blood flowing through my precocious veins. As determined as I was to sabotage my career, my parents were equally determined to salvage their son. Their two daughters (Brylirn souls untainted), married well and are sources of joy, but they abandoned the family name and were never expected to run Brylirn Foods Limited. That was left to little Alexander Sebastian Brylirn, Unlimited.

Reaching this stage of triumphant contentment with my work was a real fight. To say I had an allergic reaction to the Brylirn stores is to state the case mildly. My three memorable bouts with psychiatrists, when I was fifteen, sixteen, and seventeen, were connected one way or another to my father's well-stocked stores. Now, I can relive the episodes as if I were viewing favorite old films that get better with age.

When I was finally caught stealing from my father's largest Toronto store, I was taken to my first shrink rather than through the rigors of the justice system. Father had pull and when he pulled, he *strangled*. That first adorable psychiatrist praised my intelligence and spunkiness, then pronounced me cured after only three months of weekly sessions. Not much of a debut for an aspiring madman, but the truth was that I had grown tired of pilfering, having amassed a collection of soup cans that would have been the envy of any pensioner (father discovered my cache and personally took the cans back to one of his stores). All the cans were eventually sold, better late than never, as my father liked to say.

After that first cure, my path toward the stewardship of Brylirn Foods Limited looked smooth to my father until, for his fiftieth birthday, I handed him an envelope containing all my accumulated summer earnings, neatly cut into a thousand little pieces. Six months of twice-weekly sessions and the new psychiatrist declared that my deep-rooted aversion to money was remedied. He argued that, had I been breast-fed and not left so much in the care of hired help, I would have adored money. The fool didn't know that I found a better use for my easily earned money than playing paper-cutting games: gambling. I discovered the joys of poker in the back room with some of the older employees, guys who hated their work as much as I did but who had no real way out. They had responsibilities and obligations and kids – always that need to work for the kids.

The last enforced visit to a psychiatrist, when I was a rebellious seventeen, was the result of what my good-hearted mother called a "boyish prank" and my father equated with urban terrorism. Had I not been his only son and final carrier of the Brylirn name, I'm sure my father would have had me packed away in a grocery freezer.

During a month-long trip to Florida by my father to scout possible locations for expansion into the States — *"I think it would be grand if you managed my U.S. operations after you get a business degree at university"* — hell, I didn't even want to finish high school — I went about diligently collecting every stray and not-so-stray dog I could find and humanely sheltering the poor creatures in the large basement room that served as a museum for Brylirn Foods Limited. When my tanned parents returned, and followed the stink to the museum, amid the treasures related to the Brylirn food empire (architectural models of stores, photographs of openings and awards to dedicated employees, old cash registers, video tapes of TV commercials) they found enough fecal matter to start a grocery store of crap.

The inattentive help was summarily fired and replaced by a more vigilant crew that the Gestapo would have admired. Psychiatrist number three, a Freudian therapist who constantly chewed on an unlit pipe, was ecstatic with such a scatological case, and I enjoyed telling the man stories about my unusual sex life, which I carefully researched before each session. Miraculously, all that reading and using the library got me interested in going to university. Almost a year with Freud's clone and I was once again fully cured.

At nineteen, I did go off to university – my father's alma mater, no less – somehow reconciling my anarchistic soul with my genuinely curious and active intellect; and so, father became hopeful still another time. However, true to my saboteur's heart, I joined the school's scrawny chapter of the

Marxist-Leninist Party. I've never been much of a joiner, but for a while, that organization in the middle of a serene Canadian campus intrigued me. I tried to imagine a chapter of the Young Conservatives at the University of Moscow, but couldn't. During my third year at school, I ran in a federal election for the Marxist-Leninists. I gathered a great deal of publicity in an otherwise dull campaign after the press was alerted to the identity of the candidate's father.

During a dutiful visit home, I brought with me over five hundred colorful campaign posters and wallpapered most of the first floor with them while my parents slept. That bizarre act, my father almost might have been able to accept as a crude practical joke, but I also adorned every tree on our, oh-so-affluent street, and Rosedale wasn't even in my political riding.

MAKE THE RICH PAY ... ELECT SANDY BRYLIRN ... BRING SANITY TO THE SICK STATE.

"Why couldn't you have joined the Rhinoceros Party?" my father moaned in exasperation and all seriousness. When he came back from removing all the posters from our street's trees, he followed with one of his most eloquent lectures on the intrinsic value and goodness of work – a stirring tribute to the sheer holiness of the work ethic.

I'm *certain* that my father's last words will deal with the "value of work". This is a man who used to whisper to me when I was a child that, "Idle hands are the Devil's workshop." I used to whistle, "Whistle While You Work" as he lectured. After I got older, I started coming up with sarcastic replies or visual gags – like the embossed T-shirts I used to wear around the house: HORATIO ALGER WAS A PERVERT; WILLY LOMAN WORKED HIMSELF TO DEATH; *LIEBEN UND ARBEITEN...*

Even after I was done bringing sanity to the sick state, my father was willing to give his lunatic, communist son one more chance, if I would see this "highly recommended" psychiatrist, but I was already twenty-one and refused. I told my father that Karl Marx and Vladimir Lenin hadn't needed shrinks and those two clever fellows changed the face of the world and history. "But, could they have run a profitable chain of grocery stores?" my father wanted to know, allowing a long-buried sense of humor out.

After I received my degree in Philosophy—I adamantly refused to take a single business course, despite my father's entreaties to be sensible and practical—I moved from Rosedale to downtown Toronto, and began my search for employment that had nothing whatsoever to do with the grocery business. As for more education, I decided I'd rather learn on the street. When my father saw where I was living downtown, above a neon-lighted sex shop, he told me on the spot that he was writing me out of his will and that I was not getting back in until I was prepared to take on the responsibility of managing one of the Brylirn grocery stores: "The smallest one, in a nice, ethnic, working-class neighborhood," he stressed. I told him I didn't care for politics any longer. "Ah, idle hands are the Devil's latrine..."

***

In the first four years after graduating from university, I went through a succession of twenty-three jobs. I could have gone on indefinitely having jobs – like turning tricks – as long as my charm and stamina held out. But the twenty-third job certainly changed things for me. I clung to job twenty-three the longest, and it exerted a strange influence on my life. Yet, when I started working for Old Johnnie, I could never have foreseen just how my life was going to change.

Old Johnnie's shop was on a gray, side street, wedged between an adult bookstore that was a front for less literary pleasures and a European-style tailor shop run by an old man who had been in a Nazi concentration camp and *still* trembled each time a stranger opened his door. I liked Old Johnnie and he patiently taught me all he knew of the business he had run single-handedly for almost thirty years. I was fascinated by how Old Johnnie stoically coped with life. I guess what I liked most about the man was that he was neither wealthy nor did he ever mention the Devil. He made work—hard, careful, painstaking work—seem worth losing oneself in. I never even thought the handwritten signs he had taped around his shop were corny. 'AN HONEST DAY'S WORK PLEASES THE LORD' just didn't seem offensive in Old Johnnie's dusty place. Old Johnnie, I can honestly say, came very close to rehabilitating me.

I've been vague on purpose about the first twenty-two jobs—most of which I lasted at for less than a month—because hearing about those jobs would put you to sleep like they did me, but the twenty-third job was different. The others were pinpricks to my soul. My twenty-third job was as an assistant in Johnnie's Artificial Limb Shop, initially handling mainly paperwork, but soon becoming Old Johnnie's right-hand man, as the owner claimed with a labored smile. Old Johnnie rarely smiled or joked, but was a tireless raconteur, not unlike my father. Old Johnnie's stories, however, were rooted in fantasy and magic; he told me he had Gypsy blood.

The job didn't pay well at the start, but I liked Old Johnnie, and I did make enough to cover all my living expenses. Too much money in the bank made me uneasy, anyway. I had given up gambling years ago; very little in this world, I must admit, holds my interest for long. I tried not to

271

squander my money, and for the first time in my life, lived on a budget, keeping track of every dollar I spent.

This was the only employment I could tolerate being a subordinate at, and my impulses to be defiant or sarcastic were quelled in Johnnie's Artificial Limb Shop. From day one, Old Johnnie treated me like a friend, then after a few weeks, like a son. Twice a week, he had me over for supper with his wife, Marianne – visits I began looking forward to. There seemed to be no more peaceful or safe place on earth than Old Johnnie's small, three-bedroom house; "Paid in full," he liked to say, and not much bigger than my father's four-car garage.

Old Johnnie's wife was a huge woman, but he was slender, with a gaunt face that always seemed to crave nourishment. Yet, at home, Old Johnnie ate well and heartily. I used to wonder how such a couple could get together and remain united for over twenty-five years, with him so thin and her incredibly obese. It was the same when they were married. The wedding photographs, looking like shots of sideshow freaks, were displayed on the mantelpiece in the living room. Their heights were nearly the same, about five-foot-five or so, but there was a comic disparity in their girths; she was nearly *two* of him. My own health-conscious, squash-playing parents were trim, almost identically so. I've always associated health and trimness with wealth.

When Old Johnnie's wife asked during that first supper, "Brylirn, that's where I do my shopping, any relation?" I laughed and said it was a weird coincidence. I saw Old Johnnie's forehead furrow at my denial; he remembered the letterhead on one of my references, from a vice-president of Brylirn Foods Limited. I told Old Johnnie that my father was, "The best damn caretaker at Montreal's largest cemetery," and my mother was, "A housewife and splendid cook, you should taste her carrot cake." I was always an imaginative liar, but only around Old Johnnie, did it start to bother me. For a while, I believed he was the most honest man in the world.

I recall a great deal about Old Johnnie and Marianne, sometimes at the strangest times, and usually such insignificant incidents. Even now, I can still hear Old Johnnie's voice—which belied his sickly appearance; it was low, full, robust—talking about his dogs.

"Nothing warms up a household more than a new puppy," he commented as we started one of our meals and the proud barking mother wandered in with her three pups. "Marianne hasn't been this way since I brought our first dog home the week that man walked on the moon, way back when. Telling you straight, Sandy, that puppy excited her more than the man on the moon." Old Johnnie backed off momentarily from the steaming soup in front of him, and his eyes seemed to seek a celestial body on the ceiling. "I still can't believe it. Walking on the moon, what next? What was that first man's name?"

"Armstrong," I told him, remembering very clearly watching the event on TV with my two sisters. I was a rambunctious little kid of nine that summer, getting in trouble often but still manageable. Armstrong had walked on the moon in 1969, many years before, yet, Old Johnnie spoke as if it was happening at that moment and he was right next to the bouncy moonwalker.

As I was making excuses why I didn't want to take a puppy home with me, one of the dogs crapped on the carpet. "Bad dog," Old Johnnie scolded unconvincingly, as Marianne hurried to clean up the mess. "Toilet training them is the hardest thing," he said, and allowed a smile on that gaunt face of his.

I laughed as I thought of all the dogs using my parents' basement museum as a bathroom, years ago. The smell wafted through time and I just kept laughing. I had to explain what had so unhinged me, so Old Johnnie and Marianne wouldn't think I was really nuts. I cared what they thought. The memory of the crap-filled basement made me think of my father quoting Ralph Waldo Emerson: "Every man's task is his life-preserver." My father's indestructible aphorisms haunted me, even in the sanctuary of Old Johnnie's house. I recalled the put-down that finally stopped my father quoting Emerson on the virtue of work: "What was it the Nazis used to advertise over one of their concentration camps, Father? Wasn't it 'Work makes you free'?"

"Something like that, Alexander," my father answered, without emotion, but I knew I had pierced him deeply. I relived that triumph as I sat across from Old Johnnie and Marianne. Too bad I couldn't have come up with as effective put-downs for Carlyle or Hazlitt or Ruskin, or the hundred others my father quoted on the value and virtue of work.

As much as I liked the Artificial Limb Shop and Old Johnnie's home, I couldn't fool myself into thinking I had shaken my depression. Its return made it difficult to maintain the routine required at Old Johnnie's shop. I realize now that there is always something to trigger me, to push me from endurable moodiness to that paralyzing depression, no matter how settled or in control I get. It was discovering the "truth" that finally derailed me at Old Johnnie's shop.

I desperately wanted to stay with Old Johnnie; it ordered my day, diverted at least some of my melancholy and brooding, yet, I knew I would be lucky to finish out my first year at the Artificial Limb Shop. Still, I talked with Old Johnnie about the future. He wanted me to take over the business when he partially retired. And eventually, my benefactor started to mention over and over, that I would become co-owner of Johnnie's Artificial Limb Shop—only then it would be 'Johnnie's and Sandy's'.

I was the perfect son Nature had deprived Old Johnnie of, and I didn't want to ruin his fantasy until the last possible moment. I felt indebted to Old Johnnie for his kindness, not to mention the steady and generous raises, and a sustaining lie was the least I could repay him with. I even started to call him, "Dad". I used to call my own father, "*Comrade*," at least, as long as the term irritated him.

But things started happening around the shop that made my leaving inevitable. When Old Johnnie told me about Hungary—he had fled Budapest during the Hungarian Uprising of 1956—I was shocked. I was sure that Old Johnnie, who didn't have a trace of an accent, was Canadian. Even as I was pondering my employer's secret background, I received an even bigger jolt from Old Johnnie—or János, he had changed his name to make it sound more Canadian. For ten months, I had worked side-by-side with the man, had shared stories and evenings, but only then did I find out my employer and "Dad" had an artificial leg.

"It's nothing you want to shout from mountain tops," Old Johnnie explained, after I had accidentally kicked his leg under the table in the storage room, while we were having our lunches. The thud was certainly not caused by flesh being kicked and Old Johnnie had to answer my horrified look. I wondered how Old Johnnie could move so well, like someone normal. I could barely believe the discovery. My father kept secrets, not Old Johnnie, I had believed. Was I blind, or had he adapted so expertly? So Cunning? I had my first negative thoughts about Old Johnnie, as if he had betrayed me to an enemy. I saw my father where Old Johnnie was sitting. Once I made the discovery, I never saw Old Johnnie walk any way but unnaturally and awkwardly. And I began to detect his unmistakable accent. *Hungarian cripple*, I caught myself thinking when he angered me.

But I couldn't stay mad at Old Johnnie for long, not nearly as long as I could stay mad at my dear father. In the storage room, surrounded by the artificial legs and arms and braces hanging on the walls, eating our midday sandwiches together, I finally released what had been nagging at me since I started working at the Artificial Limb Shop.

"I thought everyone who'd come in here would be sad, pitifully despondent. I thought I'd see only gloomy faces. But hell, so many of the customers are happier than most of the people you pass on the street. It bugs me—it doesn't make sense. These people should be bitter..." I wanted what I was saying to be dramatic and important, but the more I poured out my words, the more I felt I was speaking nonsense to a stranger.

"Sandy, my lad, I learned a long time ago that hardship and bitterness don't have to go together. There are enough bitter people in this world – whole ones; two arms, two legs – who twist their faces at what they believe life's done to them. I don't even hate the Communists, and God knows, I have every right to." Old Johnnie then tapped at his artificial leg, relieved that the secret was out. He seemed to be tapping out foreign melodies and secret codes. "But when you lose an arm or leg," Old Johnnie went on, "you see the damage, you can't kid yourself about it. Loss brings out the best and worst a person has. It leaves no middle ground to flounder in. Sink or swim, isn't that what you'd call it?" He lifted his right hand and, without comment, pointed to a nearby sign:

'COUNT YOUR BLESSINGS.'

"But, how can they stay so happy?" I asked, a damn fool falling further into his folly. I kept staring at Old Johnnie's artificial leg, as if it contained answers to all my questions.

"They're not so happy," Old Johnnie answered me. "When you see an amputee with a smile, or giving you a good word, you notice; it can't be missed. Take it from me, not everyone wants pity, so they work harder at appearing all right – adjusted. Like us." He paused, realizing what he had said. To counter his embarrassment, Old Johnnie pointed to a far wall with its small sign:

'THE LORD HELPS THOSE WHO HELP THEMSELVES.'

"It's the *whole* ones who yearn for pity. They rush and fight like animals. When you're missing arms or legs, you don't rush, you fight in different ways. The way the world is nowadays, all the time rush, rush; I sometimes think it's a blessing in disguise to be slowed down and forced to appreciate what you have left. If you ask me, the whole ones are the real cripples."

"My father's a real cripple," I confessed to Old Johnnie, squeezing my eyes shut, my thoughts still assaulted by cripples. I wished at that instant that I were armless and legless.

"And he's a caretaker at the largest cemetery in Montreal?" Old Johnnie said, with unthreatening mockery.

I laughed sadly, like a man before the firing squad who's been told that the riflemen are all out of bullets... so they'll use their bayonets, instead. Finally, I told Old Johnnie the real story of my family and past, then cried until the front door clattered and the next customer hobbled in for a fitting; smiling, with a good word.

The depression grew worse for me and my attendance at work became erratic, despite my determination not to let Old Johnnie down. He began lecturing me on how I should love my father, that to respect one's father was the greatest commandment. The man I so admired even told me that he wished he were a millionaire, that having money was no crime.

I lost hold of my routine and the punctuality I had maintained for months, and began arriving late, sometimes not until noon. Caught in the jumble of my emotions and depression, once in a while, I imagined I was going to a grocery store to work. My heart just wasn't in my job. For a time, Old Johnnie tried to understand and offer support, but he blamed some of my problems on my attitude toward my father and his wealth.

I began making errors in measurements and bookkeeping and acted clumsily around the shop, dropping or misplacing things. Old Johnnie wound up doing most of the work, taxing himself unduly, the purpose of having an able-bodied assistant defeated. He told me that if his wife and doctor knew he was working so hard, he would never hear the end of it. The doctor had warned Old Johnnie that he wouldn't be as lucky with the next heart attack. I never even suspected he had a bad heart. He confessed to me that it was his heart condition that forced him to cut out smoking and get himself an assistant for the first time in his life. I began to believe that I knew nothing of consequence about my employer.

After a patient three weeks, a month before my one-year anniversary at the Artificial Limb Shop, Old Johnnie sat down with me and we had a long talk, father to son. He suggested it might not hurt if I saw a professional person, everyone has mental problems occasionally. The more I argued against getting psychiatric help, the more stubborn and insistent Old Johnnie became. To shut him up about my need for help, I lied and told Old Johnnie I would consider seeing a good psychiatrist.

Following my one-year anniversary at the Artificial Limb Shop, things seemed to grow worse. Suddenly, I couldn't stand the dozens of handwritten signs that decorated the shop and used to bother me no more than old calendar pictures. I now needed a drink or two before I could begin work, and at least two drinks before I could fall asleep at night. Worst of all, I started to find more and more of my father in Old Johnnie.

Finally, I couldn't bear going to the shop any longer, and quit my job. On the one hand, I knew that Old Johnnie was relieved; I had become a burden, a hindrance around the shop. On the other hand, I sensed that Old Johnnie was concerned that I was caught in such dark moods. On the day I quit, he brought in the name of a psychiatrist a friend had given him, a wonderful doctor who had helped Hungarian refugees having trouble adjusting to life in Canada.

The True Vocation of Sandy Brylirn

I screamed that I wasn't a refugee, telling him I hated psychiatrists more than the Devil, then apologized to Old Johnnie. I told him I didn't want to stay this way, and promised him I would seek ways out of my maze of depression, without a psychiatrist. Old Johnnie insisted we remain friends and I visit any time, his house was my house. I told him that when I felt stronger emotionally, I would come over and we would have a party and get drunk on Hungarian wine. He made me *swear* I would visit.

I never made it back to Old Johnnie's house. A few days later, I was arrested for the armed robbery of a Brylirn grocery store. For good measure, I had decided to empty my gun into the ceiling during the robbery and a ricocheting bullet hit a gold-star cashier in the arm. My father tried to make a deal with the authorities to let his disturbed son see a psychiatrist, but I had really plunged into the criminal world and the old Brylirn pull was useless. That was nearly two years ago.

All I have left to say is that, for the first time in my life, I genuinely feel comfortable working, and it *has* to be in prison. I look forward to my time in the carpentry shop. I've become one hell of a hardworking, skilled man. My Luddite days are definitely over. You should see this roll top desk I'm almost finished with. Some people want to know if there's a God, or if we're going to have a nuclear war, but all I want to know is why it took me so long to find my true vocation.

About the Authors

Gregory L. Norris is a full-time professional writer, with work appearing in numerous short story anthologies, national magazines, novels, the occasional TV episode, and, so far, one produced feature film (Brutal Colors, which debuted on Amazon Prime January 2016). A former feature writer and columnist at Sci Fi, the official magazine of the Sci Fi Channel (before all those ridiculous Ys invaded), he once worked as a screenwriter on two episodes of Paramount's modern classic, Star Trek: Voyager. Two of his paranormal novels (written under his nom-de-plume, Jo Atkinson) were published by Home Shopping Network as part of their "Escape with Romance" line -- the first time HSN has offered novels to their global customer base. Norris judged the 2012 Lambda Awards in the SF/F/H category. Three times now, his short stories have notched Honorable Mentions by Ellen Datlow. He won Honorable Mention in the 2016 Roswell Awards in Short SF for his short story 'Mandered'. Norris lives and writes in the outer limits of New Hampshire with his husband, their small pride of rescue cats, and his emerald-eyed muse. Follow his literary adventures on Facebook, or at www.gregorylnorris.blogspot.com.

Ken Goldman is a former teacher of English and Film Studies at George Washington High School in Philadelphia. Ken is an affiliate member of the Horror Writers Association. He has homes on the Main Line in Pennsylvania and at the South Jersey shore depending upon his mood and his need for a tan. His short stories appear in over 830 independent press publications in the U.S., Canada, the UK, and Australia, with over thirty due for publication in 2017. He has written five books: Three books of short stories: *You Had Me at Arrgh!!*, *Donny Doesn't Live Here Anymore*, and on Kindle, *Star-Crossed: a novella*; *Desiree*; and the novel, *Of a Feather*. Ken has received seven honorable mentions in *The Year's Best Fantasy & Horror* Anthologies. (Insert deafening applause here.) Ken's stories and books are available with a little online surfing and a mention of his name. It won't save you any money; Ken just likes to hear his name mentioned.

Catherine A. MacKenzie escapes her mundane world by writing poems and short fiction most women can relate to. Although she writes all genres, she enjoys veering toward the dark. She has been published in print and online publications and has self-published several short story collections, books of poetry, and children's picture books. Cathy lives with her husband in Halifax, Nova Scotia. The couple winters in Ajijic, Mexico, where her works have appeared in local publications. Her amazing, gorgeous grandchildren provide much joy and inspiration. Visit Cathy's website: www.writingwicket.wordpress.com.

Bruce Harris is the author of *Sherlock Holmes and Doctor Watson: ABout Type*.

Laird Long pounds out fiction in all genres. Big guy, sense of humour. Writing credits include: *Blue Murder Magazine*, *Hardboiled*, *Bullet*, *Albedo One*, *Baen's Universe*, *Sherlock Holmes Mystery Magazine*, and stories in the anthologies *The Mammoth Book of New Comic Fantasy*, *The Mammoth Book of Jacobean Whodunits*, *The Mammoth Book of Perfect Crimes and Impossible Mysteries*, and *New Canadian Noir*.

Jeremy Mays is a relatively new face to the horror genre. His first successful publication was a short story entitled, "I Walk" in the anthology *Temporary Skeletons* in February of 2014. From there, Jeremy has had several other stories published. "Midnight Rendezvous" was in James Ward Kirk's anthology *Terror Train*. Jeremy has had numerous short stories published by Horrified Press: "Onyx", "The Hunted", "Let Us to Billiards", "Do You Want Fries with That?", "Trotline", "Frozen Thoughts", "The Basement", and "A Fine Collection". His most recent short story, "Click-clack", was accepted for publication in James Ward Kirk's *Toys in the Attic* anthology, as well as another story, "Frost Bite", in James Ward Kirk's *Terror Train II*. Jeremy currently resides in Southern Illinois with his wife Jessa and his eleven children. All things related to Jeremy Mays can be found at: jeremylmays.wordpress.com.

Adrian Ludens is a radio announcer and fiction author from Rapid City, South Dakota. His newest collection, *When Bedbugs Bite*, is available on Amazon in paperback and kindle formats. Other recent and upcoming publication appearances include: *Surreal Worlds* (Bizarro Pulp Press), *Creepy Campfire Stories for Grown-Ups* (EMP Publishing), *The Gothic Fantasy Book of Science Fiction* (Flame Tree Publishing) and *The Mammoth Book of Jack the Ripper Stories* (Little, Brown).

He is an Active member of the Horror Writers Association. Visit: www.adrianludens.com.

Larry Lefkowitz's stories, poetry and humor have been widely published. Lefkowitz's humorous literary novel, *The Novel, Kunzman, the Novel!* is available as an e-book and in print from Lulu.com and other distributors. Writers and readers with a deep interest in literature will especially enjoy the novel. Lefkowitz's humorous fantasy and science fiction collection, *Laughing into the Fourth Dimension* is available from Amazon books.

Tom Larsen has been writing fiction for 25 years and his work has appeared in *Newsday*, *Raritan*, *Best American Mystery Stories*, *The Macguffin*, *Puerto del Sol* and the *LA Review*. His novels *Flawed* and *Into the Fire* are available through Amazon. Tom and his wife Andree live in the Pennsport section of South Philadelphia, home to Mummers, Flyers and that screw you slant that made the city famous.

"I wrote 'Second Chance' after reading about a NYC fugitive captured in Sausalito, CA after 28 years. It's frightening to think they live among us, but a small part of us hopes they get away clean."

Calvin Demmer is a crime, mystery, and speculative fiction author. His work has appeared in a variety of publications including *Sanitarium Magazine*, *Morpheus Tales*, and *Devolution Z*. When not writing, he is intrigued by that which goes bump in the night and the sciences of our universe. Find out more at www.calvindemmer.com or follow him on twitter @CalvinDemmer.

Gary Ives lives in the Ozarks where he grows apples and writes. He is a Pushcart Prize nominee for his story "Can You Come Here for Christmas?"

Alex Shvartsman is the winner of the 2014 WSFA Small Press Award for Short Fiction and a finalist for the 2015 Canopus Award for Excellence in Interstellar Writing. Over 80 of his short stories have appeared in *Nature*, *Galaxy's Edge*, *Intergalactic Medicine Show*, and other venues.

James A. Miller works as an Electrical Engineer in Madison, WI, during the day, developing milking robots. At night, he spends time with his family and does his best to come up with fun and creative fiction. He is a first reader for *Allegory e-zine* and member of the Codex writer's group.

Fredrick Obermeyer enjoys writing science-fiction, fantasy, horror, and crime stories. He has had work published in *NFG, Electric Spec, Newmyths, Perihelion SF, Acidic Fiction*, the *Destination: Future* anthology, and other markets.

Eric J. Juneau has been previously published in *Electric Spec* and other magazines, received an honorable mention in the 2010 "Writers of the Future" contest, and his spec fic novel *Merm-8* was premiered by Musa Publishing in Fall 2014.

Paul Stansfield works as an archaeologist during his day job, and does everything from finding 2,000-year-old prehistoric projectile points to removing 150-year-old feces from historic outhouses, and exhuming human burials—some so well preserved that the brains and other organs are still intact. Otherwise, he likes to write, especially horror fiction. He's had over 20 short stories published in magazines such as *Morbid Curiosity, Cthulhu Sex Magazine, Under the Bed, In D'tale, The Literary Hatchet*, and *Creepy Campfire Quarterly*, among others. He also has stories in three horror anthologies: *Undead Living* (Sunbury Press), *Coming Back* (Thirteen O'Clock Press), and *Creature Stew* (Papa Bear Press). His hobbies include drinking craft beer, tennis, and caring for the humongous tapeworm that lives in his intestines. His personal blog address is: http://paulstansfield.blogspot.com, and he can be reached at: paulccstansfield@gmail.com.

Jennifer Word is an award-winning poet, novelist, fiction and nonfiction writer, editor, reviewer, and publisher. She resides in Atchison, Kansas with her two children, two cats, and a lot of awesome thunderstorms. She holds a B.A. in Psychology from Pepperdine University, with minors in Education and English. She loves horror and science fiction, both written and cinema, and is an affiliate member of the HWA. She worked as an associate editor and copy editor for the horror magazine *Dark Moon Digest* from July 2010 through March 2016. She worked as a content editor for Dark Moon Books from February 2010 through April 2013. In February, 2015, she was invited to join the staff of Perpetual Motion Machine Publishing as a copy editor. She edited three separate titles for PMMP, through February 2016. In August 2016, she was invited to join the staff of Authors, Large and Small as a fiction/nonfiction reviewer, pitch and query writer, researcher, and editor. Her first official nonfiction articles reviewing and analyzing cult horror film classics will begin appearing in *Gamut Magazine* in January, 2017. Her short stories and poetry have been printed in *The Storyteller*, *The Klondike Sun*, *Dark Moon Digest*, *Dark Eclipse e-Magazine*, *Surreal Grotesque*, *eFiction*, and multiple anthologies, including: *Slices of Flesh*; *Zombies Need Love, Too*; and *Frightmares: A Fistful of Flash Fiction Horror*, all c/o Dark Moon Books; and *From Beyond the Grave* c/o Grinning Skull Press. Her current novels available through EMP Publishing, *All Because of the Cat & Others Tales* and *Once More*, can be found on Amazon in paperback and on Kindle as eBooks. You can read her film reviews, enjoy horror shorts, and watch film trailers for past, present, and upcoming horror films on her Facebook page at: www.facebook.com/JensHorrorMovieReviews/, and you can follow her on Twitter @jenniferword or @EMPPublishing.

If it screams, squelches, or bleeds, **Kristin Dearborn** has probably written about it. Kristin has written books such as *Stolen Away*, *Woman in White*, *Sacrifice Island*, *Trinity*, and had fiction published in several magazines and anthologies.

She revels in comments like, "But you look so normal… how do you come up with that stuff?" A life-long New Englander, she aspires to the footsteps of the local masters, Messrs. King and Lovecraft. When not writing, or rotting her brain with cheesy horror flicks (preferably creature features!) she can be found scaling rock cliffs or zipping around Vermont on a motorcycle, or gallivanting around the globe. Find out more about her at www.kristindearborn.com.

Bryan Grafton is a retired attorney now living in Texas.

Timothy O'Leary's award-winning short story collection, *Dick Cheney Shot Me in the Face – And Other Tales of Men in Pain*, will be released in February 2017. His stories and essays have been published in dozens of publications, and in 2016 he was nominated for a Pushcart Prize, and won the Aestas Short Story Award, among many others. He is also the author of the non-fiction book, *Warrior, Workers, Whiners, & Weasels*. More information can be found at timothyolearylit.com.

Morgen Knight is an award-winning horror/thriller writer whose short stories have appeared in numerous publications. She is a lover of macabre and enjoys searching for dark things. You can find her in Kansas City writing novels and short stories.

Read some of her work at: morgenknight.wordpress.com.
Follow her on facebook.com/writermorgenknight.

Jon-Michael Kelley's recent credits include stories in the multiple award-winning anthologies *Chiral Mad 2* and *Qualia Nous* (also a 2014 Bram Stoker Award Finalist for Best Anthology) by Written Backwards Press; Firbolg Publishing's ambitious literary series *Enter at Your Own Risk: Dark Muses, Spoken Silences*; *Sensorama* by Eibonvale Press, and *Triangulation: Lost Voices* by Parsec Ink.

Lee Duffy is retired from both the U.S. Army and the U.S. Department of Homeland Security. He is a former Army Green Beret with experience in counterterrorism, intelligence, law enforcement, and security. His debut novel, *The Dawn's Early Light*, is available on Amazon. He is currently preparing his second novel, *The Bombs Bursting in Air*, for publication in 2016.

Randy D. Rubin lives in quiet lunacy in a very old haunted house in Virginia. He is a very proud member of The Horror Writers of America and HWA-VA. He matriculated from Old Dominion University studying Creative Writing/English. He has two novellas published by Secret Cravings Press, *The Legend of my Nana, Miss Viola* and *The Witch of Dreadmere Forest*. His short story, "Tommy Kitty Cellar Son" is part of the anthology, *Suffer the Little Children*, published at Cruentis Libri Press and "This is a Troll Free Call" is in *Ugly Babies Vol. 1.* by JWK Publishing. His story, "The Water Got Mad" is part of Perpetual Motion Machine Publishing's *One Night Stand* series. He is the featured poet showcased in *The Horror Zine*'s September 2014 issue. He recently won the NECON E-Book Flash Fiction Contest last year and received an honorable mention for his haiku poetry this year. His flash fiction took second place in the January Short Fiction Contest at The Cult of Me.Blogspot.com this year. His dark passions and prose have been turned into podcasts at *The Wicked Library*, Episodes 417 in 2014; 516 last season; and 613 this year. His drabbles have appeared at *Hellnotes'* "Horror in a Hundred". And he's just getting started... His first dark poetry collection, *The Demon in My Head Doth Speak* was just released through *Eldritch Press* in February. His short story, "T-Bone" has just been published in the *Happy Little Horrors Anthology Vol 2 – Alienated* at Amazon as of Halloween 2015.

EMP Publishing will have his first collection of short stories, tentatively titled, *Warmest Regards from Austria* on the shelves in September of 2017.

A. R. Shannon is the pen name of Angela R. Sargenti, who is the author of seven eBooks. Her latest is *Meeting Mr. Pink*. Her story, "Caught Looking", appears in the award-winning anthology, *The Big Book of Domination*. For more information about her and her work, please check out her website at http://www.angiesargenti.blogspot.com.

Travis Richardson has been a finalist for the Macavity, Anthony, and Derringer short story awards. His novella *Lost in Clover* was listed in *Spinetingler Magazine's Best Crime Fiction of 2012*. His second novella, *Keeping the Record*, came out in 2014. He has published stories in crime fiction publications such as *Thuglit, Shotgun Honey, Flash Fiction Offensive*, and *All Due Respect*. He used to edit the *Sister in Crime Los Angeles* newsletter "Ransom Notes" and reviewed Anton Chekhov short stories at www.chekhovshorts.com. He lives with his wife and daughter in Los Angeles. www.tsrichardson.com.

Layla Cummins' short fiction, poetry, and non-fiction have been published in *The Saturday Evening Post, Grimdark Magazine, Crannóg, 100 Doors To Madness, GIVE: An Anthology of Anatomical Entries* & more. She was a finalist in the 2014 Sir Peter Ustinov Television Scriptwriting Award and lives in Bristol, England. Her story "The Flea Jar" first appeared in *Bugs: Tales That Slither, Creep and Crawl* and was loosely inspired by true events. Ask her why at: @laylacummins.

David Rachels has published crime fiction in *Thuglit, Pulp Modern, Plots with Guns*, and similar places. He is currently finishing work on his first story collection, *Everyone Is Ugly in the Dark*.

Jeffrey K. Blevins always views life through its morose overgrowth, paying the utmost attention to those looking back. His son, Malachai, will surely enjoy dad's story more than Jeffrey enjoys corn on macabre.

Joseph B. Cleary is a graduate of Susquehanna University with a degree in business and a minor in English. He is employed as a substitute teacher, which provides him with time to write. He lives in Westfield, NJ where he also grew up. Currently, he is working on a comic novel. His work has been accepted for publication in *Talking River Review*; *Children, Churches, and Daddies Magazine*; *Tortured Souls Vol. l*; *Frame Lines Magazine*; and *Black Market Lit*, as well as other publications. His short story, "Mick Rifkin," received honorable mention in Short Story America's short story contest.

J. J. Steinfeld is a Canadian fiction writer, poet, and playwright who lives on Prince Edward Island, where he is patiently waiting for Godot's arrival and a phone call from Kafka. While waiting, he has published seventeen books, including *Disturbing Identities* (Stories, Ekstasis Editions), *Should the Word Hell Be Capitalized?* (Stories, Gaspereau Press), *Would You Hide Me?* (Stories, Gaspereau Press), *Misshapenness* (Poetry, Ekstasis Editions), *Identity Dreams and Memory Sounds* (Poetry, Ekstasis Editions), *Madhouses in Heaven, Castles in Hell* (Stories, Ekstasis Editions), and *An Unauthorized Biography of Being* (110 Short Fictions Hovering Between the Absurd and the Existential, Ekstasis Editions). His short stories and poems have appeared in numerous periodicals and anthologies internationally, and over fifty of his one-act plays and a handful of full-length plays have been performed in Canada and the United States.

Acknowledgments

EMP Publishing would like to thank the following, in no particular order. Each one of you has supported *The Prison Compendium* and you are all responsible for helping this Volume come into being.

THANK YOU.

Amy Kimmel, FCNolan, Jenny Koenig, Jaime Metoyer, Damian Stout, Bruce Harris.

This exciting project is also being spread via Indiegogo Generosity Fundraising, to provide as many copies of TPC to as many different prison book donation programs as possible. The fundraiser will last an entire year beyond the book's release date of December 16, 2016, and EMP Publishing will mass-ship copies of the Compendium to as many prison book donation programs as our fundraising allows. Our ultimate hope is to put at least one copy of TPC into every prison library in the United States. Please visit the link below to view our Books for Prisoners: The Prison Compendium Fundraiser Project.

https://www.generosity.com/fundraising/books-for-prisoners-the-prison-compendium--2

www.ingramcontent.com/pod-product-compliance
Lightning Source LLC
Chambersburg PA
CBHW031256170626
46807CB00001B/167